MW01713848

The Golden Son

Also by Shilpi Somaya Gowda

Secret Daughter

The Golden Son

A Novel

Shilpi Somaya Gowda

HarperAvenue
An imprint of HarperCollins*PublishersLtd*

The Golden Son
Copyright © 2015 by Shilpi Somaya Gowda.
All rights reserved.

Published by Harper Avenue, an imprint of HarperCollins Publishers Ltd

First edition

No part of this book may be used or reproduced in any manner whatsoever without written permission except in the case of brief quotations embodied in critical articles and reviews.

This book is a work of fiction. The characters, incidents, and dialogue are drawn from the author's imagination and are not to be construed as real. Any resemblance to actual events or persons, living or dead, is entirely coincidental.

HarperCollins books may be purchased for educational, business, or sales promotional use through our Special Markets Department.

HarperCollins Publishers Ltd
2 Bloor Street East, 20th Floor
Toronto, Ontario, Canada
M4W 1A8

www.harpercollins.ca

Canadian Cataloguing in Publication information is available upon request.

ISBN (hardcover) 978-1-44344-679-2
ISBN (paperback) 978-1-44341-249-0

Printed and bound in the United States of America
RRD 10 9 8 7 6 5 4 3 2 1

For Anand—

My best decision, then and always.

When you counsel someone, you should appear to be reminding him of something he had forgotten, not of the light he was unable to see.

—Baltasar Gracián

The Golden Son

Maya the Harelip

Anil Patel was ten years old the first time he witnessed one of Papa's arbitrations.

Children usually were not allowed at these meetings, but an exception was made for Anil since he would, one day, inherit his father's role. As the only child present, he made himself as invisible as possible, crouching down in the corner of the gathering room. The meetings always took place here: the largest space in the largest house in this small village nestled into an expanse of farmland in western India. This room was the beating heart of the Big House, where the family ate their meals, Papa read the paper, Ma did her mending, and Anil and his siblings raced through their schoolwork before going out to play. The centerpiece of the gathering room was an immense wooden table—its top four fingers thick, its carved legs so wide a grown man's hands could not reach all the way around—a piece of furniture so substantial it took four men to lift it, though it hadn't been moved more than a meter in generations.

On this day, Papa sat at the head of the magnificent table, with Anil's aunt and uncle on either side. Relatives, friends, and neighbors stood a respectful distance away. The room was filled with people, but the subject of the day's arbitration, Anil's cousin Maya, was not among them. Maya had been born a harelip to Papa's sister, and her husband believed this to be a curse of the family into which he'd married. That Anil's uncle had agreed to come here, to hand his family dispute over to the arbiter of his wife's clan rather than his own, was significant but not surprising. Papa had a reputation for fairness and wisdom that extended well beyond their land.

Anil's uncle argued he should be released from his marriage, to be free to seek another wife, one who could give him normal, healthy children. Maya's deformity, he said, was proof his wife's womb was tainted, and that she would bear him nothing but more bad fortune and unmarriageable girls who would remain a burden. Papa's sister sat nearby, weeping into the end of her sari.

Papa's face remained impassive as he listened. He then consulted the astrologer for whom he had sent, asking him to read Maya's birth charts. The astrologer found nothing untoward: Maya was born under a good star, no eclipses had occurred during the pregnancy. Finally, Papa turned to his younger sister. *Did she love Maya?* he asked. *Was she dedicated to her husband? Would she give whatever was needed for their health and happiness?* To all of these questions, she nodded yes, still weeping. Her husband stared down at the table for so long that Anil worried he might notice the initials he and his brothers had recently carved into its edge.

"This is a very difficult matter," Papa began after everyone else had spoken. "Obviously, no one would wish for what has happened to Maya. But as you've heard from the astrologer, the problem did not come from the pregnancy or the birth. In this case, we can no more lay the blame for Maya's condition with her mother than with her father."

There was a gasp from the crowd. Anil held the last breath he'd drawn. Even at the age of ten, he understood the danger of threatening another man's pride. Yelling matches had erupted among his relatives over far less. Every pair of eyes in the room turned to Anil's uncle, who looked shocked by the suggestion he could be at fault for Maya's affliction. A deep crease appeared between his eyebrows.

"So then," Papa continued, "we must turn to the child. What do we know about Maya?"

Anil was momentarily lost. What was there to know about an infant, one who wasn't even present? Looking around the room, he could see that the others were confused as well.

"Maya," Papa repeated. "Her name means illusion. What is an illusion? Something that tricks our eyes? Something that is not as it appears? *Bhai*," he turned to his brother-in-law, reaching out a hand to his forearm, "you're too smart to be tricked, aren't you? You know your true daughter is not this harelip. You know your daughter, your true daughter, is beautiful and loyal and will bring you years of care and happiness, don't you?"

Anil's uncle stared at Papa for several moments. The furrow between his eyes softened, and very slowly he nodded his head. It was such a slight movement, everyone waited until he nodded again, then the crowd began to murmur agreement. Anil's aunt stopped crying and sniffled sharply a few times. Papa smiled and sat back. "So what we must do is uncover your true daughter. It will take a strong and clever man. Are you up for the task, *bhai*? Yes? Very good."

Three weeks later, Anil's father and uncle took Maya to the charity medical clinic traveling through a nearby town, where she underwent an hour-long free surgical procedure to repair her cleft lip. Nobody else was aware of such an option; Papa was one of the few people in the village who could read the newspaper from town. A few months later, Maya had healed completely from the surgery. When the bandages came off, the illusion was gone. In its place was a smile as beautiful and perfect as those with which Maya's three younger siblings were later born. Every year thereafter on Maya's birthday, her parents brought Papa an offering of blessed fruit and flowers.

❁

THE NIGHT Papa returned from the clinic, after Ma and Anil's four younger siblings had gone to sleep, Anil sat with his father in the gathering room, across the great table from one another, the chessboard between them.

"I've never seen them like that," Anil said. His aunt and uncle had both been in tears as they left the Big House with Maya.

One corner of Papa's mouth turned up in a weary half-smile. "Your uncle is a good man at heart. He just needed some guidance to find the right path."

"You helped him?" It came out as a question, though Anil hadn't intended it that way.

Papa wobbled his head and held up his thumb and forefinger a centimeter apart. "It was really the doctor."

His father's eyelids were beginning to flag, but Anil was eager to keep him talking. "T-tell me about it," he stammered. "Please?"

Papa rolled the pawn he was considering between his fingers before setting it down on the board. He leaned back in his chair and clasped his hands together over his belly. "There was a big tent set up outside the market, right across from the coconut stand. Fifty people were lined up outside. Inside were rows and rows of cots. The doctor came over and explained what he would do to fix Maya's lip. He showed us pictures—before and after—of other children he had treated." Papa shook his head once. "Magic. A miracle, really."

He looked up at Anil, his eyes moist. "You should be a doctor," he said. "You will do great things."

Part I

I

ANIL COULD NOT FIND THE RIGHT WORDS, NO MATTER HOW many ways he rearranged them in his mind. "Ma, please, you don't need to do all this," he blurted, regretting the words as soon as they left his mouth. Not because of the look of scorn they brought, nor because it was a futile request, but because the plea made him sound like a child rather than a man of twenty-three embarking on the journey of a lifetime.

His mother glanced over to acknowledge him before she turned back to the task of directing his two younger cousins to hang marigold garlands over the double doors. Anil knew there was no way to stem the flood of activity well underway. He had awoken this morning to the aroma of a feast being prepared, had fallen asleep late last night to the sounds of the servants struggling to lash his two enormous trunks onto the roof of the Maruti.

People had begun to arrive in the late morning after the cows had been milked, the chickens fed, and the fields tended. The rhythm of every day in Panchanagar started at daybreak, but only after the early chores were completed did anything else take place. Now, without a trace of morning dew left and with the sun blazing overhead, the dusty clearing in front of the Big House was crowded with family and neighbors. They circulated into the house for hot chai and the elaborate lunch buffet, each one seeking out Anil to wish him well. Some had familiar faces; with others, Anil struggled to find a hint of recognition behind the stooped shoulders and thinning hair that had befallen them in the six years he'd been away. He had been back in the village for only a week, but already the yearning to leave had set in.

From the edge of the porch, Anil scanned the crowd and spotted his younger sister, Piya, in the clearing below, speaking to a woman with a thick waterfall of hair down her back. As Anil approached them, Piya reached out to wrap a slim arm around his waist. "As I was saying, this whole celebration is bigger than my wedding will be." She smiled up at him and raised her eyebrows in mockery before turning back to her friend. "Of course, yours will probably come first."

The other woman tilted her head to one side, smiling barely enough to reveal a narrow space between her two front teeth, and Anil recognized her with a jolt of surprise. "Leena." He hadn't seen her in years, and never without the two long braids she'd worn as a young girl. She was now a grown woman, her nose chiseled and cheekbones high, her eyebrows arched over warm brown eyes. He cleared his throat. "It's been a long time . . . How are you?"

"She's going to leave me too," Piya said with an exaggerated sigh, "to get married."

Anil smiled at Leena. "Really?"

Leena shrugged in response. "Congratulations to you, Anil. Your parents must be very proud."

"Yes, we are all very proud, big brother." Piya squeezed herself closer to him. "This has been a long time in the making. Do you remember that little bird? The one in the coconut tree?"

"Yes!" Leena said. "We were racing to climb to the top."

"You got there first." Anil pointed to Leena. "And started throwing coconuts down at us."

"Not *at* you, *to* you. I've never seen such bad catchers. Terrible!

You scattered like ants." Leena laughed, her fingers flying up to her lips. "And that poor little bird. Oh, I felt so bad." She shook her head. "Thank God you knew to bandage up its leg until it could fly again. It would have been very bad karma for me if you hadn't saved him."

"You kept that bird in your room for weeks, no?" Piya said.

Anil nodded. The other children had been sad when it was time to let the bird go, but he had felt a swell of pride at seeing the small creature push off from the windowsill and fly away. "Yes, I fed it by hand—mashed yogurt and rice." He smiled and shook his head once. "Ma wasn't too pleased when she found all that food I'd hidden in my room."

"Okay, all this talk is making me *starving* hungry." Piya linked her arm through Anil's. "Come, let's go get some lunch."

Leena excused herself, saying she had to get home; she and Piya embraced and made plans to see each other the next day. Anil became aware that his momentary lift in mood was dissipating again as Leena walked away.

❁

AFTER ANIL finished eating, both the modest serving he'd given himself and a larger one from his mother, Ma leaned in to clear his plate and whispered, "He is awake now, you can go."

Anil stepped into the doorway of his father's bedroom. Papa was sitting upright in bed, gazing out the window. His hair, once thick and black, was thinning to the point where his scalp was visible. The white whiskers sprinkled like flour over his face could not camouflage the sagging folds of skin.

Papa turned at the creak of the door. When he saw Anil, his eyes filled with light, rendering his face recognizable again. He cleared his throat and patted the bed. "Come."

Anil sat and took Papa's hand, casually draping his fingers across the pulse point. "How do you feel, Papa?" He gauged his father's heartbeat as normal, same as the last several days.

"First class." Papa's smile widened. "It's only a pesky flu. I'll be on my feet in a day or two." He patted Anil's hand. "But your flight will not wait."

"I can change—"

His father waved his hand in front of his face as if swatting away an invisible fly. "Nonsense," he said. "This is the proudest day of my life, son. Don't make me wait any longer."

Anil began to speak, but his voice caught in his throat, so he simply pressed his hand on Papa's. His father's gift for words was not one he had inherited.

"Before you go, son, please send in Chandu."

"What is it, Papa?" Anil's youngest brother, Chandu, had still been a child when Anil left home, but his personality was apparent even then. He was often scolded for chatting in class, and had been sent home more than once for a schoolyard brawl. With seven years and three siblings between them, Anil felt more like an uncle to Chandu than a brother.

Papa shook his head. "Lately, he's fallen in with a bad crowd, putting wrong ideas into his head. Chandu is smart, but he's stubborn. He wants to find his own way. He thinks there's no room for him here. I'm trying to find him a role in the farm operations. Your brother can be successful, I'm sure of it." Anil didn't know if this was true or if his father simply lacked the ability to be objective about his own son. He rose, leaned forward to embrace Papa, then touched his feet.

"And, son," Papa said as Anil reached the door. "Take care with your mother today. This is hard for her."

HAVING SAID good-bye to his father, Anil was eager to leave. He caught a glimpse of Ma, in her parrot-green and orange sari, one of the fine silk ones she saved for special occasions. She was ambling through the crowd, holding a platter of sweets. His mother moved through life as if she were never in a hurry, unconcerned about things like train schedules and appointments, a trait Anil found maddening.

"Ma." He reached for her elbow. "We should leave soon. It's getting late."

She insisted on first performing a proper *Ganesh puja* ceremony to bless Anil on his journey. With everyone watching from the porch outside, he crossed the Big House threshold for the final time, ducking under the string of fragrant marigolds. The pandit recited prayers to remove any obstacles he might face on the road ahead, and Anil stepped barefoot between the red and white chalk patterns decorating his path across the porch and down the steps.

He watched as Ma orchestrated the distribution and loading of people into various automobiles, standing off to the side with his brothers Nikhil and Kiran. Nikhil was only two years Anil's junior, but his spindly frame always made him seem younger. "Where's Chandu?" Nikhil asked, looking around.

"Papa asked him to stay behind," Anil said.

"Well, he can't foul up too much in one day," Nikhil said. When Anil had left Panchanagar, it was Nikhil who'd become Papa's apprentice in the fields, and he was the right sort of person for the role—serious and responsible, nearly to the point of being humorless.

"Papa's wasting his time." Kiran shook his head. "No use trying to straighten a crooked branch." Kiran, who'd just finished school, had never considered doing anything other than joining the family farm. He was well suited to the physical nature of field work: strong and fast, unquestionably the best cricket player of the four brothers.

Anil glanced over at him. "Come on, you don't believe that?"

Kiran raised an eyebrow. "He's been cutting school to spend his days with a group of older louts, racing scooters and drinking toddy made from palm-tree sap."

"It's bad," Nikhil said. "I don't think Papa even knows how bad. One of Chandu's friends grows *bhang* on his grandfather's land. A bit of *bhang lassi* on Holi is one thing, but this guy adds something to make it stronger and sells it in town to tourists as some sort of herbal path to enlightenment."

Nikhil leaned down and yanked up a prickly weed encroaching on the porch. "It's just a matter of time before one of those tourists wakes up after being robbed and sends the police after that hoodlum. Not sure if Chandu's involved, but I wouldn't be surprised."

"God." Anil removed his specs to wipe a smudge from one of the lenses. He knew his brothers resented Chandu for his duty-shirking ways, though this sounded more serious. Even so, he knew Papa would be able to handle it.

Finally, after Ma had successfully accommodated no fewer than thirty-one people in four cars, it was time to go. Dozens more guests were staying behind, not for lack of desire but for lack of vehicle space. Most families had sent a delegate so Anil would feel the collective weight of their good wishes as he left home.

After everyone was seated and the car doors were locked, a nearly forgotten five-year-old cousin came running from among the thick brush, and chaos ensued until space was found for the child on someone's lap. Ma closed the boot of the car, which held enough fresh-cooked food to feed the entire family three times over, then folded her ample frame with some difficulty into the backseat. Nikhil turned the key in the ignition and drove off, stirring up a cloud of dust through which the rest of the caravan would ceremoniously pass as they left the tiny village of Panchanagar and continued for two hours on unpaved roads to Sardar Vallabhbhai Patel International Airport in Ahmadabad, the largest city in the state of Gujarat, India. Anil reached for the wristwatch Papa had given him as a parting gift. Its steel band gleamed, and its silver face was punctuated with indigo numbers and fluorescent hands. There were two dials: one set to the time here in Panchanagar, the other to the time in Dallas, Texas. Over ten hours separated his past and future homes, and it would take more than a full day in the air to traverse that distance. And yet, both measures of this journey seemed inconsequential in comparison to the lifetime he'd spent preparing for it.

❁

LONG BEFORE this day, before he was the first person to leave his village, before he was the first in his family to attend university rather than farm the rice paddies covering their land, Anil was the first son born to his parents.

Jayant and Mina Patel had four more children—Nikhil, Kiran, Piya, and Chandu. Big families were a way of life in their community. The extended clan—still known by the name of Anil's deceased great-grandfather, "Moti" (big brother) Patel—owned most of the land for more than ten kilometers in all directions from the Big House. Anil was the latest in the line of eldest sons, including Papa and his grandfather before him, and as such, the expectations of him had always been clear. One day, he would inherit his father's role as leader of the clan, responsible for farm operations, financial support, and presiding over family disputes. As a boy, Anil had followed Papa into the fields each day, learning to cultivate rice from the paddies, harvest it most efficiently, dry it in the sun, and bundle it in jute sacks to take to the market.

Anil learned quickly, as his teachers pointed out when he began attending the local school. He was the first in his class to read, the first to memorize the math tables. Every day, he left school with a stack of books tethered in twine, which he swung between his thumb and forefinger, creating a deep red indentation he took pride in inspecting after the long walk home. After working with Papa in the fields, he read his schoolbooks late into the evening, borrowing the kerosene lantern that sat on the porch outside for nighttime visits to the latrine. Once, when he forgot to replace it before going to sleep, Nikhil tumbled down the front steps and sprained his ankle, but everyone agreed later that the injury had been for a good cause when Anil took top marks in mathematics. As Anil began to excel in his studies, Papa excused him from his farm duties and, by then, his brothers were old enough to compensate for his absence.

Ever since that day Papa returned with Maya from the clinic, he and Anil shared an unspoken understanding that his path would be different. They became conspirators in building Anil into someone who could venture beyond Panchanagar and its limited offerings. Anil pored over his science books, studying the human-anatomy figures depicted in them until he could name every organ, muscle, and bone. After he outgrew the resources at school, he sent away for science magazines and ordered the *Atlas of Human Anatomy* from Jaypee Brothers in Delhi. Whenever Chakroo, the family dog who slept and roamed outside, returned with a dead mouse or rabbit, Anil sat on the porch and carefully cut it open with the smallest knife he could pilfer from the kitchen while the cook napped. By age twelve, he'd given up countless cricket games after school, and lazy summer days. There in the village of Panchanagar, after generations of farmers, surrounded by nothing but agricultural fields, Anil prepared to one day become a doctor.

Only after he arrived at medical college in Ahmadabad did Anil understand the significance of this feat. His fellow students, from wealthy families in the cities, had been professionally tutored for years:

their schools had biology labs with dissection specimens, they had shadowed their parents' doctor friends in the hospital. All they saw in Anil was a village boy, making him acutely aware of his lack of sophistication in everything from computers to popular music. Anil kept to himself and spent all his time studying, eager to prove himself as capable as his classmates.

Six years of medical college had taken him away from home, and not only physically; it had given him a taste of another world. The medical library was filled with entire sections dedicated to subjects that garnered a mere chapter in Anil's rudimentary textbook. The city of Ahmadabad bustled with ten thousand times the population of his village. It was this taste of the world that lingered in Anil's mouth like the residual flavor of sweet *paan* and enticed him to seek out a coveted medical residency in America. His professors cautioned him it would be nearly impossible for a foreign student to win a spot at a major urban hospital center, but Anil forged ahead with his applications. In the end, only three students in his class received residency offers outside India: two were going to England and Singapore, and Anil was accepted by Parkview Hospital in Dallas, one of the busiest hospitals in the United States.

"I don't know how you'll manage there all alone." Ma's words jarred Anil back to the present. "No one to cook for you, no one to take care of you. They say the food is terrible—bland and boring and so much *meat*." She spat out the offensive word as if it were the actual thing. "You'll be thin as a branch when you come back, and then how will we find you a good wife?"

Piya clucked her tongue. "Ma, stop nagging him *to death* about marriage, will you?"

Anil smiled, grateful his little sister had insisted on coming along despite her propensity to get sick on long car trips. Ma blinked a few times at Piya, as though trying to recognize her daughter. "What nonsense." She shook her head. "Son, I put some tulsi leaves and ground turmeric in the brown trunk. The turmeric will keep you well, if you take it every day. Cough, cold, stomach problems, headaches, joint pain—turmeric cures all of it. Why do you think I'm still free of arthritis, when my poor mother could barely use her hands?"

"Ma, you're too young for arthritis," Anil said. She was eight years younger than Papa, her only sign of aging a slight graying at her temples.

Ma gazed out the window, her mind clearly on her deceased mother more than on the children beside her. After a few minutes, she turned back to Anil. "And, son, please." She pressed her palms together, eyes solemn. "Don't forget your prayers every morning. God is the only one who can protect you over there."

"Yes, Ma." *Don't forget to write every week—call when you can—don't trust anybody—be careful—don't touch meat or alcohol—and come back as soon as you can.* Anil silently ran through the mantras Ma had been instilling in him for months, before remembering he would soon be far enough away to stop hearing her voice altogether.

"You can do anything you want, Anil, anything," Ma had lamented when he'd announced his decision to do his residency in Dallas. "You're so smart, so talented. Any hospital in Gujarat would be happy to have you. Why must you go so far away?"

Ma believed every step Anil took away from Panchanagar was temporary; she assumed a connection with home he no longer felt. But the problem with planting seeds, as the son of a farmer well knew, was that you couldn't always be sure where or how they would grow. Sometimes they would mutate or cross-fertilize, blown by the winds from one field to the next. A year from now, after the successful completion of his internship, Anil would stay on in America to complete a two-year residency in internal medicine, during which time he would choose his specialty for further training. By then, Ma would be used to Anil's distance and not be as distraught at the prospect of his leaving for good.

Parkview—the idyllic name conjured visions of rolling grassy hills, the state-of-the-art hospital nestled among acres of trees and flowers. There, it would not matter what Anil's last name was, what caste he came from, that his family were farmers, or how many people he bribed. In America, he could make his own way, build his own reputation. He would no longer be known as the eldest son of Jayant and Mina, or as the village boy. His colleagues would know him only as Anil Patel, and success or failure would belong to him alone.

Now, as the family caravan rolled up to the airport, Anil pushed aside any whispers of trepidation about leaving behind everything he'd known. He wanted only to look forward: past the large ceremonial meal he would share at the airport, past the many group photographs for which he'd have to pose, past the endless night sky into which he would fly toward his new life in America.

SEVERAL HOURS later, as he sat on an airplane for the first time in his life, his homeland drifting away beneath him, Anil found his mind returning to the events of the day, to his chance encounter with Leena. She had been his constant companion in the years before his studies drove him indoors. They had hidden from each other in fields of tall sugarcane, careful not to rustle a wayward stalk and reveal themselves. Leena was brave, the only one not to leap back when they came upon a family of snakes in the bushes while pretending to search for tigers. She'd been the first to challenge Anil to climb a coconut tree, using the callused soles of her feet to scramble up the narrow trunk. The first time Anil had tried it, he'd fallen on his shoulder, making his handwriting exercises difficult for weeks afterward. It was likely a torn rotator cuff, he realized later, but he'd brushed it off at the time, embarrassed to have been shown up by a girl.

One day, when just the two of them had been playing outside, Anil pulled his hand from his pocket. "Look," he said, unfurling his fingers to reveal two thin *beedis* in his palm. They were so crooked and dark, they could almost be mistaken for twigs, but Leena recognized them right away.

She peered closer. "Where did you get them?" she asked in a whisper, though they were alone outside, with no risk of being overheard. It was late afternoon, that time of day when men were wrapping up their work in the fields. The women were busy preparing the evening meal and wanted children out of the way. School was finished, and no one would be looking for them for at least another hour, when dusk set in. The illicit nature of what they were doing hung in the thick, sweet, humid air between them.

"From my uncle's house. My father sent me to deliver an envelope, but there was no one in the house. I saw the box sitting by his chair, with the lid open. There were so many, he'll never notice." Anil had been so scared of getting caught, he'd jammed the hand-rolled cigarettes into the bottom of his pocket and not taken them out until now. All day as he sat in school he'd been simmering with anticipation for the moment he could show her. "Do you . . . Have you . . . ?"

"No! Never." Leena pulled back. After a moment, she whispered, "Have you?"

Anil was surprised. Couldn't she see right through him? "No, but . . . " He repeated what he'd heard from one of the boys at school. "I've heard it can help you see figures in the clouds, and hear the flute music of Krishna."

Leena's eyes grew wider. Slowly, her lips parted into a smile and revealed the space between her teeth. Other kids sometimes teased her for this flaw but Anil had always liked it. He knew he'd got a real smile out of her when he caught a glimpse of that space.

Anil knew what she would say even before he asked. "Do you want to try it?"

They sat cross-legged facing each other in the bottom of the gully that roughly marked the property line between the many hectares of Patel family land and Leena's family's small plot, one of several that bordered the Patels'. After Anil lit the *beedis* and handed one to her, Leena took a small puff and immediately began to cough. Anil did the same after taking a puff of his. They both began to laugh, as they had trouble keeping their balance while holding on to the small cigarettes.

Leena tried again, taking a second drag and blowing it out cleanly this time. There was a shine in her eyes. Anil tried again, slowing down his inhale and controlling his exhale, until he too could smoke without coughing. The glow of the red embers on the end on the *beedis* danced before Anil's eyes. The images at the edge of his vision, the banana trees and waving tall grasses, blurred a little and he began to feel dizzy. Was Leena feeling the same effects? The ground was calling to him, and Anil lay down on his back. Leena lay down beside him and for several moments they watched the sky, the clouds drifting by.

"My father would kill me if he found me smoking this," Leena murmured, her voice soft.

"My *mother* would kill me," Anil said, referring not only to the cigarette but also to Leena's presence. "It doesn't look good," Ma had said a few weeks earlier. "You're not a little boy anymore, Anil. You can't run around playing with girls at your age." He had recently turned fourteen. Leena was almost twelve. She had not yet developed breasts, like some of the girls at school had. Girls and boys had been separated into different classrooms a few years earlier, a practice intended to enable both groups to focus on their studies but which had the opposite effect. The boys in Anil's class seemed to think of nothing other than girls, passing notes and explicit pictures in the classroom when the teacher's back was turned, sharing stories outside in the schoolyard. And, as Anil's mother never let him forget, the Patels held an important role in the community and shouldn't be socializing with a modest family like Leena's.

Anil's head was buzzing, a pleasant hum that made him feel as if someone were singing softly in his ear. His *beedi* had burned down almost to the end. He took one last puff and mashed it into the grassy hillside with his fingers. Leena's *beedi* was also gone, and she was holding her open palm up above her, tracing the outline of a cloud with her forefinger. He stole a glance at her profile, the soft curve of her nose, the sharp angle of her chin, the glint of yellow gold against her dark earlobe. She was not beautiful in a conventional way, like Bollywood stars with their rounded hips and plump lips, the kind of photos boys at school hid in their books. If pressed, Anil would not be able to explain what he found so attractive about Leena. But he loved looking at her, and when they were not together, he recreated her features in his mind, always starting with her mouth.

With the music humming in his ears and the fluffy white clouds floating overhead, Anil allowed himself to reach his hand up toward Leena's open palm. Neither of them looked at the other as their hands touched, intertwined, and drifted back down to the ground between their bodies, Anil's hand atop Leena's. Anil found himself counting beats in his head, trying to control the quickening pace of his breath. He wanted desperately to lean over and kiss her. Instead he kept counting, ever conscious of the feel of her hand beneath his.

He had counted to thirty-eight when he heard the noise. At first it sounded like the rustling of stalks in the fields, but the noises grew louder and closer, and shaped themselves into human voices. Anil stopped counting. Leena's body tensed beside him. What if it was her parents looking for her? What if it was his?

The gully was deep enough that you could only see across, not into, it when standing on either bank at a distance. One would have to walk up to the very edge to see if anyone was hiding in the basin. For this reason, it was Anil's favorite spot in hide-and-seek, but it only worked if he stayed perfectly still in the bottom of the gully, even as voices of the children looking for him echoed through the rolling fields around him. Now, a male voice, too deep and angry to belong to either of their fathers, grew closer and more pronounced. Leena began to sit up, but Anil closed his hand tightly around hers and pulled her back down. They turned their faces to each other and kept their eyes locked as the sounds grew louder. Grunts. Panting. A weak female voice, speaking unintelligibly. The male voice, louder again. Rustling. More grunting.

When it became apparent that these people had not come to search for them and, in fact, were not aware of their presence at all, Anil nodded to Leena. Slowly, they both sat up and peered over the bank of the gully, then froze, shocked. Not ten meters away, a man's bare buttocks were in full view as he moved back and forth violently on top of a woman.

It took a moment for Anil to recognize the man, one of the smaller landowners from nearby, not part of the Patel clan. He did not know the man's name, but Anil had seen his wife—and she was not this woman. From the simple cotton sari draped over her head and shoulders, and the dark skin of her bare legs, it was clear she was a servant. The man's loincloth had been thrown hastily aside and lay on the ground.

Anil and Leena sat unmoving and soundless, yet when the servant woman turned her head to the side, her gaze fell upon them. There was a vacant, haunting look in her eyes. Leena put her hand on Anil's forearm and he understood her meaning at once: *run*.

They stood at the same time, but a sharp knife of pain radiated from Anil's right foot up through his calf and thigh. He cried out and fell back to the ground, where a swarm of bees encircled his leg.

The man looked up and caught Leena standing there. "What are you doing? Bastard child! I'll kill you!"

Anil watched helplessly, holding his throbbing foot, and fumbled for his specs, which had fallen on the ground. The man stood up, unclothed from the waist down, and began to run toward them. Leena darted forward and picked up the loincloth. She held the cloth up in the air and jutted her chin out, daring him to come closer. The man stopped. Behind him, the servant woman stood up, covered herself with her sari, and hurried off in the opposite direction through the fields.

Anil could see at least three stingers protruding from his foot. He forced himself to calm his breathing and pluck them out carefully, aware of the sound of Leena's heavy breathing and the man's shouts. After pulling out the last stinger, he stood up, putting as little weight as possible on his hurt foot. He took Leena's elbow. She flung the loincloth into the air and they sprinted away, the man's shouts receding behind them.

Despite the pain, Anil could not remember ever running faster in his life, and still Leena was ahead of him all the way to the riverbank. In the morning, the banks of the river were filled with women collecting water, in the late afternoon with men washing themselves after a day in the fields. But now, at dusk, there was no one. Leena waded into the water in her clothes and immersed herself completely, plunging beneath the surface, while Anil sat on the edge of the bank, pulling handfuls of mud from the bottom of the riverbed to pack onto his foot. Afterward, they sat atop a broad, flat boulder on the riverbank while Leena slowly dried in the warm air and the cooling mud drew the sting from Anil's wounds.

They did not speak about what they had seen, or about their narrow escape. They did not acknowledge the moments before: the cigarettes, their intoxication, their intertwined hands, or the near kiss. All of it—the tender, the illicit, the innocent, and the brutal—had become entangled, and thus unspeakable.

That evening, Anil stopped to scrub his hands of the scent of tobacco at the outdoor pump before entering the Big House. When his mother caught him limping on his way upstairs to bed, Anil admitted he'd stepped on a beehive and allowed her to apply an ointment to his foot.

Soon after that day, as Anil entered adolescence, his life changed in many ways. He became more serious about his schoolwork, and gave up spending his free time outside. Most weekends, he sat in on his father's arbitration sessions rather than playing cricket with his friends. The divide between boys and girls that began in the classroom became greater as time went on, spreading to their social realm. Anil saw Leena occasionally when she walked to school with Piya, but Ma's disapproval of their friendship, coupled with his own disappointment at his cowardice, made him reticent around her.

After Anil left for medical college at age seventeen, he lost track of Leena, along with many other childhood friends. For the past six years in Ahmadabad, he'd been working to overcome the deficiency with which the small village of Panchanagar had burdened him. Although he hadn't seen Leena in many years, the time they had shared in childhood, those memories and his feelings for her, had lain dormant but not forgotten.

2

ANIL STEPPED OUTSIDE THROUGH THE SLIDING DOORS OF DALLAS/ Fort Worth airport, meeting an embrace of warm air. "Ah, just like home."

Baldev Kapoor, his new roommate, laughed and threw an arm around his shoulder. "My friend, you're in America now—*nothing* is like home." He grinned through his manicured goatee.

Anil had to admit there was some truth in this statement. The weather here reminded him of India, but little else was familiar. The airport had been a marvel of order and cleanliness. Passengers stood in straight lines and stepped politely forward. There was no jostling to get to the front, no elbowing fellow travelers out of the way, no spitting on the floors. Although Anil had come prepared with a roll of cash in his pocket, neither the customs nor immigration officers suggested a bribe to let him pass; they simply looked at his foreign-student papers and stamped his passport.

As Baldev drove, Anil stared out the windshield at the ribbon of winding highway stretched before them, the vast expanses of empty land on either side. The roads were free of bumps and debris, with clean white lines that echoed the sense of possibility in a fresh notebook page. Where were the belching cargo trucks, the scooters weaving through traffic, the ambling goats and cows?

"Where is everybody? Is it a holiday or something?" he asked Baldev, who'd been in America for several years already, having moved with his parents from Delhi to Houston as a teenager.

"The cities are another thing, but most of Texas is still wide open frontier," Baldev chuckled. "You don't want to get caught in the wrong place, if you know what I mean."

Anil had found the apartment through an advertisement posted by their other roommate, Mahesh Shah, whose Gujarati name gave Ma some reassurance. *IIT-trained computer engineer*, read the ad, *male, mid-20s, good job, financially secure, seeks two similar roommates to share luxurious apartment in Irving, Texas. Nondrinking, nonsmoking, vegetarian.* It sounded too good to be true and Anil was certain the spots would be filled, but God had been smiling on him, just as on every step of this journey. The monthly rent of six hundred dollars would be a stretch, but the apartment was only twenty minutes from the hospital and the notion of having roommates from back home was comforting.

The apartment was larger than Anil had expected, and everything appeared brand-new. The floors were covered in plush carpet the color of sand, with walls painted to a perfect match. The kitchen had gleaming tile counters and pristine electric appliances. If only his mother could see this place—but, of course, she never would. The cost of Anil's plane fare alone had required Papa to sell six head of cattle. It would be up to Anil to earn the money from his paltry resident salary for his return visits.

Baldev pointed out Mahesh's room, with its neatly made bed and adjoining bathroom; then his own disheveled room, its walls covered with posters of Bollywood starlets, a weight bench in the corner. He showed Anil the bathroom they would share in the hallway, apologizing for the arrangement. But Anil preferred it this way: after growing up with a latrine under the stars, the idea of a toilet too close to his bedroom was distasteful.

As he unpacked, Anil was surprised to find that his belongings, having occupied so much space on top of the Maruti back home, virtually disappeared into this vast room. The turmeric Ma had packed into his trunk had spilled out and stained half his clothes, which had to be thrown away. The greatest portion of his room was occupied by medical textbooks: two dozen volumes, representing all the information he'd memorized over the past six years. Unlike his classmates who'd been eager to sell their books after graduation, Anil had kept his, certain they'd be a lifeline during residency.

When he was finished, Anil stepped back to survey his new room. The sense of order pleased him; it boded well for a new beginning. He was struck by the feeling of abundance that seemed to define America. The open airport, sparse roads, this half-empty bedroom—everywhere there was more than was necessary, more than he could reasonably expect. Anil pushed away a pang of loneliness at the thought of sleeping alone for the first time in his life, having always shared his room with a brother or classmate. He focused instead on the freedom of being in this space that belonged to him—away from medical college, where he'd been saddled with his origins in the village; away from the village, where he'd been saddled with the expectations of his family.

Baldev ducked into Anil's room. "Hey, man, let's go. Mahesh is waiting outside. We're going to introduce you to the best cuisine in America." He perched his sunglasses atop his coiffed hair and raised an eyebrow. "Tex-Mex. You'll love it, one hundred percent guaranteed."

They stepped outside, and just as Baldev was locking their front door, a woman emerged from the next apartment. She wore an aqua-blue exercise outfit, and sandy-brown hair fell to her shoulders in waves. Anil thought he caught a blank, almost sad, look on her face, but when she turned around she gave them a wide smile. "Oh, hey there. Y'all must be my new neighbors." She hoisted a gym bag onto her shoulder. "I'm Amber. I live right here." She pointed over her shoulder at the doorway behind her. Her voice reminded Anil of the scent that wafted out of the kitchen back home when the cook made sweets: ghee simmering with flour was an aroma he associated with the anticipation of good things.

"I'm Dave," Baldev said in an unusually deep voice. "And this is . . . Neil." Baldev grabbed both of Anil's shoulders and shook them a little. "My friend here is a doctor recruited all the way from India. That's how good he is. Best in the country."

A flush of heat rose to Anil's face. "Well . . . that's not exactly true. I—"

"Really?" Amber turned to him. "You look so young. I can't believe you're already a doctor." She smiled and shifted her gym bag to the other shoulder.

"Not that young. Twenty-three," Anil said. "In India, we go to medical college after two years of postsecondary, so we get through school a little earlier. But we make up for it in our training years, which is why I'm here."

"I'd love to hear more about it some time," Amber said. "I think medicine is fascinating." She dropped her gym bag to the ground and leaned against the wall.

Anil was acutely aware that Baldev was eager to leave, having drifted toward the parking lot where Mahesh was waiting. But Anil wanted to stay right where he was. Most of his encounters since coming to America—at the airport, the immigration counter—had been transactional and cold. Here, finally, was a hint of warmth. He smiled back at Amber, unable to come up with anything interesting or witty to say.

"Well, this is a great place to live," Amber said into the silence that should have been filled by him. "I've only been here six months, so I haven't met too many friends yet, but there seem to be lots of young people like us. And the swimming pool is a real godsend in this heat."

"Yes, I can imagine," Anil said. He held on to the phrase *like us*, on to the idea of being grouped together with her. He had never swum in a pool before; he'd never swum anywhere other than in the river and waterfall pools surrounding Panchanagar, in his regular clothes or none at all. He made a mental note to purchase a bathing suit before next weekend. Anil was reluctant for the conversation to end, but he heard a car horn honking behind him.

"Well, it was nice to meet you, Neil."

"It's A-nil, actually."

"Ah-neel?" She looked at him for confirmation and he nodded.

"See you around." He wanted to kick himself for the meaningless words, but Amber's face brightened into a wide smile. At that moment, he decided she was more beautiful than any of Baldev's poster girls, or anyone else he could recall. Amber gathered her lustrous hair in a sweeping gesture and tied it in a ponytail as she walked toward the parking lot.

Anil climbed into the passenger seat of the blue Honda Civic and introduced himself to Mahesh, who looked just as he had in his online profile: a wiry man with eyeglasses and a mobile phone clipped to his belt. He might even have been wearing the same blue checked shirt as in that photo. As they drove out of the parking lot, Anil turned back to Baldev. "Hey, what was that nonsense with the names?"

"*Bhai*, you've got to learn to fit in here. You'll never get a girl over here if you go around acting like you're still in India, believe me."

"You're talking about that girl who lives next door, the *American* girl?" Mahesh said. "Why would you be interested in her?"

Baldev clucked his tongue and wagged a finger at Anil. "Don't you go over there and get any ideas about American girls, son," he said in a high-pitched voice. "We'll fix your marriage here when it's time." He laughed and reverted to his normal tone. "True?"

Anil and Mahesh joined in, laughing. "True, very true," they parroted, wobbling their heads as their mothers would.

ANIL HAD never tasted a margarita before, and the first frozen sip led to a searing pain in his head. "What's wrong? I ordered you a virgin," Baldev said. Seeing Anil's expression, he added, "A virgin *margarita*, you idiot. Without the alcohol."

"Oh." Anil nodded slowly. "I was thinking you really *can* get anything you want in this country." He reached for the basket of tortilla chips on the patio table. "Virgin, very good."

Baldev threw his head back and laughed. "I've already been lectured by Mr. Uptight over here how you Gujus won't touch a drop of liquor."

"I didn't say all Gujaratis," Mahesh started, "but my family doesn't—"

"Right, and you don't think all Punjabis are heathens, just those of us who drink." Baldev raised his frosty glass and took a slurp. "And eat meat," he added as the waiter placed a sizzling platter of fajitas on their table. As the odor of meat wafted upward, Anil averted his nose. "Oh, don't look so offended. It's only chicken. I knew you'd have a heart attack if I got the beef, and we can't have our doctor having a heart attack."

"Look, I'm not really a doctor yet," Anil said, "just a resident."

"Details, my friend." Baldev piled a tortilla high with grilled meat. "In America, you have to sell yourself. *Doctor* sounds better than *just a resident*, okay? Amber liked it, didn't she?" He took a bite of his fajita and jabbed his thumb into his chest. "Look at me, I'm a digital networking consultant."

Mahesh spoke through a forkful of rice and beans. "Which means he works for an electronics store, helping people plug in their computers."

"Better than sitting in your cubicle all day, writing code."

Mahesh leaned in. "Hey, you're talking to a senior software development expert."

"*Now* you're catching on, my friend." Baldev raised his glass. "To America, where you can be anything you want. Only limit is the sky."

Exactly. Anil clinked the others' glasses. *Anything I want. Regardless of what my mother-siblings-aunties-uncles-cousins-family-neighbors-clan-village want.*

Draining his margarita glass, Baldev motioned the waiter over to order another.

"Another for me too," Anil said, adding, "but no virgin this time."

Baldev leaned over to slap him on the shoulder. "Good times, my friend. We're in for some good times."

The next margarita tasted better than the first, so good that Anil drank most of it in the space of several minutes and began to feel light enough to float away. As he poured the rest of the hot salsa over his cheese enchiladas, which were spicy and delicious, his mother's warnings about tasteless food and the evils of alcohol faded into irrelevance. So far, America seemed to encompass the best of India, without the aspects he'd rather leave behind. Anil sat back in his chair, swatted a mosquito on his arm, and drew in a deep breath of Texas summer night.

THE DATE of the internship orientation had long been circled in red on Anil's calendar. Despite rising early that morning, he was late when he arrived at the hospital after navigating the complex of adjoining buildings that resembled a major airport, through pathways marked by colors and alphanumeric codes. Anil had read a great deal about Parkview Hospital, so he thought he knew what to expect when he walked through the doors that first day, bristling with excitement. But actually seeing the place was different—the vastness of it, humming with activity like some enormous breathing giant.

As Anil took his seat in the auditorium, a tall man tapped the microphone and introduced himself as the residency program director. Casper O'Brien's signature had been on every piece of correspondence Anil had received from Parkview, and it was now paired with the man standing on stage, easily over six feet tall with a booming voice. "Welcome to Parkview," he said, "one of the finest medical training programs in the country. You'll give us three years, it'll feel like six, but we'll give you back nine in experience." There were chuckles from the audience. Anil crossed and uncrossed his legs. "Our mission," O'Brien said, "is to furnish medical aid and hospital care to indigent and needy persons. What that means, ladies and gentlemen, is you're going to see it all here."

"And it won't be pretty." The low voice came from a tall blond guy in a tan blazer sitting in the row in front of Anil.

O'Brien strode across the platform, long legs moving like scissor blades. "We see over a million patients a year. We deliver more babies at this hospital than anywhere else, not just in the country but in the *world*." He stopped and held up a forefinger. "I believe there is no finer place to earn your stripes as a physician. Once we're done training you here, you'll be ready to go anywhere."

He unleashed a torrent of information—hospital procedures, staff roles, department rotations, team assignments. Anil couldn't absorb it all, but he was struck by the fact that Parkview employed twelve thousand people, which amounted to the population of his village twenty times over. He would spend his internship year rotating through a different department of internal medicine every month. There was a collective shuffling of papers as the interns were directed to find their schedules for the year.

"Well, I'm starting in Emergency," said a man on Anil's left. "Can't get much worse than that." Anil noticed he was dressed notably more casual than the others, in a shirt and cardigan rather than a suit.

Anil glanced down at his schedule again and then held it up.

"I'm Charlie Boyd." His face broke into a broad smile and he extended his hand. "Good to meet you, mate."

THE EMERGENCY room, nicknamed the welcome mat of the hospital, saw over a hundred thousand patients a year. Anil's supervisor was a stocky, muscular senior resident named Eric Stern. He had a strong New York accent and operated in a state of constant motion: walking quickly and issuing rapid instructions littered with unfamiliar terms. "Move it along, Patel." Eric ducked into Anil's examination area on his first day in the ER. "You can't spend fifteen minutes taking a history. We've got a waiting room full of patients out there. Assess and stabilize. Discharge or admit. That's your only job. What's the chief complaint here?" He glanced at the patient's chart. "Abdominal pain? Send him down to CT and go clear some more patients." In Ahmadabad, Anil would have done a thorough examination to rule out all other options before sending a patient to the one CT scanner shared by three hospitals, where lines were long and results could take days.

Within weeks, the daily rhythm of the ER became imprinted on Anil. Morning rounds began at seven o'clock sharp, after which the team dispersed to work at a frantic pace all day long—it was an incessant intake of new patients, medical histories, physical exams, admitting orders. By afternoon, the waiting room overflowed. A hundred thousand patients a year translated to a new patient every four minutes, every single day, around the clock.

In the windowless world of the ER, Anil was disconnected from the rest of his intern class. Emergency Department staff were not permitted to leave their posts to attend grand rounds or lectures with other residents, or even to go to the cafeteria. For lunch, he often settled for a protein bar from the vending machine while waiting for a consult. When the residents ordered pizza, Eric insisted upon a Meat Lover's pie, eating two slices at the same time, one flipped on top of the other like a sandwich. It was difficult for Anil to relate to Eric, so different from the physicians he'd known back in India. Loud and brash, Eric had a prominent scar on his forehead he said he'd got kitesurfing, a cross between two other dangerous sports Anil had never heard of.

Among the dozen interns and residents working the ER, Anil was surprised to see that nearly half were women. He avoided them, unsure how to behave, but was more comfortable interacting with the female nurses, as he had done in India. Anil was the only foreign student in the group, and one of the few who weren't white. Like Anil, the great majority of patients at Parkview weren't white either. Far from the bucolic paradise Anil had envisioned back in India, Parkview turned out to be the hospital of last resort for the city's poorest. Those with no health insurance, no money, and no regular doctor showed up at Parkview, particularly the ER. There was the homeless woman who listed her address as "Planet Earth" and wore, upon her disheveled nest of hair, a carefully constructed tinfoil hat, which she refused to remove for the examination. And the man reeking of liquor, with a nose reddened by a long history of alcoholism, who nevertheless insisted he hadn't been drunk when he fell down and cut his forehead on broken glass.

By the end of each day, Anil was not only physically exhausted but mentally drained. He was overwhelmed by his patients' evasion and mistrust, the desperation in their eyes and voices, the scent of urine and filth. The first thing he did when he got home, well after 10 p.m. most nights, was take a very long shower, scrubbing himself until the fragrant soap flooded his senses.

Interns were expected to study at home in the evenings, and Anil had been accumulating a reading list. Every night he left the hospital with the intention of working through his list, but after being on his feet for twelve hours, he'd barely make it through the first topic before falling asleep. When his alarm sounded at 5 a.m., he'd wake up in bed, surrounded by books, with his specs and the overhead light still on.

⊗

"HAVE YOU seen Eric Stern?" a nurse asked Anil, the only white coat in the vicinity of the triage desk before morning rounds. "I've got an urgent patient."

"I can take it," Anil said, reaching for the chart.

"You sure?" She peered at his ID badge. "It's not a minor."

Anil took the chart. He'd been looking for an opportunity to present his own case on rounds, to make an impression on the attending. Behind Curtain 6 he found John Doe, a young man dressed in street clothes, his head fallen to one side and his mouth hanging open.

"Sir?" Anil shook the patient's shoulder and shone a light into his eyes. His pupils were constricted, his respirations shallow. No alcohol on his breath, nothing on his body other than a few residual marks of healed scabies on his arms. Anil's pulse raced as the differential diagnosis ran through his mind. *Brain stem hemorrhage. Pulmonary embolism.* He tried hoisting the patient up but was surprised by how limp and heavy his body was. The patient dropped back onto the hospital bed with a thud, his head falling to the other side.

Anil yanked open the curtain and yelled for an intubation cart, just as the ER attending rounded the corner with Eric and the rest of the team.

"Patel, where you been?" Eric barked. "Rounds start at seven o'clock. Sharp."

"I-I-I have a critical patient here," Anil said. "Might n-n-need to intubate." He felt a rush of shame as he sputtered out the words.

"Whoa," the attending said. "Slow down. Let's see what we have here. How's his breathing?"

"Shallow respirations—"

"But he's breathing independently, right? Let's check his airway." The attending placed a tongue depressor deep into the patient's mouth and John Doe, in his first visible sign of life, gagged on it. The attending turned to the rest of the team. "From that reflex, we know he's protecting his airway. No need to intubate." He shot a look at Anil. "Heart rate?"

Fifty-five, Anil recalled, but *f*s were the worst for him. He could already feel them stopping up behind his lips, ready to trip over each other if he opened his mouth, so instead of speaking he watched the attending listen to the patient's heart with his own stethoscope. "Heart rate's fifty-six—normal. What else? BP?"

"I di-di-didn't check." Anil tried to breathe slowly as the heat rose to his face.

The attending turned to the rest of the team. "Can anybody who paid attention the first week of med school tell me the initial steps for a nonresponsive patient?"

The tan-blazer guy from orientation spoke up. "Airway, breathing, circulation." *Trey Crandall*, Anil read on his name badge.

The attending turned back to Anil. "ABC. Sound familiar? And did you notice anything in your physical exam, Dr. Patel?" A hard edge had crept into his voice. "You *did* do a physical exam? Anything strike you as unusual about the patient's arms?" He grabbed John Doe's wrist and held it up for everyone to see.

"Recent s-s-scabies infection . . ." Anil's head was burning, and there was a pulsing pain behind his eyes. He searched his memory for anything that might have developed from scabies, rummaging in his pocket for the index cards he'd prepared for this rotation.

"Scabies?" The attending smirked. "Anyone else?"

The mood at Curtain 6 turned somber as the urgency of the patient's medical condition was replaced with Anil's public humiliation. The incessant beeping of a monitor behind the next curtain marked a few moments before Trey Crandall jumped in, eager to fill the void created by Anil's squandered opportunity. "Track marks?" he offered.

The attending dropped the patient's arm and pointed at Trey. "Bingo! This type of patient is a frequent flyer in our ER, Patel. These marks are obvious signs of an intravenous drug user. I bet his tox screen will come back positive for gamma-hydroxybutyric acid. High doses of GHB, also known as Liquid E, can cause rapid unconsciousness. He'll be up in an hour or two, screaming and cussing like everyone else. Until then, roll him on his side so he doesn't aspirate, and check his vitals every half hour."

As the team filed out behind the attending, Eric Stern stopped directly in front of Anil. "Getting a little ahead of yourself, Patel. Next time, tell the triage nurse to page me when you don't know what the hell you're doing."

On his way out, Charlie placed his hand on Anil's shoulder. "Okay, mate." The unexpected touch caused Anil's eyes to fill. He bit down on his tongue.

ANIL WAS five years old when he first began to stammer. At school, the cruelest children taunted him. The worst of the lot was a large, dim-witted boy named Babu, whose father was a known drunkard who couldn't hold a job, though he had once worked as one of Papa's field hands. Whenever the teacher's back was turned, Babu made hissing sounds at Anil, until the other boys joined in and they resembled a pack of angry snakes.

One day, as the students began filing out of the classroom, the teacher asked Anil to stay behind—Babu launching one last hiss at him. The teacher held out a thick volume, bound in fabric too fine for a schoolbook. Anil ran his hand over the tightly wound threads of the indigo cover. He fanned through the pages, releasing a musty odor.

"Do you know it?" the teacher asked.

Anil nodded, recognizing the title from his father's collection—the autobiography of Mahatma Gandhi.

"Practice reading those passages I marked. When you're ready, you can do a recitation for the class."

This notion terrified Anil but he dutifully took the book. Each afternoon he left the Big House, walked around the rice paddies, over the low hill, and out to his favorite banana tree, where he stayed until the sun sank low in the sky. He sat under that tree and read the passages his teacher had marked until the words came smoothly and were committed to memory. Finally, Anil stood under the tree, performing the passages for an audience of crickets and toads. Then he knew that, at least in one isolated place, with one set of words, he could speak clearly. In this way, Anil was able to largely overcome his stutter by the age of nine, and with that accomplishment, he learned he could do anything.

❁

AT THE end of the shift, Anil sat in the workroom as Charlie changed out of his scrubs. "I can't do it," Anil said. "I've been working toward this my whole life and now I'm f-f-f-failing." He closed his eyes and rubbed at them.

"C'mon, mate," Charlie said. "You just had a bad day."

Anil shook his head. "You didn't see Stern's face. I'm going to fail out of the program. I'll have to go home, and I won't be qualified to practice, and all the training programs in India are already closed." He pictured the expression on Papa's face if he went home a failure.

Charlie pulled up a chair across from Anil and sat on it backwards, his chin resting on the top edge. "Listen, mate, take a deep breath. One day at a time. What do you have to do for tomorrow? Finish today's reading and prepare for rounds, right? So let's do that. Don't worry about anything else tonight, okay?"

Beginning that night, Anil and Charlie went to a nearby diner to work through their reading lists every day after leaving the hospital. They kept their books in their cars and met up in the same burgundy vinyl booth in the back corner, away from the kitchen and the other patrons. Their regular waitress was a thin older woman named Joy whose raspy voice intimated a lifetime of smoking. She learned their orders: the meatloaf platter for Charlie, and the same without meatloaf for Anil. The mashed potatoes and vegetable medley were unremarkable, but at this diner Anil had discovered gravy, which he poured over everything, along with one of the many hot sauces kept on the table.

"Mate, this is amazing!" Charlie exclaimed a couple of weeks later when Anil presented him with a full set of his color-coordinated index cards, each containing notes of symptoms, differential diagnoses, recommended tests, and treatments. "How . . . When did you do all this?" Charlie flipped one of the cards over, glancing at the journal references on the back.

Anil shrugged, a little sheepish. "I started in medical college and just keep adding to them." He hadn't made a practice of sharing his notes, given how competitive medical college had been. But Charlie was different, easier to get along with than many of the other interns. Perhaps it was the relaxed nature he claimed was endemic to all Aussies, or that he was older than the rest of the class. Charlie had worked as a biomedical engineer in Sydney for several years and was planning to apply to business school when he went to America to go backpacking in Monument Valley. With his experience in the Australian outback, Charlie was soon leading expedition groups through the canyons. During that year, spent in close proximity to both nature and people, Charlie decided climbing the corporate ladder at a medical-device company wasn't for him after all, and applied to medical school instead.

"Seriously, Patel, this is a secret weapon." Charlie fanned through the stack of cards. "We'll have the ER mastered in no time. Thank you, mate, really generous of you to share these." He reached over and slapped Anil's shoulder.

Anil smiled as he picked up a bottle of bright green chili sauce and untwisted the cap. "No problem." He was happy to do something for Charlie, the only one of his peers he felt he could trust. One day, a few weeks earlier, when he had been changing scrubs in the locker room after getting soaked by a wayward urine catheter, he'd overheard some guys talking as they tossed a football back and forth on the other side of the room. "Have you seen that foreign guy on rounds?" a disembodied voice said in between the thwacks of the ball being caught. Anil froze in place, one foot hovering over his pant leg.

"Who?" He recognized Trey's unmistakable baritone.

"Patel. He's got these little index cards with notes from every obscure journal article. Can't think on his feet, can't answer a question worth a damn. You should've seen the attending take him apart when he wanted to look something up before answering." Anil held his breath, terrified someone would walk around the lockers and see him there, pantless.

"Besides," a third person said, "even when he has an answer, who the hell can understand him?" All three of them broke into laughter, the dissonance reverberating in Anil's ears. He didn't know if it was his accent they were mocking, his stutter, or his inadequate presentations, nor did it matter.

Anil expected things to improve after his first rotation in the ER, but he came to discover that each monthly rotation had its own particular horrors. The ER was only the worst in terms of the sheer volume of new patients to clear every day. The general medical wards were an incessant juggling act of demanding patients. Gastroenterology offered frequent opportunities to be vomited upon, as well as the occasional explosion of diarrhea. Every month brought not just a new realm of medicine but a new set of supervisors to challenge and humiliate him, and a new set of peers eager to step over each other to score points.

A sense of utter exhaustion had overtaken Anil's life. Fatigue unraveled itself into a full-body experience: First his head became foggy, then his shoulders sagged and he found himself leaning against the wall. At some point, his eyes began burning and watering, for which he kept tissues and eye drops in his coat pocket at all times. After he'd been on his feet for twelve hours or more, he felt a deep ache in his knees, which would stay with him all night if he was on call, and which could not be alleviated except by eight hours of undisturbed sleep, whenever it finally came.

Six days a week, Anil roused himself in a haze and returned to the hospital, determined to prove he could do this job for which he'd so long prepared. He had expected to work hard during his internship, and this he didn't mind, but he did miss hearing words of praise once in a while, or the inner satisfaction of getting something right. He missed feeling appreciated, or simply respected, by patients. In India, his grateful patients had brought him so many sweets that Anil gained three kilos in the first month. Here, his patients were distrustful and combative. Whether this was equally true for all doctors, or worse for Anil, he couldn't be sure.

Within a few months, Anil had given up the elusive hope of finding proficiency in his work. Instead, he developed ways of coping: moving through his patients with brisk efficiency, remembering them by condition or room number instead of learning their names. Charlie's advice to get through one day at a time became his new mantra. Every night, Anil revisited the impish blue Krishna calendar pinned to his bedroom door, wondering, before placing a black gash across the date, if this daily glance at the deity would qualify as prayer in his mother's eyes. Midway through his internship year, his hierarchy of goals had changed. Just like the human body under duress needs oxygen and fluids before all else, Anil was now just trying to survive.

3

Leena tried to maintain a neutral expression as Piya grinned and clutched a pillow to her chest. "Come, come! Tell me," Piya said, making herself comfortable on her bed.

Leena sat at the other end of the bed, facing Piya, her legs outstretched. She shrugged but a smile crept through regardless. Piya had always been able to draw things out of her, despite being two years younger.

They had been friends from the time they were old enough to stray out of their neighboring homes and find each other outdoors. Leena had no brothers or sisters, so she relished the company of Piya and her siblings. Anil was the unspoken leader of their little group, always looking out for his four younger siblings and setting rules of play that were fair to everyone. Leena couldn't say quite why she and Anil had gravitated toward each other in the first place. Perhaps it was because they were both quiet as children: she, an only child, accustomed to playing in her own imagination; Anil more absorbed with his books than with rowdy games of cricket like the other boys and reluctant to speak because of his stutter. Whatever the reason, when he discovered a waterfall at the end of the river, she went with him to swim under it. And when she wanted to climb the tallest coconut tree on the land, he followed. After a while, they could spend an entire afternoon together without many words.

Piya slapped Leena's knee. "Tell me *everything*, hear? Every little detail. Come on. What's he like?"

Leena shrugged again. "I . . . I don't know, really." It was true, she knew almost nothing about the man who might become her husband in a few weeks' time. She had met Girish once, and things had moved quickly since then.

A few months earlier, Leena's parents had decided it was time to seek a husband for her. She was twenty and had finished her schooling. Leena enjoyed living with her parents, helping her mother with the cooking and their home, some days accompanying her father in the fields. The land surrounding them was her true home: the green expanses of the rice paddies, the soaring trees, the rise of the mountains in the distance. Leena was in no hurry to get married, or to leave her parents on their own. Her father had begun suffering from one ailment after another: he was short of breath, his knees were weak, and his back became sore after a few hours in the fields.

But Leena knew it was time: she might still feel like a girl, but she was the right age to marry, and in a few more years she would be too old. Besides, she didn't have many other choices. She had barely scraped her way through the tenth standard at school; she wasn't a good student like Anil, though he'd tried to help her with her studies when they were younger. "How about this?" he would say, explaining a math problem in a new way. Anil studied harder than anyone, as if he were propelled by an inner motor toward some distant horizon he alone could see.

Nor were there any prospects for Leena to earn a living. Farming was the way of life in their village, and it was largely men's work. When the harvest was good, her parents worked in tandem: her father moving up and down rows to gather the vegetables, her mother carrying them in vessels back to the large terrace that wrapped around their small house, where she sorted and cleaned them. Leena's mother would rub the eggplants until their purple skin gleamed; she wrapped the long beans in tidy, even bundles. When Leena's father returned from the market, he often reported selling his stock immediately and at the highest possible price. Her mother smiled as she rubbed warm coconut oil on her husband's tired feet. Her father praised his wife for her talents of presentation at the market. Her father's land was productive but modest: it was enough to sustain them, but her parents could not go on supporting her forever. Perhaps, if she could have a marriage like theirs, it would be worth it to leave her parents. As content as Leena was being their daughter, she wondered if something even better might await her.

They all thought it best to find a boy from a family who lived nearby. There were not many eligible men in Panchanagar. Her parents spent several months looking, but all the boys they found were too young to get married, so old that everyone knew something was wrong, or otherwise unsuitable. Her father, though hardworking, was not a rich man and could not afford the dowry the best families were asking.

So they began to inquire about boys in villages farther away, relying on the introductions and suggestions of people who were merely acquaintances or barely known in their circle. Soon, families came with their sons to visit, and each time, Leena and her mother spent all day preparing. They ensured every corner of their small home was cleaned and filled with the aroma of chai brewing. Leena's mother, known for her delicious homemade sweets, always had a tray of freshly prepared *boondi laddoo* or pistachio *bhurfi*.

"Come, you must know *something* about him," Piya said. "One thing, besides his name."

Leena cast her eyes up toward the ceiling and rocked her head back and forth as she thought. "He likes his tea sweet, *too* sweet," she giggled.

The day Girish had come to visit, he wore a crisp white *kurta-pajama* with tan embroidery around the neckline. Right away, Leena noticed how neat his hair was. It looked as though it had been freshly oiled, and the pale line of his part was straight as a ruler. That a man would take such care in his personal grooming was surely an indication of how he would care for his wife.

Rather than addressing Leena directly, out of respect for her as an unmarried woman, Girish asked her mother for three full spoons of sugar in his tea. What could it mean, Leena wondered, that he possessed such strong tastes?

His parents sat on either side of him on the divan. His father was a tall man with a straight nose and dark sagging skin under his eyes that made him look as if he were perpetually tired. When Leena leaned forward to offer the tray of chai, he peered directly into her eyes for several breaths before taking his cup, and Leena had the strange sensation that he was trying to see inside her. He spoke only to her father, posing all sorts of questions. *How often did Leena fall ill? Which of the foods she prepared were his favorites? Did she know how to mend clothing? Had she ever raised her voice to her parents?* His questions came quickly—one after another, like the popping of mustard seeds in hot oil—and then, just as suddenly, they stopped and he sat back on the divan, blowing across the surface of his chai while he looked over at his wife.

Girish's mother was a plump woman with an equally round face who wore her hair in a large bun. Her ample belly spoke of a household where food was abundant and hardship scarce. Once she began, she spoke without pause about how smart her son was, how hardworking, how respectful: a good boy with excellent prospects, a bright future and his choice of brides. He was the middle of three sons and his mother was very proud; this seemed to Leena a good thing, even if the woman came across as somewhat boastful. Perhaps if Leena had a son one day, she would feel the same way.

When Girish's mother finally stopped speaking, she ate an entire *laddoo* in one bite and drank down most of her chai in a single, long gulp. Leena noticed her parents exchange a smile; their guests' cups were empty and they had each consumed several sweets. Leena's father took the opportunity to ask his questions, inquiring about the quality of the farmland in their village, what type of accommodations Leena would have in the family house, and the nature of the eldest brother's wife. He had managed only a few questions before Girish's family had to leave, to return to their village before nightfall.

Piya clapped her hands together. "How exciting! He sounds handsome, yes?"

Leena wobbled her head, her smile unrestrained now.

"What will you wear for the ceremony? And what kind of jewelry?"

"Ah, don't be ridiculous!" Leena said, slapping her friend's knee. "You're getting ahead of yourself." And yet, Leena knew her parents were downstairs in the gathering room at that moment, working out arrangements for a possible wedding ceremony with the village pandit and Piya's father, Jayant Patel, who her father held in high regard. Now, for the first time, Leena allowed herself to feel excited, letting her mind slip into what might lie ahead.

4

Anil awoke with a start. It was always the same dream that haunted him: he was home, visiting from medical college, and Ma shook him in the middle of the night. "Come quickly, the midwife is calling. Papa's waiting in the car." When Anil stumbled into the car outside, Papa explained that one of the villagers was in labor with her third child and the midwife had sent for help.

Anil thought of explaining to his father the limitations of his relevant experience. He'd only spent two years studying medicine, and only in books and laboratories. He had no clinical experience with patients, nor any obstetrics training. He hadn't attended a childbirth or seen a woman in labor. He had never, in fact, seen a woman unclothed for any reason in his twenty years. But he swallowed these words, knowing he was still the most qualified person for such a task and that Papa was counting on him.

It was eerily quiet when they approached the house, the warm night air still and devoid of the cries Anil would have expected from a woman in the throes of labor. Inside, he saw her, laying on the floor, panting, her hair matted with sweat and her eyes closed. An older woman he assumed to be her mother sat behind her, propping her up. The sheets upon which the young woman lay were soaked through with blood and other fluids. Her knees were parted, and the midwife was squatting between them, blood dripping onto the floor around her. "I can see the baby's head," the midwife said. "But it will not come out." She shook her head. "Her first two babies came with no problem."

Papa nudged Anil forward. The midwife turned to him, her mouth puckered tight. Next to her were two pails of water, a pile of cloths, and a few rudimentary tools, including a pair of ancient forceps. Anil washed his hands in the hottest water he could get from the cistern, and dried them on a clean cloth as he gingerly kneeled down next to the midwife. In Gross Anatomy, he'd dissected a cadaver from head to toe in concert with each chapter of his textbook, but this was entirely different.

The young woman's legs were spread wide, her thighs trembling and her genitals swollen nearly beyond recognition. The midwife wiped away some blood and pointed to the crown of the baby's head, an ovular patch covered in fine black hair pressing against the mother's pubic bone. To Anil's shock, she thrust her fingers into the birth canal and traced its circumference before indicating, with her blood-covered hands, the size of the baby's head. Anil looked around the room: there was no equipment to use, nothing with which to sterilize, no medicine.

Suddenly, the midwife grabbed Anil's wrist and held it tight, as if she sensed he was about to run off. "Do something, quickly, or else they will both die," she whispered. He followed her eyes to the floor, where a small pool of blood was forming around their feet.

Each time he had the dream, the diagnosis came easily—when the warm blood dripped onto his sandals, or when the veiny lump of tissue obscured the opening to the cervix. Placenta previa was not an uncommon condition and would have been easily identified with a prenatal ultrasound, if the woman had had one. Always, the same terror rose within him. She would never make it to the hospital in time. What was he to do on the outskirts of the village in the middle of the night, perform a C-section with an unsterile kitchen knife?

The young woman's eyelids began to falter and her body shuddered. The profuse volume of blood had become visible to her mother, who began moaning for God to save the baby. Anil said a silent prayer as he reached for the decrepit forceps. How long had it been since they'd been used, or even properly cleaned? He maneuvered the forceps into the birth canal and around the baby's head. It took a surprising amount of strength. Anil felt the tension in his shoulders, the straining of the muscles in his arms, but finally the baby's head emerged, then the shoulders, and the midwife leaned forward and pulled out the baby. She clutched it to her bosom and cleaned out its mouth and nose while Anil watched anxiously. A small, animalistic cry came as the baby took its first gasps of air. Anil closed his eyes and took a deep breath.

It was a few moments before he discerned another kind of shrill scream mixed in with the baby's cries. He looked up to see the older woman slapping her daughter's face, which had gone pale. Her eyes had rolled back, and her body was limp. A gush of warm fluid spilled onto Anil's feet; she was hemorrhaging blood.

Anil grabbed the remaining cloths from the floor and packed them in, applying as much pressure as he could, but the blood seeped through. He looked around frantically, then tore off his shirt and used it against the tide of blood. The older woman was crying loudly, pleading with Anil to do something. His hands were lodged against her daughter's body. He had no blood to transfuse her, no drugs to clot her blood. Even if he could stop the hemorrhaging, she'd lost too much blood already. If she didn't go into shock, she would almost certainly develop an infection. But he stayed in that position, pressing with all his strength—with his hands, his arms, his shoulders—against the young woman's body as he watched the life drain out of her and onto the floor.

When she died, Anil felt it in his hands. There was nothing left to strain against. He stood up and backed away from her lifeless form, his body covered with her blood. The older woman cradled her daughter's head in her arms and rocked back and forth, moaning. Anil turned toward the door and saw his father, holding a pile of clean towels and wearing an expression of disappointment Anil had not seen before.

Anil washed himself at the pump outside the house, trying to scrub away the sticky blood from between his toes, scrape it from underneath his fingernails. At this point, the dream often departed from the reality of what happened that night. Sometimes, the older woman followed him outside and beat her fists against her chest, wailing that he had killed her daughter. This time, the young woman's husband was waiting outside with a string of jasmine buds. Anil was forced to look into the man's bloodshot eyes and tell him his wife was gone. "What good are you?" the distraught man cried, then his hands were around Anil's throat, squeezing tighter until Anil woke up gasping for air.

In actuality, what passed that night in Panchanagar was both milder and more haunting than what Anil imagined in his nightmares. The young woman's mother appeared outside as Anil was trying to clean his hands. He readied his apology, braced himself for her wrath. She walked toward him, put her palms together, bowed her head, and fell to the ground to touch his feet. "Thank you, Doctor Sahib, for saving my grandchild."

A wave of shame swept over Anil, not only for his own failure but also for his home in this uncivilized corner of the world where the practice of medicine was nothing but an illusion. It was then, Anil knew for certain, that he could not stay in Panchanagar. He would strive to practice the highest level of medicine he could—far, far away.

5

It seemed to Leena that everything happened very quickly after that day at the Big House. Within a week, the wedding preparations had begun. There were meetings with the astrologer and the pandit. Leena and her mother selected wedding saris, jewelry, and henna designs for her hands and feet. Despite her parents having told her to choose whatever she wanted, she picked out smaller earrings and a less ornate necklace after seeing her mother wince at the more elaborate pieces.

There was such a flurry of activity and excitement, Leena barely had time to consider how much her life would change in the days ahead. Lying in bed at night, she closed her eyes and pictured her groom's face from their single encounter. She repeated his name, softly, to herself. She tried to recreate his voice from the few words he'd spoken. What would his laugh sound like, how would his arms feel around her? Although she knew little about this man, Leena trusted her parents, who approved of the boy and his family, as did the pandit who had compared their horoscopes.

On her wedding day, Leena followed the pandit's solemn instructions during the ceremony, even as she tried to catch glimpses of her groom's long fingers, his prominent shoulder, the faint shadow of his freshly shaved face. She greeted people as they pressed coins and coconuts and rose petals into her hands, wishing her well in her new married life. Within the swirl of activity and emotion, Leena hardly knew how to feel, until she saw the unadulterated joy on her parents' faces. But after the festivities were over, when it was time to say good-bye to the only home she'd known, she could not help but weep and cling to her mother.

THE RIDE to her husband's village was long, nearly two hours. Leena sat next to her mother-in-law in the car, staring at the back of Girish's head, studying his hand gestures and facial expressions for clues about this man with whom she would spend her life. Her body brewed with equal parts anticipation and nervousness.

It was dusk when they finally arrived. Through the fading daylight, Leena could see that the cotton crop in the fields was overgrown and withered, while the family house was quite large and looked as if it had once been grand. Girish opened the car door for her and carried her single large trunk into the house. She followed him, stepping carefully across the porch, avoiding the wooden planks that seemed to be disintegrating.

As Girish entered the house ahead of her, two children came running to greet him. A small boy clutched at his leg while an older girl wrapped her arms around his waist. Girish stopped to ruffle the boy's hair and kiss the girl's head, then called out, "Rekha! Come take these rascals. I'm tired." Leena was touched by the obvious affection the children had for Girish, and he for them—a good sign, she thought.

Girish's elder brother's wife appeared from a hallway leading to the back of the house and grabbed each child by the wrist, scolding them as she took them away. Leena was eager to get to know her new sister-in-law. Rekha had been kind during the wedding functions, complimenting Leena on her hair, her jewelry, her outfits. She seemed like the kind of person with whom Leena could have an easy friendship, perhaps even a sisterhood.

"Come," her mother-in-law said once they were inside, and she led Leena into a small bedroom converted from a sleeping porch, just big enough for the bed and metal cupboard it contained. "You will be comfortable here," she said, as if reading Leena's concern. The older woman turned to Leena and held her face firmly in her plump hands. "You call me Mother, okay? I don't stand on formality. No need for 'Memsahib.'"

Leena was touched by the gesture, though she had never considered calling her new mother-in-law "Memsahib," as a servant would.

Her mother-in-law smiled widely, revealing an open space where one of her back molars should have been. "Come now, child. Say it."

Leena looked down for a moment and summoned a smile. "Yes . . . Mother. Thank you."

The older woman opened the metal cupboard and shuffled some items around inside. "You can put your things here." She pointed to the newly cleared shelf. Then she leaned down, opened Leena's trunk, and began lifting out the saris her mother had carefully wrapped. "Hmm," she said, fingering the gold embroidered border of one. "Whatever doesn't fit here, I can keep in my room for you. These silk saris, you won't need them for everyday wear." She collected a few of them in the crook of her arm and squeezed through the narrow space to the door. "When you're done, come to the kitchen. Almost time for dinner."

Leena turned back to the cupboard, filled with her husband's clothes. She ran her palm lightly over the stack of folded shirts and lifted one to her face, trying to detect its scent. Who was this man? And where was he? She had expected him to be here with her in their first hours alone as a newly married couple.

After unpacking her belongings and stowing her trunk under the bed, Leena went to look for Girish when she heard someone calling to her. "Leena, come." Rekha was beckoning to her. She led Leena to the back of the house and into the kitchen. "There's the stove," she said, pointing. "Fuel is by the dose. Don't waste it, it's costly." Rekha moved briskly around the kitchen, showing Leena the cooking vessels and utensils, and where the grains and lentils were stored. She pulled down the tin of spices from one of the upper shelves. "Watch carefully. Sahib has particular tastes, so you need to learn. I'll show you today. Tomorrow, you'll do the cooking yourself."

Leena was startled by Rekha's brusqueness, the sudden change in her demeanor. She must have been tired from the wedding and the journey, worried about getting food prepared for everyone. "I will help, don't worry. I can prepare the rice?" Leena offered.

"The rice first, then the chapatis," Rekha said without a hint of warmth. "The dough is there. Sahib likes his chapatis very thin, so don't tear them."

Dinnertime, instead of the relaxed occasion to which Leena was accustomed, was a tense affair. Rekha served their father-in-law, whom she called by the honorific title "Sahib," then stood waiting off to the side for his reaction. If the dal was not spicy enough or the chapatis had grown cold, Leena was dispatched back to the kitchen. She ended up spending most of the mealtime there, reheating food and making adjustments to suit Sahib's tastes. When Leena finally rejoined the table, the men had finished eating and Sahib was rising from the table.

"Rekha, the mango pickle is still not soft," he said. "It's like chewing on rocks. Are you trying to break my teeth, you worthless girl?" He dropped the metal spoon with a clang against the pickle jar, overturning it. "Clean it up!" he bellowed as he left the table.

Leena gently touched Rekha's forearm in silent support.

"Well?" Rekha spun around and barked at her. "What are you waiting for? Don't just stand there. Clean it up!"

LATER THAT night, Leena lay in bed, dressed in the new cotton gown her mother had packed in her trunk, waiting for Girish to join her. Weary from the long journey and the wedding festivities in the days before, her eyelids grew heavy.

She was aroused some time later by the pressure of Girish next to her. She opened her eyes and started to sit up, but he pressed her back down on the bed. "Shh," he whispered and shifted his body on top of hers. Leena's mother had told her what to expect, so she was prepared for the pain, clenching her nails into her palms to keep from crying out. When it was over, Girish rolled onto his back, and Leena felt a rush of satisfaction at having performed her first wifely duty. Perhaps now she could begin to know him.

The next morning she tried to engage Girish by asking him about the farmland and the crops they grew. "Do you raise any sugarcane? My father says it's his favorite crop. Very hearty, even though the bugs like it too."

Girish did not see her smile, nor did he respond as he combed his hair in the mirror with great concentration.

"I've never seen cotton bushes before. Is it very difficult to harvest?" Leena tried again.

Girish gestured with his hand for her to move aside so he could get into the cupboard. She opened the doors and chose a shirt for him, holding it out. "No. Just let me get it," he said, tossing the shirt she'd chosen back into the cupboard.

"What are you doing today? Will I see you for lunch?"

"God, so much talking," he said. "Before I've even had my tea."

"I'm sorry," she said. "I'll go prepare it." As she walked through the house, she noticed things in the light of day she hadn't seen the prior evening: paint peeling off the walls, dust accumulated in the corners.

The tables and shelves were largely bare, devoid of the trinkets and decorations she would expect to fill such a large house.

She found Rekha in the kitchen, annoyed with Leena for her late arrival. "You think you can sleep all morning? There's work to do. Tomorrow, you get up when you hear the rooster crow the first time, understand?" Rekha turned away. "Worthless girl," she muttered as she left.

❁

THAT EVENING, Leena decided to try a different approach with her husband. She prepared two cups of warm milk with saffron and slivered pistachios and went to find him. The men's voices were coming from outside and she followed them, pausing at the door to rebalance the tray in one hand. Girish was sitting with his two brothers around a small table holding a bottle of amber liquid. Her husband tipped a full glass to his lips, took a swig, and wiped his mouth with the back of his sleeve.

"What's the best thing about marrying a leper?" Girish asked, then answered himself. "She can only give you lip once!" He took another drink.

His brothers laughed, and the younger one reached over to refill Girish's glass. "She's bad, huh?"

Girish shook his head. "Never shuts up."

"I know one thing you can shove into her mouth to make her shut up." The elder brother stood halfway out of his chair and launched his hips forward, gesturing crudely to his crotch. Girish threw his head back and slapped the table with his hand.

Leena closed the door. The glasses of warm milk, which now had a skin across its surface, clattered on the tray as she walked quickly back to the kitchen. She emptied the glasses, washed and dried them, and put everything back in its place, leaving no trace of her presence.

Leena went outside through the back kitchen door and into the washroom, where she began heating the water. In the morning, there had been no time for this step, and Leena had bathed quickly with cold water. Now, her muscles aching and her head throbbing, she longed to wash away the things she'd heard her husband say.

After her bath, Leena redressed in the same clothes to walk back to the house and into the bedroom, locking the door behind her. She undressed again, opened the metal cupboard, and pulled out a clean cotton nightgown. Remembering thr rose-scented talcum powder her mother had packed in her trousseau, Leena reached to the back of the cupboard but could not find the slender canister. She took everything out of the cupboard, her clothes and Girish's, all their toiletries, but the rose talc was not there.

Leena was pulling her empty trunk from under the bed when there was a sound outside the bedroom door. The door was forced against its jamb, the knob rattling back and forth. "Hey!" Girish slurred from the other side of the door. "What is this? Open the door, woman!"

Leena, still naked, fumbled back to the cupboard for her nightgown and clumsily pulled it over her head while Girish banged at the door. She opened it, confused between the shame and anger that rose within her.

"What is this?" he said, his eyes narrowed. "Don't ever lock that door. This is not your house, understand?"

"I was getting dressed." Leena retreated, pulling the gown up at her neck.

A smirk bloomed across Girish's face as he moved toward her. "What a shame."

Leena reached for her comb on the nightstand and began to pull it through her tangled hair. "I'll be ready for bed in a few minutes."

"I'm ready now," he said, reaching for her nightgown. He took one of her hands and moved it toward his belt. "See?" He grinned.

Leena yanked her hand back and turned away from him. She climbed into the bed and continued pulling at the tangles with the comb so hard her scalp burned.

"What?" Girish crawled on top of the bed after her. Leena pushed him away. He stopped and looked at her with bloodshot eyes, as if weighing a decision. Then he pinned both of her hands above her head with one of his. Leena was surprised at the strength with which he held her down. She remembered the day she and Anil hid in the gully, smoking *beedis*, the terrible scene they'd witnessed. She'd never expected to be treated the same way by her husband.

The next morning, her shoulders and wrists sore from the force Girish had used against her, Leena rose and went to the washroom to bathe. As she arrived, Rekha was leaving, clad in a clean sari and carrying her old clothes in a bundle. As she stepped back to let her sister-in-law pass, the distinct fragrance of fresh roses lingered in the air.

When Leena returned to their room, Girish offered a halfway apology for the night before. "You shouldn't have provoked me, locking the door and running away from me. I'm your husband. As long as you show me respect, you'll never have reason to complain. Understand?"

"I want my rose talc back," Leena said without turning to face him.

"What?"

"I put a can of rose talcum powder in the cupboard. Right there." She pointed. "It's gone. I think Rekha took it."

Girish stared impotently inside the cupboard for a few moments, then slammed the metal door shut, startling her. "Why must you always make so much trouble?"

6

Anil's new assignment was in the Intensive Care Unit, known for being a particularly brutal rotation. ICU patients were quite ill to begin with and often suffered a rash of new complications in the hospital, so they could go from stable to crashing at any moment. His first night on call, Anil paid close attention as a fellow intern signed out her patients to him in the break room. Jennifer was a short, perky girl with flaming red curls, who wore glasses with invisible frames that disappeared into her pale skin. Huddled over her sign-out sheets, she spoke in bullet points. "Dina Jimenez. Sixty-two. Hispanic female. Motor vehicle accident." Jennifer tapped the chart with the end of her pen. "Brain-dead. Son's on his way from Arizona. If he shows up tonight, ask him for the DNR."

Anil nodded, tuning out his apprehension. He had never asked a family member for a do-not-resuscitate order—permission to remove life support—but he was certain he could handle it.

Jennifer flipped to the next chart. "Lyndon Jackson. Fifty-four. Black male. Keep an eye on him, he's a mess. AIDS, kidney failure. Came straight from dialysis in respiratory distress, then his right lung collapsed. Just a mess," she repeated. "He's intubated. If his O_2 drops, you'll have to call Renal. I asked the nurses to check his temp every two hours and watch for infection. If you suspect pneumonia, get a chest X-ray. And he's on a rule-out protocol for MI, so you'll have to check his EKG for changes at 2 a.m." She shook her head. "Hopefully, he won't crump before morning.

"Last one." Jennifer pointed her pen to the final name on her list. "Jason Calhoun. Fifty-seven. White male. Diabetes and hypertension. Went in for his regular physical yesterday and the internist felt something in his abdomen, so he did an ultrasound. Aortic aneurysm. Eight centimeters," she announced with pride, as if she'd discovered it herself.

"Eight?" Anil craned his neck to see the details. An average aorta was two centimeters, was classified as an aneurysm at three, and required surgery when it reached five centimeters.

"Yeah, can you believe that? No abdominal pain or anything. Lucky guy." Jennifer pushed the thin gold arch of her glasses up the bridge of her nose. "Had an angiogram today and he's clear, so he's booked for surgery in the morning. We're just babysitting him overnight. Shouldn't give you any problems." She traced her finger down the chart. "I ordered two milligrams morphine every two hours. He was complaining of back pain when he came out of Recovery. Probably just sore from lying on that hard-ass angio table. Then again, I'd probably fall asleep if somebody let me lie down for a minute." Her laugh, sounding more like a loud bark, reverberated through the break room.

❁

THE SENIOR resident on call tonight with Anil in the ICU was Dr. Sonia Mehta. She seemed taller than her diminutive size as she breezed into the break room and poured herself a cup of coffee. Her surname suggested she might be Gujarati, but Anil didn't venture to ask. Sonia Mehta was unlike any Indian woman he'd met, and she made him uncomfortable. Her hair was short around the sides and fell down a little over one eye, a style that might look pretty on an American woman. Under her scrubs, she wore a fitted long-sleeve black shirt, a functional uniform of sorts. Reportedly, as code leader last month, she'd run twelve codes in one night and lost only two patients. Another intern had breathlessly described watching Sonia perform a risky bedside pericardiocentesis—inserting a long needle directly into the sac enveloping the heart to remove lethal fluid—saving the patient right there in the ICU.

"Ready for your first night on call in the ICU, Anil?" Sonia sat next to him on the olive-green couch that carried the residual scent of human sweat and stale pizza.

"Yes, definitely," Anil said, looking up from his papers. Sonia's large almond-shaped eyes were framed by dark lashes; small silver hoop earrings hung from her ears. He wondered why she didn't wear gold like other Indian women. There was a flutter of attraction in his stomach and he immediately tightened his abdominal muscles to quell it. She was his superior, a third-year resident and a legendary one at that.

"Listen," Sonia said. "I know some residents say it but don't really mean it. If you need help, call me."

"Thanks," Anil said. But in this place, calling for help was admitting failure, and he certainly wasn't going to admit failure to a woman like Sonia Mehta. Among the conflicting emotions Anil felt toward her, his determination to prove himself took precedence.

❁

AT THREE o'clock in the morning, the ICU was an eerie netherworld: completely dark except for the fluorescent lights seeping out from the central station into each patient's trapezoidal area. Most patients were asleep, but the wheezing of ventilators and beeping of monitors created a continuous soundtrack. Anil checked on his patients one more time, determined to stave off any problems overnight, then found Sonia at the central station, looking just as she had at the beginning of the shift, her skin smooth and her eyes clear. After nine hours, Anil knew his eyes were blotchy and stubble had surfaced on his chin. He rubbed it self-consciously as he gave her a report on his most critical patients.

"Lyndon Jackson, kidney failure, has a slight fever. I was about to send him down to Radiology to check for chest infection when his O_2 dropped to seventy-three, so I paged Renal to come dialyze him emergently. I'm ordering a portable chest X-ray to check for infection."

"Good," Sonia said. "He's so compromised, we need to be vigilant about pneumonia."

Anil jotted a note in the chart. "The diabetic woman you admitted earlier from the ER, I ordered an additional blood draw because her most recent blood sugar was borderline." It was a precaution, but he'd tried to anticipate anything Sonia might ask for. "Jason Calhoun, abdominal aneurysm. Just some discomfort from the angio table. I upped his morphine and gave him oxygen. He's going for surgery soon."

"Good." Sonia's pager beeped and she glanced down at the screen. "I have to head back to the ER, might be a while," she said, walking toward the elevators. "Hold down the fort and page me if you need anything."

Moments later, while Anil was filling out charts at the central station, a high-pitched beeping sounded through the unit. "Seizure in seven!" a nurse called out. She and Anil ran toward the patient, whose body was convulsing violently. The nurse grabbed his shoulders, and Anil helped roll the patient onto his side. Foaming saliva was drooling out of the corner of his mouth, and his eyes had rolled back so only the whites were visible. The nurse wrapped her palms on either side of the patient's head to keep it steady while Anil held the man's wrists together. As soon as a second nurse arrived, Anil shouted to be heard over the monitors. "Gi-gi-give him point one milligrams of lorazepam." The nurse injected the medicine through the patient's IV, but the convulsions didn't stop. Both nurses, struggling to restrain the patient, were looking to Anil for direction. The patient's skin was beginning to turn a bluish tint and he knew there was risk of brain damage if the seizure lasted much longer. He called out for the nurse to try another anti-seizure medicine. Within a minute, the patient's limbs gradually stopped jolting.

When Anil released the man's wrists, he felt the dampness in his own armpits and around his neck. He closed his eyes and breathed deeply a few times, then proceeded to examine the patient carefully for injury. When the patient regained consciousness a few minutes later, Anil asked a few questions and, miraculously, other than being slightly disoriented, the man appeared unaffected by the violence that had wracked him. The same could not be said for Anil.

By the time the seizure patient was finally stabilized, it was 4:30 a.m. The nurses were doing their last rounds, checking vitals for the night, and morning labs would be back in an hour. Anil leaned over the counter of the central station, trying to rub away the dull ache in his temples. It might easily have been remedied with one cup of strong chai, but the Parkview cafeteria carried only weak Lipton tea bags, brewed in barely hot water carrying the trace flavor of coffee. He decided to lie down in the call room for a few minutes.

"Dr. Patel?" Another nurse called out to Anil as he passed the counter. "Mr. Calhoun's blood pressure is down again—mid-nineties. Pulse is up and breathing's up to thirty."

Anil removed his specs and rubbed his eyes with his thumb and forefinger. "He's probably dehydrated. Give him a bolus of saline to help his pressure and flush out the angio dye. He's going to surgery in a couple of hours. Let me know how he responds. I'll be in the call room."

Anil didn't remove his shoes or white coat before stretching out on the call-room bed. His eyes burned behind their lids when he closed them, but he was too tired to reach for the drops in his pocket. He felt the slightest bit of relief that none of his patients had crumped. Jennifer would be happy. Sonia would be proud. Despite his sore, wobbly knees and the dryness of his eyes, Anil would survive his first night on call in the ICU, along with all his patients.

ANIL WAS aroused by an unfamiliar voice. Woozy, he opened his eyes to see a pyramid of white light casting into the dark of the call room. He squeezed his eyes shut and opened them again, blinking rapidly to focus on the stout figure in the doorway.

"Dr. Patel?" came the voice from the door.

Not another seizure, Anil thought.

The figure spoke again, the muffled words traveling to his ears as if through water. "Dr. Patel, I bolused Mr. Calhoun but his pressure's slightly lower. Low nineties now."

Anil sat up and focused in on the nurse. Falling blood pressure in an aneurysm patient meant one thing. But how could it be a rupture? He'd checked for that. He swung his legs out of bed and grabbed his specs. "Where's Dr. Mehta?"

"Running a code." The nurse followed him down the corridor. "Should I page her?"

"Yes, but let's get a CT first." If the CT scan showed blood in the abdomen, it would mean the aneurysm had ruptured. It was the first thing Sonia would ask him, and he needed to have an answer. "Call CT and tell them we've got a STAT patient." A new rush of adrenaline coursed through Anil's body when they transferred Mr. Calhoun to a gurney, but as they headed down the hallway toward the elevator, a feeling of horrible dread filled his chest. "Page the vascular surgeon operating on Calhoun today," he called out to the nurses' station. "Tell him we might have a rupture."

As they waited for the elevator, Anil examined Mr. Calhoun's abdomen again, gently palpitating the area around his navel. Just as before, there were no signs of a rupture: no mass in the abdominal area, no rigidity, no pulsating. What had he missed? Inside the elevator, Anil watched the floor numbers light up in descending order, and silently repeated one of his mother's mantras to himself.

A MIX of relief and shame washed over Anil when the elevator doors opened on the basement level and he saw Sonia Mehta waiting there. The nurse rattled off stats as they rolled out the gurney. "Abdominal aortic aneurysm. Pressure's seventy-four, down from ninety a few minutes ago. Gave eight milligrams morphine and opened fluids. Going to CT to check for a rupture."

Sonia ran alongside the gurney. "Dr. Patel, anything to add?"

"No . . . I mean, I don't know how I mi-missed it. I checked for signs of rupture. I checked t-t-two times with a f-f-f-full examination."

The cardiac monitor alarm sounded. "Too late for a CT now," Sonia said. "Did you call the surgeon?"

"Yes," Anil said, hoping to prove some level of competence. "We paged him from the ICU."

Sonia swung the front end of the gurney down the next corridor. "We'll have to go straight to the OR and hope the surgeon gets here in time." They traveled through the bowels of the hospital, along dimly lit corridors that snaked their way around the basement. By the time they reached the operating room, the patient's breathing was ragged.

"Pressure's down to sixty." The nurse's eyes were locked on the blood pressure monitor.

"Deanna, go look for any surgeon inside," Sonia said to the nurse. "Tell them we have a ruptured triple-A bleeding into the retroperitoneal space." She reached for the patient's wrist. "And get a crash cart!" she called as the OR doors swung behind the nurse.

Sonia stepped up onto the lower railing of the gurney. "Starting compressions."

"Sh-should I get the crash cart?" Anil asked.

"No." Sonia pressed down on the patient's chest in an even rhythm. "You stay here."

Deanna reappeared with the crash cart, shaking her head. "No one inside, but they're paging another surgeon in the hospital."

"Patel, get up here and take over," Sonia said from her perch on the gurney. Anil stepped up and counted the rhythm of his compressions while Sonia charged up the defibrillator. "Stand back." Anil raised his hands. She placed the paddles on the patient's chest, and his limp body jumped in response, then flatlined again. Anil resumed compressions, alternating with Sonia's use of the defibrillator. They tried for several more minutes to resuscitate Mr. Calhoun, until Sonia shook her head, paddles in hand. "It's no good," she said. "I'm calling it." She glanced down at her watch. "Time of death, 5:29 a.m."

Anil stepped back from the gurney and bumped into the cement block wall. Sonia turned to him, her voice rising. "Why didn't you call me earlier? When did his pressure start falling?"

"I di-di-didn't"—Anil struggled to get the word out—"I didn't sus-suspect a rupture. The intern last night said his angiogram went fine, he was just uncomfortable from lying on the table." His face flushed. "He didn't show any signs of rupture. No rapid decrease in pressure, no pain in the abdomen, no rigidity or masses. I examined him twice."

Sonia picked up the chart from the end of the gurney and flipped through it. "Morning labs show a drop in hematocrit." She handed him an unfamiliar yellow lab slip and continued to read from the chart. "His pressure was up to one-seventy after the angiogram at 3 p.m. yesterday, and fell slowly through the night until it was eighty this morning." She nodded to the nurse. "When I was finally paged."

Anil shook his head slowly. He could feel sweat patches at his armpits. "I-I-I didn't see those labs. He was fine after the procedure, he was stable. I just didn't suspect . . . there wasn't a sudden drop in pressure to indicate a rupture—"

"No, there wasn't a sudden drop," Sonia interrupted. "There was a gradual drop because it was a slow leak." She pointed to a spot in the chart. "His aortic wall was thinned to less than a millimeter. Anything could puncture it. Like a catheter."

Anil put his fingertips to his temple and rubbed.

"The angio procedure yesterday must have created a small perforation in the aneurysm," Sonia explained. "He was slowly bleeding into his retroperitoneal space, beneath the gut. That's why you couldn't feel it in the belly. He was bleeding out slowly, all night long. Twelve hours, maybe more. Ruptured aneurysms don't always have a classic presentation. That's why it's important to do a CT if you suspect one. It's simple, takes ten minutes." She handed the chart to Anil and turned to the nurse. "Deanna, you'll call the morgue? We'll head upstairs and start the paperwork."

Anil stared at the unmoving figure of Mr. Calhoun. Sonia pressed his elbow and led him away. "Let's go."

They didn't speak in the elevator as others filtered in and out. Back on the ICU floor, Anil followed, numb, as Sonia walked briskly to the break room. She pointed to the olive-green couch where they'd sat hours earlier. Anil sat. She remained standing. "What the hell, Patel? Why didn't you page me when you were in trouble?"

"I should have caught it," Anil said. "I should have ordered a CT earlier."

"Yes, but you're not always going to catch everything the first time you see it. You need to learn when to ask for help. As your supervising resident, I need to trust you're being completely straight with me."

"I wasn't keeping anything f-f-f-from you," Anil protested, "I-I was just trying—"

"To handle it all yourself. I know," she interrupted. "Rookie mistake." Sonia jabbed thumb into her chest. "These patients are *my* responsibility. When something goes wrong, it falls on me. Listen, Patel, you think you're the first smart guy to walk in here? Every single intern at this hospital was top of their class in med school. Everyone is used to having the right answers. No one gets this far otherwise."

Anil rubbed at his forehead, shielding his eyes.

"This is different from school," Sonia said. "You can't know all the answers yet, and you won't find them in your books. The only way you're going to learn here is by watching and doing." She leaned toward him. "Anil, in this place, the consequence of your not knowing the right answer isn't a bad grade. The consequence is *somebody dies*. You've got to check your ego at the door, and change your goal from having the right answer to learning everything you can. Understand?"

Anil nodded without looking up. He was desperate for her to leave the room.

Sonia sat down on the far arm of the couch. "Look, this was a tough case. It wasn't the normal presentation of a rupture. It's not easy to identify a small perforation, especially where he was bleeding. But you've got to know when you're in over your head. I didn't call you out in front of Deanna because these nurses can sniff out incompetence a mile away, and if you lose their respect this early, you'll never make it."

Sonia stood up. "I'll page you when Calhoun's family gets here.

They'll have questions about his final hours, if he was in pain, so think about what you'll say." When she reached the door, she turned back. "Listen, it's tough to lose your first one. Don't beat yourself up too much. Just make sure you learn from it."

❁

ANIL GLANCED up at the clock over the door after Sonia left. Rounds began in an hour. He hadn't yet checked morning lab results or seen any of his patients, yet he'd already managed to kill one. And there was no doubt in his mind that he had killed Mr. Calhoun, no question it was his fault. If only he'd checked the hematocrit, ordered a CT earlier, recognized the pattern as a slow leak, not the big rupture described in his textbooks.

If only.

Anil had seen other patients die at Parkview, many others, but Jason Calhoun was the first who was his fault. Sonia could have berated him publicly, yelled at him for not telling her about Calhoun's falling pressure, for allowing his pride to lead to a fatal mistake. She had been kinder than he deserved, and it was worse this way. Now she recognized he was stupid and worthless.

Anil's temples were throbbing. The coffee pot in the break room was nearly empty. He poured himself the last muddy dregs and drank it straight, wiping the residual grounds of coffee from his tongue with a paper napkin. Through the window, he could see the first glow of morning sun illuminating the sky. The same warm light was slowly fading into darkness over the fields of Panchanagar. The cook would be shuttling back and forth to the table with platters of food. The scent of chapatis, served piping hot from the flame, reached out from Anil's memory. Papa would be sitting at the head of the table, consecrating the meal with a prayer. Anil struggled to retain the image of Papa last year, sitting with his impossibly straight back and holding his chin high as he listened to the mealtime banter at the table. A more recent picture of Papa, with stooped shoulders and sunken cheeks, crept into his thoughts, and Anil tried to banish it. In this place, surrounded by illness and disease, it was easy to think of everyone in terms of their ailments.

The door to the break room opened and a nurse poked in her head. "Dr. Patel, Mrs. Jimenez's son is here." She lowered her voice. "Dina Jimenez, the DNR?"

Anil pressed his eyes closed and saw the image of Mr. Calhoun's still body. "Be there in a minute," he said. After the door closed, he removed his specs and rubbed his eyes before standing up. He'd already killed one patient today, and now he would have to persuade this man to let him kill another.

7

The pattern of communication became etched between Leena and her husband. Girish barely spoke to her unless he needed something; he did not seem curious about her the way she was curious about him. Other than when they lay together at night, Leena spent little time alone with him. While her husband went off with the other men, Leena spent her days under the direction of her mother-in-law, who managed the house, and Rekha, who was in charge of the kitchen.

Leena had never been afraid of hard work. At home, she and her mother did everything themselves. Leena had always taken pride in performing a job well: rolling a stack of perfectly round chapatis, polishing the furniture until it gleamed, scrubbing the stains out of the wash. In her new house, it was different: no matter how hard she tried, she could derive no satisfaction from her work. Leena did all the cooking, but under the control of her sister-in-law. Rekha told Leena exactly what to do, standing over her shoulder to watch. If Leena failed to chop the vegetables in precisely equal pieces or missed one tiny stone in the dried lentils, Rekha would strike her hand with a rolling pin.

Leena prepared every meal like this, under a threatening hand. When everyone came to the table, it was Rekha who served the food and accepted their compliments on the cooking while Leena remained in the kitchen, preparing hot chapatis. Once everyone's bellies were full, Leena was allowed to join the family at the table and eat from what was left. Many times, she did not even get to taste all the food she'd cooked. After the meal, Leena cleaned the dishes and scrubbed the kitchen by herself.

With nine people in the house, it took at least two hours to prepare and clean up after each meal, but even then Leena was not allowed to rest. In the few hours between meals, Rekha sent her to Mother, who put her to work washing and hanging clothes on the lines outside, sweeping the floors, and making the beds. Although it was hard work, it was also somewhat of a relief for Leena. Whereas Rekha was bitter and mean, Mother was simply blind in her devotion to her sons and her belief that their wives should serve them. In this way, at least, she treated Leena and Rekha with equal disdain. Mother often grumbled about all she had done for her own husband when she was a young bride, though their relationship appeared to be nothing like Leena's parents', the way Sahib spoke to her like a servant or dismissed her with a flick of his hand.

From the moment her feet touched the floor in the morning, until the end of the day, when her back ached and her feet were sore, Leena worked and worked. In the afternoon, when the house needed to be quiet while everyone else napped, she was sent out to the fields to collect cotton under the hot sun. She tried to accept her duties without complaint, but she couldn't understand why she was being treated in such a way, as if she were not a member of the family, not even allowed to share meals with them. Perhaps it was a test of her will. If she worked hard enough, cooked well enough, scrubbed the clothes clean enough, one day they would invite her to join them at the table. Every day, as Leena waited in the kitchen, she listened for the voice of her father-in-law or husband. But the only time she heard her name, it was someone asking for a fresh chapati, or telling her to bring the rice.

The only people in the family who treated her kindly were the children, Ritu and Dev. Ritu was nine years old, a serious girl with thick hair that was always tangled; Dev was a spry five-year-old with mischief in his eyes. They often played together in the small cellar next to the kitchen. Rekha chased them away when she found them there, but when Leena was alone in the kitchen, she gave them small steel bowls and tumblers to play with. She enjoyed hearing the sound of their laughter, and even their bickering, while she worked. Although she was their aunt, they called her *didi*, elder sister.

❁

ONE MORNING, a few months into the marriage, as Leena was cleaning scalded milk from the bottom of a pot, her eyes filled with tears. Her mother-in-law had chided her for letting the chai boil over while she was busy slicing mango. She had called Leena a stupid girl, worthless. As Leena scrubbed at the brown residue with steel wool, the odor of burned milk rose around her and those names echoed in her ears. She saw her hands, the skin no longer supple but cracked now, calluses on the palms, knuckles covered in scabs. Tears slipped down her face.

"*Didi*, why are you crying?" Ritu asked. Leena shook her head and wiped her face on her arm. When she turned back, both children were standing at her elbow. "Don't cry, *didi*," Ritu said.

"Do you want a chocolate biscuit?" Dev asked. "I know where the jar is. I can reach it if I climb on Ritu's back." He made the wild motions of a monkey climbing with his hands, one of which had a large, dark birthmark on the back. Leena had tried to look at it once, gently taking his hand and outlining the jagged egg shape, but Dev had pulled his hand back and run away.

At his offer, Leena laughed. "It's okay, monkey, I don't need a biscuit," she assured Dev, but he remained skeptical, ready to pounce on his sister's back if she changed her mind.

Ritu took Leena's hand and rested her head against Leena's arm. "Don't go away, *didi*," she said. "Please don't go away."

Leena kissed her disheveled hair. "Don't you worry, sweet girl. Now, go play outside while I finish the dishes." After the children had left, the sounds of their laughter continued outdoors, but tears kept sliding down Leena's face.

❁

NIRMALA WAS applying almond oil to her hair when she spotted the vehicle through the sunlit bedroom window. Three men emerged from the car. She was filled with excitement, quickly followed by panic, at the sight of Leena's new husband, his elder brother, and their father. Since she was not dressed for guests, Nirmala called out for her husband, Pradip, to greet them while she quickly tied up her hair. When a daughter's in-laws made their first visit after the wedding, it was customary to have a celebratory meal and exchange gifts. She thought of what she might have in the kitchen to serve them.

It had been a few months since Leena's wedding, such a joyful occasion for all of them. On the morning of the wedding, she and Pradip had proudly presented the dowry to the groom's father. It was more money than they had ever seen in their lifetime, and it graced their hands for only a few moments. After counting the bills, the groom's father nodded. *This will give our happy couple a good start in life*, he said and gave the signal for the marriage ceremony to begin. For the rest of the night, Nirmala did not worry about money or any other concerns that had weighed on them before the wedding day. Now, she missed Leena's daily presence, but she took comfort in knowing they had sent their daughter to her new home with pride.

By the time Nirmala came out to the drawing room, the men were already seated and Leena's father-in-law was speaking. They were disappointed in Leena, he was explaining. She was not carrying her share of work in the family, was not enough of a help to her elder sister-in-law and mother-in-law. Her cooking skills had been overstated, he said, when in fact she was slow and sloppy in the kitchen and needed to be told how to do everything. Leena showed no interest in household responsibilities as a good wife should, preferring instead to spend her time playing with the children.

Listening from the edge of the room, Nirmala felt a hollow space expanding inside her, as she'd felt after Leena had been born, when her taut belly was deflated of the life it had carried. Who were they talking about? This girl didn't sound like her daughter. Then again, Leena had a strong mind, which could sometimes veer toward disobedience. She remembered her daughter as a young girl staying out late to play in the fields for hours after she should have been home.

And marriage was hard. Nirmala recalled her own early days of marriage: the sudden intimacy of a man of unfamiliar scent moving on top of her, the confused unlearning and learning of the ways of her husband's family. For months after her own wedding, she'd ached to return to the comfort of her parents and siblings at home. But in time, this yearning had dulled. At some point, though she couldn't say exactly when, it had been replaced by the ease she came to feel in their home, the companionship she found with her husband, the creation of their own family.

Next, the elder son spoke up, offering examples of how Leena didn't treat his wife, Rekha, with respect. And Leena's husband complained about the way she rubbed coconut balm on his feet only grudgingly. They had been deceived about the kind of girl they were getting in Leena, her father-in-law said. If they were now expected to train her in the basics of housekeeping and cooking, they would need to be compensated. Five hundred rupees a month.

Nirmala covered her mouth to stifle a gasp. They were already scraping to get by after paying Leena's dowry. She tried to make the sack of flour last longer by rolling smaller chapatis, and she hadn't bought market vegetables in weeks. How could they possibly come up with another five hundred rupees a month for this man? Impossible.

She saw the same awareness on Pradip's face as he assured the men Leena would come around. *His daughter was a good girl*, he said, *always helpful at home, and she would learn how to adjust to their ways. Just give it a little time*, he pleaded. Nirmala heard the hint of desperation in his voice and hoped the other men couldn't. *We have a gift for you*, he said to Leena's father-in-law, *something for your lovely wife, for all the guidance she's giving our daughter.* He lifted his chin toward Nirmala, who went and knelt by his chair, and he whispered for her to bring one of her gold wedding bangles. When she hesitated, he nudged her on, grinning like a rich man who owned a tree upon which gold bangles grew.

While the men drank their tea, Nirmala went to the bedroom, opened the cupboard, and reached up to the highest shelf. She pulled down the cardboard box that held the few precious pieces of jewelry her parents had given her for her wedding. From another section of the cupboard, she took a white handkerchief she had just embroidered for Leena, pressed and folded into a small square. Nirmala wrapped the gold bangle in the handkerchief. If she could not be there to wipe her daughter's tears, this would have to do.

8

Through the fog of sleep, Anil became aware of the phone ringing. The clock read 3:00 a.m. and he was due back at the hospital at eight. He fumbled for the phone next to his bed. "Hello?"

"Anil?" came the faint male voice through the line, then louder, "Anil *bhai*?"

"Yes. What is it?"

"*Bhai* . . ." The voice, which Anil now recognized as Kiran's, broke off into a muffled cry. There was a shuffling through the line as the phone changed hands.

Anil sat up in bed and turned on the lamp, his eyes wide open, his pulse beating rapidly. "Kiran? What is it?"

"Anil, Nikhil here." Nikhil's voice was clear. "Anil, listen. This morning, Papa . . ." Nikhil paused for what felt like minutes while Anil's mind churned with the possibilities. "Papa's gone, *bhai*. He passed this morning."

Anil's heart thumped in his ears. His eyes focused in on the gold lettering on the tattered brown spine of the *Physicians' Desk Reference* book on the windowsill until it became a blur. Finally, he blinked and the words came back into focus.

"He was complaining of chest pain and breathing trouble after his nap. We did just as you told us—we put the nitroglycerin tablet under his tongue and took him straight away to the hospital. By the time we got there . . . they tried to save him, but the doctors said it was too late, *bhai*. He's gone." Nikhil's voice caught and the receiver was muffled on the other end.

Anil slowly opened his left hand, releasing the fistful of pillow he hadn't realized he'd been clenching. He cleared his throat, strode toward the closet, and yanked open the accordion doors. "I'll come as soon as I can. I'll go to the airport and see—"

"Son?" His mother's voice came through the line.

"Ma?" Anil said, his voice cracking. His hand rested on the suitcase in his closet.

"Listen to me, son. I don't want you to worry about coming here right now. It will be difficult for you to leave, and we have so much family here. Your brothers will take care of the cremation rituals tomorrow—"

"Tomorrow?" Anil said. There was no way he could reach Panchanagar by then.

"*Beta*, you know we can only keep the body a few hours at home. Already it's very warm here. The pandit has chosen an auspicious time tomorrow morning. We had to make the arrangements, knowing you probably couldn't come. Please, don't stress yourself, son. You have so many worries already. We will keep the ashes until you come in the summer, and make a pilgrimage to the Ganges. Your father always wanted to see Varanasi." Ma's voice faded into the kind of long silence they rarely had during these expensive calls.

Anil sat back down on the bed, staring at the suitcase in his closet. He closed his eyes and saw the hot sun burning behind them, the sun that ripened mangos within a day at the Big House, the sun that would not be patient with his father's body. He pictured himself going to Casper O'Brien for permission to leave, or trying to get a seat on one of the packed flights to India. His mother was right. He would not be there to light the cremation pyre for his father. Who would hold the blazing torch to the bed of branches upon which his father's body would be placed? Nikhil or Kiran? Perhaps all three of his brothers together. Or would one of his uncles carry out the responsibility in Anil's absence?

After hanging up the phone, Anil walked over to his desk and opened the drawer, pulling it out as fully as the catch mechanism allowed. He rummaged through pens, paper clips, and scraps of paper, finding the boarding pass for his flight from Ahmadabad to Dallas the previous June and an envelope his mother had sent containing herb tablets to alleviate headaches. Then he heard it, rolling to the back of the drawer and bumping lightly into the edge. He reached back into the recess of the narrow drawer, scraping his knuckles on the metal runners inside. His fingers touched the smooth felt lining at the bottom of the piece, and he pulled it from the drawer.

He had held this king countless times, yet he never failed to appreciate the beauty of its chiseled shape, the way the hand-carved tiny cross at the top was impossibly symmetrical. In the dim light of his room, the rosewood appeared almost black. Anil closed his palm tightly around the familiar shape and weight, and a vivid image of Papa rushed to his mind: sitting across the broad wooden table, his brow deeply creased in concentration, contemplating his next move.

Anil had been eight years old when his father returned from his monthly trip into town with a chess set. Sitting at the table, they had deciphered the instructions together, learning the names of the pieces and how each moved around the board. They began to play together in the evening, staying up so late Ma would turn off all the lights except the one right above the table. He and Papa could play an entire game without more than a few words, stopping only at the end to dissect their respective strategies.

"Anil *jan*," Papa said one night. "Do you know where this game came from?"

"You said a British traveler left it behind." Anil studied the board, trying to save his rook from Papa's advancing bishop.

"Hmm, yes, that is true." Papa chuckled. "But the game of chess, did you know it originated in India in the sixth century?"

Anil dragged his eyes from the board to look up at Papa.

"Yes, it's true. As the tale goes, in ancient times there was a raj who loved to play games but was bored easily, so he asked a poor mathematician to invent a new game for him. The man returned with a game played on an eight by eight square board with two armies, each led by a king, where the object was to capture the enemy king. The raj was so delighted with this new game, he told the inventor to choose his own reward." Papa took one of Anil's pawns with his knight. "Do you know what he asked for?"

Anil shook his head.

"He asked for one grain of rice for the first square of the board, two grains for the second square, four grains for the third, and so on, doubling the number of rice grains for each square on the board." Papa raised his eyebrows and smiled. "Ah yes, you think it doesn't seem very wise, does it? That's what the raj thought too, so he agreed quickly to the offer, thinking he was getting a good deal."

Anil turned his attention back to the board and slid his rook over to protect his king.

"Anil *jan*, do you know how much rice that is?" Anil started some rudimentary counting on his fingers, but his father didn't wait for his reply. "A heap of rice larger than Mount Everest. Over eighteen billion *billion* grains of rice. There was not enough rice in the whole kingdom to pay the inventor, so the raj had to hand his kingdom over to the poor mathematician, who became the new raj." Papa smiled and moved his bishop within striking distance of Anil's king.

Another time, Anil had been close to winning until he made a careless move with his queen. He got angry when his father wouldn't let him take back the move only moments after he'd seen his error. "You can't do that, Anil," Papa had said. "Not in chess and not in life. You can't undo a mistake after it's made. Choose wisely before you move." Anil closed his fingers tightly over the dark rosewood piece. The other king, the light-colored sandalwood that Papa always played, had gone missing the summer before he left India.

From that memory flowed another, of puddling the rice paddies with his father: wading through shin-deep water, an extra step Papa insisted upon to ensure optimal growing conditions for the rice. Then came a vision of Papa looking old and fatigued, the day Anil had left Panchanagar. He reached to remember their last conversation on the phone. Anil found himself growing numb, unable to shed a single tear. Then, remembering how Papa serenaded Ma when she cooked his favorite dishes, terribly out of tune until she chased him out of the kitchen with a rolling pin, Anil laughed out loud, which in turn led to uncontrolled sobbing.

The first signs of trouble had appeared during Anil's last year of medical college—Papa had temporary episodes of chest pain and shortness of breath when he walked up the hills around their land. By then, Anil had known enough to recognize the possible symptoms of angina. Papa insisted he was fine but, as a precaution, Anil brought home baby aspirin, beta-blockers, and nitroglycerin, and showed Ma how to administer each of them. He had been planning to take Papa to Ahmadabad for a full workup when he returned home this summer. A stress test to determine if there were reversible areas of ischemia. A blood test to see if he had high cholesterol that could be treated with a statin, one small pill for pennies a day.

At some point, Anil must have fallen asleep, since he awoke to the blare of his alarm clock, always set at the highest volume. When he opened his eyes, he was dazed for a moment, his mind empty. The first thing in his field of vision was the watch Papa had given him, and he remembered everything in a rush. His raw eyes stung as he tried to focus in on the dials. It was six thirty in the evening in Panchanagar, where his family was preparing for the cremation ceremony. But in Dallas, it was seven o'clock in the morning and time for him to return to the hospital.

Anil sat at his desk with an untouched bowl of cereal next to him and counted the days on the calendar he'd pulled off his door. Nine days since he'd heard his father's voice, had disregarded the strain he noticed through the phone line. Two hundred and one days since he'd left Panchanagar, since he'd perched on the edge of Papa's bed and felt the long narrow bones of his hands. One hundred and fifty-nine of those days he'd spent working inside Parkview. During that time, he'd treated over a thousand patients, yet all the while he was thousands of miles away from the one patient who had needed him most.

Anil had not been there to save Papa, nor would he be able to perform the rites of cremation, his most sacred duty as his father's eldest son. But he could not stay away now. And he could not step foot back into that hospital, regardless of the consequences. Interns were not permitted to change their schedules, they were not allowed to take leave without authorization. All of this had been clearly spelled out at orientation. And yet Anil didn't give a damn when he picked up the phone to book his flight.

❁

LATE THAT night, Anil inched his way down the aisle of the jumbo jet, blocked in front by an elderly woman wearing a green batik sari and nudged from behind by an impatient father holding a baby with gold-studded earlobes. As other passengers fretted about finding space in the overhead bins or their proximity to the lavatory, Anil stashed his backpack under his seat, pushed off his shoes, and stared out the window. Phosphorescent rows of white lights spelled out a runway in the distance, where an airplane glided silently toward the ground. He would be in India in less than one day. It seemed like a nominal amount of time to traverse the globe and land in a different world, but in the past year, Anil had learned how long one day could be.

One day was long enough for a stable patient to sustain cardiac arrest and be pronounced dead while his wife dashed home to change her clothes for the first time in days. It was long enough for Anil to go from feeling energized at the start of a new shift to completely drained, reaching into the foggy recesses of his mind for basic mnemonic devices learned at medical college. Long enough for Calhoun's aneurysm to rupture and slowly kill him from the inside, while Anil missed the signs. And some days were long enough to leave him questioning why he'd ever believed he could become a doctor.

Anil unfolded the acrylic blanket and pulled it up to his chin to ward off the chill penetrating the oval airplane window. He would have to face the absence of his father, feel the void left by him everywhere: the empty rocking chair, the table where they'd played chess, the bed where Papa had suffered his fatal heart attack. Anil closed his eyes, not wanting to see any of those familiar places vacated.

ANIL EXPECTED one of his brothers to be waiting for him at the airport in Ahmadabad, but his throat tightened at the sight of his mother, transformed into a widow by her stark white sari, standing next to Nikhil. When he leaned down to touch her feet in respect, she caught him by the shoulders and embraced him tightly, then placed her palms against his cheeks, rough with two days' stubble. Anil regretted not cleaning himself up before boarding the plane. He'd become neglectful about his appearance the past several months—forgetting to brush his hair and wearing yesterday's rumpled clothes.

Nikhil took his suitcase and Ma held his arm as they walked to the car. She seemed to have aged ten years since he'd left last summer. Ma had never looked like this, not even the year drought had cut their harvests down to a trickle. For three months that year, she'd fed the children first, then Papa, and herself last, one modest meal in the evening.

"It's good you came, *bhai*," Nikhil said as he stowed the suitcase in the boot. "We knew you would, even though she said not to." He nodded toward their mother, who had settled herself into the car. "It means a lot to her."

As soon as they pulled up the winding dirt road leading to the Big House, Anil sensed something was different. The towering coconut trees lining the road had bicycles propped up against them. Several cars, rather than the usual one or two, were parked in the dusty clearing before the house. And even before the Big House came into view, he glimpsed numerous yellow flames flickering around its perimeter. Anil rolled down the window: dozens of people lined the front porch, holding candles and lanterns at three o'clock in the morning. A wave of shame swept over Anil as he realized his family had waited up to welcome him home.

After greeting dozens of relatives, Anil retired to his room, where the servant had already unpacked his suitcase. "Shall I draw a bucket of hot water for a bath, Anil Sahib?"

The servant had addressed him with the term of respect formerly reserved for his father, and Anil felt an unexpected twinge. "No, I'll wait until morning." The servant wobbled his head, as if Anil's response had no impact on him either way. Anil had been chided for making this same gesture on rounds. *Yes or no, Patel*, an attending had demanded. If only he could feel as indifferent as the servant, who now closed the door quietly behind him.

Anil walked over to the window and cranked it open, hearing the familiar squeal of scraping metal. His diploma from medical college had been framed and mounted over the chest of drawers, no doubt by his mother. He touched it and found the glass clean, free of the layer of fine dust that accumulated on surfaces here every day.

One item remained on top of the bureau. The chess set looked strangely democratic without its two kings as visual peaks. Anil unzipped the small pouch of his backpack, pulled out the rosewood king, and placed it on the pale wood square where it belonged. He looked at his pieces, mapped out a few moves in his mind, then on the board. He moved his pawn, followed by his rook. His father would have responded with his knight. *Underrated, very powerful*, Papa used to say about his favorite piece. Anil placed his finger on top of the knight. A dull ache radiated through his chest and began tightening his throat. He turned away from the chess set without resetting the board.

Anil climbed under the gauzy mosquito net draped over the bed and listened to the rhythmic squeaking of the overhead fan. The chirping of the crickets and the earthy smell of the air wafting in through the open window were as deeply familiar as the sense of obligation he felt here. That night, Anil dreamed he was running up and down the corridors of the hospital, unable to find the room to which he'd been paged. When he found himself at the dead end of a hallway, he woke up, drenched in sweat, his heart racing.

MA CONSULTED with the astrologer to find an auspicious date to travel to the Ganges to scatter Papa's ashes, and Anil booked his return flight accordingly. Until then, his days were occupied with receiving relatives and friends who came to pay respects, and eating meals so elaborate that one ran into the next. After having subsisted on a meager diet of cheese pizza and sandwiches from Parkview's cafeteria, Anil's appetite now barely had a chance to recover between meals.

Anil was not prepared for the steady stream of questions from his family and visitors. When they weren't satisfied with his curt responses, he finally gave the answers they wanted to hear: he told them about how advanced the hospital was, the wise and kind doctors who taught him, the grateful patients. He described the world he'd expected to find when he left Panchanagar, the one that now barely existed in his mind. Each time he repeated the varnished account of his life in America, it became a little easier.

Although Anil's family accepted his version without question, Anil knew he wouldn't have been able to lie to his father. But neither would it have been easy to disappoint him. At times, the guilt over how he portrayed himself compounded the shame he already bore. Other times, when he heard his mother boasting about him to relatives, Anil allowed himself to sink into this version of reality, to savor feeling successful and respected again.

One morning, Anil came downstairs as lunch was being served. He took the empty seat next to Kiran. "Where's Chandu?" he asked, accustomed to being the last one himself.

"Still sleeping," Kiran said, raising an eyebrow. "He was up late playing cards."

"Again?" Anil filled his plate and began to eat. He'd noticed Chandu's curious behavior but was reluctant to mention it to Ma in the aftermath of Papa's death.

"Ma said Pushpa Auntie's moving in with her son," Piya said. Pushpa Auntie, one of Papa's widowed aunts, had lived for years in a small house close to theirs.

"So who'll take her cottage, then?" Kiran asked. "Or will it sit empty?"

"Nikhil's got his eye on it, don't you, *bhai*?" Piya nudged her elbow into her brother's ribs. "I don't know why you're in such a hurry to get married."

"What hurry? I'm already twenty-one," Nikhil said.

Anil's mouth was burning. He must have lost some of his tolerance for spice after all those dull cafeteria meals. He took a long drink of *lassi* and studied Nikhil's expression. "Really, *bhai*?"

"Why not? What's there to wait for?" Nikhil reached across the table for the bowl of bright green coriander chutney. "Except you." He nodded at Anil.

Anil's hand was suspended over his plate. "You don't have to wait for me. I don't care." Ma appeared with a pitcher of water, making her presence known by clucking her tongue.

"She cares." Nikhil cocked his head toward their mother.

"In due time, son." Ma rested a hand on Anil's shoulder. "You boys will have your pick of brides, God willing. After our mourning period is finished, Anil will come home, and we'll start looking. Then you will be next." She squeezed Anil's shoulder and he sat back, no longer hungry.

"Well, don't start looking for me anytime soon," Piya said. "I'm in no hurry."

Kiran leaned forward in his chair and kicked her under the table. "Don't worry, I don't see too many suitors lined up outside. I think you're safe."

Piya laughed and kicked him back. "And you should talk? Who's going to want you, with those table manners? It's like eating with some kind of jungle animal."

Anil stood from the table to go clean his hands. As he held his palms under the running water, trying to rinse away the guilt, he realized that in his father he'd lost his only champion. Now he was left with his mother's expectations and his brother's hopes laced with resentment. Anil couldn't bear to cause any of them further disappointment. His path, so clear before, was now shrouded by Papa's death.

Mina Patel took private satisfaction in hearing her children bicker and tease one another. She could recognize their voices and inflections from the next room, even anticipate what each might do next, a skill that had proved invaluable when they were younger.

She had reason to worry about each of them from time to time, particularly Chandu, with his affinity for trouble. Perhaps it was natural for him to seek some way to distinguish himself from his older brothers, who had already excelled in all the usual ways: Kiran as an athlete, Nikhil in farm work, and Anil always the best student. Mina had not been concerned about Anil in many years, not since he was afflicted with that terrible speech habit as a little boy.

But it was her eldest son she now worried about most. Anil did not look well. He was thinner than when he'd left home and it showed, particularly in his face. There were dark shadows beneath his eyes, which themselves looked vacant. The boy was mourning the loss of his father, of course, as they all were. There was an enormous hole at her very core, and Mina did not expect to feel complete again for a very long time, if ever. But Anil seemed changed in a way that went beyond grief. Something intrinsic to his being had been destroyed over there in America, his insides hollowed out like a gourd. Mina's mind ran with the possibilities of what could be troubling her son. Simply considering the countless corruptions of the West—meat, alcohol, drugs, girls—was enough to give her a headache. Anyone could see that country was not good for her son.

Later that evening, Mina went to Anil's room. He'd been sleeping an inordinate amount since he'd come home, another sign he was not well. She touched his cheek with the back of her hand, the way she used to check for fever when he was a child. "You're not eating well over there, son? You've lost weight." If Jayant could see his son now, would he still believe America was such a good idea?

"I'm okay, Ma," Anil said. "Just tired. Jet lag."

"Son." Mina sat down at the foot of his bed, noticing his forehead was creased with lines. "I didn't want to speak about this when you were over there." She cleared her throat and looked down at her hands as she spoke. "Your papa, before he passed . . ." Her throat clenched with the words, and she had to breathe deeply to continue. "He couldn't manage the disputes lately, son. Some people have been waiting for months."

"Oh, Ma, I don't think I can." Anil shook his head. "There must be someone else. What about Manoj Uncle, or even Nikhil? He's old enough now."

Mina noticed the dimple in his chin that had appeared when his face began to mature out of childhood. She touched it with her thumb, reminding herself. "He wanted it to be you, son." Mina was careful not to overstep what Jayant had said. She wanted to tell her son it was time to give up this foolish dream now that his father was gone. But Jayant had warned her not to hinder Anil's medical training in any way, not to ask him to come home. She had promised her husband she would ask only that he fulfill this one role, as best he could.

Anil let out a long breath, erasing the crease in his forehead. He looked at her for several moments. "Okay, Ma. I'll do what I can while I'm here, but I can't make any promises about when I go back."

Mina smiled and stood up. "Day after tomorrow, then. We'll hold a meeting. I will let everyone know."

The Disputed Well

As people began to trickle into the Big House on Thursday morning, Anil ducked into the kitchen under the pretense of getting another cup of tea when what he really needed was a moment to collect himself. The entire village had come to depend on his father's wisdom and judgment, and the idea of stepping into that role filled Anil with dread.

By the time he returned to the gathering room, most of the chairs were filled, and a dozen people were standing against the walls. Only a few faces were familiar to him. His mother was standing in the back corner of the room, and he followed her gaze to the magnificent carved wooden armchair that sat like a throne at the head of the table. He pulled out the chair, the sound of the heavy legs scraping against the stone floor drawing everyone's attention.

Anil sat down and folded his hands on the table. "Let us start with a prayer." He bowed his head and recited the blessing his father had always used to open these gatherings. When he looked up afterward, his mother nodded. "All right, who would like to begin?"

A man named Jagdish, seated to his right, spoke first. "Anil Sahib, I would be most indebted for your counsel." He went on to explain his dispute with his neighbor, Bipin. "On my land, I grow rice, only rice. Just like your esteemed father, rest his soul, I tend only one crop and I do it well. For years on my land, it has been nothing but rice, only rice—"

Anil gestured with his hand for Jagdish to pick up the pace.

"As you know, Anil Sahib, for rice you need more water, plenty of water, so much water. For years, I saved money. Three months ago, I built a well on my land to deliver water to my fields. Eight thousand rupees I spent, out of my own pocket, to build that well. I had to procure the pipes, the tank—" He counted off the items by touching his thumb to the tip of each finger.

"Okay, I get it," Anil interrupted. "So what's the problem?"

"Now, after all my hard work and money, this scoundrel"—Jagdish pointed an accusing finger at a tall, thin man seated across the table—"Bipin wants to steal my water for his lousy sugarcane!"

Bipin jumped out of his chair. "Your water? *Your* water?" he shouted. "Oh, I'm sorry, *Bhagwan*." He pressed his palms together in mock prayer and began to genuflect. "I didn't realize God himself was living right next door to me. All the water, the soil, the air belongs to you. How dare any of us try to take it from you?" His red-lined eyes were bulging from their sockets.

"Okay, let's all calm down." Anil motioned for both men to sit down and tried not to be distracted by the mumbling from the perimeter of the room. "Now, Bipin *bhai*, it seems very clear to me Jagdish *bhai* invested his own money to build this well and he has a right to use it as he wishes. Perhaps you can build your own well if you'd like one."

"And does he have a right to run those pipes for his well under *my* land? Heh?" Bipin leaned forward in his chair and narrowed his eyes at Jagdish. "I know what you did, you old donkey! I spoke to that fellow you hired to dig up my land at night, when you thought no one would see. You think I don't know about the reservoir of water under my land? Heh? My soil has always been better than yours, just like my crops. So you see, Anil *bhai*, who's stealing now?" Bipin sat back in his chair and folded his arms across his chest.

Anil looked over at Jagdish, who stared at the table and muttered something about where Bipin could put his sugarcane, but offered no audible defense against his neighbor's accusation.

The cook appeared, placing a steaming cup of tea on the table, and Anil took a sip. The hot liquid burned his tongue, leaving a raw, prickly feeling. He pushed the cup away. "Okay." Anil spoke slowly, waiting for something insightful to come to mind, as he did when asked a tough question on rounds. "Does anyone else have something to say about this matter?" Around the room, various people were whispering to one another. Anil summoned the confidence he'd learned to project even when he didn't have the answer. "Well then, although the well belongs to Jagdish, it seems the source of water may come from Bipin, so the only fair solution is to share the well water equally. Jagdish, you use the well on Monday, Wednesday, and Friday. Bipin, you use it on Tuesday, Thursday, and Saturday. On Sunday, we'll give it a rest." Anil looked back and forth between the two men, pleased with his solution.

"But Thursday is market day, I can't—" Bipin began to protest.

"And my rice needs more than—" Jagdish interjected, and soon they were talking over each other, their voices rising again.

"Listen." Anil raised his voice to be heard above them. "*Bhaiya*, this is a fair solution and I expect you both to cooperate. Okay? Good." Both men still looked unsatisfied. Jagdish again said something unintelligible, and Bipin shook his head and stood up from his chair.

After the dueling farmers departed, others came forward with their disputes. Anil did his best to mediate for a woman whose husband had gambled away most of the couple's money in nightly card games. But he didn't have any greater success talking this man out of his addiction than he'd had with the heroin abuser who'd come to the Parkview ER with heart palpitations, certain he was dying. The gambler and his wife continued to bicker loudly as they left the house.

Next, there was a pair of unmarried sisters in their forties who lived together in the family home but couldn't stand each other's cooking. One sister had furtively brought samples of what she deemed to be the other's worst dishes as proof: indistinguishable brownish heaps of mushy lentils and vegetables in a tiffin carrier. She offered a taste to anyone in the room as evidence for her grievance but found no takers. Anil proposed they take turns using the kitchen, so each could prepare her own meals, but even as they departed, leaving the offending tiffin behind, Anil knew they'd soon be fighting over the kitchen utensils or who used the last of the rice.

He tried his best, but all of the arbitrations ended more or less as unsatisfactorily as had the first one, between the two farmers. Anil remembered his father having to bear others' complaints and tears, but Papa had been better suited to this task than Anil seemed to be. When people left Papa's table, they were more peaceful than when they arrived; some were downright joyous with his father's decisions, and everyone was respectful. Anil didn't know how to navigate conflicts for these people, some of whom he hadn't seen since he was a boy. He was well aware that no one in Panchanagar thought of him as an individual or valued his personal opinion. To them, he was just Papa's eldest son. His only qualification for this role was one he'd done nothing to earn.

THE MEETING took longer than expected, and by the time it was over, it was time for the midday meal. Anil stood, watching everyone file out of the Big House. As the room cleared, a figure moved toward him. It was Nirmala Auntie, Leena's mother, her face etched with lines. How long had it been since he'd seen her? She held a parcel at her side, wrapped in thin white cotton and tied with a plain string.

Anil put his hands together and bowed slightly. "*Namaste*, Nirmala Auntie."

"I would like a word with your mother if she's available," she said.

"Of course," Anil said. "Let me get her."

He found his mother in the kitchen, instructing the cook on the preparation of lunch. She grabbed the narrow rolling pin from the sheepish man and shook it at him before demonstrating how to roll out the dough. "Ma." Anil touched her arm. "Nirmala Auntie wants to talk to you. I think she brought a gift."

"What nonsense?" Ma's elbows shot out behind her as she rolled. "The nerve of that woman, coming here at a time like this, when we are still in mourning." She spoke without turning to look at Anil. "Crying about their problems, when we have enough of our own." Ma plucked another ball of dough from the pile and flattened it between her palms. "Everything has fallen apart since your father died." Ma pressed the rolling pin down on the dough. "I can't manage it all." She shook her head, her mouth puckered.

Anil felt a sudden protectiveness. "How can I help, Ma? What can I do?"

"Just take care of it, Anil, please. I can't handle any more unpleasantness right now." She walked into the cellar and returned carrying an improbable number of potatoes in one hand. "Just don't let them off the hook. They can't afford to repay their debts, when they've brought it all on themselves. If they were dealing with the moneylender, he would not be so forgiving."

Nirmala Auntie was standing in precisely the same place when Anil returned to the gathering room. He gestured to the table. "Please, sit down." He wished he'd asked the servant to bring out some tea but didn't dare return to the kitchen now. "I'm sorry, my mother's not feeling well," he said, even as the sound of her voice carried above the din of clanging pots. "But maybe I can help. I understand there's the matter of a debt?"

The expression on Nirmala Auntie's face was wiped clean—not a muscle moved. Her hands rested atop the white-clothed parcel in her lap. She stared at him without speaking.

Anil cleared his throat. "Let us work something out," he said, reaching for the notepad he'd left on the table. He was accustomed to dealing with situations out of context; it had become a regular part of his daily routine to take over patients midstream and diagnose ailments with incomplete histories. "The current payment is . . . ?"

"Two hundred rupees."

"Okay, two hundred rupees a month—"

"A week."

"Oh, I see," Anil said, scribbling out the numbers. "Eight hundred rupees a month. And what kind of payment can you afford?"

Nirmala did not answer him. Anil was growing weary of feeling that he was disappointing everyone who sat down at this table with him. "How about four hundred rupees a month?" He looked up from his notepad after scratching out a few calculations.

Nirmala Auntie closed her eyelids for a long moment, then nodded once.

"Good, then." Anil slid the paper over to her. "Please say hello to Uncle." Why hadn't the man come himself to discuss such money matters? "And Leena as well."

Shortly after Nirmala Auntie left, the servants came to arrange the table for lunch, and Anil was ushered outside before he could tell Ma what had been decided about the debt.

"Was that Nirmala Auntie?" Piya came up behind him on the porch. "I haven't seen her in ages. God, I miss Leena," she said. "You know she got married a few months ago?"

"Oh?" Anil said. "No, I didn't know." *To whom?* The question lingered on his lips. It felt as though he'd been in America much longer than six months.

Piya jabbed her elbow lightly into his ribs. "All the good ones are getting snapped up. Better not wait too long."

Anil groaned. "Yes, Mother."

"Hey, good job today," Piya said.

Anil shot her a wry smile. "Thank God for the blind devotion of my kid sister. Even if it is misplaced."

She smiled. "Papa left a big chair to fill. But you will, brother. You will."

After Piya left, Anil stood on the porch alone, looking out over his family's land. In the clearing below the Big House, villagers were gathered, discussing the morning's affairs. It was a burden, this business of orchestrating people's lives, solving their problems. And it was one he wanted no more today than when he'd left here. The ripples of his father's death were radiating into all of their lives. For years, Papa had given Anil a protected space to pursue his career, and now it was up to Anil alone to maintain it.

Part II

9

ANIL SAT IN THE OFFICE OF THE RESIDENCY PROGRAM DIRECTOR, Casper O'Brien, studying the family photo on his desk: a tanned O'Brien with a sunny-haired wife and two adolescent boys on the beach, framed by palm trees—everything appeared perfect, even the rough-and-tumble way the two boys were holding each other, as if pausing from a friendly wrestling match to smile for the camera. On the shelves behind the desk, interspersed with the usual medical books and hospital-issued binders, sat a basketball on a stand, and a framed photo of O'Brien, hanging from the rim of a hoop. The kind of life suggested by these images—professional success, athleticism, the model family—was so unattainable, so distant from his own reality, Anil couldn't take his eyes from them.

The door swung open and O'Brien strode over to his desk and sat down. "You left us in a very difficult position, Patel. Our patients count on us. We count on *you*. Do you understand the impact on this program when an intern leaves for two weeks without notice? December is our busiest time. Do you have any idea what your peers had to do to compensate for your absence?"

Anil shook his head, unwilling to risk speaking, knowing the words would not come out as he intended, if at all.

"I'm sorry about your father. We'd have given you a few bereavement days if you'd told us. But disappearing for two weeks and just leaving a voice mail." O'Brien shook his head. "We couldn't even reach you on your pager." He leaned forward over his enormous desk. "Look, bad things happen in life, but we have to keep working through them. That's the nature of the medical profession, and you'd better get used to it." He rocked back in his brown leather chair, the springs squeaking with the movement. "I feel compelled to remind you, Anil, the internship year is a probationary period. It's a time for us to figure out if you can make it in this residency program, in this profession. You should think about that too. Because from what I've seen so far"—he pointed vaguely at some papers on his desk, probably Anil's monthly evaluations—"it's not at all clear. You'll have to prove it to me."

❁

ANIL RETURNED to work with a renewed sense of purpose. He did not want to go home, and he certainly didn't want to go home a failure. He owed it to Papa to make good on their tacit agreement, now even more than before. Anil knew, even if no one else did, what Papa wanted most was for him to see this lifelong effort through, for Anil to fulfill his dream of becoming a doctor. With each day marked off on his Krishna calendar, and each passing week, Anil's resolve hardened. He was the first one to rounds in the morning, followed up on every patient before the end of his shift, ran down each lab result and consult before collapsing in one of the empty call rooms at the hospital. Despite so little free time, grief was his constant companion, filling up the small pockets of his day with fond remembrances and sudden longings that caused an ache under his ribs.

He still joined Charlie at the diner a few evenings a week, but only to study. The meatloaf platter without meatloaf had lost its appeal, as had many other simple pleasures. One evening, Charlie ordered slices of pie for both of them. Anil enjoyed two bites of the tart-sweet berries before pushing his plate away. He jammed his hand into his pocket for the inhaler he'd been carrying around for weeks. It would have been such a small thing to box it up and ship it off to India the first time he'd heard Papa short of breath on the phone. It wouldn't have prevented his fatal myocardial infarction, but it would have been something—something to make his father more comfortable, something to let him know his son was thinking of him across the oceans. Anil slid the hard plastic edge of the inhaler under his fingernail and pressed down on it until he felt pain, which brought him a satisfaction sweet berries in his mouth could not.

Charlie drummed his fingers on the newspaper sitting on the table. "Hey, did you hear about Miami? Twenty-eight cases of dengue fever this year. First cases reported in the US in over two hundred years. Isn't that crazy?"

Anil craned his neck to see the article. Dengue, a mosquito-borne illness, was prevalent in India. He'd treated many patients with it in Ahmadabad, but not a single one in Dallas.

"They think it's because of global warming that these tropical diseases are spreading to new geographies." Charlie flipped the newspaper over. "Isn't it fascinating—the way viruses move across the world, the constant race to find the right vaccine?"

"Maybe you should think about infectious disease as a specialty," Anil said. "You can do a research project to feel it out."

"Yeah, that's not a bad idea," Charlie said. "People are starting to form research teams. I wasn't even going to think about it until second year, but apparently some of our eager classmates are already petitioning for sponsors at the hospital."

"How about something with MRSA?" Anil suggested. Every hospital in America was concerned about the resistant strain of staph bacteria appearing in their facilities, creating publicity and legal troubles.

"I read that several hospitals have been doing small-scale studies to reduce risk factors. Maybe you could collect them all and do a retrospective study. You could put together a list of proven steps hospitals could follow."

"Yeah, I like it." Charlie tapped the end of his pencil against the table. "And they'll love it at Parkview. Free research that also solves a PR problem. What do you say, mate? Want to work on it together? We'd make a great team."

Infectious disease wasn't really Anil's area of interest: it reminded him too much of India and he'd rather work on first-world medical problems. But Charlie looked so keen, and it would be fun to work together. "Sure, let's do it," Anil said.

ANIL'S PAGER buzzed against his hip, displaying a number he didn't recognize. When he called from the nearest hospital phone, the ward nurse who answered told him Dr. Mehta wanted to see him. Anil took the elevator to the sixth floor and waited in the ward staff room, drumming his fingers against his knee.

"Patel," Sonia said, entering the room. "You're back. How was India?"

"Uh . . . it, uh, was okay." Anil stumbled for words. How had the news traveled through the hospital ranks?

"Casper give you heat?" she asked.

"Uh, Dr. O'Brien? Yeah."

"Well," she said, pouring herself coffee, "for what it's worth, I think you did the right thing."

Anil cleared his throat and nodded. This whole conversation was putting him off balance.

"It can feel like Parkview's the whole world, but it's not, of course,"

Sonia said. "I'm sure it took guts and O'Brien will make you pay for it, but you absolutely made the right call to go home." She flashed him a brief smile.

"Uh . . . thanks," Anil said. This couldn't be why Sonia had paged him?

"Anyway, I wanted to let you know the department's chosen Jason Calhoun's case for the next M&M conference. You know what that means?"

It was a rhetorical question, since every intern knew and feared being called in front of the M&M. The morbidity and mortality conference, open to all physicians and residents, was intended to be a nonpunitive forum to review medical errors, with the goal of improving learning and patient care. Senior residents referred to it as the firing squad.

Sonia explained that she and Anil would present their case and be subjected to inquiry from their peers about the complications and errors that had led to the patient's death. "We should probably get together once or twice to review the chart, make sure we have everything covered." They agreed to meet up again toward the end of the week. Despite Sonia's assurances that everything would be fine, Anil left the staff room with an anxious energy coursing through his body.

The Shared Mango Tree

After thirty-six hours straight at the hospital, Anil was relieved to find no one home when he returned, but the phone began ringing soon after he entered the apartment.

"Oh, Anil, thank God. I've been calling for half an hour," Ma said when he answered. "We chose this time, no? Are you ready, son? Everyone is gathered here, waiting for you."

Anil sank onto his bed. Before leaving India, he'd agreed to hold an arbitration session by phone every month or so, to be scheduled on his days off and to last no more than an hour. He'd have preferred to hand off the role to someone else, but Papa's death and his own disappointment had left him on the shores of the Ganges feeling he owed something to his father's memory and his family. Now, after his reprimand from Casper O'Brien and the looming specter of Jason Calhoun, he didn't have much confidence in his own judgment. "Ma, is it important or can it wait?" he said, summoning the triage skills that now defined his daily routine.

"Just talk to Manoj Uncle," Ma whispered. "He and your cousin have been fighting over that mango tree on their property line. Manoj Uncle's dog left his pile outside your cousin's house, and he's threatening to retaliate. You know your cousin has a temper. I'm worried he'll do something violent."

THE MANGO tree had been there for years, decades even, without causing any problems between the neighbors. Manoj Uncle, not technically an uncle but a family friend, had lived on the same plot of land for as long as Anil could remember. He and his brothers had played there, along with their cousins, who lived in the neighboring house. As boys, they would climb up to pick the unripe mangos, still green and hard as rocks, using them as balls in their cricket games. In the summer, when the golden fruit ripened on the tree, they shook the branches and enjoyed the spoils. They tore off the stems and squeezed the fruit pulp from the skin right into their mouths, competing to see who could consume the most. When they'd had their fill, the boys gathered up the remaining mangos from the ground and pelted them at each other until they were covered in sticky sweetness and flies began to swarm. They were wasteful, Anil was ashamed to remember, the way children can be with things they have in abundance. Only when something was precious did it become valuable. *Mangos. Sleep. Approval.*

The mango tree had grown mature in recent years and now produced two or three crates of fruit every week. Since its roots were on one property and its branches on the other, both parties claimed ownership, and tempers rose along with the price of mangos during the last drought. Anil listened to Manoj Uncle describe how his neighbor snuck outside early in the morning to collect the fruit and squirrel it away inside his home. "Like a thief, he creeps out there, I tell you—very careful not to make a sound. He *knows* he's stealing from me."

Anil's cousin complained that Manoj Uncle had neglected the tree for years, never taking any responsibility for pruning or watering it, but now acted as if he were its sole and rightful owner. "I'm the one who groomed that tree, Anil," his cousin said. "I nursed it back to health. Last month, I even removed a wasp nest from its branches, and got so many stings for my trouble. Why shouldn't that fruit belong to me? Without me, that tree would still be small and weak, producing nothing."

Anil's eyelids threatened to close. He imagined the fragrance of the mangos, the tangy-sweet flesh smooth on his tongue. What he would give for one of those mangos now, just one small bit of pleasure. He rolled over and glanced at the clock radio, glaring at him with its red eyes, and mentally calculated the REM cycles left before the alarm would sound. *Were they really fighting over a fruit tree?*

"You both deserve praise for nurturing such a productive tree," Anil said. "But two or three crates of mangos are too much for either of your families, no? They will spoil if either of you keeps them, and it would be a shame to waste such delicious fruit. So here is my advice: every morning you meet at the tree at ten o'clock to collect and divide the mangos equally. Manoj Uncle, as I remember correctly, Auntie makes wonderful *kulfi*, does she not? Cousin, perhaps you can have your mother make her spicy mango pickle, and the two of you can exchange your gifts."

There was silence on the other end of the line, which Anil took for agreement. Then his mother came back on. "Thank you, son. I'll handle the rest; we'll do it another time. And, Anil?"

"Hmm?" he murmured as he turned off the light and pulled the covers over him.

"Please don't forget your prayers."

Anil had not uttered a word of prayer since Papa's death. Ma would be disturbed to know how infrequently religion entered his thoughts. In the ICU, when he'd taken Mrs. Calhoun to see her husband's body, draped with a white sheet, he'd stood to the side with the social worker as the new widow stepped tentatively toward the table and stroked her husband's head. She kissed him gently on the forehead and smiled before her face crumpled and she fell onto his chest with a heart-piercing wail that Anil could hear echoing even after he left the room to pace the corridor outside. When he returned, a priest was holding a rosary and blessing the body. The wife's expression was pained, her eyes searching every inch of her husband's corpse for an explanation.

Anil was grateful for the presence of the priest and social worker to help shoulder the woman's grief. But was God there in that cold room filled with metal machines and halogen lights? It seemed unlikely. Anil was used to the idea of a capricious God, a spiritual order in which death often came to the undeserving. He'd seen the destructive hand of Shiva in the earthquake devastation of Gujarat, and in the slow death of a disease-ridden body. It wasn't that Anil thought God merciless for taking Calhoun at fifty-seven, leaving behind a widow and three fatherless children. He simply didn't sense God's presence there at all. The man had suffered a ruptured aneurysm because of Anil's oversight. His death was caused by a catheter tip and human error. The whole concept of God had been irrelevant.

10

Before she got married, Leena's mother warned her the first year would be the hardest. Leena kept this in mind when her new life was not what she expected: the dilapidated house, the untended lands, the ceaseless toil. She worked hard in the hope that things would get better. Yet, no matter how quickly or carefully she worked, her sister-in-law and mother-in-law were always displeased. They always found some corner unswept or some shirt stain uncleaned. Even as Leena's cooking improved and she overheard the men around the table complimenting her dishes, Rekha grew more spiteful.

Girish acknowledged her only when he wanted something; otherwise, it was as if she didn't exist. If he didn't like the way she folded his clothes or something she said, or if he had too much to drink, he pushed her up against the wall. Leena learned to tilt her chin down right before he did this, so the back of her head did not get slammed against the concrete. If he wanted to get her attention as she walked by, he grabbed her wrist so tightly she could see the impression of his fingers on her skin afterward.

At night, in bed, he did the same thing, clamping her hands above her head while he moved on top of her. His eyes were often closed but Leena kept hers open. She wanted him to know, when he opened his eyes, that she was still there, she was watching.

Leena couldn't understand why he would want to be close to her if he despised her so. Perhaps it was like the way he oversweetened his chai, using too much sugar because he couldn't tolerate the natural bitterness of the tea leaves. When he was finished with her, he turned away and told her to get out. Leena would go to the washroom and clean herself quietly with cold water. Only when she heard his snoring did she return to the bedroom. She was terrified of becoming pregnant and kept a careful count of her cycles, as her mother had taught her to do before the wedding, telling Girish it was her womanly time of the month when she needed to keep him away.

One evening, Leena was returning the clean, folded clothes to her in-laws' bedroom when she noticed something had fallen underneath the cupboard. She bent down to pick it up: a white handkerchief embroidered with a beautiful peacock in tiny, even stitches she immediately recognized as her mother's. It was dusty from the floor but held its perfect square creases. Leena clutched the kerchief and ran to find her husband. She was hungry for news of her parents. She had not seen them since the wedding and had had only a few short phone conversations under the watchful eye of her mother-in-law.

She found Girish in the parlor, playing cards with his brothers and two other men. Normally, she would not have disturbed their game, knowing how easily he was angered, but this time she could not help herself. She rushed in, waving the handkerchief. "Where did this come from?" she asked. "Did you see her, my mother?"

The men's laughter and conversation halted, and their eyes turned to Girish. Slowly, her husband looked up at her, his face darkening. He stared at her for a moment, jerked his head in the direction of the door, and turned back to his cards.

Leena stood there, wanting an answer. Wanting her mother. "Tell me," she pleaded so softly she could barely hear her own voice.

Without glancing her way, Girish waved her out of the room. "Deal the cards," he snapped at one of his friends.

Amid the noise of the men resuming their game, Leena backed out of the room and closed the door behind her. She returned to their cramped bedroom and crawled onto the bed, clutching the handkerchief to her face, breathing in the sandalwood scent that reminded her of her mother. She didn't know what had happened, where or why or who had seen her parents, but she knew this: her mother had sent her love. Lying in the shelter of her bedroom, Leena could hear her brother-in-law in the next room yelling at Rekha—a string of names and meaningless insults she tried to block out. Leena slept in the same position all night long, and the next morning, she tucked the handkerchief into her sari blouse and carried it with her all day, pulling it out periodically to inhale its fragrance. It gave her the strength she needed as the situation in her husband's house grew worse.

In the kitchen, Rekha swapped out the thin rolling pin for the thicker one and carried it with her at all times. If Leena didn't work quickly enough, she snapped the rolling pin against her forearm or shoulder. Leena began to wear a sweater over her sari, even on the warmest days, to cover up the bruises on her arms and to protect herself.

As a distraction from the daily misery, Leena began to allow her mind to wander as she worked. She thought of her father working happily in the fields, her mother singing as she busied herself in the kitchen. She pictured them taking a break from their work to share a simple meal of lentils and rice, garnished with fresh cilantro her father had brought from the garden. At times, she envisioned herself as a younger girl, roaming the terrain outside their home. The daydreams first came to her while she was performing mundane tasks like scrubbing clothes in the washbasin or chopping vegetables. As she ate alone on the floor of the kitchen, she imagined that she was sharing meals with her parents, passing vegetables and yogurt to them, smiling at companions who were not there. Soon, she was escaping into the fantasies any chance she could, even when her husband mounted her in their bed at night.

One day in the kitchen, Leena was remembering the Holi celebrations she enjoyed as a child, her father rousing her in the morning by calling through her window. When she ran outside to find him, he would be waiting to douse her with handfuls of colored powder. Leena always squealed as clouds of turquoise and magenta engulfed her. Her father pretended to run away as Leena and her mother chased him, but in the end he was also covered from head to toe in a rainbow of colors, and the arrival of spring had been properly greeted.

The crack of a rolling pin against Leena's knuckles made her gasp.

"Stupid girl!" Rekha snapped. "Don't you smell that?" She yanked a pot off the open flame. "Stupid, slow girl. Mind wandering to God knows where when the rice is burning right beside you." She slid the lid off the pot and tilted the vessel toward her. "Look at that!"

"I'm sorry, I'm so sorry," Leena said as the scent of burned rice flooded her nostrils.

"Sorry?" Rekha grabbed Leena's wrist and twisted it toward her. "You *should* be sorry!" she shouted. "Sahib is very particular about his rice. You can't just scrape this off. You'll have to start over, and now dinner will be late!"

Rekha yanked Leena's hand to the stove and held it over the open flame. Leena felt the sear of the heat against her skin and tried to wrest her hand away, but Rekha's grasp was firm. The sharp ache of burn spread through Leena's hand, and an involuntary moan escaped from her. When Rekha finally let go, Leena cradled her hand against her chest and looked at her sister-in-law in disbelief.

"Now that you know how it feels to be burned, maybe you'll take greater care with the food." Rekha glared at her. "Hurry up, clean this pot and make some new rice. I'll have to go tell Sahib why dinner is late."

With tears streaming down her face, Leena filled a small steel pot with cold water and immersed her hand in it. After a few moments, she found a clean kitchen towel and, recalling how Anil had bandaged the injured bird's leg, gently wrapped her hand, crisscrossing the ends of the towel to hold it in place and tucking in the end at her wrist.

For weeks afterward, there were blisters on the palm of Leena's hand. She could cope most of the time, except when she had to roll chapatis and the pain was unbearable. She was vigilant about Rekha and her whereabouts, never turning her back when her sister-in-law was present. Leena's mother-in-law was no better: the old woman was feeble and couldn't strike with as much force as Rekha, but her tongue was her sharpest weapon. Leena came to prefer Mother's tepid slaps across the face or on the bottom to the terrible names she called her. *Stupid. Lazy. Ungrateful.* One day, she called Leena *garbage*, which quickly became her favorite pet name for her daughter-in-law. Even after the bruises and blisters healed, those cutting words remained.

Leena began to look forward to the days she was sent out to the fields. Picking cotton was difficult work, the nettles leaving her arms scratched and her fingers bloody, but at least she could escape the evil occupying the house. What was she doing to arouse such anger? She remembered her mother's counsel about being compliant to her new family. Leena didn't know if her experience was unusual or normal for a marriage. She had no older sisters to ask, and she'd been the first of her friends to wed. Her parents had made great sacrifices, having handed over their life savings for her dowry. Leena knew she had to find a way to make the marriage work.

11

Anil opened his eyes to the bright sunlight streaming through his bedroom window and grabbed for his alarm clock. Why hadn't it rung? Boisterous voices came from down the hall, and he remembered it was Saturday: he had the day off and his roommates were home as well. As Anil lay in bed waiting for his heart rate to subside, he thought, as he had every morning for the last several weeks, of the morbidity and mortality conference at which he would have to appear.

Anil had already mentally revisited Jason Calhoun's case many times. It was easier to decipher what had gone wrong without the chaos and exhaustion of that night. He had been biased by what the other intern, Jennifer, had told him—Calhoun just needed babysitting and pain meds. While Calhoun's blood pressure was dropping precipitously, Anil was distracted by the patient with seizures and the one with kidney failure. And although the presentation of the ruptured aneurysm had been atypical and subtle, the fact remained that Anil had simply missed it.

There was nothing anyone could say to Anil at the M&M conference that he hadn't already tormented himself with. He'd even prepared himself for the probability that he would stammer his way through the whole meeting. There would be public humiliation, of course: Trey Crandall and his buddies never missed an opportunity to witness others' mistakes. But Anil's real concern was being on trial in front of Casper O'Brien. Thinking about what he would have to face in just a few weeks, Anil was tempted to stay in bed, but he swung his legs over the side and stood up. He was not going to squander away his first day off in two weeks.

Baldev let out a holler and dropped his game controller when Anil entered the living room. "Oh-ho, what are they doing to you at that place?" He playfully slapped Anil's cheek.

Anil shook his head. "Believe me, you don't want to know. But today, I'm free."

"Well then, let's go make the most of it." Baldev smacked Mahesh, still engrossed in their video game, on the back of the head. "Come on, look at this beautiful day." He pointed toward the sunlit window. Anil looked out at the wide swath of clear blue sky, the fresh air he'd been denied inside the hospital, its antiseptic environment to which he would return the next morning.

As they discussed where to go, Anil realized he'd forgotten his pager in his car and went to retrieve it. Jogging back through the parking lot, he spotted Amber emerging from her car in black running shorts and a fitted pink top. He stopped, his heart pounding from the physical exertion of running, or the heat, or her proximity, he couldn't be sure.

"Hey there." Amber took a long pull on her water bottle. "I just got back from the lake. Have you been out there? Looks like you're a bit of a runner." She smiled.

"What? Oh me, no." Anil shook his head, smiling. "Just forgot my pager." He held it up in his palm.

"Oh, too bad. The lake is my favorite place to go running in Dallas. I go there every weekend." Amber wiped perspiration from her upper lip. "Hey, would you like some tea? It's pretty hot out here."

Anil followed Amber into her apartment, a smaller mirror image of his, with an identical kitchenette and living area, and the same long hallway leading to the bedroom.

"Your roommate, Dave?" Amber called out from the kitchen. "He seems nice."

It took Anil a moment to realize she was referring to Baldev. "Oh yeah, he's great. There are three of us, actually." Anil glanced around the apartment, stunned at how different the same space could look. Amber's couch had four matching pillows propped neatly in the corners. The dining table was a clean white circle, its surface free of the papers and dishes that cluttered theirs. A small glass jar of flowers sat on the kitchen bar.

"You're lucky to have roommates," Amber said. "Must be nice to always have someone to do things with. I don't really know anyone in Dallas, except for a couple of people at work."

Anil heard clattering from the kitchen, and was unsure what to do. In India, offering to help someone, particularly a woman, with the common hospitality task of making tea would be considered an insult.

"I didn't realize how hard it would be moving to a new city and trying to make friends." Amber appeared from the kitchen, carrying a tray with two tall glasses filled with ice cubes and a pitcher of dark liquid. "Here we go." She set the tray down on the table and began to pour from the pitcher. "It's unsweetened, but I have sugar if you like. Lemon?" She looked up at him. "Oh, what? Is something wrong?"

"Oh, no, no." Anil shook his head and let out a chuckle. "It's just . . . when you said 'tea,' I assumed you meant hot tea, like chai. I'm still figuring things out here." He laughed again at his mistake.

"Hot tea? In this weather?" Amber looked at him like he'd proposed climbing Everest, then she began laughing as well. "What are you, a glutton for more punishment than 110 degrees?"

"No, no." Anil wiped a tear from his eye as he tried to stop laughing.

"We drink hot tea in India to cool down. No, really!" he said, seeing the dumbfounded look on her face. "It's a scientific fact: when you take in hot liquids, you reduce your body temperature." He shrugged. "Either that, or a billion people have been making the same mistake for centuries."

Amber shook her head. "Well, I don't know about that, but in Texas we drink our tea ice-cold all year round."

Anil took a sip from the glass she'd poured. "Mmm. Very refreshing. Maybe you're onto something with this iced tea."

Amber smiled as she sat down. "So why did you decide to become a doctor?" She filled her glass from the pitcher and topped up his as well.

"That is a very long story," Anil said. "And I don't want to bore you."

"The first time I really understood what doctors did, I was ten years old. Dr. Jupiter."

Anil raised an eyebrow. "That was his name?"

Amber smiled. "No, not really. It was Juniper, but I couldn't pronounce it, so he told me to call him Dr. Jupiter. He saved my momma's life. Probably saved mine too."

"What happened?"

"I found my momma passed out on the bathroom floor. Scared me half to death. Thought she was dead. She was in a diabetic coma, but we didn't know that yet. Dr. Jupiter diagnosed her with type 2 diabetes. She was thirty-two."

Anil swirled the ice cubes around in his glass and waited for her to continue. He'd learned from interviewing patients on sensitive topics when to speak and when to listen.

"I had to start giving her insulin injections because she couldn't stand to do it herself. Dr. Jupiter taught me how. He also told me I had to eat better and start exercising if I didn't want to end up like her." Amber looked over at Anil and smiled. "I was kind of a pudgy kid back then."

The image was hard to reconcile with the slender woman before him, but Anil just nodded for her to continue.

"He was so calm and confident, and it was such a scary time. My momma was sick, and my dad didn't know what was going on. Dr. Jupiter sat us down and explained everything. He knew how to make things better. Gave me my momma back when I thought she was gone." Amber took a long sip of her tea, then placed her glass down carefully on the table. "I think it's pretty amazing what you do every day, the difference you make in people's lives."

Anil's fingers slipped on the condensation on his empty glass. No one had been impressed about his being a doctor since he'd left India. At Parkview, he always felt stupid for how little he knew. He swallowed hard. "Thanks. Thank you."

Amber smiled. "So what are you up to on this beautiful Saturday?"

"Oh," Anil said with a start. "I should be getting back. My roommates are cooking up some big plans for my day off." He stood up. "Thank you for the tea. It was perfect. I'm a convert."

Amber walked him to the front door. "See you soon?"

When Anil returned to his bedroom, he could hear the shower running through the wall that bordered Amber's apartment. Such an innocent sound—the cascade of water against tile—but imagining her on the other side of that wall, his mind filled with thoughts not innocent at all.

Back home, the rules of behavior had been clear. In medical college, boys and girls largely kept to themselves. Most of Anil's generation expected to have their marriages arranged by their families. Parents submitted portfolios and took out matrimonial ads. Family trees, diplomas, medical records, and astrological charts were compared. Prospective brides and grooms were interviewed for suitability, and when a marriage was arranged, the couple had a few chaperoned meetings. The notions of flirting and dating were foreign to Anil.

The closest Anil had come to such interactions was with Sujata Lakhani, his lab partner in medical college. Sujata was fair and pretty, and wore colorful glass bangles that tinkled on her wrists. They spent hours next to each other in the lab, hands and shoulders touching as they worked, and Anil came to know the scents of her soap and hair oil, the mixture of sandalwood and coconut. The crook of her elbow became familiar to him, as did her thin forearms, the parts of her body that he could gaze at undetected as they sat next to each other. She was a serious student, but he could make her laugh if he said just the right thing. At night in his hostel, Anil imagined what her body looked like under the *salwar khameez* and those tinkling bangles as she moved above him.

One night at the library, he nearly asked her to join him for dinner, but he never worked up the courage, and by graduation Sujata's parents had arranged her engagement to a surgeon in Ahmadabad. Anil had seen the man once, after their graduation ceremony, and was surprised he was not as tall or handsome as Anil would have expected.

And what did Leena's husband look like? Ever since Piya had mentioned her marriage, Anil found himself wondering about this, trying to picture the man who stood beside Leena at their ceremony, joined to her by a knotted shawl. She must have made a beautiful bride.

ANIL AND his roommates spent the afternoon at the apartment complex's pool, which was filled with other young people, most laughing and talking rather than swimming. Mahesh sat in the shade reading a newspaper while Baldev surveyed bikini-clad girls behind his mirrored sunglasses. After they returned from the pool and showered, Baldev proposed going to a karaoke bar. Mahesh, who loved belting out Bollywood tunes in his car, agreed immediately.

"But I can't sing," Anil protested.

"Everybody can sing after a few beers," Baldev said. "One hundred percent."

The bar was crowded with young people, all of them happy and beautiful. Music pulsed through the floorboards, which were covered with broken peanut shells. The peanuts sat in large barrels at both ends of the bar, where they could be scooped into small paper cups by patrons who alternately ate them or threw them at the stage in disapproval.

Both Anil and Mahesh were amazed at the open vats of peanuts, free for the taking. Back in India, street vendors sold these same nuts in rolled newspaper cones for a few rupees. A bearded old man sat on the street corner near Anil's hostel, making a living—indeed a whole career—off the very same commodity given away here. And not just given away, thrown away.

Anil had been reticent about singing even before they'd arrived, before he'd seen others get pelted off the stage with peanuts. But after he and Baldev finished one large pitcher of beer and began a second, he started to come around to the idea. After that first margarita, Anil had tried drinking beer a few times with Baldev, and he preferred its gradual effect to the margarita's quick impact. He couldn't remember ever feeling this way: loose, warm, and happy. Unencumbered. His head was pleasantly spinning, and all thoughts of the hospital drifted away. How wonderful it was to be somewhere no one expected anything of him, except to drink down his beer and sing a song.

They took the stage to the opening beats of the Village People's "YMCA." It was a good choice by Baldev, a crowd-pleaser and one that required no real musical talent. The three of them swayed together on stage, arms around one another's shoulders, as the audience sang along, throwing their arms up in the air to spell out the letters. There were so many pretty girls in the crowd, jumping and bouncing and smiling at Anil, encouraging him to sing with gusto. Not one peanut was thrown during their performance, and the crowd cheered wildly when they finished. After they had settled back into their booth, Anil felt at once elated and thirsty.

"So, Mahesh, you think you'll hear this week?" Baldev turned to Anil. "He's up for a promotion at work. Senior . . . what is it?"

"Senior software group manager," Mahesh said proudly. "There's no reason I shouldn't get the position over the two other guys on my team. They pal around with our manager, but I'm better."

"Well, I wouldn't leave it to chance," Anil said. "You should put together your case on paper. Ask for a meeting with your manager and lay it out for him. Just be calm and clear, not aggressive. Tell him you'd really like the position and you believe you're the most qualified." Anil nodded in response to Mahesh's skeptical expression. "You should, Mahesh. It doesn't matter if you're better. What matters is his impression of you." Anil wished he had followed this advice himself—with Casper O'Brien, or Sonia Mehta in the ICU, or Eric Stern in the ER—before he'd made so many bad impressions.

"The doctor's right," Baldev said. "Impression is everything in America. Talent, not so much. Why do you think I do so well? Customers love me." He leaned forward and said in a conspiratorial tone, "Especially the ladies."

"This promotion would give me a very respectable income," Mahesh said. "Six figures. With that and a green card, I'll have no trouble finding a wife."

"Wife?" Baldev cried. "What about us?" He leaned back in his chair and slapped his chest with both hands. "You're only twenty-five. Live it up while you can. So many beautiful women in America. All shades of skin, all colors of hair, all shapes and sizes. Why not sample a bit and see what you like?"

Mahesh looked as if he'd bitten a lemon. "I don't need to *sample*, I already know what I want. A petite, fair-skinned, well-educated, vegetarian Lohana Gujarati girl."

"From a good family," Anil added.

"Of course." Mahesh nodded.

Anil drained his pint glass of beer and slapped the wooden table. "Well, I'm going to do it," he announced. "I'm going to ask her out."

"Amber?" Baldev reached over and pounded Anil on the back. "That's my man!"

"Amber, the neighbor girl? Why?" Mahesh sipped from the straw in an oversized red Coca-Cola cup. "What's the point?"

Anil shared a smile with Baldev, who raised his eyebrows a few times. Mahesh was still thinking of propriety and his parents back home composing his matrimonial ad. Anil knew he could be sent home from Parkview in a few months, the American dream pulled right out from under him. He felt an urgency, almost a desperation, to yank it back before it escaped his grasp. Baldev was right—this was the land of opportunity in all things, including women. Why not partake in the offerings while he was here? Why not enjoy himself, for once in his life?

❁

THE DATE with Amber was two weeks later on a Friday night. Anil worked feverishly all day and traded favors with two other interns to ensure he could leave the hospital by six o'clock. He'd made a reservation at a restaurant he'd heard Trey and his friends discussing as the perfect date spot.

When Anil and Amber arrived at Daniele Osteria, they were directed to an obscure basement entrance and passed through a sweeping black curtain. Once his eyes adjusted to the dim light, Anil understood what Trey had meant. The dining room held only a dozen small tables, around which couples were closely huddled. Candles encased in red glass created a soft glow, which illuminated diners' faces and little else. The hospital ward at night was brighter than this restaurant.

Amber said she preferred white wine, so Anil struggled with the thick leather wine list, organized by country and varietal rather than by color. The waiter, a short bald man with a dark moustache and strong accent, tapped his pen impatiently while Anil flipped back and forth through the pages, trying to find the right section and something remotely affordable.

"Can we get some garlic bread?" Amber asked.

"No, madam." The waiter chuckled and shook his head. "Not possible."

Anil leaned toward him. "Surely you can make some garlic bread?"

The couple at the next table looked over. "It's okay," Amber whispered to Anil.

"No garlic bread," the waiter repeated. "Only authentic Italian cuisine." He joined the fingertips of his right hand, touched them to his mouth, and kissed them before turning away.

Anil turned to Amber. "I'm sorry—"

"No—really, it's okay." Amber's cheeks were reddened, the effect accentuated by the candlelight. "It's better anyway. I really shouldn't be eating refined carbs."

A couple of awkward moments passed while Anil tried to focus on the wine list again. In frustration, he put it down on the table. "I mean, what kind of Italian restaurant doesn't serve garlic bread?" he said, louder than intended.

Amber tried to suppress a giggle but couldn't. She clamped a hand over her mouth to stifle the laughter, and the effort to do so was so ridiculous, soon Anil was laughing with her. A few more patrons in the restaurant looked over at them.

When the waiter disappeared into the kitchen, Anil leaned close to

Amber. "Hey, you want to get out of here?" Still covering her mouth, Amber nodded. They slid out of the leather booth and snuck out of the restaurant.

In the parking lot, they both finally burst into unrestrained laughter. "I mean, even Olive Garden has garlic bread!" Anil was bent over, his hands on his knees. "Oh no," he said in a mock Italian accent, "we only serve *authentic* Italian cuisine." He kissed his fingertips and released them to the sky in a dramatic gesture.

Once they'd calmed down and caught their breath, he led Amber back toward the car and held open the door for her. "Now, let's go find some place real."

❁

THIRTY MINUTES later, they were parked on a quiet overpass over the major freeway dividing the city of Dallas into east and west. They sat on top of the hood of Anil's car, eating burritos from a local taqueria, while a steady stream of cars raced below them.

"See?" Amber pointed out a set of headlights coming toward them with dangerous velocity. "You can tell by the shape of them. That's a Ford F-150."

"Wow, you have a real talent for this." Anil peeled down the foil wrapper of his bean-and-cheese special.

Amber shrugged. "My brothers and I did this a lot as kids. Except it was a dusty country road instead of a big freeway, so we had to wait a long time in between cars." She described the East Texas ranch where she'd grown up, with its horses and cattle. Amber spoke about her father and brothers, who were avid hunters (deer in the fall, quail in the spring), and how she'd spent hours in the kitchen with her mother. "Momma is a great cook, at least when it comes to frying. She makes the best fried chicken, fried okra, hush puppies. Believe it or not, that was my favorite meal growing up—three different fried foods on one plate." She shook her head. "You can see how she ended up the way she did."

"Does she have her diabetes under control now?" Anil asked.

"She usually remembers her insulin, but she's lost some vision in one eye, and her kidneys are weak." Amber stared out at the oncoming traffic, her face alternately illuminated and darkened by the glare of headlights. As he watched her, Anil was struck once again by the innumerable forms the human body could take: how the simple features of eyes, cheekbones, nose, chin, and mouth could be arranged so many different ways to create a face—one plain, another beautiful. When he'd first started observing surgeries in Ahmadabad, it was reassuring to concentrate on these commonalities of the human body. Whether the patient was an elderly woman or a young boy, rich or poor, regardless of caste or religion—below the layers of skin, fatty tissue, and muscle—everyone had the same organs arranged in the same way.

He pulled another beer bottle from the paper bag, twisted off the cap, and offered it to her. "And the rest of your family?"

"Daddy has high cholesterol, but he still eats his fried eggs and bacon every day." Amber shrugged. "They're pretty much all like that. My little brother's twenty-two and he's already prediabetic. All he keeps in his trailer are doughnuts, beer, and soda." She shook her head. "Ten years old—that's when I made up my mind, after I found Momma on the bathroom floor. I was not going to end up like her. My school had three sports teams for girls, and I joined them all. I guess that's when I became a fitness nut, as Momma calls me."

"And you still are."

Amber nodded. "I love being a personal trainer, helping people lead healthier lives. Not the way you do, of course. I'm not saving any lives."

"Don't sell yourself short," Anil said. "It's hard to get people to change their lifestyle. I have this conversation with patients every day—get more exercise, eat a better diet, quit smoking." He shrugged. "Most of them never change, and there's not much I can do." This was an oddity about America he'd noticed—the fitness equipment commercials on TV at all hours, the exercise gyms in every strip mall, a whole industry dedicated to keeping people healthy. And yet, most of his patients suffered from obesity, high cholesterol, hypertension, and diabetes: a parade of ailments brought on by the excesses of the Western lifestyle. "It's hard to break those family habits," he said.

Amber took a long drink of her beer and exhaled. "That's for sure. My family thinks I'm crazy for moving here. Most of my friends stayed in East Texas to start families. Momma was worried about me moving to Dallas. She thinks big cities are full of bad things and bad people." Anil noticed her jaw tighten. "They don't get it—I can work in a world-class fitness center here and take nutrition classes at night. I can't do any of that in Ashford." She pointed at another set of headlights. "See that one? Ram pickup." She sighed. "And the worst part? My mom was kind of right. It *has* been hard for me here. I feel like I'm on my own a lot of the time. But I can't tell my family that, because they're expecting me to give up and come home." She tilted the bottle up to her lips, then put it down and spoke instead. "It's just so different here. I feel so out of place sometimes, like I don't know the rules."

"Like asking for garlic bread in a swanky Italian restaurant?" Anil said.

"Exactly." Amber laughed. They toasted with their beer bottles and both took a drink.

"I feel the same way," Anil said. "I mean, this is a new country for me, of course. But even at the hospital, which should be familiar—even there, I feel like I'm missing something everyone else seems to know."

"Yeah." Amber nodded. They drank their beers and identified a few more sets of headlights. "So," she said, "your turn. Tell me about where you're from."

"Ah, well, I'm from a very small village," Anil said, "more than a hundred kilometers, or . . . about seventy-five miles, from the nearest city, Ahmadabad, which you probably haven't heard of."

Amber shook her head and smiled. "So, I guess that means you're kind of country too." The moment seemed right to lean over and kiss her, but as Anil was summoning up the nerve, a car horn blared on the freeway below.

At the end of the evening, they agreed to go for a run by the lake on Anil's next day off. In the intervening week, Anil revisited his medical textbooks to refresh his academic knowledge of female anatomy, and borrowed some of Baldev's naughty movies to fill in the practical details he was determined to put to use.

THE FIRST step, Amber announced after seeing his old sneakers, was to go shopping. In under an hour, she had Anil fully outfitted: new shoes with shock absorbers and contoured insoles, a moisture-wicking shirt, shorts made from recycled plastic bottles, even new lightweight socks. Anil stood in the fitting room staring at the transformed image of himself in shades of gray and electric blue, all of which would collectively cost him half a month's rent. He admired himself from different angles, seeing himself as Amber might, and left the store in the new outfit, carrying his old clothes in the shopping bag.

They drove to White Rock Lake, on the east side of Dallas, the opposite end of town from where they lived. Beautiful mansions graced the perimeter of the lake, each of them set back from the road by a vast expanse of manicured lawn. It was a perfect day for running outdoors, sunny and clear, but not too hot yet. As they walked toward the paved path encircling the lake, the immensity of White Rock came into view.

"Wow." Anil stopped, taking it in. Crystal blue water stretched out before them, interrupted only in the far distance by several narrow docks. Water birds grazed on reeds just a few feet from the path.

"Isn't it beautiful? Even if it is man-made," Amber said. "It's nine miles around." She stood on one leg, grabbing her other foot behind her. "But don't worry, we don't have to run the whole thing. Not today anyway." She smiled and pulled a device from her pocket. "I'll even give you an edge, my iPod." She then raised Anil's shirt sleeve and wound a Velcro strap around his upper arm, fixing it in place. "Ready?"

As the pulsing music filled his head, Anil pushed forward to keep pace with the rhythm. He marveled at the minuscule device on his arm that allowed him to run in his own world, immersed in music from hers. As they passed the magnificent houses, he imagined how each one looked inside, picturing himself in the tall foyers, climbing the grand stairways.

Anil lasted for only three miles at Amber's pace, and one more at a slow jog. He collapsed in the shade of a large tree, breathing heavily and layered in a thin film of sweat. He felt the same exhilaration he remembered feeling running through the fields as a child, the burning in his lungs and the wind in his face. Only, back home, he ran in bare feet—no shock absorbers, and certainly no iPod.

"Anil, I want to thank you." Amber sat upright beside him, breathing normally.

He squinted at her from his place in the grass. "For what, slowing you down?"

She smiled. "For being a gentleman. Most guys would have been all over me by now, and you haven't even kissed me yet. I feel like you're interested in really getting to know me. It's nice, for a change." She smiled, turning back to the lake.

Anil sat up, his heart and breath not yet back to their normal pace, his head swirling with dehydration and the possibility of what was about to happen. Emboldened, he reached his arm around Amber's shoulder, appreciating her beauty as she continued to gaze out at the lake. Gently, he turned her face toward him, leaned in, and kissed her. It was a moment he'd pictured many times, but he'd never imagined it would take place outdoors in public, both of them covered in sweat. When their lips parted, he smiled. "Sorry. Am I no longer a gentleman?"

"Hmm, not sure." Amber smiled. "Let me think about it." She leaned in and kissed him again, and this time it lasted for quite a while.

Afterward, they lay back in the grass, Amber's head resting on Anil's chest. Anil watched the leaves rustling overhead in the light breeze as slivers of sun warmed his legs. It was the happiest he'd been in the eight months since he'd moved to Dallas. The rest of his internship year still loomed before him, but he could begin to envision a life beyond his residency: a specialty private practice that afforded him one of these beautiful homes, running around the lake in the morning with Amber, living to his own soundtrack.

❁

AFTER THAT day at the lake, which turned into the first night they spent together, Anil and Amber slipped into a pattern of seeing each other whenever their schedules allowed. His night shifts and her early-morning training sessions made it challenging, but at least once or twice a week they spent the night together at Amber's apartment, a precious few hours that more prudently should have been spent on sleep. Amber did not seem to mind Anil's inexperience; indeed, she enjoyed their slow mutual exploration, and Anil appreciated that she never made him feel self-conscious. Even when he came home from the hospital exhausted, Anil had energy for her, to explore the contours of her body and to release into the pleasure of her company. She re-energized him and propelled him through another day or two, or five, until he could see her again. The thought of seeing Amber at night sustained him through day after grueling day at the hospital.

"I love hearing you talk about your work," Amber said to Anil once.

"You mean, the way I complain about it all the time?" Anil said.

"I mean, your dedication to it. The way you think of it not just as a job but as a calling." She took his hands. "You're different, Anil. You're different from almost everyone I've ever known, the way you take life seriously, the way you believe in achieving something great."

Anil shrugged, self-conscious about his ambition. "Everyone in medical college was like that. It's so competitive. You need confidence to get through."

"I never really considered going to college." Amber fiddled with the hem of her nightshirt, and he could see she was embarrassed. "Hardly anyone in Ashford does. Maybe a star football player every couple of years. By the time I thought about it, it was too late."

"It's not too late. You can still go, if you want," Anil said.

"Anil, come on. I barely have a high school diploma from a third-rate school in East Texas. No one in my family has ever been to college."

"So? I'm from a tiny village halfway across the world. No one in my family ever went to college, before me."

Amber's expression morphed into something softer. "Really, you think I could?"

"Yes, of course. You're smart, you work hard. You have an innate curiosity about human physiology and nutrition. There's no reason you can't go to college and earn a degree." When Amber looked down, Anil asked, "What? Did I say something wrong?"

"No." She shook her head and looked up at him with watery eyes. "It's just . . . no one's ever said that to me before. Not my parents, not my teachers."

Anil reached over and grabbed her hands. "Well, you'll just have to show them."

Amber began to look into undergraduate programs at local universities, and Anil loved seeing her confidence bud as thick application packets arrived over the following weeks.

As the morbidity and mortality conference approached, Anil grew anxious about the presentation of Jason Calhoun's case. When he couldn't sleep at night, Amber listened patiently, without question or judgment, to his recounting of the events. Somehow, Amber was able to look past his failings to some good and strong inner core she alone seemed able to see. It was during that dark period that Anil knew, with a certainty he hadn't felt about anything since coming to America, he was in love with her.

He told her so, one Sunday morning as they lay together in her bed after making love, a term he finally, truly understood. A draft came through the open window and Amber reached for her clothes on the floor, but Anil held her tightly in his arms until she relaxed into his embrace. It was a spontaneous declaration of love, whispered in her ear, and he immediately worried it was too hasty, coming just a few months after they'd started dating. But Amber, her eyes glistening, told him she loved him too.

When they were like this, the two of them alone in the world, no one else mattered and all his troubles receded to the background. Anil imagined this life with Amber stretching into the future, the protected universe of their love rendering the rest of the world irrelevant.

In the end, after all Anil's worrying, Sonia took the weight of responsibility at the M&M presentation, explaining that her team had missed the subtle signs of the ruptured aneurysm not only because it was a slow leak but also because the blood accumulated in the retroperitoneal space rather than the abdomen, making it difficult to detect through physical examination. She recommended a new protocol to flag blood pressure drops in aneurysm patients, to counteract the shift nature of the work, in which patients were handed off between teams and such gradual changes could be unintentionally overlooked. Anil stood by, prepared to face questions, but Sonia shielded him from most of them. Only Casper O'Brien asked Anil what he'd personally learned from the case. Anil was ready with the response he and Sonia had discussed, about having learned to order CTs and check hematocrit levels more aggressively with aneurysm cases.

In May, six weeks after the M&M conference, Anil received a nondescript letter confirming his second year of residency, the same form letter received by all sixty-five of his fellow interns. He did not join Charlie and the others at the Horseshoe Bar, where they gathered to commemorate the end of their internship year. There was no sense of accomplishment when Anil placed the check mark on the calendar that signified his biggest career milestone to date. Despite years of study, Anil had been unprepared for what he faced at Parkview: working under extreme pressure to treat patients who didn't resemble what he'd learned in his books. The professional camaraderie he'd expected was supplanted by senior doctors who took pleasure in humiliating him, and by peers who preferred to compete for their favor.

Amber surprised him with a bottle of sparkling wine and was disappointed when he didn't feel like celebrating. Anil didn't know how to explain to her that mere survival was not what he'd hoped for when he'd come to Dallas one year ago.

12

It was a particularly hot day, and Leena had come in from the fields to get a glass of water when little Ritu tiptoed into the kitchen. The girl could not stand to rest with her brother and the adults during the afternoon nap; she simply had too much energy to lie still for that long.

Ritu's face was sticky with sweat, and her hair was a tangled mess. She followed the glass of water with her groggy, listless eyes. Leena gave her the glass, watched as she drank, and filled the glass again from the clay cistern above the sink. "Come," she said. "There's a breeze outside."

They sat on the steps and Leena poured water over the little girl's head, soaking her hair. Slowly, she pulled a comb through each section, holding the hair away from Ritu's scalp as she removed the knots. Ritu giggled and squealed as Leena worked, pressing a hand over her mouth so as not to wake those inside. Finally, her hair was smooth and glossy. It was impossibly thick; even when slicked back with water, Leena could barely wrap her palm around the whole lot. Leena separated Ritu's hair into several sections and began braiding it.

When Ritu asked, "What's the name of that song?" Leena realized she was humming a song her mother used to sing, but she couldn't remember the words, only the tune. Once Leena had finished one braid, Ritu ran her fingers down her cool woven hair and smiled. "I love you, *didi*," she said.

Sweet Ritu. Leena hadn't heard those words since she had left her mother's arms on her wedding day.

"Please don't go away," Ritu said. "Don't leave us like before. Promise?"

Before Leena could respond, Rekha came out the back door. "What are you doing out here? Why isn't the afternoon tea ready?" She grabbed Ritu by the hand to take her inside. The girl cried out, but Leena smiled and gestured for her to go.

Leena never saw Rekha show her children any love or affection. Most of the time, she acted as if they weren't there, and showed interest only when they were with Leena. Girish's elder brother was also erratic with them. The other day, Dev had jumped into his father's lap as he sat in the parlor, and Leena had watched the man bounce his son playfully on his knee, then grab his hand and mock his birthmark, teasing the boy that he hadn't washed himself properly after using the latrine. Leena turned away in embarrassment for Dev and retreated to the kitchen, where she put aside two chocolate biscuits for when he would come into the kitchen later, sullen.

As Leena waited for the milk to boil for afternoon tea, she thought about the curious thing Ritu had said outside. But she was only a child; there was no reason to believe the imaginings that filled her mind.

Those children were the single ray of happiness in Leena's life. Every morning, Ritu ran to the kitchen and wrapped her small arms around Leena's waist. Her sweet face, with its round cheeks, bloomed with happiness, and Leena came to depend on that innocent smile.

Leena hadn't received any more gifts from her parents, nor had she been allowed to visit them. She knew her husband and father-in-law had been to see them at least one more time, because she'd heard them discussing it afterward. A few times, when Rekha was napping, she secretly telephoned her mother, but their conversations were always the same. Leena said she missed them and wanted to come home for

Diwali. Her mother spoke in a whisper too, though there was no need to hide on her end. *Be good and stay strong*, she said.

One evening, when the rest of the family was going out to a wedding, Leena was told to stay home to finish the ironing. Her mother-in-law came out of her bedroom wearing one of her best saris and earrings that resembled delicate gold waterfalls running over ruby and pearl pebbles. Leena recognized the earrings at once: they belonged to her mother—one of the few pieces of jewelry she owned. She had worn them on Leena's wedding day.

Surely, there must be some mistake. Leena moved closer to her mother-in-law to look, and when she was shooed away with a wave of the hand, Leena noticed the etched gold bangles on the old woman's wrist, which had also belonged to her mother. They departed then, all of them—her husband, his brother and his wife and children, their parents—and Leena was left alone in the house. She tried to do her best with the ironing, but she kept seeing those gold and ruby waterfalls before her eyes instead of the petticoat she was pressing. Rather than the sizzle and crackle of the iron, she heard only the tinkling sound of the two gold bangles on her mother-in-law's wrist. She picked up the phone and dialed her parents' number over a dozen times, but each time there was no answer.

Leena knew in her heart that something was terribly wrong. She worried that her mother was dead and her husband's family had not told her. Or that her mother was ill and asking for her. Leena burned two blouses and one petticoat that night while she formulated a plan in her mind.

The next morning, Leena bathed and dressed in a special sari, one her parents had given her at her wedding. She wove fresh jasmine buds into her hair and applied *kajal* to her eyes. After Girish rose and went to take his bath, she made the bed, tidied the room, and then sat waiting for him. When he returned, she began.

"I was thinking perhaps I could go visit my parents for Diwali. I haven't seen them since the wedding."

"Hmm," Girish grunted as he dropped his towel and reached for the fresh clothes she held out.

"It's still two weeks away. There's plenty of time to prepare—"

"That's a long drive. You expect me to lose a full day's work to take you there and back?"

Leena did not point out that Girish barely worked at anything other than playing cards and eating meals. "No, of course that would be asking too much. I'm sure my father would be willing to come and fetch me. I could call him today?" She desperately wanted her father to come and see this house, this land, to tell her whether she was wrong to expect more.

"And you'll leave Rekha and my mother to do all the work while you're gone? That's pretty selfish, don't you think?"

Leena bit her tongue. Rekha and Mother had been perfectly capable of caring for the household before she'd arrived. "It's just a few days. They can manage better without me in their way."

Leena had thought through all of this the night before. It was not an unreasonable request—to go see her parents for a few days after being here nearly a year. She had chosen the early morning to speak to Girish because nothing had happened yet to sour his mood. She'd anticipated his arguments and readied answers that would not anger him. What was the worst that could happen? He could slam her up against the wall, or pin her arms behind her back, as he had before. Leena was prepared for that; she was willing to endure it if it meant getting to go home.

But with Girish's reaction, Leena could see she had miscalculated. Her question, her very presence, was enough to enrage him. By his expression and the way his lip curled up at the corner, she knew that he wanted to hit her.

Leena stepped out of the bedroom. "I should get the tea started before the others wake." Girish followed her into the kitchen. Her hands shook as she lifted the heavy cistern outside to the water pump. Her arms had grown strong from doing this task every morning, but now they trembled as he watched her.

Outside, the horizon was streaked with pale pink and deep orange, and the birds were calling to each other. The air felt very still; it was going to be a hot day. Leena was lowering the cistern below the water pump when she heard the door creak open behind her. She did not turn around. She would not give Girish the satisfaction of seeing fear in her eyes. She would do her work, as she always did.

Leena gripped the thick iron lever and began pumping it up and down, relaxing into the familiar rhythm, using the strength of her legs to take the pressure off her arms. The lever groaned, and finally water began to trickle, then pour, into the cistern. It was because of the water that Leena did not hear the liquid splashing at her feet and onto her sari. She did not hear it, nor did she feel anything. She smelled it first, the sharp familiar scent of kerosene.

When the pungent odor entered her nose, she dropped the lever and turned around. Girish stood there, holding the square tin from next to the kitchen stove. With a wild lurch of his arm, he splattered the last of the oil at her, then tossed aside the empty tin. His eyes were narrow and their black pupils glinted at her. He was chewing lazily on something.

Leena opened her mouth, then closed it again without speaking. She had gone too far, crossed him, she now understood. Slowly, she began to move away from Girish, taking small steps backwards. He advanced on her, as if they were joined by an invisible rope. He reached into his pocket and, in a movement too quick for Leena to follow, lit a match, the orange flame flickering at the end of his finger. His lips opened into a sneer, and Leena was struck by how his expression transformed his face. It was so clear to her now—this man was evil. How had she not seen it before?

Leena never saw him throw the match. She believed there was still time to turn and run. She must have closed her eyes for a moment, or looked up to the heavens to pray for mercy, because when her eyes opened, she saw Girish's back as he walked toward the house. Bright flames licked up at her feet—bright yellow, deep orange and red, the same colors of that morning's radiant sunrise.

Warmth at first, as the flames crept toward her. They leaped to the hem of her sari, soaked through with oil. Heat, scorching heat, was spiraling around her. Leena looked about frantically. Girish had poured a ring of kerosene on the ground around her. She was trapped in a circle of fire, with nowhere to go. Her eyes burned with smoke. Her throat tightened. She was so tired of crying, tired of not crying. She wanted to lie down on the ground and close her eyes.

Everything was spinning around her, then the ground came up hard under her cheek. Searing pain in her foot unlike anything she had ever felt before, climbing up her leg. A sickly odor she had never smelled—thick and sweet and oily. It penetrated her mouth and nose; she choked on it. The odor of flesh burning. Her flesh. Leena tried to stand, but her foot was aflame. She crawled away from the fire, but it followed her. It was engulfing her. She tore off her sari and stumbled toward the well, lifted her foot and sank it into the cistern. With a sizzle and a crackle the fire went out, steam and smoke rising into the air. The odor infiltrated her nostrils and her eyes. Her hand went to her blouse and retrieved the peacock handkerchief. Leena covered her nose and mouth and tried to breathe.

Then, she ran. Although she could hear the fire burning behind her, she did not turn to look. Singeing pain radiated up her leg, and the near nakedness of her body shamed her. But it was the smell that most overcame her, the smell that burrowed deep into her nose and filled her mouth like a thick oil. With every breath, it moved deeper into her, flooding her with its pungency.

Leena ran until she was past the boundaries of her in-laws' land, until the crops changed from cotton to sugarcane. The dirt road between the farms was empty of vehicles. It was still early morning and most people hadn't yet risen. When she could run no longer, she walked along the edge of the road, wearing only her sari blouse and petticoat, burned off below the knee. She was humiliated to be seen this way, in her undergarments, but what choice did she have?

And where could she go? As the first house came into view, Leena felt a wash of relief. But she didn't know anyone who lived around here. She had been kept inside her in-laws' house since she'd come; she hadn't met any neighbors other than Girish's friends, and they would not help her. She would have better luck with a stranger. But without her clothes, any stranger would take her for a beggar, or worse.

Leena walked on, past that first house and then another, trying to ignore the pain of each step shooting through her left foot and up her leg. She walked toward the rising sun, to the east, toward Panchanagar, but her village was over a hundred kilometers away. Even if she knew the way there, and even if she walked all day, she would not reach it before nightfall.

Finally, when she could bear the pain no more, she sat down at the edge of the road and folded her foot onto her lap, forcing herself to look at it. The skin covering her ankle and calf was burned an angry shade of red and covered in blisters. On the top of her foot, where the flames had started, the skin looked as if it had already turned to gray ash. Dirt and leaves were embedded in the wounds.

Holding her foot that way, inspecting it closely, Leena could not avoid the odor. She turned her head to the side and held the kerchief to her nose, seeking the scent of sandalwood. She knew she could not walk for much longer on her foot, but she had to keep going. Leena hoisted herself up and began to walk again.

She was unaware of how much time passed, but less than a hundred steps later, she came upon a simple house: whitewashed with a wooden door, it reminded her of her own. Outside, marigolds grew on both sides of the door. Their bright, frilly blooms were welcoming, their fragrance happily overpowering. The plants were robust, full of new buds. Their dead leaves had been pared away, and the soil below was moist. Someone inside that modest house took great care with those flowers, Leena knew. A woman, perhaps, who would take pity on her.

13

ANIL EMBARKED ON HIS SECOND YEAR OF RESIDENCY IN THE blistering heat of summer, and soon found his new role to be a meaningful improvement over intern. He was now impervious to the gritty nature of Parkview and its patients. The new batch of interns and med students, in their wide-eyed fear, helped him see how much he'd learned over the past year.

Anil had been supplanted at the bottom of the hospital food chain, but he was now responsible for teaching his team of neophytes. As an intern, he hadn't appreciated the demands of this role. In addition to his own patients—he always kept the most complex cases for himself—Anil had to demonstrate procedures and monitor his interns' work.

There were many ways to fulfill the teaching requisite of his job. To do it well, Anil learned, took a great deal of time and energy, neither of which were ever in excess supply at Parkview. And along with his new responsibilities came increased expectations. There was no leeway to commit beginner mistakes; he could not squander the second chance he'd been given.

One of the marked benefits of being a second-year resident was that Anil could occasionally leave the hospital at the end of his shift, having assigned the follow-up work to his interns. Tonight, he pulled into the parking lot at home while the sky was light, looking forward to spending the evening with Amber. When he went to retrieve the mail from the group mailboxes, two other neighbors were already there, blocking his access. They were big guys, one dressed in an oil-stained jumpsuit, the other in a cutoff T-shirt exposing both tattoo-covered arms.

Anil waited for them to step aside. When the tattooed one turned around and saw Anil, his eyes narrowed. "We in your way?" He slapped his friend on the shoulder. "Look, Rudy, this guy can't get to his box. Ain't that a shame?"

Rudy turned around and folded his arms across his barrel chest. Neither man made any movement away from the mailboxes.

"No problem." Anil smiled and held up a hand. "I'll wait 'til you're done."

The tattooed one stared at Anil. "We done, Rudy?"

"Yeah, we're done." Rudy turned his head a fraction and spit on the ground.

The men stood there for another long moment, then the tattooed one took a step toward Anil. "What's your name?" he sneered. "Osama?"

It was a moment before Anil understood his implication. "No, i-i-it's Anil." He straightened his back. "Doctor Anil Patel."

Rudy stepped forward again. Anil fought the urge to step back. He was close enough to smell the dank sweat and cigarette smoke lingering on the man. "I-i-is that right?" he mocked. "Well, if we need any extra towels, we know who to ask, right, Lee?" He jabbed his elbow toward his friend. "I bet this guy's got a whole closet full." Rudy laughed, pushing past Anil. Lee shot Anil a menacing look before following his buddy outside.

Anil drew in a deep breath and exhaled as he collected his mail, trying to rid his nostrils of the men's bodily odors. After entering his apartment, he locked the door behind him and took a long, hot shower until he no longer felt shaky.

Outside of that incident, Anil settled into a comfortable routine at home. When their schedules aligned, he and Amber studied together in the evenings: he with his medical books and journals, she with her SAT preparation tome. She was planning to apply to the undergraduate program at a local university where she could take a part-time course load while continuing to work at the club. Although he was drained after a day at the hospital, Anil looked forward to these evening study sessions since they held the promise of falling into bed together at the end of the night.

For most of the summer it was too hot to run outdoors, but he and Amber went to White Rock Lake to walk or have a picnic. As they strolled around the perimeter, holding hands, they picked out the houses they would like to live in: combining the gray brick of one house with the black shutters of another, selecting planters of geraniums and a wooden swing for the front porch.

Occasionally, on the weekends, all four of them—Amber, Anil, Baldev, and Mahesh—went out together. Mahesh found an old theater nearby that played the latest Bollywood releases on Saturday nights. Anil was a little uneasy about two distinct parts of his life coming together, but they wound up fitting comfortably: Amber loved the film's song-and-dance numbers and downloaded the soundtrack to her iPod before they left the theater. She was happy to go along when Mahesh suggested going out for *chaat* afterward. In furtive snatches of Hindi, when Amber got up to refill her cup numerous times during the spicy meal, Baldev teased him about getting serious with her and Mahesh warned him not to. But Anil was too happy to take either one of them seriously.

IN SEPTEMBER, as the oppressive heat of summer finally began to relent, Anil started his rotation in the Cardiac Care Unit. When he arrived in the CCU the first day, he was pleased to see Jennifer, the red-haired intern he'd worked with during the ICU disaster the previous year. She'd been shocked to hear Jason Calhoun died of a ruptured aneurysm, and Anil was grateful for her blameless reaction.

Anil and Jennifer were chatting, waiting for rounds to begin, when Jennifer stopped mid-sentence, her gaze traveling beyond Anil's shoulder. A girlish smile crept onto her face and she held up one hand in a small wave. Anil turned around and his shoulders tightened.

"Hey, folks." Trey towered over Anil by at least six inches, his broad chest and muscular arms filling out his crisp blue dress shirt. He offered them a roll of mints, and only Jennifer accepted one.

A larger crowd than usual was gathering in the CCU. "What's going on here?" Anil asked. Two senior residents were huddled off to one side, studying their notes.

"Tanaka's leading rounds today," Trey said. "Department head. Heavy hitter."

"I've heard he's tough." Jennifer smiled as she pursed her lips over the candy. Her demeanor left Anil feeling inexplicably betrayed.

Dr. Tanaka arrived precisely at seven o'clock. Anil noticed he was of mixed descent, his stiff dark hair and eye folds diluted by the Caucasian milkiness of his skin, making Anil feel something of a kinship. Morning rounds commenced without any preliminaries, and both senior residents seemed nervous. When Dr. Tanaka spoke, it was in a surprisingly low tone. Some attending physicians practically bellowed on rounds, as if standing in front of a lecture hall, but Tanaka spoke so softly everyone had to step or lean in to hear while they scribbled down notes. The rest of the team modulated their voices after Tanaka, so they all became part of the same intimate discussion.

⊛

Several weeks later on morning rounds, the team was standing outside a patient's room when one of the senior residents asked Trey to present the case for him. Jennifer and Anil exchanged a glance at the unusual move.

Trey stepped forward. "Patient is a forty-six-year-old female, obese, with a history of type 2 diabetes and smoking, who presented to the Emergency Department yesterday with shortness of breath. I was called to the ER last night to admit her. The cardiologist on call was consulted by phone and recommended the patient get a ventilation/perfusion lung scan for suspicion of pulmonary embolism." Trey paused until Dr. Tanaka nodded for him to continue. "Labs weren't back yet, but my assessment was that the patient was experiencing an acute myocardial infarction and should be taken to the cath lab for a stent."

Dr. Tanaka held up his silver-plated pen, a gesture that was always his precursor to speaking. "This is very important. The symptoms and EKG results can look similar for an MI and a PE, but they have different management paths, and we may not have long to decide." He turned back to Trey. "What led you to this assessment?"

Trey cleared his throat. "It was the combination of everything I observed—the EKG alone could have pointed to PE, but her chest pain, bradycardia, and diaphoresis, together with her risk factors, suggested an acute MI." Trey shifted his weight from one foot to the other. "Also, as I was leaving, she . . . the patient grabbed my wrist and said, 'Doc, please help me. If you don't do something, I'm going to die.'"

A prickle traveled up the back of Anil's neck. Dr. Tanaka's eyebrows arched above the rim of his glasses and he looked around at the rest of the team. "Doctors, this is of great diagnostic value. Remember this: when a patient tells you she's going to die"—he lowered his voice further—"pay attention."

Anil was confounded by this guidance. How many times at Parkview had he been warned not to take a patient at face value? The addict who feigned back pain to secure narcotics, the prostitute who claimed she always used protection, the street teen who denied taking amphetamines. How many times had a patient come into the ER insisting he was having a heart attack when it was simply indigestion? Sound diagnosis was built on the objectivity of clinical assessment and inarguable test results, not a patient's desperate utterings.

Tanaka nodded at Trey. "Please go on, Dr. Crandall."

Dr. Tanaka hadn't referred to anyone on the team by name until then, and Anil realized this was not an oversight but a sign of his indifference to the rest of them. Trey continued with the rest of the case presentation. He'd gone to the ER resident and suggested an alternative course of action, but no one was willing to overrule the first cardiologist. As a junior resident, he had little say in these matters. Anil would have followed the senior doctor's instructions, and by Jennifer's strained expression, he knew she would have done the same.

But Trey had been so confident in his own assessment that he'd hunted down another cardiologist in the hospital. "I showed him the EKG and told him I had a patient with a pile of risk factors who said she was going to die," Trey said. "He grabbed the phone and told the cath lab to get ready. By the time we got there, the patient was arresting, but we were able to shock her back. Once she was stable, they put a stent in the RCA. It was touch and go for a while, but she made it." Trey handed the chart back to the senior resident.

Tanaka held up his silver pen. "Doctors, sometimes we have to make decisions without all the information we'd like, without even seeing lab results. In these cases, you need to trust your instinct. But first"—he paused as he pointed his pen around the circle of listeners—"you need to develop your instinct, which comes from seeing many patients over many years. It's rare for a young resident to make a call like this, but because Dr. Crandall did, he saved this woman's life." He aimed the pen in the direction of the patient. "Good work, Dr. Crandall." And they all followed Dr. Tanaka in to see the patient who owed her life to Trey's unrelenting confidence.

Trey's case presentation served as a challenge to the rest of the team. Over the next few weeks, the other residents and interns began pushing to make their own diagnostic choices and fighting to defend them. Anil tried to get into the game, but making and defending assertive calls did not come naturally to him.

IN THE last week of his rotation in the Cardiac Care Unit, Anil finally had a chance to present a patient to Dr. Tanaka.

"So the EKG shows no abnormalities, but the patient is experiencing distress and chest pain," Dr. Tanaka said. "Other considerations?"

"High cholesterol and family history of heart disease," Anil replied.

"Your recommendation?"

"Perform an angiogram to see if there are any blockages."

"Yes, good." Tanaka nodded. "Send her to the cath lab, and scrub in if you want to observe." Anil was stunned by the invitation as junior residents were rarely allowed into the sacred chamber of the Cardiac Catheterization Lab.

Before entering the cath lab, which felt like an operating room, Anil donned a lead apron over his scrubs, surgery cap, mask, shoe covers, stiff plastic face shield, and sterile surgeon's gown. Inside, the patient lay on the table, draped with sterile cloths so that only a small patch of skin near the groin was exposed. Prominently mounted above the table was an enormous monitor. A hushed intensity fell over the room when Tanaka issued instructions for the junior cardiology fellow to make an incision at the groin, insert a needle into the femoral artery, thread in the guide wire and the sheath. While he manipulated the catheter, every pair of eyes in the lab was trained on the monitor. Images began to emerge on the screen—grainy at first, then clearer. The artery became visible, a clear white branch against a black sky.

All measurements of the artery were within normal range. "I want to take a closer look at the LAD with the IVUS," Dr. Tanaka said. He turned to Anil to explain. "The intravascular ultrasound catheter is a marvelous technology. It enables us to see from inside the blood vessels out."

Moments later, Anil understood what Tanaka meant. The image on the monitor was the opening of a deep tunnel. Once the catheter was inserted, it looked like they were traveling down the artery, as though they were actually inside the body, with the ability to see into the corners of its life systems. Anil could not take his eyes off that view into a mysterious world. It must have been how Cousteau felt the first time he traveled to the depths of the ocean and saw what no one had seen before: vast expanses of life and nature functioning in all their beautiful complexity. Anil heard a weak moan and remembered the patient on the table.

"Look at that," Tanaka said. "Significant plaque buildup in the left anterior descending." The heart monitor began beeping loudly and bright red numbers flashed on the screen. Dr. Tanaka took a step forward, and Anil instinctively moved back. He deciphered the signals on the monitor as ventricular fibrillation. The patient was in cardiac arrest.

The team moved quickly, Tanaka conducting the players in the room like an orchestra. It was like no code Anil had seen. As the situation grew more stressful—the patient's heart was losing oxygen and her brain, lungs, and kidneys were at risk of damage—Dr. Tanaka grew calmer and so did everyone else. Anil felt his own sense of panic slowly abate. Every one of his senses was heightened: he could hear the whirring of the machinery, smell antiseptic in the air.

After numerous tries with the defibrillator, the flatline finally responded with a jump to indicate that the heart had resumed its natural rhythm. Once the patient was stable, Tanaka inserted a new catheter to dilate and stent the blocked artery, which had caused the patient's heart to stop. Anil watched on the monitor as the vessel was reopened and protected, and a pump was used to help stabilize blood flow to the heart. With his work finished, Dr. Tanaka moved to the head of the patient's table and explained what had been done to repair the failings of her heart. "You're better than new," Dr. Tanaka said, smiling as he patted her shoulder.

"HE FOUND the blockage just in time and literally brought her back from the brink of death," Anil said to Charlie as they sat in the Horseshoe Bar later that evening, pint glasses in front of them. For the first time in his residency, Anil felt like celebrating. He couldn't contain the sense of exhilaration he'd felt, the thrill of seeing the inner workings of the body, the rush of adrenaline he'd experienced in that room.

Charlie emitted a low whistle. "Sounds amazing. But a fellowship in interventional cardiology is four or five more years. And you still get called into the hospital all the time. Why'd you want to do that to yourself?"

"Twenty years ago, that woman would have died on our doorstep," Anil said, "and Tanaka just gave her ten or fifteen more years with that stent. Imagine being able to do that, do *something*, for everyone."

Every day in the Cardiac Care Unit, Anil was surrounded by patients who'd suffered the symptoms of a heart attack. When someone described the crushing chest pain or feeling suffocated, he imagined what his father must have gone through in his final hours.

Anil had not looked closely into his patients' eyes before, but now he found it impossible to look away. When the oxygen mask was applied or the cardiac monitor started beeping erratically, he saw bewilderment in his patients' eyes and felt their silent trust planted like two ominous weights on his shoulders. Above all, he saw fear distilled to its purest form. While he still had to look up their dosage levels, the irrelevant details of their personal histories burrowed into his mind, like the MI patient who'd been an office janitor for forty-three years and met his wife at a school dance. And he could never forget his patients were the fortunate ones—in a world-class hospital filled with doctors and equipment, not an isolated rural village hundreds of kilometers from the nearest medical facility, which itself was years behind in technology. In that lab, with those catheters, stents, and balloons at his fingertips, Anil could be the kind of doctor who dealt in life rather than death. This was why he'd come to America.

"Okay, mate." Charlie shrugged. "I hope you still feel that way when you're camping out in a call room five years from now. It's competitive, though, only five or six fellowship spots at Parkview. I've heard of a few people applying already. Not to mention Trey, and you know he's in for sure."

Anil took a long sip of beer. "Trey? Why?"

"His father? The legendary Dr. Crandall—cardiologist, swanky private practice in Highland Park, sits on the Parkview board."

Anil stared into his sepia-toned beer. That explained Trey's remarkable performance: always ready with his answers on rounds, never scrambling for a test result, never flustered like every other resident at one time or another. Trey had been bred for this job.

"Well, the department head invited me into the cath lab," Anil said. "That's got to be worth something."

"You should try to work on a research project with Tanaka. Come up with a really great idea to take to him," Charlie said with a thin smile.

"What about our project?" Anil said. He and Charlie had been making steady progress on their MRSA retrospective study. They were at a critical juncture where they'd have to complete the analysis of their data set soon, a big investment of time.

"Come on, I know that's not really your cup of tea." Charlie swirled the last inch of beer in his glass. He looked up and met Anil's eyes directly. "Look, mate, you shouldn't count on me right now. I might have to step away from the project for a bit. I don't want to let you down. It might be good if you had something else going on, something you're really into."

"What? Why?" Anil said. "Charlie, what are you talking about?"

Charlie shrugged. "I've got some problems back home I need to take care of. I'm going to have to take a job in the evenings when I'm not at the hospital, at least for a few months," he said. "My sister's in a bit of money trouble. She's pregnant with twins, and her husband was laid off a couple months back. Turns out there aren't many jobs these days for a thirty-six-year-old miner. My parents are working-class folks, you know, don't have much money to spare. I'm supposed to be the big earner in the family, the one everyone's counting on." Charlie signaled to the bartender for two more pints. "You know how expensive kids are? Twins!"

"So what are you going to do?" Anil asked.

"Between us, mate?" Charlie leaned closer. "I'm going to drive a gypsy cab in the evenings. This guy in the parking garage hooked me up. I can use my own car and set my own hours. He said I can make four hundred dollars a night on the weekends."

"At night, after your hospital shift?" Anil said. "When are you going to sleep, Charlie?"

He shrugged again. "Well, at least I'm used to being awake all night. Driving a car will be a breeze compared with running triage in the ER. And ten grand will make a big difference to my sister in the next few months." He nudged Anil's shoulder with his own. "Don't worry, mate, it'll be fine. But I won't have much time for the research study for a while. I'm sorry."

"It's okay," Anil said. "You do what you need to do. Take as much time as you need. I'll keep things going with the data analysis, and you come back to it when you can." Charlie cocked his head and began to protest, but Anil interrupted him. "No arguments. *Mate*."

Charlie smiled in a way that was almost convincing.

14

LEENA HAD BEEN AT HER HUSBAND'S HOME FOR OVER A YEAR, but Nirmala still felt her absence anew every day. Early one morning, Nirmala awoke from a terrifying dream: she and Pradip were traveling to the market to sell their crops when giant black crows swooped down and tore open the burlap sacks with their beaks, scattering rice all over the road. She was watching herself sift white grains out of the dirt when the phone trilled in her ear, waking her from the nightmare.

When her husband went to answer the phone, Nirmala peeked out the window. The burlap sacks were still in the back of the truck, ready for their trip into town later that day. They were going to the market twice a week by then, to sell, in addition to their regular crops, anything of value they could muster: eggs from their chickens, milk from their cows. Nirmala hadn't made Pradip's favorite stuffed-eggplant curry in months. The additional dowry payments to Leena's in-laws had crippled them. From the bedroom, Nirmala could hear only a few words on her husband's end of the conversation, but from the tone of his voice, she knew something was wrong.

They arrived at the house with marigolds out front nearly two hours later, and a tiny old woman opened the door, her body frame shrunken to the size of a child. She wore wire-rimmed glasses on a perfectly round face, and her white hair was pulled back into a small, tight bun. Without a word, she stepped back to let them enter and nodded toward Leena, asleep on a bedroll on the floor.

At the sight of her daughter, Nirmala began to cry. Leena was wearing an unfamiliar sari made of unadorned white cotton, the kind worn by widows. Her feet and calves were wrapped with strips of the same white cloth. Nirmala pictured the old woman with a cupboard full of plain white saris, having given away the colorful ones when her husband died.

"She is a brave girl," said the old woman. "She did not cry once when I cleaned her wounds. Your daughter has endured a great deal."

Tears poured liberally down Nirmala's face, dripping off her chin and running down beneath her blouse. She took a few steps toward Leena and knelt down several feet away, reluctant to disturb her. The deep golden color of her daughter's skin attested to her time in the sun; the slight protrusion of her upper lip concealed where her teeth parted underneath. Nirmala's eyes traveled from the familiarity of Leena's face to her bare arms, which appeared to belong to someone else, covered as they were with scabs and bruises. The skin under one wrist was crinkled red from burn. Nirmala drew in her breath.

"I treated the wounds, but she will need a doctor," the old woman said. "The burns are . . . severe."

Nirmala stood up. "Thank you for your kindness." She pressed her hands together and bowed her head to the old woman. Filled with gratitude for this stranger, Nirmala felt cries rise in her throat. Her shoulders trembled as she wept silently, then dropped to the ground to touch the old woman's feet. A hand on her shoulder beckoned her to stand again.

"There is no time for your pain, child," the old woman said. "You must focus on hers."

Oh, how Nirmala longed for her own mother. She wiped her face with the loose end of her sari and looked around the room, which contained two chairs and a small table. The old woman lived modestly, yet she had given Leena one of her saris and torn up another to dress her wounds. Nirmala dug out her coin purse, but the old woman pushed her hand away so firmly she did not try again.

Nirmala didn't want to impose on the woman any longer, but she couldn't bear to awaken Leena. She realized Pradip was no longer in the room, and through the open door she could see him pacing in front of the house. He was a small man, but he could have an outsized temper. He was probably thinking of confronting Leena's in-laws, whose home was a couple of kilometers down the road. Nirmala would have to convince him to put his anger aside. Just like her pain, it would have to wait until after they brought their daughter home to recover.

Pradip did not speak when Nirmala came outside, nor on the long and slow drive back, throughout which Leena moaned from the pain. He would not say anything after they returned home, although Nirmala begged him to, sensing the tempest brewing inside him. Was it sorrow he felt for Leena, or anger toward her husband's family? Did he feel shamed about the failure of her marriage or guilty about his role in the arrangement of it? Nirmala didn't know the particular nature of the emotional turmoil Pradip suffered, but in the following days, even as Leena's physical wounds slowly began to heal, her husband grew more and more distant.

For the first few days, Nirmala nursed Leena as if she were a child. She helped her sit up in bed, fed her grains of rice with her fingers, held a small cup of water to her lips. She waited by her daughter's bedside until Leena fell into a restless sleep, listened for her cries during the night, and checked on her upon rising in the morning.

When Leena was well enough to speak again, Nirmala asked her what had happened. Darkness clouded her daughter's sweet face as she described having done the work of two servants at her husband's home. "I tried my best, Mama—I sweetened the rice with ghee like you taught me. I scrubbed the clothes in the hottest water." Leena held up her chapped, blistered palms in a helpless gesture. When she tried to explain what finally drove her to leave, about the burns covering her legs, Leena could not finish the story before being wracked with sobs, and Nirmala held her close until she could breathe evenly again.

After Leena fell asleep that evening, Nirmala went to Pradip and told him everything. Waiting for his response, she grew anxious. "We have to go to the police, no? Tell them what happened?"

Pradip shook his head. "We can't. We are just as guilty." He explained that the law clearly stated that, in dowry cases, both sides must be prosecuted: both the givers and the takers of the dowry. The Indian government had taken a hard line in their attempts to ban the practice. If they reported the groom's family, he explained to Nirmala, they too would be punished. He would certainly go to jail, perhaps Nirmala as well. They couldn't take the risk of leaving Leena alone after what she'd already endured.

AFTER RETURNING to Panchanagar, Leena stayed in her small room, grateful to be back in the shelter of her parents' home and the care of her mother. She saw and spoke to no one else, until the day Piya stopped by the house. From her bedroom, Leena heard her mother's voice thanking Piya for the bag of ripe oranges she had brought from the Patels' abundant supply.

Yearning for her old friend, Leena ignored all caution and rose from her bed, then hopped tenderly out to the front room. She was surprised to see that her mother had not even invited Piya into the house and was already closing the front door on her.

"Wait, Mama," Leena called out. "Piya, is that you?" Leena caught a flare of anger on her mother's face as she hobbled over to the front door and opened it again to reveal Piya halfway down the steps. She watched as her friend's expression cycled through surprise, then joy, and finally sorrow when she took in the gown shorn at Leena's knee, her leg wrapped in bandages. Leena was filled with shame at showing herself this way, but in the next moment, Piya rushed to her side.

Her mother had already turned away and retreated to the kitchen. Piya helped Leena back to her room, where they sat together on the bed. Piya gripped Leena's hand and her eyes swelled with tears as Leena explained what she had endured over the past year at her husband's home. "I never knew it was possible for people to be so unkind. To treat me as they did. I tried so hard . . . and still . . ." Leena's body trembled as tears streamed down her face. "I let everybody down. My parents, my husband, my in-laws. How will I ever show my face again? What will people think of me?"

"Leena." Piya held both her hands and looked directly into her eyes. "You had no choice, you had to leave. What kind of a life was that for you? Living like a second-class citizen, like a servant?" Piya shook her head and squeezed Leena's hands. "It's over now, behind you. No one needs to know. I won't tell anybody, and neither should you."

Leena nodded, still unsure of herself but longing to believe Piya. The prospect of returning to that house terrified her, but even if she stayed with her parents, her life would not be the same as the one she'd been sad to leave. Abandoning a marriage was shameful, regardless of the circumstances. Once people in the village learned she had run away from her husband, from her new home and family, Leena would be shunned. The reasons for her leaving did not matter. She would be blamed for it, and marked by it, for the rest of her life.

"Please. Not even your family, Piya," Leena said. "Not . . . not even Anil." A forgotten memory from childhood flashed through her mind: the look of disappointment on his face when she'd scored poorly on her math test after weeks of his help. She couldn't bear his pity now.

"No one," Piya agreed. "Listen to me," she said, gently touching Leena's wrapped leg. "The only thing you need to worry about is getting better."

Dilip the Loyal Servant

Anil sat at his desk at the day and time prearranged with his mother, waiting for the call from Panchanagar. When the phone rang, he answered while doodling in his notebook.

"Anil," his sister whispered through the line.

"Piya." Anil was pleased to hear her voice. "How are you?"

"Listen, Ma will be here in a minute, but I have to ask you a question first."

"I'm listening."

"What's the best way to treat a burn?"

Anil put down his pencil. "Burn? What happened?"

"Nothing, never mind. Just tell me—I've read about applying turmeric powder and mustard oil. Does that help?"

"Piya, did you get hurt? You should see a doctor."

"No, no. I'm fine."

"Who then?" Silence on the line. Anil rolled the pencil between his fingers. "Okay, then. How bad is it? Superficial? Redness or swelling? Any blisters?"

"Blisters, yes." Piya hesitated before adding, "And some of the skin is black."

"God, Piya." Anil exhaled, scanning the shelf of textbooks over his desk. "Those are second- and third-degree burns. You really need to consult a doctor."

"I thought that's what I was doing," she snapped.

"Okay, okay," Anil said. "Wrap the skin in clean, dry cloth. Change the dressing once a day, and clean the wound with a salt-water solution. Don't apply anything else, no other ointments or creams, until the blisters have healed and there's no risk of infection—"

"Ma's here," Piya interrupted. "She's going to tear the phone from my hand. Thanks, brother."

When Ma came on the line, she explained there were three disputes to be presented that day. First were parents who disagreed on a name for their newborn daughter. The girl's mother wanted to follow the advice of the village astrologer, who had prescribed not only the first sound but also the ending sound and the number of syllables the name should include. They could find only one name within such strict constraints, which also happened to be the name of a certain Bollywood star known for her sultry roles and loose hips. The father objected to this name, believing it would harm his daughter's reputation when it came time to marry.

Anil had little patience for navigating between one set of superstitions and another, but he was able to convince the astrologer to relax one of his three requirements for the name without marring the child's destiny. With the help of the chorus gathered at the Big House, a new name was soon found, acceptable to both the parents and the Vedic charts.

The next dispute featured a young boy who'd been caught stealing dried areca nuts from his father's supply. It was a common practice for villagers, particularly men, to chew on the stone-hard nuts, thinly sliced and wrapped in betel leaves. The *paan* acted as a mild stimulant and left a telltale reddish stain on the lips and teeth, which is how the seven-year-old had been caught. In Ahmadabad, Anil had seen all the fanciful forms *paan* could take—it was sold prepackaged with crushed tobacco leaves at street stalls, wrapped into triangles with sweeteners and coconut, even rolled into large cones and frozen into ice *paan*. At medical college, he had witnessed the damage this habit wreaked: mouth ulcers; gum deterioration; cancer of the mouth, pharynx, esophagus, and stomach; exacerbation of asthma; increased risk of diabetes. But it was not the health dangers or the addictive properties of areca nuts that concerned the boy's father. It was that the boy had stolen from his personal stash, and he wanted Anil to choose an appropriate punishment.

Anil knew it was futile to warn those listening in Panchanagar about the risks of the centuries-old practice. They might trust him to be their arbiter, but they would never believe an ingredient used in ayurvedic remedies and religious ceremonies was harmful. As a penalty, Anil recommended that, for the next month, the boy spend an extra hour each day working the fields instead of playing cricket. He would've liked to admonish the boy's father for his ruinous personal habit but chose to reserve his energy for the last dispute.

The final arbitration of the day promised to be the most difficult, not only because it was a sensitive issue but also because it was between his own brothers: Nikhil, who'd been carrying on the business of the farm after Papa's death, and Chandu, who'd just finished school and joined his older brothers in the family farm operations. Anil had noticed on his last trip home that his youngest brother, Chandu, had grown into the most sociable of them, staying up late every night to play cards with the children of the field servants. There was usually a clear delineation between the Patel family and the servants, most of whom were of the untouchable caste. The household servants used a separate entrance at the back of the house, and ate their meals on the porch outside. The field hands used the water pump outside to drink from and wash themselves. Anil had always been polite to the servants, and played with some of the children when he was young, but that came to an end when he started school and they joined their parents in the fields.

"Anil *bhai*, you remember Dilip?" Chandu asked.

"Yes, of course." Anil pictured the field hand, a small, wiry man with dark skin, weathered like the husk of a palm tree. "He's still there?"

"Yes, but he's getting quite old. Before he can't work in the fields at all, I think we should give him some land, a small piece of land for him and his family. He's worked hard on our land for thirty, maybe forty years, but he owns nothing. He has nothing to pass on to his three children. It's a small gesture for a loyal servant."

"Well, it may be a nice gesture, but it's a bad idea." Nikhil's voice came through the line. "Listen, Anil *bhai*, you know the way things work here. Our family owns the land, the servants work for us. We treat our servants fairly—we pay them a good wage, we give them one day every week to rest, we feed them, we give them a place to sleep, a special meal on Diwali. That's more than many other landowners do for their workers. Papa was always very clear on that, treating the lower castes with dignity."

"Dignity?" Chandu spoke up. Anil pictured them struggling over the single phone receiver in the Big House. Or was Ma holding it between them? Were others still present, or had the crowd dwindled, since the quarrel was limited to the Patel family? The thought of Ma watching his brothers argue compelled Anil to bring about a resolution as quickly as possible.

Chandu continued, "Dilip *bhai* has worked for our family his whole life, and what does he have to show for it? He lives in a home owned by us. He has no property, no savings—what can he leave his children? Nothing."

"He doesn't need to leave anything to his children," Nikhil said. "His children work for us. We give jobs to all our servants' families, even the weak and stupid ones."

"That's your problem, Nikhil." Chandu's voice grew louder. "You think untouchables are all stupid."

"No, not all, brother," Nikhil said, "but some are. Just like some landowners are stupid, as seen in our own family."

Anil covered his mouth to stifle a laugh.

"Listen, Anil, you understand," Nikhil said. "This is not the way things work. If we give a piece of land to Dilip, why not to someone else? We have two dozen field hands—are we going to give them all a piece of land? Then who will be left to work our land? The system is based on everybody filling certain roles. If we don't follow the rules, it falls apart. Our land is valuable only if we have people to farm it."

"So we should keep everybody in their places forever? That's what you believe, Nikhil? Dilip *bhai*'s family is destined to be servants through every generation? His sons, and their sons, none of them will ever have any opportunity to make progress? They should accept their lot in life, down on their hands and knees in those fields all day, working under the hot sun, slaving away for you?"

"Not for me, Chandu, for us. *All of us.* That's how this works. Maybe if you'd spent more time with Papa instead of playing cards, you'd have learned some things."

Anil took off his specs and placed them on the desk. He rubbed his eyes. "Chandu, how did this all come about? Was this your idea, or did Dilip ask you for the land?"

"*Bhai*, what difference does it make?" Chandu said. "The question is whether we want to sentence this man to a lifetime of servitude because of his caste. How would you feel, Anil, if you knew you had to perform the same drudgery every single day for the rest of your life, with no hope for anything better?"

It was a question Anil had struggled with many times since coming to Parkview. Quite often, the only source of light through the darkness of his residency had been the certainty it would come to an end. When day after day was filled with anxiety, pressure, and fatigue, at least he could keep crossing off those days on his calendar.

"Yes, Chandu, I see your point," Anil said. "So tell me, if you had your way, where would we take the land from? Out of whose share should this gift come? Would you be willing to take it from your share?" Papa had left most of the land to his four sons—Anil, Nikhil, Kiran, and Chandu—in equal measure, as was traditional in property rights. Less customary was the fact that Papa had also designated a smaller plot for Piya's future wedding dowry.

Anil scribbled around Dilip's name in his notebook as he waited for a response. Had they lost the phone connection?

"I don't think of it that way, *bhai*," Chandu finally said. "Everything here belongs to all of us. Dilip works for all of us, like Nikhil said. We don't make those kinds of divisions."

Anil stopped doodling and laid down his pencil. He took in a slow, deep breath. His little brother was right, of course. Anil closed his eyes, the unswallowed pill of regret settling in his throat. He recalled the time a teenaged Kiran had charged through the Big House looking for a music tape. "Where is my *Rangeela* cassette? Has somebody taken it?" Kiran had asked, disturbing the books and papers on the table.

Papa had put down his newspaper and cleared his throat. "Son, in this house there is no such thing as 'your cassette' or 'my cassette.' Everything belongs to everyone. There is no place for 'yours' or 'mine' in this family, understand?" It was his younger brother who'd been chastised that day, but they had all grasped the message. Only Anil had forgotten.

"Brothers, this is a complicated situation," Anil said. "I realize it will affect many people, so I want to give it some more thought and come back to you with a decision."

After working out the arrangements for the next call with his mother, Anil closed his notebook and considered the possibilities. They could give Dilip the opportunity to earn the land at a favorable price with his coming years of service, but that would likely take too long.

Perhaps Chandu could let him win the parcel in a card game? No, Ma would undoubtedly object to the use of gambling as a solution. He was bound to anger someone, no matter what he advised. How was he to make this decision for them, from all the way over here? Irritation bubbled up inside him, percolating into anger. Whatever he decided, Anil knew it was not he, but his family, who would live with the consequences, and it was this idea that weighed on him as he sat at his cluttered desk, thousands of miles away.

He recalled something his mother had said last summer about Chandu playing cards with the servants. *It doesn't look good*. The phrase sounded innocuous, even well-meaning, but it grated on him in a visceral way. Ma had used the same words many years earlier warning Anil about his friendship with Leena. He shared his brother's ire now at her condescension.

THE QUESTION of what to do about Dilip was still troubling Anil later that evening. As he sat with Amber on her couch, swapping cartons of Chinese food, he explained the situation.

"Your family has servants?" Amber asked, sipping her wine. "Isn't that like modern-day slavery?"

"It's not *slavery*," Anil said. "They're . . . workers. They're paid, and given a place to live and meals while they work. It's a system that's worked for generations."

"Well, slaves were given room and board too." She passed him the noodles. "Look, I'm not blaming you for the way it is, I'm just saying maybe it's time to change."

Anil reached for his wineglass and took a deep sip.

"What if you could make life better for all those people?" Amber said. "Change their lives, and their children's lives?" She traced her fingertip around the rim of her wineglass. "What do you think your father would do?"

Anil rested the carton of noodles on his knee. He'd been thinking a good deal about that himself, recalling how Papa had been trying to find a role for Chandu, a way to fold him into the family business. As reckless as his younger brother had been in the past, Chandu was now making a genuine effort to be involved with the farm operations. He'd come to the table with a serious proposal. Perhaps Anil would need to make a contentious decision in order to make things better, something his father had never been afraid to do.

"Anyway, it doesn't matter what he would do," Amber continued. "They want to know what you think." She reached across the couch and combed her fingers through his hair.

Anil smiled at her touch, but he knew this role he'd inherited had nothing to do with who he was as an individual. He doubted anyone back home wanted his personal opinion, but since they'd put him in this position, he would give it to them. His time in America had shown him that the prospect of a lifetime of grueling work without reward was unthinkable. By the last sip of wine, Anil had made up his mind. They would give Dilip the land.

Amber cleared away the remnants of their dinner and brought over a pint of ice cream. Anil lodged another pillow behind his lower back, which had been aching all day. He wondered if he had herniated a disk from standing on his feet so much in the CCU. "So, you're going home again this weekend?" he asked, trying to keep the disappointment from his voice. He had only two weekends off a month and he counted on spending them with her. Outside the hospital, Anil was always at a loss about what to do on his own. "I thought we could go to the state fair on Saturday. It's the last week."

"I know. I'm sorry." Amber laid a hand on his knee. "Maybe you can go with the guys?"

Anil shook his head. Mahesh refused to go to the State Fair of Texas on the basis of the costly tickets, and Baldev claimed there wouldn't be enough eligible women in attendance to make it worthwhile. Plus, Anil wanted to go to the fair with a Texan. Apparently, they sold fried butter on a stick. "But you went home two weeks ago. Why again so soon?"

"I just . . . have to." Amber pulled her hand back into her lap. "Didn't I tell you I was going a while back? I thought I did."

"Why can't you go next weekend, when I have to work anyway?" Anil dug his spoon into the ice cream, aiming for the nuts.

"I can't, I have a . . . thing." Amber looked down at her hands and began inspecting her nails.

"What kind of thing?" Anil tilted the ice-cream carton toward her but she shook her head.

"Just a, like a . . . a family thing."

"What kind of family thing?" He placed the carton on the coffee table and laid the spoon down gently beside it.

Amber held a pillow in front of her chest and looked down as she spoke. "My sister's getting married. I just . . . I should have told you earlier, but I knew you wouldn't enjoy it."

"I can come with you," Anil said. "I have the whole weekend off." Charlie had gone to a wedding with a nurse at the hospital and reported that Texas weddings were a sight to behold.

"Oh, you don't want to come," Amber said. "It'll be boring. I'll have to be with my sister the whole time, and my family—"

"I'd love to meet your family," Anil said. It wasn't particularly true, but he didn't want to face an entire weekend without her. In the past six months, his relationship with Amber had grown from a pleasant distraction into something he needed desperately, as much as food or sleep. He'd been planning to go to the library this weekend to read through cardiology journals for research ideas to pitch to Dr. Tanaka.

But he would gladly give up that time to be with Amber, knowing he would have to make it up with some late nights when he returned. He moved closer to her and lifted her hair to kiss her neck. The scent of her was tantalizing. Anil unbuttoned her blouse and slipped it off her shoulders.

15

Soon after Leena's return, her in-laws began phoning, demanding to know why she had run away and accusing her of starting the kitchen fire in her clumsiness. Nirmala knew Pradip wanted to shout at them, to blame them for mistreating his only child, but he spoke politely on the phone, bargaining for time while they sorted out what to do. He explained that Leena needed time to recover from her injuries and it was best for her to heal at their home, where she would not be a burden to her new family. Leena's in-laws in turn demanded that either Leena return to fulfill her marital obligations or the remaining dowry be paid in full to compensate them for her abandonment.

One day, as her daughter still lay defenseless in bed, Nirmala heard a car pull up outside their home. It was those bastards, she saw, feeling herself shake with rage. As Pradip returned from the fields to intercept them, the back door opened and slammed shut, and Nirmala caught a glimpse of Leena running away from the house. Somehow she had managed to get out of bed by herself; she was running on bandaged feet, on wounds that had not yet healed.

A few moments later, Leena's father-in-law and brother-in-law were inside her home. Girish, the coward, had not come with them. "It's been long enough," the father-in-law said. "Where is she? Let us see her!"

The man's pride was injured, Nirmala could see. A runaway daughter-in-law did not reflect well on any of them. "She has not yet recovered." Nirmala tried to keep the venom rising within from infecting her voice. "She is resting."

"Please, will you have some tea?" Pradip offered, but they didn't want tea, or even to sit down in the drawing room. Nirmala stared at her husband, trying to warn him with her eyes that Leena had left.

"Why doesn't she come out and explain herself to us?" Leena's brother-in-law asked.

"It would not be proper for Leena to see you in her present condition," Nirmala answered. "Not worthy of the respect you deserve." She clenched her left hand into a tight first, using her fingernails against her palm to keep from crying out the truth.

"Hmm," said the older man, picking up a small silver figurine of Ganesha, the elephant-headed god who warded against disaster, from a small table at the front door.

"Please, Sahib," Pradip said. "Please, take it as a small token of our appreciation."

Nirmala's stomach curdled. The older man slipped the figurine into his pocket without acknowledgment. He and his son proceeded to wander through the drawing room, into the kitchen, and around the rest of the house. Nirmala followed them as they took whatever they wanted: food from the kitchen, a lamp from the drawing room, even a bundle of harvested crops from outside. Nirmala could not watch as they took her wedding saris, after they had already taken all her jewelry.

At last they left, after assurances from Pradip that everything would be resolved soon. He had said what was necessary for them to go peacefully, without Leena or the money for which they had come, but Nirmala was disappointed at the way her husband had begged and appeased the very men who had frightened their daughter into running.

Leena came back only after the men were gone, her bandages covered with grass and mud. Nirmala had to unwrap her legs, clean the wounds carefully, and wrap them again: a terrible pain Leena chose to endure rather than see those men again.

That evening, after Leena was safely asleep, Nirmala and Pradip spoke in hushed tones about what to do. The other family wanted an additional ten thousand rupees for Leena's freedom. Even if they sold every single possession of theirs—every stick of furniture and farming implement—it would not bring in ten thousand rupees. Leena's in-laws had already taken everything of value.

"I can sell my homemade sweets, and make jars of pickles for the market," Nirmala offered.

"And where will we get the money for all that ghee and sugar?" her husband said. "Those things are expensive to buy up front." He shook his head. They had already paid nearly eighty thousand rupees to this family. Their savings were gone, and the debt they'd taken on was crippling them, depleting their crop income as soon as it came in. "Maybe it would be different if she went back." Pradip spoke slowly. "They must miss her, the way they're calling and coming around. They might treat her better now that they realize her value."

Nirmala stared at her husband, a stranger for the first time in twenty-four years. "What are you saying?" She rose from the bed on which they sat together and took a step back from him. "What are you saying?" The words caught in her throat as it thickened. "You would send her back there?" Her voice was a low, angry whisper. "Your own *daughter*?" She expected to see anger on his face, or frustration, but it looked like something else—a blank stare of resignation.

"I don't know, it might be the only way." He turned his eyes away from hers. "Nirmala, you know as well as I do she'll be ostracized if she stays here. What kind of life is that?"

"*Never*," Nirmala said. "There must be another way."

"Yes," Pradip said, rubbing his fingers together in a mindless gesture. "Yes, I'll figure something out."

IN THE week following that visit, Nirmala often woke up in the middle of the night and found Pradip out in the drawing room, sitting upright in a chair, staring out the window. He sat there for hours, until the first hint of daylight, then went out to the fields and worked without break until the last rays of sun had drained from the sky. Had she not brought water and food to him in the fields, he would not have eaten or drunk all day.

This continued, day after day, until Pradip's face grew thinner and his eyelids began to sag. He seemed intent on working himself to death. Nirmala worried about her husband's health. She worried about Leena, ready to escape like a caged animal out the back door whenever a car drove up to the house. She worried what that vile family would do when they returned, expecting their payment. And she worried what her husband, with all that anger brewing inside him, might do to them.

16

The night before they left for the wedding, Anil stayed up all night to finish the data-analysis segment of the MRSA research study. He'd barely seen Charlie in the past couple of months, and when he did, the guy looked absolutely wiped out. Anil was determined to keep pushing their project forward until Charlie could come back to it.

He and Amber left for Ashford late Friday, after Anil's shift. Unsure what the appropriate attire would be, he packed nearly everything in his closet, including a pair of new cowboy boots he'd bought online. He chose a gift for Amber's parents, the largest potted plant in the hospital gift store, despite its inflated price. It was a rare specimen, its green leaves covered in tiny pink spots so perfect, they appeared to be painted on.

"Okay, now, the men will probably ask you to go hunting," Amber said, her hands on the steering wheel. "So just say you don't have your hunting clothes."

"I don't have hunting clothes," Anil repeated. "Don't worry, I'll be fine." He reached over and rested a hand on Amber's thigh as she drove. He found himself unduly excited about their first trip away together.

It was well after dark by the time they arrived in Ashford. The ranch house was set back from the road and surrounded by a large fenced-in pasture. As Amber pulled up the long gravel drive, two oversized dogs came bounding down the steps. They leapt onto Amber when she got out of the car. "Hi, Dixie, hey girl," she said, patting one of them.

The other dog charged toward Anil when he got out of the car, and he put up his arms in defense. Amber laughed and grabbed the dog's collar. "Down, Mason!" She pulled the dog away. "Sorry, they're always a little excited to see me."

The screen door swung open and a short, plump woman leaned into the small pool of yellow light cast by the porch lamp. "Amber, that you, honey?"

"Hi, Momma," Amber said in a singsong voice. She climbed the porch steps and embraced her mother, who looked much as Anil had expected, and nothing like Amber. "Momma," Amber turned to him, "this is Anil."

Anil stepped forward and held out the plant. "Hello, Mrs. Boxey. This is for you."

"Oh, bless your heart." Amber's mother accepted the pot and held the screen door open for them. "Your daddy and brothers are out back, honey. Your sister's upstairs fussing over her dress. Go on up there and talk some sense into her, would you?"

"Okay, Momma, in a minute." Amber touched Anil's elbow. "Come on, I'll introduce you first." He followed her through another screen door to the backyard, where a group of men were sitting on plastic lawn chairs around a small fire pit. They all held beer cans in foam holders of various colors, and a few were smoking cigarettes.

"Ber-Ber!" The gruff voice came from a large man in a fishing vest with short-cropped hair. He pulled Amber down onto his lap, where she almost toppled over.

Amber laughed. "Hi, Daddy."

A younger man, presumably one of her brothers, reached over and yanked her ponytail. "Chuck!" Amber squealed and righted herself. "Daddy, y'all? This is Anil." She gestured behind her chair to where he stood.

The bloodshot eyes of six men turned to Anil. Chuck took a swig of his beer. "So you're the doctor, huh?"

"Yes. Well, training to be a doctor." Anil walked around the circle of chairs to Amber's father. "Mr. Boxey," he said, extending his hand. "Nice to meet you."

"What's your name again?" Amber's father's arms were wrapped around Amber's waist. He did not free one to shake Anil's hand.

"Anil, Daddy," Amber said, turning her head to face him. "Ah-neel."

"Hmm."

"Amber?" Her mother's voice cut through the screen door and smoky air. "Becky is positively going to have a fit over that dress zipper if you don't get up there soon."

Amber hoisted herself off her father's lap and touched Anil's shoulder as she passed. "Be right back."

"Get used to that, man." Chuck punched the guy next to him in the shoulder. "Becky has a fit over something every dang day of the week. Welcome to your life."

Anil was introduced to the groom, who had strong, callused hands, and to Amber's two brothers, Chuck and Frank. "Burger and Hot Dog, that's what I like to call these two meatheads," Mr. Boxey said. "Pull up a seat, doc." There were no more chairs, so Anil perched on top of a plastic cooler.

"What time we leavin' tomorrow, Pops?" Frank asked.

"Before first light," Mr. Boxey said. "Five o'clock, I think."

Chuck swigged his beer. "You comin' on the duck hunt, ain't you, doc?"

"Me?" Anil asked. All he could think about at the moment was sleep, after pulling two extra-long shifts in a row.

"Yeah, it's a tradition. Men go hunting, women get their nails done or whatever. You're a man, ain't ya?" Chuck glanced around the circle, grinning.

"Unfortunately, I don't have hunting clothes." Anil tried to smile politely, despite images of guns and dead birds and bloody feathers coming to mind.

"Well, that's okay, Frank's got extra clothes you can use." Chuck flattened a beer can under his boot. "What's the matter? Don't have a queasy stomach, do ya, doc?" There were guffaws of laughter around the circle.

"No." Anil eased the cooler he was sitting on back from the fire pit, which was blowing smoke into his eyes. *Queasy stomach?* This morning he'd treated the pus-oozing gangrenous foot of a diabetic patient, for God's sake. "It's, uh . . . I'm just not into h-hunting. I . . . I'm a v-vegetarian, actually."

Mr. Boxey screwed up his face. "You're *what* now?"

Chuck leaned backwards in his lawn chair, dangerously close to tipping. "Whatever *that* means." He swung forward and stood up, tossing the butt of his cigarette into the dying embers. "Well, I'm goin' to kick it, boys. Guess I'll see all you real men in the morning." The others around the fire drained their beers and began to disperse. Anil stood and followed them into the house.

"Would y'all look at this beautiful plant he brought us from Dallas?" Mrs. Boxey held up the pot as they passed by the kitchen. "Isn't that special?"

Chuck grunted. "Looks like it's got the chicken pox."

Mrs. Boxey swatted his arm. "Now, you be nice, hear? This boy is smarter than all the rest of y'all put together."

Anil smiled at Mrs. Boxey, bent down to get his overnight bag from the front door, and followed the others toward the staircase.

"Oh no." Mr. Boxey clamped a heavy hand down on Anil's shoulder. "You're staying in Chuck's trailer, out back." One side of his lip curled up into a smile. "Can't have you too close to my little girl, case that vegetarian stuff rubs off on her." He chuckled.

The trailer was small, and filled with the odor of cigarette smoke and stale beer. Chuck showed Anil to the couch, then disappeared behind a gaudy-patterned curtain to his own bed. It wasn't long before Chuck's loud snoring began and continued all night.

THE WEDDING was small, no more than a couple of hundred guests who all seemed to know one another. Since Amber was attending to her sister, Anil was largely left on his own. He didn't even recognize Amber when she walked down the church aisle, her hair in a big pile of stiff curls, wearing a pale green dress that reminded him of hospital scrubs. He didn't realize it was her smiling at him, trying to catch his eye, until she had passed him by.

At the reception afterward, Anil joined the guests flocking to the hunting lodge. All the family members were still at the church, posing for photographs. With a beer in hand, he made his way to the patio and tried to relax. He forced himself to smile and say hello to the other guests, but no one engaged him in conversation. There was no chance of anonymity here, as there would have been at a wedding back home, with thousands milling around. Here, Anil stood out like a rash—the only person at the lodge who wasn't white, other than the black servers.

When Amber found him at the bar more than an hour later, Anil was on his third beer and his head was buzzing. "There's my handsome date. How you doing?" Anil wanted to steal her outside, to have just a few moments alone on the back patio to remind himself who they were together, but Mrs. Boxey was approaching them with a large redheaded woman. "Oh God, it's Momma and her best friend," Amber said.

"Well, there you are," the redhead said. "Amber darlin', don't you look just beautiful?"

"Hey, Mrs. Tandy." Amber embraced the woman. "How are you?"

"I was just tellin' your momma, you look as beautiful as a bride yourself today."

Mrs. Boxey beamed, and Anil smiled back to acknowledge Amber's beauty, even if it was shrouded by the ridiculous costume she was wearing.

Mrs. Tandy leaned toward Amber and whispered loudly, "Now, don't you worry your little sister beat you to the altar."

"Don't you worry," Mrs. Boxey repeated, squeezing Amber's arm.

"Your momma says you're just waitin' for the right man." Mrs. Tandy winked. "You know my Billy still asks about you. Goes fishin' with your daddy every Sunday after church."

"Mrs. Tandy," Amber reached out for Anil's arm, "this is Anil. He came with me from Dallas." Anil stumbled a little as she tugged him forward.

Mrs. Tandy turned to Anil, clearly noticing him for the first time. "Oh? Why, hello." She extended a limp hand. "You're from . . . Dallas? Is that where your people are from?"

Anil gently tried to shake her lifeless hand. "Well, from India originally, but I've been in Dallas a few years." He used his best drawl. "I'm a real Texan now. Even got my own boots."

"Oh?" Mrs. Tandy nodded slowly. "Well, you are lucky. I just burn like a match in the sun. I sure wish I could tan nice and good like you."

Anil, perplexed by her comment and foggy from the beer, was trying to figure out how to respond.

"Wasn't it a lovely ceremony?" Mrs. Boxey piped up.

"Yes, yes it was," Anil said. In truth, he was surprised at how short and somber it had been: a few words from the priest, a song, and vows, all in under twenty minutes. "Short and sweet. Doesn't take much to get married over here, does it?" His words slipped out easily. "In India, the ceremony goes on for days and days. Maybe that's why our divorce rate is so much lower than in this country." He wondered if a few beers would always keep his stutter under control.

"Oh, look." Mrs. Boxey clapped her hands together. "Becky's gettin' ready to throw the bouquet. You better get on over there, Amber!"

❁

FOR DINNER, Anil was seated at a table of family friends, along with Mrs. Tandy and her son Billy, who interrupted his stories of high school football triumphs only to pick food out of his teeth with a fingernail. After several beers and no food, Anil could feel the alcohol saturating his mind, his stomach, his skin. He felt a modicum of empathy for the patients who showed up at the Parkview ER ill from drinking. Although there was little on the buffet Anil could eat, he filled his plate with fried chicken and ribs to stave off any more questions about his vegetarianism, carefully eating only the mashed potatoes and gravy.

Three hours later, Anil sat alone, eating his second piece of spongy wedding cake, watching Amber dance the Texas two-step with Billy Tandy. He was glad he hadn't embarrassed himself by attempting those dance moves himself. And yet, watching her move in perfect synchronicity with Billy, Anil couldn't help wish it was him with whom Amber looked so natural. After the music had finished playing, the plates of wedding cake had been cleared, and the farewells said, the crowd at the hunting lodge thinned rapidly. Anil and Amber walked back to her parents' house in silence. When they reached the foot of the driveway, Amber took off her shoes and stood barefoot on the blacktop, her hideous green pumps now dangling from one hand.

"You didn't want me to come here, did you?" Anil said. "You didn't want your family to meet me." A lump began to form in his throat. "Charlie went to two weddings last summer with a nurse at the hospital, and they'd only been on a couple of dates. We've been together over a year," he said. "Fourteen months."

Amber nudged at a pebble with her bare toes, rolling it back and forth on the pavement. "I'm sorry, Anil. I just knew this wouldn't be fun for you."

"For me? Or for you? You're ashamed of me."

"No." Amber looked up. "It's not you. It was never about you, Anil. Never." She shook her head. "It's just . . . my family. I was afraid what you'd think if you met them."

"They didn't even know about me before, did they?" Anil asked.

Amber kicked the pebble away. "What do you want me to tell them? It doesn't matter, Anil." She choked on tears. "That you're a doctor, you're brilliant, you speak better English than me? . . . They're not going to get any of that. They're just *hicks*, okay?" She sat down on the ground, right there in the middle of the one-lane road, and drew her knees up under her chin. "Everyone in this crappy little town. This isn't Dallas, you know."

Anil wanted to laugh at the absurdity of her statement. In two years, he had not experienced Dallas as the bastion of cultural tolerance. Amber was starting to cry, and one part of him wanted to wrap his arms around her, bury his nose in the fresh apple scent of her hair. Another part wanted her to feel the same kind of pain he did at that moment. Anil sank to his knees a few feet away. Amber was rocking back and forth in the dark, her chin resting on her knees.

The blare of a horn sounded in the distance, and headlights flashed over their faces and away as the vehicle turned. When she spoke again, Amber's voice was muffled. "Have you told *your* family about me?"

Anil exhaled. "Amber, my father just died. It isn't the right time."

"Your father died before we met."

"Exactly, and there hasn't been a good time since then." Anil had just booked his trip to India for the short break between his second and third years of residency, two months from now. He hadn't yet considered whether to tell his family about Amber. "It's not that easy, Amber." He turned away, picked up a fallen tree branch, wishing desperately they could be back in Dallas, carrying on as normal, spending the evening stretched out on Amber's couch. He remembered the first time he'd sat with her on that couch, after their first run at the lake, how she curled up under his arm and they kissed for what felt like hours, until the light pouring in the window dimmed to gray and they realized they'd spent the entire day together, effortlessly.

Amber had been his first kiss, his first sexual experience, and his first girlfriend. Now, he knew, she would also be his first heartbreak.

17

Every day when Piya came, she unwound Leena's bandages and cleaned the wounds. It was a painstaking process, removing the charred layers of skin, during which Leena tried to keep from crying out. Once Piya had redressed Leena's leg with fresh cloths, she would stay for another hour, sometimes two. She brought Bollywood magazines and regaled Leena with stories of film stars' antics. She read to Leena from her Enid Blyton books; some days, they played cards. Piya never once made her feel pitied. Leena's mother tolerated Piya's visits, though she did so with more reluctance than warmth, never offering Piya tea or sweet lime juice.

Leena took Piya's counsel to focus on her recovery and barely moved from her bed. She was beginning to feel better—until that day she'd heard a car door slam outside, then a voice she'd recognized. A prickling feeling had traveled through her body.

Without thinking, Leena was on her feet and rushing toward the back door, then blazing across the ground, aware of but unencumbered by the pain in her foot, the chafing of her leg. She didn't stop until she reached the gully between the Big House and her family's land. She carefully picked her way down through the branches and stones to the bottom of the gully, buried herself under the dried leaves, and lay there completely still but for her rapid breathing. The spot had been

Anil's favorite hiding place when they were young. He would gamble on other children being too lazy or careless to find him there, and he was often right. Leena had not been to the gully for many years, yet her feet had taken her there instinctively. As she lay in the gully, panting and staring up at the clouds overhead, she felt safe again, but she knew it would be fleeting. She could not outrun her problems. Leena had made a commitment to her marriage, her parents had made great sacrifices, and she had ruined it all by running away. What else could she have done to make the marriage work? And why hadn't she, before things went so wrong?

Later that night after she'd returned home, Leena had heard her parents arguing through the thin walls. They hadn't raised their voices, but the sharp-edged tone of their words revealed the underlying fracture.

Leena recognized that the house to which she'd returned was not the same as the one she'd left a year earlier: the chapatis had grown smaller and the yogurt thinner, and they'd eaten few vegetables other than potatoes and onions. Her father rose earlier each morning to go out to the fields and no longer came in to share meals with Leena and her mother. Once, when Leena rose in the middle of the night to get a drink of water, she saw her father in the drawing room. It frightened her, his ghostly figure, and she returned to bed without speaking to him.

Her mother had changed too, becoming joyless in her household duties. No longer did she sing under her breath as she chopped vegetables or kneaded dough. Most curiously, she had suddenly taken on the impossible task of clearing the house of the dust that accumulated everywhere, the thin layer of earth that blew in through their open doors and windows along with the cooling breeze. Every morning and every night, her mother set to work on the floors and furniture, first with her broom, then with damp cloths. Leena had stopped offering to help with this task, sensing it involved some sort of demon her mother was determined to expunge. She had developed an equally fierce protectiveness over Leena, tending to her daughter as if she were a fragile thing. Leena used to help her mother prepare every meal, but now she was sent out of the kitchen, and sometimes out of the house itself.

It was the distance between her parents, the strife that had erupted, for which Leena felt responsible. As their only child, she had spent a lifetime serving as the bond between them, the one clear manifestation of their union. When she was a young girl, she had slept between them, and swung between their arms when they walked together. She found herself thinking often about those days, when she could spend all day outside, exploring the hills and valleys surrounding their home. The coconut trees beckoned to her, inviting her to find the small bumps and ridges along their tall, smooth trunks to use as perches for climbing. From the top of those trees, she could see miles of pasture and pick out the tiled roofs of everyone's houses. It gave her a sense of comfort to see everything she knew and loved in the world in a single frame. When the sky grew dark, her father would come looking for her, calling out her name playfully, pretending he didn't see her hiding in the fields.

As she grew older, Leena acquired her mother's oval face and her father's smiling eyes. She inherited her mother's precision in stitching, and when she ate spicy food, the edges of her ears grew red like her father's. Leena had always understood herself in relation to her parents, and their foundation had been steadfast. Their home and their plot of farmland were modest compared with that of other families, but it had always been enough for the three of them. When Leena was younger, she occasionally wished for a sister or brother, but over time this yearning faded away, replaced by the special link she had with each of her parents, the simple reassuring knowledge that she was at the center of their love.

Now that it was beginning to unravel, Leena could blame only herself.

⊛

NAVRATRI CAME and went without dancing or music; they celebrated Diwali quietly at home. Leena's parents avoided village gatherings and festivals, and did not invite anyone to their home. Leena knew they were protecting her, but she also felt like a shameful secret. When relatives or friends came by the house unexpectedly and were surprised to see Leena, her father explained she had taken very ill, and had come home for a short period to recover.

Was it true? Would her father send her back to her husband—to the marriage to which she'd committed, and for which they had sacrificed so much? Although it seemed unbearable to her, this was what everyone probably expected. She was not the first bride to suffer mistreatment at the hands of her in-laws. The thought burrowed deep into Leena's consciousness like an insect: Did her father believe what happened was her fault?

⊛

AS SOON as Leena could walk on her bandaged feet, she went into the fields every morning as the sun was warming the air. She left her sandals on the terrace, preferring the feel of the damp earth under her feet, the soil molding under her arch and in the spaces between her toes. Every step reminded her she was home. She found stray reeds that had fallen from viney palms: long reeds, golden as the sun, dotted with drops of morning dew. Something about the way they hung by one last thread to their mother plant made Leena inexplicably sad, so she began to gather them up, and soon her sari was filled.

At home, she laid out the reeds on the balcony and smoothed them with her palms.

Leena could not explain what she intended to do with these reeds, but it brought her comfort to see them gathered on the balcony, in a pile that grew larger every day. Only later did she discover how flexible the reeds were when they were damp, how she could bend and twist them without breaking. She began to weave them together into mats, then braid them into stronger layers. One day, she made an entire basket out of the reeds, out of material that had been discarded in the fields.

Leena presented the basket to her mother, filled with vegetables from the small garden behind the kitchen, where her father cultivated the family's favorites: small delicate *tindora*, fragrant *methi*. Her mother smiled and placed the basket in the corner of the kitchen. The next day, Leena found the vegetables bundled with the crops her father was taking to sell in town.

The only time Leena's parents left her on her own was when they made their weekly trips to the market. One day, Leena begged her parents to take her along with them, and they reluctantly agreed. She was tired of feeling like a prisoner at home, cut off from the rest of the world. Those friends and relatives who'd learned of Leena's return had not come back to check on her or to bring food, as her mother had done so many times for ailing neighbors.

When they first arrived in town, Leena worried it had been a mistake to come. The market was a chaotic jumble of people, a cacophony of sounds that left her feeling jarred, as though she'd forgotten how the rest of the world carried on outside her parents' modest home, their small piece of land. But despite her initial unease, something propelled Leena forward into the vibrating core of the market. She left her parents at their vegetable stall with a promise to return soon and moved slowly, tentatively, from stall to stall, appraising the array of goods for sale: hand-stitched leather sandals, textiles of every color, small bottles of perfume, and brass pots. The sounds of crowing roosters, hawkers' calls, and bargaining chatter faded into a low hum as she moved through the crowd.

"Leena?" The hum was broken by the sound of someone calling her name. Leena turned. Piya was across the walkway, moving toward her. Her cheeks were flushed as she held up her bags. "We just finished our shopping," she said.

Mina Patel, standing next to Piya, wore an expression of curiosity. "Leena," she said. "You've come home? To visit your parents?"

Warmth spread from Leena's neck to her face. "Yes, Auntie, for a visit." She dropped her eyes to the ground.

"How generous of your husband to let you go during the holidays," Mina Auntie said. "You must be returning soon, no?"

Leena's knees weakened under her. "I . . . I'm not . . . sure."

Piya reached over and squeezed her hand. "Well, I'm happy to have you back."

"Leena!" The voice came from behind her, and Leena spun around to see her father waving.

"I'm sorry, I have to go." As she turned to leave, she caught Mina Auntie's eyes narrowing. Leena rejoined her parents, whose scant load of crops was already depleted.

"Did she say anything to you? Mina Auntie?" Leena's father asked once they were in the car. "What did she say?"

"What does it matter what that woman has to say?" her mother snapped.

Though curious, Leena did not ask what they were talking about. She was by now so accustomed to the sharp talk between her parents, she was just grateful they said little else to each other on the rest of the ride home.

18

EVERYTHING AT THAI PHOON WAS A DEEP SHADE OF PURPLE: the walls, the napkins, even the highchairs. There was no mistaking this restaurant for the stark white hospital cafeteria where Anil consumed so many meals, and for this reason alone, he loved it.

"I told you not to get serious about her." Mahesh scooped rice onto his plate. "From the first day, I told you she'd be trouble."

Anil couldn't shake the deep unrest he'd felt the previous weekend with Amber's family, and how it infected the way he saw everything—even her accent, which he used to love, now reminded him of her brothers. They hadn't talked about it since they'd returned, as if neither of them could bring themselves to face the ugliness that had erupted that weekend. But a cool distance had settled between them, one they both maintained without acknowledging.

Anil now spent his free time at the medical library working on the research proposal for Tanaka, an excuse Amber readily accepted. His idea was to analyze data from patients who presented at the Parkview ER with cardiovascular symptoms and map the key indicators to treatments that would lead to the best patient outcomes. The proposal was bold in scope and would yield valuable information for Parkview if he could secure a mentor to help him orchestrate the cross-departmental cooperation needed. Dr. Tanaka, as head of the Cardiology Department and respected throughout the hospital, would be the ideal sponsor for this research, and Anil hoped to convince him of this.

Baldev reached for the pad thai. "Man, I'm telling you, you should ask that Dr. Sonia out," he said. "Mahesh, you should see this woman he works with. Totally hot, in a naughty teacher sort of way." He turned to Anil. "And, I think she likes you."

The week before, Baldev had come by the hospital to borrow Anil's house key after misplacing his own, where he'd met Sonia in the break room, then flirted with one of the nurses and left with her phone number. "Dude, you're crazy," Anil said. "She doesn't like me, and I can't ask her out. She's practically my boss."

"So?" Baldev said. "This is America. I'd ask my boss out if she was hot."

"You don't work with any women," Anil said.

"Exactly." Baldev pointed his chopsticks at Anil. "Consider yourself fortunate. Don't squander that opportunity, man. I did, however, meet an interesting new client this week. She was all alone in a big empty house in Plano—husband at work, kids at school."

"Kids?" Mahesh held a half-eaten spring roll suspended in front of his mouth.

"Yeah, she was like forty or something. But still good-looking. Takes good care of herself, if you know what I mean. And she was very appreciative of my work. She said she'd call me back to rewire her bedroom." Baldev moved his eyebrows up and down. "You know what that means."

Mahesh shook his head. "I'm telling you, you could both have your pick of girls back home. My parents started putting the word out for me last month."

"Too bad you screwed up that promotion," Baldev said. Anil jabbed an elbow at him. "What?" Baldev said to Anil. "He should've listened to you, that's all."

Mahesh shook his head. "Yeah, lesson learned. You were right, Anil. Next performance review, I'll go in with a list of my accomplishments and start building my case." He shrugged. "Anyway, my parents are already getting a lot of interest."

"Yeah, so have you seen any of these girls yet?" Baldev teased. "Their pictures? Or do you just get astrology charts and that nonsense?"

"My mother's screening them first," Mahesh said. "She wants to separate the serious prospects from the girls who just want to come to America. You've got to be careful about that. Everyone wants to come over here, until they realize there are no servants to do the housework."

"Well, go ahead and settle down if you want." Baldev tipped back his beer. "Not me. I'm not getting married 'til I'm thirty. *At least.* One hundred percent guaranteed."

THEY SANG along to the *Delhi-6* soundtrack blaring through the overtaxed speakers of Mahesh's Honda Civic all the way home. Mahesh pulled into a parking spot but waited until the song was finished to switch off the ignition. In the quiet that ensued, Amber appeared in the frame of the front windshield, waving at them.

"Well hello, Miss Amber." Baldev leaped out of the car, leaving Anil stranded in the rear seat, groping for the front-seat lever to liberate himself. He stepped out of the car in time to see Baldev, lubricated by music and beer, take Amber's hand and bow formally to her. She was dressed in athletic gear, and Anil felt a wrench of guilt over having fun with the guys while she'd been working late. "What brings you out at this hour?" Baldev said.

Amber's hair was coming loose from her ponytail, and her eyes looked weary. "I have a new client who can only meet at 9 p.m." Her bag slid off her shoulder and landed at her feet. "And I have to be back at six tomorrow morning."

"Oh no," Baldev said. "Has the good doctor rubbed off on you, with his work-around-the-clock nonsense?" He threw one arm around Anil's shoulders and the other around Amber's. "I've been trying to teach him. You must drink the sweet nectar of life." Baldev slapped Anil on the back, then playfully pushed him away.

"Here he goes," Mahesh grumbled. "Our daily lesson in the philosophy of hedonism."

Anil reached down to pick up Amber's backpack and gestured for her to go ahead. They walked toward the complex, Baldev leading the way, his arm slung around Amber and leaning conspiratorially toward her. "Miss Amber, you come spend some time with me, I'll show you how to enjoy life. You like dancing? I have some good moves on the dance floor." He did a funny little quickstep, and Amber giggled.

Anil heard the sounds first: laughter and cursing, followed by the shatter of breaking glass. He slowed his pace and looked down the empty passageway to where the sounds were coming from. A moment later, two men came into view around the corner. Anil recognized Rudy, wearing a wide-brimmed black cowboy hat, and his tattooed friend, Lee, both holding beer bottles.

Mahesh stopped in place when he saw them. Anil reached out to grab Baldev by the shoulder, but his friend was too far ahead. Baldev and Amber stepped into the bright pool of security lights lining the perimeter of the complex. Anil and Mahesh stood shrouded by darkness a few feet away. Anil's ears filled with buzzing from the lights overhead, and there was a pulsating in his throat. He recalled the time his family had gone to see a reenactment of the epic *Mahabharata* when he was young, where he watched the scene play out before him on a lighted stage. The same feeling of dread had occupied his chest then, as he anticipated the bloody battle scenes.

It took a moment longer for Lee, staggering down the passageway, to notice Baldev and Amber. "Well, whatta we have here?" He took a swig from his beer bottle and let out a loud belch. "Hey, Rudy," he yelled over his shoulder, louder than necessary. "Look here, it's Foxy Boxey." His tattooed arm bulged out from his T-shirt sleeve as he swung the six-pack. Anil saw that only two bottles were left. "These guys bothering you, Amber?"

Rudy stopped a few feet away, tipped his hat back, and peered at Baldev, his bloodshot eyes darting between him and Amber. "What the fuck?" Rudy said. Then he repeated it, shouting this time, holding both arms up in front of him. "This guy?" Rudy stomped the pavement, and Anil noticed the thick black heels of his cowboy boots, the swirled embroidery pattern on the toe.

Mahesh moved closer to Anil, so their shoulders were touching. "We should go," he whispered. Anil nodded imperceptibly without taking his eyes off Rudy and Lee. He moved one step closer to Baldev and Amber, and Mahesh followed behind, a timid puppy.

Rudy threw his arms up in the air and dropped them to his sides. "So this is your boyfriend, Amber, huh?" He jerked his chin toward Baldev. "This is the guy you been ditching me for? A fuckin' towel head?"

"Rudy, please—" Amber's voice was muffled. She shook her head.

"Listen, gentlemen." Baldev smiled and stepped in front of Amber. "There's no problem here. We're just walking the lady home, okay?" He held out his hand to Rudy.

Rudy slapped it away. "Yeah, well, I think there is a problem, *nigger*." He jabbed his finger into Baldev's chest. "Problem is, you've got your stinkin' Paki hands all over this girl, and I don't like it." Rudy rammed the heel of his hand into Baldev's chest, causing him to stumble backwards.

Anil stepped forward, grabbed Amber by the wrist and pulled her back toward him. The rhythm of his heart was thumping in his eardrums.

"Oh, you too, punk?" Lee bellowed at Anil, waving his beer bottle in front of his face. "Hey, Rudy, this towel head thinks he can get a piece of her too. Get your hands off her. You hear me? You guys are *sick*, you know that?" He spat on the ground, then stood squarely in front of Anil.

Anil dropped Amber's wrist and put his hands in the air. "I'm not touching anybody. I think Amber can go. No need for her to be here." He glanced toward Amber and nodded his head in the direction of her apartment. Her brow was ridged and her eyes held the same fear he'd seen many times in his patients.

"Yeah, go on, Amber," Rudy said. "We'll take the trash out for you."

Anil kicked the backpack toward her and jerked his head again. Amber's lower lip was trembling, and a small sob escaped from her throat as she reached down for her bag and slowly backed away, until she disappeared around the corner.

Rudy drained his beer and hurled the empty bottle sideways against the wall, where it shattered inches from Baldev's feet.

"Listen, gentlemen." Baldev's face broke into its signature wide smile as he relaxed his posture and put his hands in his pockets. "You can't blame Amber for enjoying our company," he slurred, rocking back on his heels. "I have a way with the ladies. They find me irresistible, right guys?" He turned to Anil, smiling and nodding.

Anil was frozen, uncertain how to react. Baldev could talk his way out of any situation. Perhaps his usual charm would work here, and in a few minutes they'd all be back in their beige apartment, laughing about it. Slowly, Anil nodded back at his buddy.

Baldev was facing him, a grin on his face, when out of the corner of his eye, Anil saw Rudy lunge at Baldev. He grabbed Baldev's shirt with both fists and slammed him up against the brick wall, glass crunching under his boots.

Behind Anil, Mahesh cried out, invoking a God whose mercy was absent at that moment. Anil made a movement toward Rudy, adrenaline flooding out any sense of caution in his brain, but he found himself facing Lee, a massive wall of a man. "You better stay outta the way if you don't wanna get your ass kicked all the way back to I-raq, Osama."

Anil pushed against Lee's muscular arm, but his efforts were futile. As he watched impotently over Lee's shoulder, Rudy drove his fist into Baldev's abdomen. Baldev doubled over and groaned.

"Get up, boy." Rudy kicked Baldev behind the leg, causing him to stumble forward onto his knees, his palms landing in the shards of glass. Baldev began to crawl away slowly on the pavement. Anil could hear the sounds of broken glass scratching under his knees. "Where you goin', boy?" Rudy followed Baldev a few paces, a smirk on his face, then raised his boot and positioned his heel squarely above the center of Baldev's back. He looked at Lee and grinned.

Mahesh whimpered. Anil squeezed his own eyes closed, then forced himself to open them again just in time to see the thick black heel crash down. A terrible cracking sound pierced the air and Baldev was flattened onto the pavement, facedown in the glass, his arms and legs splayed out around him. Blood trickled down his forehead and he gave a low moan. Anil's mind traveled back to when he was seven years old and the servants had trapped a rabbit that had been raiding the crops. The injured animal, its hind leg caught between two sharp wires of the homemade trap, had emitted the same sad sound of defeat.

Anil thrust himself forward again and, taking Lee by surprise this time, managed to push past him. He tried to grab Rudy by the back of his shoulders, but ended up with two fistfuls of his shirt. Anil had no idea how to fight, his only education coming from watching staged

Bollywood fistfights, but what he lacked in skill he made up for in unbridled fervor. He tried to pull Rudy away from Baldev, but his own shoulders were yanked and suddenly he was flying backwards. Anil saw a glimpse of Lee's stained yellow teeth for a fraction of a second before time slowed down and everything went quiet, save for the humming in his ears. He watched Lee draw back his clenched fist, then saw it coming toward his head.

There was an explosion of pain in the left side of his face. Anil heard a crack he hoped wasn't his fragile cheekbone, and tasted blood in his mouth. He fell to the ground, slamming his right elbow on the concrete, and immediately rolled over into a fetal position, arms wrapped around his body and cradling his elbow. He took a couple of breaths, and when he tried to open his eyes, the left eye resisted, opening only partway.

Anil staggered onto his knees and leaned over the grass, certain he was going to be sick, but nothing came up. Mahesh was kneeling in front of him, his forehead touching the ground, repeating an unidentifiable mantra over and over.

Anil turned to look over his shoulder. Lee had hauled Baldev up off the ground and was holding his arms behind his back while Rudy drove his fist into Baldev's gut, over and over again. His friend's head hung off to one side in a way that looked unnatural; blood streamed from his forehead and down his cheeks. Anil touched his own temple, and his fingers came away coated scarlet.

"So, you learn your lesson, towel head? You gonna keep your stinking Paki-nigger hands off Amber?" Rudy shouted, linking together his racist invective in one illogical string. "Huh?" Rudy bit his lower lip, flared his nostrils, and kicked Baldev in the shin, but got no response. Baldev's eyes were swollen shut and his chin hung down on his chest. "Huh, did ya?" Rudy leaned down until his face was within a few inches of Baldev's, as if to inspect his handiwork up close, then made a horrible retching sound, drew back, and spat in Baldev's face. Still no reaction.

Lee released Baldev's arms, and Baldev slumped to the ground. His head landed on the pavement with a thud. Lee nudged Baldev's rib-cage with the toe of his boot, as one would test a suspicious-looking rodent to see if it was alive. "Yeah, I think he learned his lesson." Lee took a few steps away and leaned down to pick up the six-pack.

Rudy turned toward Anil and Mahesh, both crouched on the ground several feet away. "You tell your buddy here to leave Amber alone, and you niggers too, if you don't want to end up like him." Rudy kicked Baldev's limp arm. "Go home and stay with your own fucking kind!" He straightened his cowboy hat, which had somehow managed to stay on during the brutalities. "If I see any of you with her again"—he pointed a threatening finger around to each of them—"I'll put you in the fucking morgue, got it?"

Lee pulled the last two bottles of beer out of the six-pack, handed one to Rudy, and together they swaggered off toward the parking lot. Anil waited until the two men were out of sight, then rushed over to Baldev, lying motionless on the pavement.

"Oh God, oh God, oh God," Mahesh repeated in something between a prayer and a cry.

"Mahesh!" Anil snapped. He clapped his hands once. "Go tell Amber to call an ambulance. Get some towels and blankets and the first-aid kit from the closet." Mahesh hesitated. "Go! Now!" Anil cried. Mahesh ran off.

Anil leaned close to Baldev's mouth and placed his palm on his friend's chest. He watched it rise and fall long enough to calculate his breathing rate in the normal range, then observed for another minute, monitoring the way his chest moved. He laid two fingers on Baldev's carotid artery and felt for his pulse, closing his eyes to count the beats. *Airway clear, breathing shallow, twenty breaths per minute, pulse fifty-six.*

When he opened his eyes, Amber was kneeling across from him, on the other side of Baldev. Her eyes were shot through with red vessels, and her face was streaked with tears. "Ambulance is on the way," she said in a hoarse whisper. "I called the police as soon as I got inside. It's been at least five minutes. I thought they'd be here by now—" She choked on her words and started to cry. "Oh God," she sobbed. "Is he going to be okay?"

"Baldev?" Anil lightly slapped each of his friend's cheeks. His face was covered in blood, and tiny shards of brown glass were embedded in his forehead, the left side of his face, and chin. A deep gash sliced across the corner of one eyelid, and the flesh around both eyes was swollen and bruised. "Baldev? Can you hear me, *bhai*?" As Anil wiped his bloody hand across the front of his shirt, a shooting pain traveled from his right elbow down to his wrist. He tried to pry open one of Baldev's eyelids.

Mahesh stepped forward and sank to his knees, holding out a stack of blankets and towels without speaking. Amber grabbed one, a cheery yellow-striped towel Baldev had bought for the pool. "Should I put this under his head?"

"No," Anil said. "I don't want to move him. He might have a neck or spinal injury." He took Baldev's wrist and felt for his peripheral pulse: weak but steady. He held Baldev's hand up to the light, but Mahesh stood in the way. "Get out of the light!" When Mahesh didn't move, Anil glanced up. Mahesh wore a vacant expression. "Take him over there," he said to Amber, nodding toward Mahesh. "He's in shock. Make him sit down and put his head between his knees."

As Amber urged Mahesh to the side, Anil inspected Baldev's fingers and hands. He pressed on a fingernail, watching for any response from his friend. "Come on, *bhai*, open your eyes."

"He won't open his eyes?" Amber called out. "What does that mean? Is he unconscious?"

"Possibly. His eyes might just be swollen shut." Anil pressed gently on Baldev's brow bone. "He has so many other injuries, we have to be careful." He rubbed his own forehead, then grabbed Baldev's hand again and pressed as hard as he could on his thumbnail. "Baldev, come on, man. Give me a sign."

An indistinct moan, barely audible, came from his friend. Anil leaned in toward him. "Okay, I heard that. I heard you, Baldev. Do you know where you are?" Anil placed his ear next to Baldev's mouth, but if a response came, it was drowned out by the wailing of the ambulance siren in the distance. "Amber, go out to the street! Show them where we are."

Amber glanced at Mahesh, who was sitting on the grass, head hanging between his knees, a blanket draped over his shoulders. Then she sprang up and ran across the parking lot, waving her arms overhead.

"Stay with me, *bhai*," Anil said, gripping Baldev's fingers. "I'm right here." He looked over at Mahesh, who still had his head down and was rocking back and forth. "I'm right here with you." As the ambulance approached with its blaring siren, neighbors began gathering in the passageway. Amber ran up, her face glistening with sweat. A medic jumped out of the ambulance and Anil stood up to meet him. "Anil Patel, PGY-4 at Parkview," he introduced himself. "Is the Parkview ER accepting?"

The medic pulled on latex gloves. "Yup. That where you wanna go, doc?"

Anil nodded. "Patient suffered severe and repeated trauma to the chest, back, and face. Possible neck or spinal injury, so you'll need to put him on a board." Anil hammered out stats as the medic moved toward Baldev, while Amber tried to hold back the spectators. "BPM twenty. Pulse fifty-six. Minimally responsive. GCS below eight: E1c,V2, no motor response yet." Anil was relieved neither Amber nor Mahesh could decipher his medical shorthand describing Baldev's dangerously low level of consciousness. He caught Amber's eye and pointed at Mahesh. "Make sure he drinks something with sugar."

A second medic brought over the back board and, working in unison, the two of them stabilized Baldev's head and neck and transferred him to the board. "Step back, clear out, folks," one yelled to the gathering crowd.

Anil climbed into the back of the ambulance after them. Before yanking the doors shut, he called out to Amber. "Hey!" he yelled, unable to say her name. "Follow us to the hospital."

19

In the ambulance, they gave Baldev oxygen and IV fluids, but he remained unresponsive except for a few muted groans escaping from the back of his throat. When they pulled into the Emergency bay at Parkview, the trauma team was waiting outside. The medics carried out Baldev's gurney, relaying his vital stats. Anil looked around for the ER team leader and spotted a familiar stocky figure: Eric, the extreme athlete, pizza-sandwich eater, senior resident from Anil's inaugural rotation who'd witnessed his inexperience firsthand.

"Patel!" Eric called at him across the gurney. "Dispatch radioed it in. Friend of yours?"

Anil nodded. "Severe trauma to chest, abdomen, and back. Multiple lacerations to face and hands. Glass shards still embedded." He ran alongside the gurney through the hospital doors.

"Weapons?" Eric asked.

Anil's vision swirled with the embroidery pattern on the toe of the cowboy boot, the beer bottle shattered under bare skin, the clenched fist as hard as a brick. The taunting voices echoed through his mind. *Nigger. Paki. Towel head.*

"Christ," Eric said, shaking his head. "Your buddy really took a beating."

They arrived in one of the trauma rooms, where a team of nurses and residents swarmed around Baldev's gurney, pushing Anil out to the periphery.

"Okay, Patel, we'll take it from here," Eric said. His eyes traveled from Anil's face to his bloody shirt. "You should get checked out too. Wait in Exam 2—"

Anil shook his head. "No. I'm staying here." A nurse leaned past him to attach EKG leads to Baldev's chest. "It's not my blood, it's his." Both words and courage came easily for once. "Listen, Eric, I think he may have traumatic pneumothorax caused by a fractured rib on the right side."

Eric put his stethoscope into his ears and listened. "No shortness of breath. Did you hear something with the scope?"

In his mind, Anil saw the thick black heel crashing down on Baldev's unprotected spine. He heard the reverberation of the crack ring in his ears. "No," Anil said. "But I noticed his chest rising unevenly when I checked his breathing, a little lower on the right than the left."

"Okay." Eric wrapped his stethoscope around his neck. "Let's get him to Radiology for a CT scan. We can also rule out spinal injury, and see if he has broken bones—"

"No!" Anil interrupted. The nurse looked up at him, surprised. The rules of seniority clearly dictated Eric make the calls here; Anil was not even on duty tonight. "We can't wait for a scan," Anil continued. "He might need a chest tube. We should do an ultrasound right now. Right here, bedside."

Eric stared at him for a moment. The protocol for a stable patient was a CT scan, and they were both well aware of it. Anil mentally prepared his defense. He knew he was crossing the line with Eric, two years his senior. And he didn't give a shit.

"All right, Patel. We'll do it your way," Eric said. Over his shoulder, he bellowed, "Get me an ultrasound and chest tube cart."

AMBER AND Mahesh were in the ER waiting area when Anil came out. As he crossed the room, other patients eyed his blood-stained clothes. Mahesh was staring at the floor, tapping his feet, a can of 7UP balanced between his knees. Amber leaped out of her chair when she saw Anil and threw her arms around his neck.

Mahesh stood up, looking weary but no longer dazed. "How is he?"

"He's badly injured," Anil said. "But he should make a full recovery."

Mahesh exhaled, put his hand on Anil's shoulder, and bowed his head slightly toward the floor. Amber covered her entire face with her palms and began crying.

"Fortunately, there was no damage to his neck or spine," Anil said. "He does have a broken leg, a dislocated knee, a torn rotator cuff, and two fractured ribs, which caused his lung to collapse."

Amber's mouth dropped open, and she covered it with her hand.

"I know it sounds bad, but it could have been much worse. He regained consciousness briefly and was fairly lucid, so we don't suspect any brain damage."

Mahesh's face contorted, as though he hadn't considered this possibility. "What did he say?"

"He knew his name and what year it is," Anil said. "He remembered what we ate for dinner at the restaurant and . . . what happened in the parking lot afterward."

There was a long silence while they all considered whether this memory recall of Baldev's was good or bad. Finally, Amber spoke. "Can we see him?"

"He's under pretty heavy sedation for the pain right now," Anil said. "We're admitting him to the ICU, and he'll probably stay there a few days. You should go home and get some rest. I'll call you tomorrow when he wakes up."

"Okay," Mahesh said. "I'll call his parents and his office."

"Yes, good," Anil said, relieved to see Mahesh back to his reliable self. He couldn't bear any more responsibility this evening.

After Mahesh and Amber left, Anil returned to the central desk where Eric stood, writing Baldev's admitting orders. Anil waited for him to finish, bracing himself for censure.

When Eric looked up from his papers, his gaze rested on Anil's battered cheek for a moment before he spoke. "Good call, Patel."

Anil swallowed, a knob rising in his throat.

"On the ultrasound, it was a good call you made," Eric explained. "I was more focused on possible spinal injury, but that occult pneumothorax would have expanded with ventilation. And without the chest tube, it probably would have escalated to tension pneumothorax in the CT scanner, which would have been . . . well, you know." Eric scribbled his signature on the papers. "Really, really bad."

The sliding doors delivered a gust of wind and Anil crossed his arms, cradling his elbows. He became aware, for the first time, of a throbbing pain on the left side of his face.

"Not to mention, the fractured rib could have punctured his diaphragm if we hadn't found it until he got to Radiology," Eric said. "You saved your buddy, Patel. You probably saved his life." He reached out one of his muscular arms and put a hand on Anil's right shoulder. Anil winced. "Come on, man, you've gotta let somebody take a look at your face and arm—"

Anil shook his head. "After he's admitted. Should I page ICU?"

"I already did. Your friend's in good hands," Eric said. "Mehta's on call. You can wait for her down here if you want." He held out the admitting orders to Anil. "Page me if you need anything." He touched Anil's arm lightly as he walked away. "Anything, okay?"

THE TRAUMA room where Baldev lay sedated was otherwise empty; the nurses, interns, students, and extra equipment had all been cleared out, leaving behind the wheezing and beeping machinery. Anil grazed his hand on Baldev's shoulder and down along his arm. Less than an hour ago, he had made a one-inch incision into the chest under the armpit and inserted an intercostal drain to relieve the gas, which had leaked into the pleural cavity. In that moment, when he found the right position for the tip of his scalpel and felt for the opening between the ribs, he had not thought of it as Baldev into whom he was cutting.

Baldev, with the big grin and the hearty laugh. Baldev, who had challenged Mahesh to eat as many raw jalapeños as he could earlier that night at the restaurant, then ate one more himself, just for fun. Baldev, who had taught Anil to lift weights, play videogames, and talk to girls. Baldev, who had warned Anil on his first day in this country not to get caught in the wrong place in the great state of Texas. How were they to know the wrong place was right outside their own home on a pleasant spring night? How were they to know the wrong place would find them?

A shudder traveled through Anil's body and he stepped backwards, away from the gurney and the patient who lay there. The patient who was not just a patient. The way they referred to everything in the hospital—the patient, the pneumothorax, the fracture, the seizure, the bowel obstruction—it was as if medical conditions were disconnected from the people who suffered them. Anil leaned against the wall of the trauma room and moments later, Sonia Mehta came flying through the swinging doors. He was unaware he'd been crying until he saw the look in her eyes, which lingered not on the injuries to his face or his bloodied clothes but on his wounded eyes.

Sonia approached the gurney and studied Baldev's face, his injuries. She lightly touched his forehead, the one small spot not covered with a bandage, then walked over to the wall where Anil stood. "I'm so sorry."

With his good hand, Anil rubbed his forehead and looked down at the floor. He shook his head, slowly at first, then faster, and bit down on his lower lip.

"Eric told me what happened." Sonia moved closer and peered at him. "Are you all right?"

Anil cleared his throat. "Fine. Just superficial lacerations." He gestured with his right hand and felt the sharp pain there again.

"That's not what I meant," Sonia said. She watched him for a moment, her eyes searching his face. "You." She tapped his elbow gently with two fingertips. "Are *you* okay?"

Anil stared at the floor and chewed on his lower lip, trying to stem the emotions erupting inside him.

Sonia swiveled and leaned against the wall beside him. She stared up at the ceiling. "I had to spend a couple of nights in the hospital once, as a patient. It was awful. I was a terrible patient. But I learned more about medicine from that experience than anything else in my residency. Everyone tells you not to get personally involved with your patients, but sometimes you have to. And sometimes you should. Not too involved or you'll lose objectivity or burn out. But it's good to remember that each of these patients we treat is a real person—with dreams and talents, and a family and friends who love him."

Anil looked up at the ceiling. He took deep breaths. *In and out. In and out.*

"I can't imagine what it was like for you to be there, Anil," Sonia said. "But you could help him because you were."

"But I didn't help him," Anil cried. "Those guys, these . . . huge guys, they kept punching him and kicking him, over and over again. I couldn't do anything." He pounded his heel into the wall behind him and took a deep breath to steady himself. "Nothing," he said softly. "I just stood there and watched it happen."

"You helped him the best way you could." Sonia nodded toward the gurney. "You helped him *here.* I know this might be news to you, Patel, but you are not perfect. You're not going to be good at everything. So you can't win a street fight, so what? Who gives a shit? You can do this." She held her hands up, indicating the trauma room. She rotated toward him and Anil met her warm brown eyes. "You're *good* at this."

Anil breathed slowly, trying to absorb her words so they could heal whatever was now broken inside him.

"Now," Sonia said, pushing herself off the wall. "Let's get him upstairs." She walked toward one end of Baldev's gurney, Anil moved to the other, and together they pushed it through the doors of the trauma room.

After they boarded the elevator, Sonia looked Anil up and down. With a quick movement of her head, she flipped away the hair that had fallen over one eye. "You look like shit, Patel," she said. "And you're going to scare my patients. Once we get your friend settled, we're going to clean up your face and get an X-ray of that arm." Anil didn't protest this time. There were blades of pain shooting through his right arm, and his head was throbbing around his eye socket.

❁

As it turned out, Anil needed four stitches on his cheek and another two outside his eyebrow, all administered by Sonia's assured hand. There was something very calming about sitting passively on the hospital bed, allowing her to clean and treat his wounds. "So, is everything okay now?" he asked, after Sonia numbed him with topical anesthetic. He held her eye for a moment, before she looked away. "After your hospital stay, is everything okay?"

Sonia rolled her stool sideways to get some gauze from the counter. "Yeah, fine. It was a long time ago." She rolled back. "Hold still."

Anil flinched at the pinch of the needle on his cheek. "Sorry, was it unprofessional for me to ask that question?"

Sonia finished sewing up his cheek before answering. Did he detect a slight smile as she ripped off her latex gloves? "You think I stitch up all my junior residents for free, Patel? We're already way past professional."

An X-ray confirmed Anil had sprained both his wrist and elbow in the fall onto the concrete, and he would have to wear a brace on his right arm until it healed. Casper O'Brien gave him a few days off to recover at home, but Anil refused to take the painkillers Sonia had prescribed. It seemed unfair to numb the pain of the few mild injuries he had sustained while Baldev was suffering in the ICU and would endure weeks of pain and rehabilitation.

❁

THE NEXT day, Anil was sitting by Baldev's side in the ICU when he was paged to the visitors' lounge. Amber was waiting there for him, perched on the edge of a chair. Her hair hung in a limp ponytail, and she wore sweats and no makeup. She looked as if she hadn't slept at all. Anil held open the door that separated the visitors' lounge from the inner chamber of the ICU and Amber followed him back to where Baldev lay sleeping. She gasped when she saw his discolored face, the bandaged eye, the swollen lip. "God," she said, covering her mouth. "Has he woken up yet?"

"Yes, and he's fine, just sleeping a lot, which is normal." Anil pulled over another chair and they sat together, listening to the steady drum of Baldev's heart monitor, the robotic breathing of the ventilator.

Amber reached over and took Anil's hand in hers; he could feel her body relax with the gesture, but his did not respond the same way. "Have you . . . do you want to get some food in the cafeteria?" she asked. "Have you eaten anything today?"

Anil shook his head and stood up abruptly. "No, you go ahead. I've got some things to do." He glanced at his pager. "See you later, okay?"

Despite the leave he'd been given, Anil spent most of his time at Parkview, sitting in the ICU with Baldev or consulting with his physicians on his progress and treatment plan. When he came home after dark, for a change of clothes or a few hours' sleep, he parked his car illegally along the red curb right outside their front door and sprinted the few steps to safety. He was fully prepared to get a parking ticket, or even to find his car towed come morning, but neither ever transpired. How many other criminal activities went unpunished every day?

At home, Mahesh took care of everything that needed to be done. Before Baldev's parents arrived from Houston, he readied Baldev's bedroom, taking down the posters of women from the walls, removing the obscene magazines and movies, putting fresh sheets on the bed. Once they arrived, he made chai for them the proper way, boiling loose tea leaves together with water and milk on the stovetop, rather than simply using the microwave as he normally did. He drove them to the hospital every day, and to the Hindu temple afterward, where the pandit performed special prayers on Baldev's behalf.

As he observed Mahesh's frenetic activity in those first few days after the attack, Anil wondered if they each suffered guilt in inverse proportion to the physical injuries they'd sustained. Anil felt bad compared with Baldev, and Mahesh, without a scratch on him, was worse still. Anil thought of Amber and wondered how she was faring, but he couldn't bring himself to go see her, couldn't justify spending time away from Baldev's bedside, dividing himself like that.

When he finally went to her apartment a few days later, Amber opened the door, stepped into his arms, and began to cry. She couldn't seem to stop crying. Anil held her tighter, trying to protect against the sobs that wracked her thin frame. "I can't stop thinking about it," she said, once she had composed herself slightly. "I have these nightmares, then I wake up and you're not here." She clutched his forearms. "God, I've missed you." Anil walked her over to the couch and sat her down. Amber rested her chin on her knees, shuddering with halted breaths. "Momma says this just proves big cities are full of trouble. She wants me to move back home."

Anil waited to feel something in reaction to the idea of Amber leaving, but he was numb. "Maybe . . . maybe she's right," he said. "If you don't feel safe." *With me*, he didn't say. *If you don't feel safe with me.* He'd seen a different person in Amber the night of the attack. Under the fluorescent lights of the parking lot, the sunny woman he knew was replaced with a frail young girl. Anil felt responsible in some way for her transformation. Something had broken, in them and between them, and he was not sure it could be mended. He closed his eyes, trying to think of something to say, and felt her hand drop away from his arm.

Amber began to cry again. "I wish everything could just go back to the way it was."

"How can it?" Anil whispered, his eyes watering. "How can things ever be the same?" They wept together, holding each other on the couch where they first made love, until their eyes and hearts were raw to the point of pain. "I want you to be happy, Amber. You deserve that."

Amber nodded, saying she wished the same for him.

He kissed her tear-stained face for the last time.

Then he left.

❁

FOR THE first few days afterward, Anil felt as if his ribcage had been hollowed out whenever he thought of Amber, gone from his life.

The police came to the hospital and took statements. When Baldev regained consciousness, they asked if he wanted to press charges against

Lee and Rudy, but he declined. Anil knew from the look in his eyes and by his nervous laugh that Baldev was scared. He knew it too because he had the same fear himself, of what could happen if he was caught in the parking lot at night, or went to check the mailboxes in the morning. Once Baldev was moved out of the ICU and onto a regular ward, Anil returned to work at the hospital. Some residents offered condolences and sympathetic looks, while the senior staff treated him with the same disregard as always, which Anil found oddly reassuring. Life at Parkview would go on as it always had, despite his world having been upended.

Over the next several weeks, even as Baldev's medical condition improved—as his lungs re-expanded and pulmonary function resumed—it was clear to Anil that something about his friend had changed. The mischievous glint in his eyes had been replaced with a certain heaviness, and even when he smiled at Anil's weak jokes, there remained an underlying sorrow in his expression. Baldev would undergo surgery to repair the torn tendons in his shoulder, and to restore his patella to its former condition, but Anil did not know whether his friend would ever be the same again.

He began a new rotation in the emergency room, which was mercifully busy and left him with little waking time at the end of the day to think about anything, including the loss of his first love. Eric Stern gave him interesting cases and asked Anil to present them to the attending on rounds. He spent as little time as possible at home, grabbing dinner at the hospital or at the diner with Charlie, who had finally stopped moonlighting as a gypsy cab driver now that his brother-in-law had secured a new job. Anil spent his infrequent days off with Mahesh, who distracted him with bootlegged copies of the latest Bollywood features. He became accustomed to sleeping alone again, but was always reminded of how empty his bed was when he woke in the morning. Whenever he felt a pang over Amber, he thought of Baldev's pain and reminded himself that this was a punishment he deserved.

Anil didn't drive out to the lake for over a month, and when he finally did, he was surprised to find it populated with individual runners like him, dodging between baby strollers and avoiding bicyclists. The times he'd gone there with Amber, he'd somehow formed the impression it was all strolling couples, enjoying the private cloak of their love. He began to go to the lake every weekend, pushing himself to improve both his pace and endurance, finally making it all the way around the nine-mile perimeter. He no longer cared to imagine what was inside the beautiful houses that lined the path. When he ran, he focused on the pounding of his feet on the pavement and the beautiful rhythmic pumping of his lungs—the grace of his perfectly functioning body.

Amber was gone, and Baldev lay broken in the hospital. All that was left for Anil was medicine, the one thing that had brought him here in the first place. He continued to work on his infectious disease project with Charlie, even as he was finalizing his proposal to take to Dr. Tanaka for a cardiology research study. It was crazy to undertake two research efforts during his residency, but Anil would not abandon Charlie, nor would he give up his dream. He would have to work twice as hard, and without Amber in his life, he now had the time to do so.

Part III

20

Nirmala woke in an empty bed. There was a folded slip of paper on Pradip's pillow, and as on the day the phone rang with news of Leena, Nirmala felt a terrible sense of foreboding.

She climbed out of bed and ran past the bedroom where Leena lay asleep, out of the house, and into the fields. The earth was still damp. The crops had been cut back so severely, it was possible to see quite a distance, but Nirmala ran up and down each row, calling his name—hoping, even as dread filled her chest and her calls turned to cries, that she would find him there.

When she reached the far edge of their property, Nirmala stood, breathing heavily, looking back at their home. She turned and walked, more slowly now, toward the riverbank. It was the river that made their soil so rich and fertile for growing crops, the river from which they used to collect water years ago before the well was built. On hot days, her husband would take a dip in the river after a long day working in the fields, and she knew she would find him there now.

As she drew closer, she saw him, dressed not in his field clothes but his good white *kurta-pajama*, the one he'd worn to Leena's wedding. His body was floating in the middle of the river, bobbing peacefully like a piece of driftwood. Nirmala waded in to retrieve him, the layers of her sari forcing her to move slowly through the water.

THREE MONTHS after returning to Panchanagar, Leena knelt in the same dirt she'd felt under her bare feet nearly every day of her life, staring at the pile of ash that used to be her father.

"Just you and me now, little lamb." Her mother used the pet name Leena had not heard in years. If only she could rewind the clock to that time, when her father used to hold her in his lap and her mother braided her hair and tied ribbons at the ends.

Leena shut her eyes tightly against the final wisps of burning smoke. She had been worried about the odor, but it was the smoke that broke her, penetrating the crevices of her eyes, forming tears she could not stem once they had begun.

After a final prayer, her mother scooped the warm ashes into a steel vessel. They had not called the priest to perform the rituals, nor any relatives to attend the cremation ceremony. It was only the two of them, and they would have to rebuild their life without the man who had been at the center of it.

As a widow, her mother would be expected to withdraw from public life, to wear white and no jewelry or makeup. *To be invisible.* With a shock, Leena realized her mother had already been living this way, ever since Leena had returned to Panchanagar. All her jewelry was long gone. There was no money for new saris, not even plain white cotton ones. They had been living in seclusion since Leena had left her husband, and now her mother had lost her spouse as well.

As she mourned the loss of her father, Leena grew anxious about her and her mother's ability to survive without him. They could not possibly do the farm work her father had done, and even if they could, their land had been yielding less and less as her father crowded it with more crops and eliminated fallow periods over the past year. Before his death, he had broken all his own principles about farming, as if his judgment had disintegrated before the rest of him. The land would come back if they tended it, but it might take years, and until then, Leena and her mother would have to find another way to support themselves.

The week after her father's death, Leena and her mother made a trip to the town market with the last of their harvested crops. When everything had been sold, the last customer, a rich Memsahib, asked Leena if she could buy her empty basket to carry home her vegetables. The next morning, Leena collected armfuls of damp reeds from the fields and sat down to weave more baskets. Within a week, Leena had finished eight baskets, and when she and her mother returned to the market, to Leena's astonishment, they sold every last one: to students balancing books on their bicycles, customers at the market who bought more than their arms could carry, even a flower vendor to carry her garlands. Leena and her mother came home with over three hundred rupees, and had a feast of five-vegetable curry to celebrate. The next morning, Leena showed her mother how to weave and they began to work together, making and selling baskets.

Their good fortune continued for several months. Leena and her mother were earning a decent living. They could afford to keep their kitchen stocked with grains and lentils, to buy fresh vegetables each time they visited the market and new sandals to replace their worn ones. Their newfound self-sufficiency continued until Leena began to notice more women coming to the market with baskets for sale, and prices began to fall. Weaving baskets was a tradition in some villages, with whole families working together to produce hundreds of baskets every month. Leena could not keep up with them, especially with her mother's failing eyesight, and soon the disquiet about their future set in again.

Around the corner from the market, a few hundred paces from where they sold their baskets, was an alleyway between two tenement buildings. The ground-floor windows of each building were framed with colorful curtains. Women in garishly bright saris and heavy makeup could be seen sitting inside the windows. As evening fell, the women migrated outside—standing in the doorways, leaning against walls. The first time Leena happened upon the alley, she didn't understand what it was. She was intrigued by those women—mocking each other across the alleyway, allowing their saris to fall shamelessly from their shoulders, using the kind of language she'd heard only from men. A bald man with missing teeth sat on a stool outside and called out to her, trying to grab at her clothing as she walked by. Leena ran all the way back to the market. She didn't tell her mother what she'd seen, but Leena found herself wondering afterward how much those women earned.

❁

ONE DAY at the market, Leena saw an old woman selling clay pots. They were simple and sturdy but very small—the size of the *diyas* used to light a single oil flame at Diwali. Leena asked the woman why she was selling *diya* pots when Diwali was long over.

The old woman smiled. "This is all I can make with my stiff fingers, child. Years ago, I used to make enormous vessels"—she illustrated by holding her frail arms into a wide circle—"huge pots to store dry grains and lentils after the harvest, to keep water cool in the summer. But I cannot do it any longer with this pain." She held up her gnarled hands.

When Leena told her they had come from Panchanagar, the old woman's eyes brightened. "You are near the river," she said. "Your clay should be very fine." She told Leena how to dig for it, two hands below the surface of the earth. "Cover it with damp burlap. Keep it wet or you will lose your chance to shape it. Water keeps the clay like a young child, while the sun makes him into an old man." Leena's mother thought the old woman might be weak in the head, but her voice was strong and her meaning clear.

The next morning, Leena went to the banks of the river and dug into the soil until she reached the hard-packed clay. Burrowing her fingers below the cool surface, Leena felt like a child again, though it took great strength to pry the clay from the earth bed where it rested. She collected enough to fill the small steel urn they used to make yogurt—three or four handfuls.

Leena neglected her duties for the rest of the day. She sat outside with the urn of clay and a vessel of water and played like a schoolgirl—kneading the clay, rolling and shaping it with her hands. It was the end of the day before she noticed the clothes were still hanging on the line and her mother had cooked the entire evening meal herself. Leena felt guilty, but her mother pushed her out of the kitchen, saying she was happy to see her daughter smiling again.

Over the next few days, Leena discovered how many ways there were to shape clay using only her two hands. As the old woman had told her, she had to add plenty of water to coax it to softness—but not too much or the clay became sticky and uncooperative. Leena pressed it into a ball and then rolled it between her palms until it was perfectly round and smooth, like the shiny seed of a chickoo. She held it loosely between her flattened fingers and moved them back and forth until small clay ropes formed, the length of her hand, then of her forearm and even longer. Leena coiled the ropes around and around, like a cobra, and formed a drinking cup. The next day, she borrowed the wooden pin they used to make chapatis and rolled out some more clay. From the large, smooth clay sheet, she cut out a circle to form the base of a pot, and a long rectangle to form the sides, using water to join the various pieces together.

When Leena went back to the river to find more clay, she learned to dig deeper into the ground until she reached the purest clay, from which she could stretch out a ribbon the length of her smallest finger. She was so enraptured with this cold dark clay from beneath the earth. There it had always been, beneath their feet, their home, their crops, and their roads. The old woman had been right: the best clay was near the river, where the soil was rich, in the shade of the banana trees, where the rains accumulated and the sun did not parch the ground.

The next time she and her mother went into town, Leena brought the drinking cup she'd made of coils, and the flat-bottomed pot she'd rolled like a chapati. When she showed them to the old woman at the market, the woman smiled. "My dear," she said, "you haven't yet learned the real secret of clay."

"Secret?" Leena thought she'd already learned the power of transforming a hard lump into something useful with only her hands, water, and the sun.

"Yes," the woman said, "the magic of spinning your clay on a wheel."

Leena listened as the old woman told her what to do. After returning to Panchanagar, she found an old wagon wheel and rubbed it all over with a stone until its surface was smooth. She took a flat steel lid from one of the kitchen pots and secured it to the center of the wheel to create a seat for the clay. She applied cooking oil to the long axle so the wheel could spin freely, and buried the axle deep into the earth. It took some time to position the wheel so it was level. Then she used a long stick between the spokes as a handle to get the wheel spinning quickly. Only once Leena had practiced this quite a bit and could keep the wheel spinning for a few minutes on its own did she place a lump of clay in the center. She spun the wheel so it was going very fast, and sprinkled some water onto the clay.

The moment her two hands touched the misshapen lump, Leena felt the truth of the old woman's words. When she closed her palms over the clay, the bumps and imperfections seemed to melt away. With more water and her thumbs pressed firmly into the top of the smooth mound, she created a well in the center. Another sprinkle, one palm placed inside the well, another outside, and she widened the well to make its walls stand up straight.

As the wheel slowed down, the magical feeling started to slip away. The clay shape began to show its imperfections. Leena spun the wheel again with the stick, applied more water to her hands, then placed her fingertips on either side of the base of the clay. She moved her fingers up the side, slowly and very gently. The structure was vulnerable now, its walls less than a finger's width. Before Leena knew what had happened, her fingertip had torn a hole in the wall of the pot. It wobbled and fell onto itself, still spinning, looking like a hunchbacked man.

Over the next several weeks, Leena continued learning how to work with the clay. It was a process that began violently: to remove the air bubbles, she had to knead the clay with force and slam it down repeatedly on the terrace. It took all the strength she had in her arms, and her shoulders ached the next day, but Leena took great satisfaction in the sheer aggression of it. But once the clay began to take shape, it required a progressively lighter hand, only the softest touch of a single finger was necessary to even out the thin upper rim of her piece.

Leena learned how to change the strength in her hands, how to adjust for the feel of the spinning clay. The true magic of the pottery wheel was in its power and speed—with it, she could make smooth, beautiful pieces in a few minutes, but could also ruin one in seconds. One moment of lapsed concentration, the wrong angle with her wrist, a slip of her finger and it was gone. Clay might be forgiving, but the pottery wheel was not.

Some days, she used the other techniques of rolling the clay, or coiling ropes to make vessels, but Leena made her best creations spinning on the wheel. Inside the house, she kept an entire shelf lined with wobbly and misshapen pots from the early days when she was first learning to use the pottery wheel, but also from those days she lost focus. Others might consider them ugly or useless, but Leena liked to keep them as a reminder of what she'd learned.

Many more pieces—bowls, urns, drinking cups—were good enough to sell at the market, and Leena soon began to earn more than she had from the baskets, nearly as much as her father had from their farm crops. That first day at the market, Leena had not been looking for an old woman with a bent back, but she was drawn to her tiny, perfect creations. With her wistful words, the old woman had given Leena a gift. When Leena sat down at the wheel, she knew it was where she belonged. Not only was it her craft and her livelihood, it was her salvation.

Once, Leena had hoped for more from her life. Now, after the torment she'd lived through, the wounds still carried on her body and in her memory, it was an unspeakable gift to be able to live on her ancestral lands, in her family home, and support herself and her mother. Gradually, she emerged from the seclusion of their home, accompanying her mother to village gatherings, though others there still largely avoided her. When Leena saw her cousins and school friends, their lives full and busy with husbands and children, domestic chores and village gossip, sometimes she felt a deep longing. In time, she learned it was better to avoid these people, to retreat to the things that brought her solace: her mother, their home, the pottery wheel. That other kind of life was not her karma.

21

FOUR WEEKS LATER, WITH BALDEV STILL IN THE HOSPITAL recovering from knee surgery, Anil completed the second year of his residency and returned to India for the trip he'd planned months earlier.

Now, as he sat on the porch of the Big House, a light breeze rippled through the fronds of the coconut trees lining its perimeter. Anil closed his eyes and enjoyed the sensation of the breeze caressing his face. With a cup of chai warming his hands, he allowed himself to sink into the newfound pleasure of being home. He'd sensed the difference as soon as he disembarked from the plane in Ahmadabad, when he slipped easily into the throngs of bodies jostling around the baggage belt, another unremarkable person in this country of millions; no one looking at him, no one noticing he was different.

The front door creaked open behind him and Ma stepped out onto the porch, carrying a tray laden with fresh cups of chai and a stack of warm *paranthas*. She nodded her chin toward the fields—Nikhil was walking back to the house for a morning tea break. He was darkened by the sun, his bare arms sinewy with muscle. Anil stood up to greet his brother, waving one hand high over his head.

They sat together on sturdy wooden chairs on the porch, shoulder to shoulder, looking out over the land that now belonged to them. Ma poured two cups of tea, straining out the gingerroot and crushed mint leaves. Anil raised the cup to his lips and inhaled the fragrant cardamom.

Ma stood between her two sons, one hand on each of their shoulders. "This is how it should always be," she said before retreating into the house.

Anil blew on his tea to cool it down.

Nikhil tipped his cup to pour a small amount of tea into his saucer, drank it in one gulp, and filled the saucer again. "You should tell her you're never coming back, so she can stop pining for the day." His voice was cold.

Anil turned to his brother and watched him slurp another saucerful of tea. "I didn't say I'm never—"

"Well, are you?" Nikhil stared straight out at the land, his dark eyes glinting like coal. "Or are you going to keep telling us what to do from your comfortable life in America?"

Anil put down his teacup, still full, next to Nikhil's empty cup on the tray. *"Bhai?"* His younger brother had never spoken to him this way. "Is something wrong?"

"You think you know more, sitting over there in your fancy hospital with your smart doctors? You think you know how we should do things over here?"

"Listen, *bhai*, I don't want that role," Anil said. "I've tried telling Ma I don't want it, but she won't listen." Just that morning, Ma had told him she had scheduled an arbitration session for the following day. "What nonsense," she'd replied when he protested he wasn't up for it.

"You know what it's been like here since you decided to give Dilip that land?" Nikhil's voice grew louder. "Each and every other servant has come to me asking for his own plot. Men who've been here less than a year and get drunk at lunchtime, even they think they deserve a piece of our land. This land"—he swept his arm in a circle—"that's been in our family for generations, that none of us would even own today unless Papa had died too soon. When I refused those other men, they went on strike for three days, all of them. Kiran and I were left to do everything, which we couldn't, of course." He paused. "We lost some crops."

"Strike?" Anil cried. "What do you mean 'strike'?"

Nikhil shook his head. "They didn't call it a strike, but they all claimed illness at the same time, three days in a row. I knew they weren't sick; they were playing cards down on the riverbank, but what was I to do? How does it look if I try to force a sick man to work?"

Anil reached for his cup. "So, what did you do?"

"I fired them," Nikhil said.

"What?" Tea spilled over the edge of Anil's cup, burning his thumb.

"I had to. They were of no use. They had to go."

Anil sank back in his chair and rubbed his forehead. "All of them?"

Nikhil nodded, staring straight ahead. "Even Dilip's sons."

"Why them?" Anil said. "Surely they didn't strike. After what you did for their father?"

Nikhil shook his head. "They were getting into fights with the other men. You can't expect men to do the same job and treat them differently. People will get upset, it's only natural. I couldn't afford the same problems with the new crew, so I fired them all. We lost three or four hectares on the west side to spoilage before I could find new workers."

"Oh God, Nikhil. I'm sorry." Anil twisted in his chair toward his brother, but Nikhil did not turn to face him. "I had no idea—"

"Yes, you did," Nikhil interrupted. "I told you what would happen if you gave Dilip that land. I warned you." He laid his head back against the chair and his voice dropped. "But you knew better."

Anil closed his eyes, remembering the discussion, recalling Nikhil's warning. He removed his spectacles and rubbed at his eyes. "Why didn't you tell me this earlier?"

"I know you're doing very important work over there, saving lives and all." Nikhil's voice was laced with such hostility it was unrecognizable. "What I do here?" Nikhil threw his arms out in front of him. "I know it's not so important, not so interesting for someone like you, *bhai*. I'm just trying to take care of Papa's land, to make a living, to support our family. It was hard enough before—every day I have men out with injuries, or down with fever, or preoccupied with family problems. Some don't show up at all when they're drunk. It's not an easy job, managing it all."

"I know, and I want to support you, *bhai*." Anil's voice sounded softer than he intended. He tried to muster the strength to say more: to acknowledge how important Nikhil's responsibility was, to appreciate how well he performed his work. But his words seemed insufficient.

Nikhil slapped his hands on his knees and leaned forward to stand up. "*Bandar kya jaane adark ka swaad*," he said, then strode down the steps of the Big House. It had been one of Papa's favorite proverbs. *What does a monkey know of the taste of ginger?* One who can't understand can't appreciate.

As Anil watched Nikhil return to the fields, he began to understand how much the natural order of things at home had been disturbed. When Papa was here, he'd managed to hold it all together, but his absence had created a wake of imbalance and simmering tensions. Anil had always believed he was right to pursue what he wanted, what his father had wanted for him. But Papa would not have wanted this.

In some ways, it would be a relief to come back home. Ever since the attack, Mahesh had been carrying on about how there was no way they would ever really belong in America, not the way it was possible in India. Anil disputed this assertion, pointing out the immigrants of all types who were successful in America. But when he pictured Baldev in the hospital, lying in traction as his body rebuilt new bone tissue and cartilage, unease stirred within him. He didn't find much consolation in knowing the same thing could have happened to anyone with dark skin in the South. And yet, Anil felt he belonged, more than he'd belonged anywhere, in that catheterization lab. He'd never been more alive, more driven, more purposeful. His hands literally tingled with the desire to start doing what he was meant to do.

"More *paranthas*?" Ma returned to the porch. "I'm so happy to see you eating, son. You're getting some of your weight back." She held out the plate to Anil, but he held up a palm.

Ma sat down in the chair vacated by Nikhil. "Son," she said, her voice softening to a whisper. "You haven't been eating … the wrong kind of food over there, have you?"

Anil understood her question despite its ambiguity. "No, Ma, I haven't. Only vegetarian."

"Ah, good." She sat back in the chair, patting the armrest. "You must not forget your Indian values."

His mother could rest knowing he hadn't eaten meat, yet there were so many other corruptions about which she did not even know to ask. Perhaps she would tolerate the drinking and nightclubs, but if she knew about Amber, never mind the sexual extent of their relationship, Ma would certainly come unhinged. Anil told himself he'd been sparing her by keeping Amber from her, but now he could see he'd also been sparing himself. He'd been a coward, just as he'd accused Amber of being with her family.

Anil watched Nikhil showing two field hands how to pull the old tiller between them, a task he and his brother had shared themselves when they were younger. He had made things harder for Nikhil with his long-distance counsel, and this he regretted, even if it had been his father's wish and at his mother's insistence. His involvement, however remote, had done nothing but muddy the situation.

Piya came out to join them on the porch. "There you are." She accepted a cup of tea from Ma and sat down.

"I'm going to start preparing lunch," Ma said. "Manoj Uncle and your cousin will be coming this afternoon. They have begun juicing the mangos from the tree that splits their property. Every weekend, they bring mango *lassi* for all of us at the Big House." Ma laid a hand on Anil's shoulder. "Thanks to you, they have found a way to share the fruit."

"Mmm, those mangos are delicious," Piya said. "Good job, brother."

"What about those two farmers," Anil said, "with the water well?"

Ma clucked her tongue. "They're still at it, fighting like billy goats. Some days, I can hear them all the way over here."

"And Nirmala Auntie?" Anil asked. "Is the new payment schedule working out?" When Ma did not respond, Anil turned around to look at her, but she simply walked back into the house without a word. "What was that about?" he asked Piya.

Piya craned her neck to watch their mother until she disappeared from view. "You know, Ma's general aversion to anything remotely scandalous." There was a note of bitterness in her tone. "It's so sad. They've had such a tough time since Leena came back."

"She came back?" Anil said.

Piya nodded. "And then her father died a few months ago. Everyone said he died from the shame over Leena's broken marriage."

Anil looked at his sister, who was gazing out over the fields. "God, I didn't know." Even if he'd made an effort to keep up with the happenings in Panchanagar, bad news like this was rarely spoken of. Most people, including Ma, preferred to brush unpleasantness away, as if, by sweeping it outside with the dust, it could be forgotten. As if, by acknowledging the existence of something unsavory in their community, they might be tainted by it themselves.

Piya placed her teacup back on the tray. "Personally, I think he died of a broken heart. His only daughter, his only child."

"What happened?" Anil asked. "With . . . Leena, with her marriage?"

Piya picked up her cup and took a long sip before responding. "It didn't last long. She doesn't like to talk about it." She stood up and touched him on the shoulder. "I better go see if Ma needs help with lunch. I'm sure there's a feast under preparation for you."

After Piya left, Anil felt restless and decided to go for a walk. Something stirred inside him as he digested the news, and he couldn't identify what it was. Crossing the fields, Anil spotted in the distance a coconut tree, its outline distinguishable from those around it. He recognized its grotesquely crooked trunk, which reportedly had survived being maimed by a wild elephant. As kids, they'd called that tree "the cripple" and used it as a meeting spot for cricket games.

Anil retraced the familiar paths of his childhood: down along the coconut-tree lane toward his old school, the dirt road over which his rickety bicycle had taken him twice a day. He circled back and over the low rolling hills to the banana tree where he had recited his lines as a child. That tree, which they'd named "the peacock" because of its perfect semicircle of branches, was taller now. Anil laid his palm against the smooth trunk of the tree, under which he'd sat for hours, wrestling his own demons.

Too unsettled to sit now, Anil continued walking. Trees he hadn't noticed in years became recognizable again—"the elephant," with its wide-eared fronds, "the dwarf," shorter than its neighbors. Anil found himself at the end of the lane. In the distance, next to the riverbank, stood a familiar house with a large terrace. Peering closer, he made out the rows of earthenware pots clustered on the terrace. Among them was a figure in a yellow sari. Leena sat on a low stool, her eyes focused downward, her hands covered in slick brown clay. Her head moved rhythmically with her hands as they sculpted; she seemed to be in a meditative trance.

The farmland surrounding Leena's house was barren, stripped of its crops, of its tools and equipment. Anil's main recollection of Leena's father was seeing him work in his fields from dawn to dusk, good-naturedly shooing them away when he caught them playing hide-and-seek in the crops. He was a man who had taken great pride in his small plot of land.

There had been one time, Anil recalled, when Leena's father had found him hiding in the crops all alone. He was six years old and had been cornered after school by a few of the older boys who wanted the sweets Ma had sent for Diwali. The boys had surrounded him outside the school and taunted him until he stammered out a weak response: "L-l-leave m-m-me a-a-lone!" Mocking his stutter, the boys closed in on him. Anil dropped the metal tin he'd been clutching and covered the front of his pants with both hands, but not before wetness trickled down his legs. As the boys howled with laughter, Anil sprinted away.

Not until he could see the Big House up the lane did he stop and, breathing heavily, crouch down in the fields belonging to Leena's family. How could he go home empty-handed, his shorts wet, stinking of his own cowardice? Anil sat in the dirt, his skin itchy and burning, determined not to move until he had a plan. He panicked when Leena's father, cutting down sugarcane with a long knife, approached him, but Anil curled forward into a ball and waited until the footsteps receded. He thought he'd eluded notice, but not long afterward, Papa came walking down the lane, found Anil in the fields, and knelt down next to him. He touched his palm to Anil's tear- and dirt-stained face. "Shall I carry you?" he'd said, and without a word about Anil's soiled clothes, Papa had lifted him up and carried him home on his shoulders, like a hero.

Now, Anil watched Leena gently touch the upper rim of the piece on her wheel. In the space of the few minutes he'd been standing there, she had created a bowl with her bare hands. In the space of the two years since he'd last seen her, they had both lost their fathers. He began to walk again, drawing closer to the terrace, until he was only a few feet away.

LEENA BECAME aware that someone was watching her, and looked up to see Anil Patel standing at the bottom of the house steps. "Oh." When had he come back? She slowed the wheel with her inner knee. She was not accustomed to having visitors other than Piya.

"I don't want to interrupt," Anil said. "I-I-I . . ." He drew in a deep breath. "I just came home for a visit, and I heard about your father. I wanted to pay my respects, to you and your mother."

Leena was caught by his words. She looked down, noticing the hem of her sari coated in dust. What a simple thing he was offering, yet hardly anyone had done so in the past few months.

"I'm sorry, I must be disturbing you—"

"No, it's fine." Leena stood up slowly. She was never quite certain of people's intentions anymore. Was it Piya who'd sent her brother? What had she told him? "My mother isn't home, but I can make us some tea."

Anil smiled. "If it's not too much trouble."

Leena forced a smile in return. "I should probably take a break. This one's giving me some difficulty." She gestured to the half-finished pot on her wheel. "It's supposed to look like that one." She pointed to a large footed urn that stood waist-high. "It's for a hotel in the city. They've asked for a matching pair, to put at the front entrance. For um . . . umb . . ."

"Umbrellas?" Anil offered.

"Yes, that's it. Um-ber-el-las," she pronounced slowly, and they both laughed at the peculiar word and the absurdity of tourists trying to shield themselves from the monsoons.

Anil walked slowly around the terrace, looking at Leena's clay bowls, urns, platters, and pots, all in various stages of completion. "You made all of these with your hands?" he asked.

Leena pulled her sari close around her, feeling exposed with her work sitting out in the open. "Please, come in." She entered the house, conscious of how small it was as he followed her inside. Their home was more of a cottage, with a small drawing room in the front, the kitchen behind it, and two bedrooms on the opposite side of the hallway. It was a simple layout, a square split into four quadrants, each room with its own purpose. Unlike the Big House, with its open rooms and immense furniture, this home was built to accommodate only a few people.

Leena put milk and water to boil on the stove and gestured for Anil to sit at the small table. It felt familiar to have him there—reminiscent of the many times her mother had fed them as children—but also strange to see his adult frame perched on the low stool. She wondered if the ways in which she'd changed were as obvious to him as his changes were to her.

"There must be a hundred pieces outside," Anil said. "How long did that take you?"

Leena shrugged as she stirred tea leaves into the pot. "I've been preparing for the busy season. First Diwali, then weddings, then all the tourists come to town. Many of the vendors sell half their wares for the year in those couple of months. Some of the more experienced vendors—the shawl-*wallah*, the jeweler—they bring extra supplies and men with them in the morning and set up in different parts of the market, acting like different merchants, pretending to be competitors. Sometimes they cheat the tourists by setting a very high price and driving them to the other stall across the market, where they think they're getting a better deal." Leena placed two cups of tea on the table, along with two steel plates, each holding *thepla* and a dab of orange-colored pickle.

"I remember this." Anil smiled. "Your mother's sweet mango pickle." He rolled up the savory flatbread and dipped it into the sweet, milky chai. "Mmm."

Leena joined him at the table, reaching for the end of her sari to wrap around her shoulders. The tea was too hot to drink. She still made it as her father had liked it, boiled rapidly for a full minute at the end. Somehow, it felt like a betrayal to prepare it any other way.

"When I first started making pottery, I thought the monsoons were a terrible time," Leena said. "It was impossible to build a fire under the ground to bake the clay. But I've learned this is the best time for me to spin pots. My clay stays moist for weeks, it's more forgiving. If I make a mistake, I can just form it back into a lump and begin again the next day." She heard herself rambling but continued on anyway. "By the end of the monsoons, when the soil is dry again, I'll have over a hundred pots, and they bake more evenly all together underground."

Anil cleared his throat. "Leena, I . . . I'm really sorry about your father." He put his hands in his lap, then around the cup, then back on the table. "He was a good man."

His hesitancy, the awkwardness of his movements made something rise within her, a bubbling of resentment toward everyone who hadn't paid proper homage to her father. "Yes, he was," she said with emphasis, as if she were disputing his statement rather than agreeing with it. "He was." She stood and collected their empty plates.

"I still think of my father every day," Anil said. "But it gets a little easier with time. It helps to have my family around, people who knew him and loved him like I did."

Leena busied herself with the dishes, keeping her back to him, biting the inside of her lip to keep from speaking. What did he know of her grief, the grief she and her mother suffered alone—without the company of friends, without the solace of other family? Without all the people who would rather pretend they no longer existed than acknowledge the shame she'd brought on them?

Anil cleared his throat again. "What are those pieces over there?"

He was pointing to a corner of the drawing room barely visible from the kitchen doorway. It was easy to miss the shelf holding a dozen ceramic pieces, since the pale shade of dried clay matched the backdrop of the whitewashed walls. "Those?" Leena said. "Those are my mistakes." She dried her hands on a towel and leaned against the sink.

A small smile tugged at the corner of Anil's mouth. "C-c-can you show me?"

Leena hadn't heard him stammer since they were children. She recalled the way he'd been teased in school, how quiet he'd been before he'd learned to overcome it. She took a long, deep breath before answering. "Yes." She took another full breath in, then out, deliberately slowing down her speeech as she used to do. "Come." She walked into the drawing room and knelt down in front of the shelf. Anil sank down to his knees next to her. There was barely enough space for the both of them, wedged as they were into the corner.

Leena had never shown these pieces to anyone. They were unfinished and unglazed, she explained. Most people preferred pottery when it was sturdy and colorful. "But I think it's most beautiful at this stage." Leena picked up a wide, shallow bowl and rested it on her knee. "It's still porous like this—not really useful for anything, but you can see everything—the small swirl in the bottom where I began, and these lines going up the sides—those are my fingertips." She traced a circle around the inner rim with her third finger, then tilted the bowl toward him. "Feel," she said, and he did, moving his fingertips over the minute ridges formed by hers. "This bowl was perfectly round until I bumped the rim and it went oval." Leena smiled and replaced the bowl on the shelf, where it sat unevenly, its base trembling for a few seconds before it came to rest. Other pieces were tilted, one had a jagged hole in the side, a few had collapsed in on themselves. "It's more delicate in this form, more vulnerable."

"What about this one?" Anil picked up a small drinking cup. "It looks perfect."

"There's a crack around the bottom," Leena explained, turning it over to show him. "I didn't notice until after it came out of the fire. It happens quite a lot as the pieces dry out: you can't always see the cracks, but you can feel them with your fingers." She took Anil's finger and guided it around the base of the cup. After she let go, she still felt the touch of his skin like an electric current. "Sometimes I can repair a crack when the piece is wet, with a thin liquid mixture of water and clay. But before I learned that, I lost many pieces." She held the drinking cup up and laughed. "I probably had a full set of these cracked cups, a dozen or more."

She caught a look of sadness drift across his face. "I can't imagine," he said, "having to throw away such beauty."

She shook her head. "I didn't want to. The first few times I found a cracked piece, I tried to apply a thick paint all over and bake it again, but the crack grew bigger from the heat and pressure of the second baking. Then it was *really* of no use. Or if I dropped it, it would break along that line, even if it was invisible. You can never fix it completely. Clay has a memory. Once it's scarred, the heat helps it remember. It's always the weakest point, where there's been a fracture."

Anil was watching her intently as she spoke. "Same with people," he said, returning the cup to the shelf. His eyes were glistening as he began to speak; words poured out without his pausing for breath or to see her reaction. He told her the story of his friend, the men who had attacked him and how he could not stop them, the ambulance, the emergency room, and how his friend now lay in a recovery room, healing but still broken. Anil's voice cracked as he spoke. When he finished, she sat with him in silence for several moments, a stillness interrupted only by bird calls and the rustling of leaves outside.

"It must be hard for you over there," Leena said.

Anil nodded, and they sat without speaking for a few moments longer. "Sometimes it is. But other things are . . . incredible. They have more advanced equipment on the ambulance than in the entire hospital here. The homes are new and beautiful, with electric appliances in the kitchen, and they have these huge indoor shopping centers. Look." He pulled a small white square out of his pocket and held it up between two fingers. "This holds ten thousand songs."

Leena watched him as he spoke about the musical gadget, noting the tousle of wavy hair, the boyish smile, the small dimple in his chin she didn't recognize. As heat rose to her face, Leena turned away and began replacing the imperfect pottery pieces on the shelves.

"There's an arbitration meeting tomorrow," Anil said.

Leena reached for the end of her long braid and twisted the tail of it around her finger. "I know. My cousin Brinda and her husband will be there."

"So you're coming?"

Maybe she imagined it on his face, a slight smile. Leena shook her head. "No, I think it should be a private matter when a married couple discusses their problems, not for everyone to hear."

"Then why are they coming?" Anil looked slightly annoyed.

"What other choice does she have? There is no court around here, no police." Leena's voice rose in pitch. "Her in-laws won't hear a bad word against their son, her parents don't want to make trouble. It's good she has someone who can listen to both sides. But I don't think it's right for others to watch." She smoothed out her sari against her legs. "I . . ."

"What?" Anil asked.

Leena shook her head, keeping her eyes focused on the golden line at the edge of her sari, how perfect and unblemished it was. Why open up her wounds, why expose them, now, to him? And yet, in the space of Anil's own brokenness, Leena felt some shelter, some relief from the isolation that had engulfed her in the past several months.

Anil touched her wrist lightly, and again she felt the spark. "Tell me."

Leena dropped her gaze, willing herself not to care about his reaction. "I wouldn't have wanted that. When I was married, I wouldn't have wanted to discuss my problems in front of others." She didn't know how much he knew, what Piya might have told him. "My marriage did not turn out as I expected. There . . . there was no resolution, except to leave." She compelled herself to look up at his face, expecting to see pity or perhaps scorn, but his expression betrayed neither. Anil held her gaze but said nothing. She smiled at him a little, and he smiled back. The edge of Leena's foot began to tingle, then her ankle. She tried to move it discreetly beneath her sari, not wanting to disturb their position on the floor of the drawing room, cramped between the shelf of ceramic pieces and the chairs. Anil shifted his position to accommodate her, and something clattered onto the stone floor. Leena leaned over to pick up the wooden piece rolling on the floor.

Anil put his hand to his pocket. "Oh."

Leena inspected the piece closely, turning it around between her fingers. It was a rich shade of brown, carved from mahogany or rosewood. "It's from a game, no?" She moved to stretch her legs and stand up, and he followed.

"Chess. I used to play with my father." He described how the game worked, how capturing the opponent's king was the goal. "I lost the other king piece, the sandalwood one that was Papa's. We always played the same colors. I took this one to America, hoping I could find a matching piece."

"You won't find it." Leena handed it back to him. "It's one of a kind, carved by hand."

❁

As he left the house, Anil slipped the chess piece back into his pocket and tightened his grip around it. It struck him as a cruel thing for her to say, but she was probably right. It seemed absurd, now that he'd said it out loud, that he'd been carrying the piece around for so long.

Anil walked back up the lane and crossed the fields. As he stood on one edge of the gully that ran between the Big House and Leena's family home, he was surprised by how much smaller it was than he remembered. The small valley had been formed over the years when the monsoon rains forged the path through the land. As kids, they'd lain down at the top of one hill, arms flat against their sides, and took turns rolling down, seeing how far up the other side they could get. In the monsoon season, it was their unspoken practice to run from their homes at the sign of the first big rain and meet at the gully, which made for an excellent splash pool when filled with water.

During a malaria outbreak in their area, Anil's parents wouldn't permit their children to romp around in pools of water where mosquitoes might gather. Anil remembered being ten or eleven years old, standing with his forehead pressed against the window, watching the torrential downpour and thinking it was the single most unfair pronouncement his parents could make. Three children died that year, including one infant. Anil never knew whether Leena had been allowed to play in the rains or not, whether she had waited there for him.

How had he and Leena ended up so far apart, after starting in the same place? He tried to make sense of the tangle of emotions rising within him, things he hadn't felt before, with Amber or anyone else.

❁

"THERE YOU are!" Piya was waiting on the porch when he returned. "I've been out here for ages looking for you. Ma's got lunch ready. God, brother, I can barely recognize you at a distance. Look at you, with your cool hairstyle, your fancy clothes."

Anil brushed a hand through his hair, which had grown longer than normal during the turmoil of the last few months. He glanced down at the electric blue athletic gear he'd worn this morning with the intention of going for a run and realized it was even worse than Mahesh had claimed. Not only was it impossible to truly belong in America, but he didn't fit in here anymore either. He was a dweller of two lands, accepted by none.

The Unbound Marriage

The next morning, Ma woke Anil hours before the arbitration session was to begin. She had become very particular about the rituals beforehand: allowing enough time for everyone in the house to take a purifying bath and do a *puja* together, ensuring Anil ate a proper meal with plenty of carrots and beets to sharpen his brain. There were a great many people coming today, Ma warned him, and the meeting would probably take several hours.

Throughout the morning discussions, the servant brought Anil fresh tea, and although he was already alert and no longer hungry, Anil kept a cup nearby to sip on. It gave him something to do while he listened to the argument between two neighbors over noisy chickens, followed by an uncle and nephew fighting over a new litter of goats. As he jotted down notes in his book, he came to notice that most of the disputes followed a pattern.

Many were about the division of resources: plots of land, the family home, a parental inheritance. In these cases, it was important for everyone to feel as if they were being treated fairly. The key was to identify something one party valued more than the other, and use that as a basis for dividing the property or, as Papa had often done, to find a creative solution. Anil was pleased about resolving one of the morning's disputes between two daughters over their late mother's diamond flower earrings, the ones she'd worn every day. He suggested they take the earrings to a jeweler and have them made into two pendants, which each daughter could wear on a chain near her heart, a daily reminder of their mother's love.

Other people came with interpersonal disagreements: between parent and child, husband and wife, siblings and neighbors. The incidence of quarrels among in-laws alone was enough to warn anyone off marriage for good. Anil always knew he was dealing with one of these disputes when the parties came to him for one issue, then raised complaints from several years, even decades, ago. A man in his twenties lashed out at his elder brother for failing to defend him on the cricket pitch when they'd been children. An elderly woman held a grudge against her daughter-in-law for not preparing a sufficiently elaborate meal after the wedding, twenty-some years earlier. How could people remember such things?

With his own memory limited to what he needed to know for current patients, Anil found this type of enduring recall remarkable. These arguments were rife with hurt feelings and deeply rooted emotion, and Anil had learned it was important to keep the discussion respectful and calm. He had to make sure each person felt truly heard by the other. When this transpired, there was usually enough latent love in the relationship for some reconciliation. Not all wounds could be mended, of course, and in those cases, Anil prescribed a way for the parties to get some distance from each other. He saw how feelings between people could easily shift from affection to spite, and was reminded of his conversation with Nikhil on the porch the previous day.

Finally, there were disputes arising from the recommendation of another counselor: the local astrologer, the ayurvedic doctor, or even the *vastu shastra* expert who advised people on how to arrange their homes in positive alignment with the universe's energy. These were the arbitrations Anil found the most intolerable; it was difficult to argue against some ethereal thing that had no factual basis. How he wanted to shake these people who sat before him, convinced that a case of arthritis had been caused by a northeastern-facing bedroom, or that diabetes could be treated effectively with bitter melon. It wasn't spiritual faith to which Anil was opposed—he'd seen such belief help people in the hospital, bringing them comfort when science had failed—it was superstition. He resented having to debate an argument when its inherent defect was so evident.

Two hours of arbitrations passed, and Anil was beginning to tire when the next group sat down at the long table. A buzz of whispers rose in the room as a young woman, her sari wrapped around her shoulders, sat on one side of the table, three men of varying ages by her side. On the other side was a young man, who stared down at the table, with an older couple next to him.

Anil assumed, from the way they avoided each other's eyes, it was the young woman and man who were in dispute. One of the three men spoke up first, introducing himself and the others as the father and brothers of the young woman. Anil watched her face as her brother spoke. She met Anil's eyes and held them. "What is your name?" he asked her, interrupting her brother.

"Brinda," she said in a clear voice.

Anil turned to the young man, fidgeting with the hem of his shirt. "And you?"

"Sanjay," he answered.

Anil laid his palms down on the table and spoke to the crowd gathered in the room. "Since it is almost midday, let us take a break for lunch and rest, and we will return here in two hours' time." He looked at his watch. "Two o'clock, okay?" He pushed the heavy chair back from the table and stood up.

Brinda's brother, the one who had spoken before, began to protest. Anil held up a hand. "Two o'clock, see you all then." His voice carried through the large room as people shuffled out the doors. Ma stood in the back corner, nodding to people on their way out.

Sanjay and his parents stood to leave, but Anil held up his hand to keep them in place. Once the room had cleared, he sat back down. "Brinda and Sanjay, I'd like you to be my guests for lunch," he said. "And your families, of course." He turned to Ma. "We will take our lunch here, please." She nodded and disappeared into the kitchen, where she could be heard barking instructions to the servants.

Anil leaned forward and spoke softly, obliging the others to lean in as well. "Brinda, it was your idea to come here today?" When the young woman nodded once, Anil said, "Very well, I'd like to hear from you first." He held up his palm to her brothers and father. "Don't worry, you will all have your say."

Brinda explained that she and her husband had been married for over a year and had not yet bound their marriage. In describing this, she used the Gujarati word meaning to tie something together, like a bundle of sticks, and Anil wasn't sure what she meant. Brinda read the ignorance in his eyes and tried another word, an English word. *Consummated.* The marriage had never been consummated. He and Brinda were the only two people in the room who knew the unambiguous meaning of that word. She had used the Gujarati euphemism to spare her husband embarrassment, and this told Anil a great deal.

"It is not a real marriage," Brinda said. "We discussed having children, a family, when the marriage was arranged. It is . . . important to the marriage . . . to me." Brinda's father and one of her brothers watched Anil carefully, ready to break in with their own grievances. The second brother stared across the table at Sanjay. Despite the linguistic differences, the air was thick with tension.

Ma burst into the room, two servants trailing behind her; they placed large *thalis* covered with colorful mounds of food in front of each guest. Anil noticed she had used the good silver *thalis*, the ones engraved with their family name and which she brought out for special guests and occasions. Anil smiled at her as she bustled about, breaking up the tension in the room.

Once the others began to eat, Anil leaned toward Sanjay and said quietly, "*Bhai*, come with me."

He climbed the stairs to the second story of the house and down the long corridor, Sanjay lagging a few steps behind. Anil stopped outside his bedroom and stood against one wall. He held out his hand for Sanjay to stand against the opposite wall. It was not much of a meeting room, but it would have to do. At least they were out of sight and earshot of the others.

"I need to ask you some questions, okay?" Anil said. "Personal questions."

Sanjay nodded, his eyes focused downward.

"*Bhai*, whatever you tell me will stay between us. No one else will know."

Sanjay nodded again. His eyes drifted upward and in them Anil saw a combination of shame and fear. Anil took a deep breath and began asking questions, the type of questions that no longer made him uncomfortable, about Sanjay's means of arousal and sexual history. He asked as a clinician, with empathy but without judgment.

Sanjay's shoulders relaxed and his hands unclenched as he explained how many times he'd tried and failed since his wedding night. When he'd heard enough to make a diagnosis, Anil reached out and placed a hand on Sanjay's shoulder. "It's not your fault, *bhai*."

But, like a water pipe that had finally burst and was gushing uncontrollably, Sanjay could not stop. The man had been torturing himself with speculative theories about his manhood, and punishing himself for the normal pleasuring activities he'd enjoyed as an adolescent boy. He had worked himself into a state of anxiety that would have impaired any man's ability to perform sexually. Finally, when Sanjay's well of penance was depleted, Anil repeated himself: "It's not your fault." He shook his head several times for emphasis. "Come with me."

Anil walked into his bedroom and slid his large suitcase out from under the bed. Crouching down on the floor, he rummaged through the plastic bag of medicine samples and first-aid supplies he'd brought with him, some as preventative measures for himself, others to leave behind for his family. He shuffled through the asthma inhalers, quinine for malaria, antidiarrheals, the sleeping pills for his flight home. In his preflight rush, he had thrown into his suitcase more drugs than he and his family could possibly use. Finally, he found the small blue pills he'd brought for one of his uncles, because of their lesser-known use in treating pulmonary hypertension. He counted out three sample packets and gave them to Sanjay, along with clear instructions. "Don't take more than one pill at a time. Come back tomorrow, tell me what happened, okay?"

After Sanjay, Brinda, and their respective families left the Big House, Anil sat alone at the head of the long wooden table while Ma reheated his lunch in the kitchen. He ran his palm over the lumpy knots in the wood and the indentations that marred its surface. Each one told the story of meals consumed, books studied, chess matches won and lost, and problems solved. For the first time, Anil understood why Papa had wanted him to play this role. Who else could have helped Sanjay like that today? Not even his father, who probably would have sent him to the astrologer or the ayurvedic doctor, with predictably bad results. Not even Papa.

22

After lunch, while the others in the Big House napped, Anil walked down the lane toward Leena's house. He found her on the terrace, sitting with her legs wrapped around the base of the large urn she'd shown him yesterday, sanding down the top edge with the rough side of a piece of palm bark. Her hand moved in quick, sharp movements in a single direction, sending off a fine white ceramic dust that coated her face and arms. She was unaware of his presence until she stopped sanding to cough from the dust.

"I wanted to thank you," Anil said, "for your help with my arbitrations this morning."

"Me?" She smiled, tilting her head to the side. "I didn't do anything."

But without her, Anil never would have thought to clear the room of spectators, to separate Sanjay from those in front of whom he couldn't speak openly. "Can I ask a favor? Can I borrow some of your bowls and cups?" Anil asked. "Not your good ones." He waved his hands at the rows of pieces in various states of completion on the terrace. "The ones from inside are fine."

Leena's face opened slowly to her gap-toothed smile, and her hand moved reflexively to cover her mouth. Anil wondered how she could be self-conscious about her appearance. He preferred the full smile that revealed her imperfectly spaced teeth; it was as if she were sharing all of herself when she smiled like that. She steadied the urn carefully on the balcony and stood up into a powdery cloud. With her hair dusted white, Anil had a glimpse of how she might look as an old woman. Still beautiful.

She retrieved a large serving *thali* from inside the house and filled it with ceramic pieces from the shelf, some of them noticeably damaged, others with their invisible flaws. "What is it all for?"

Anil smiled. "Come by the Big House in the morning."

❁

THE NEXT day, Anil awoke early on his own to the calls of the rooster and gradual warming of his bed sheets from the sun. After four days, his body had finally settled into the once-familiar routine of Panchanagar.

Downstairs at the breakfast table, his brothers were surprised to see him so early. Kiran and Chandu took a second cup of tea to sit with Anil while he ate breakfast, but Nikhil pushed his chair back from the table and announced he was heading out to the fields.

"Listen," Anil said to Nikhil, "if you have any field hands with injuries, send them up here on their break. I'll take care of them."

Nikhil raised one eyebrow, the rest of his facial expression remaining unchanged, then left.

❁

ANIL RETRIEVED the suitcase from under his bed and asked Piya to help him outside on the porch. Together, they cleared away all but two of the chairs and set out, in Leena's various clay dishes, the medical supplies: syringes, bandages, gauze, antibiotics, medicines, and disinfectants. Anil asked Ma for a few steel urns of boiled water and a stack of towels.

"Leena!" Piya called out, waving. Anil turned to see her walking toward the house.

"What's all this?" Leena stood at the bottom of the steps, surveying the transformation of the Big House porch into a makeshift medical clinic. She held a hand to her forehead to shield her eyes from the sun.

"We could use some help," Anil said, "if you want to stay." Before Leena could answer, someone began shouting his name. He turned around and saw a man running toward the Big House.

"Anil *bhai*! Anil *bhai*!" The man was waving both of his arms overhead as he ran. It was Sanjay, from yesterday's arbitration. He bounded up the porch steps two at a time and landed, breathless, a few feet from Anil. He put his palms together in *namaste* and bowed deeply, fell to the ground to touch Anil's feet, then jumped back up like a gymnast. "It worked, Anil *bhai*. It worked just like you said it would. I am a happy man. A very happy man." Sanjay beamed. He lowered his voice. "Brinda too, she is very, very happy."

Anil looked over Sanjay's shoulder to see Brinda walking toward them, carrying a bowl overflowing with coconut, fruit, and flowers. With her eyes averted in a shy smile, Brinda handed the bowl to Anil and went off with Leena, their arms wrapped around each other's waists.

"Anil *bhai*, do you have any more?" Sanjay pulled one of the empty sample packets from his pocket and waved it in front of him.

"Uh, yes," Anil said, stunned by the wholesale transformation of the man. He set down the enormous fruit bowl. "Let me go find some."

❁

Before they'd even finished setting up, the first field hand arrived, with a hand laceration that had become infected. Anil drained the pus from the wound, then showed Leena how to clean it with iodine, treat it with antibiotic ointment, and bandage it to prevent further contamination. More servants arrived from the field and neighboring homes, and within an hour there was a queue of people down the steps and into the clearing in front of the Big House. A familiar anxiety stirred up inside Anil; he felt a pressing need to move quickly through the line, but no one else seemed to feel the same way.

Anil examined the patients on one side of the porch; Leena assisted him when needed, and showed patients to the other side of the porch when they were ready to leave. Piya traveled up and down the queue, inquiring about people's ailments and moving the urgent ones to the front. Even Ma, who had initially been skeptical about relinquishing her towels, dispatched her servants to carry trays of water cups out to those waiting to be seen.

As lunchtime approached and passed, and Anil refused to take a break, Ma brought food outside and hounded them to eat something. Anil took a few bites when his stomach growled, glancing up after each patient to mark their progress against the human chain stretching down the lane.

In some ways, it felt oddly similar to his frenzied shifts in the Parkview ER. And yet, it was nothing like that. People waited patiently in line under the hot midday sun: the men draped white handkerchiefs atop their heads, while the women used the ends of their saris. The patients introduced themselves by explaining how they were connected to the Patel family: a distant cousin of Papa's sister's husband, a neighbor of one of the field servants, the elderly grandmother of one of Kiran's cricket teammates. Only after they had made the connection clear to Anil did they reveal their ailments. Often they thanked Anil, and God, before he'd done anything to treat them.

As the day wore on, Anil treated a field servant who had a broken rib from a donkey kick, two others suffering with seriously infected wounds, and six members of a neighboring family afflicted with what was probably a mild case of malaria, who took all the chloroquine Anil had brought with him. Anil and Leena worked until after his brothers came in from the fields, and once the sun went down, they kept working by the light of a single lantern. When the line had dwindled to a small handful of people, Piya joined Leena in bandaging up the minor wounds. They saw the last few patients after Ma had finished cooking the evening meal and everyone inside the Big House had begun to eat.

The sky was an inky blue, save for the glowing aura of the moon and a sprinkling of stars. Anil could barely make out Leena's face as they cleaned their hands and instruments in vessels of hot water. But in her dusky outline, he filled in the details from glimpses he'd stolen all day: the graceful arch of her eyebrows, the tiny gold stud on the side of her nose, the full lips that parted to reveal the gap between her teeth. She had smiled several times throughout the day, despite the strenuous work and heat. Perhaps she was becoming less conscious of it.

As Anil lay in bed that night, his body ached all over with pleasant weariness. After dinner, Nikhil had pulled him aside and thanked him for treating his men. "That was one of my best men, the one with the infected cut on his hand. With everything going on, I thought he was just complaining like the others, but he was in real pain. The look of relief on his face when he came back to the fields today . . ." Nikhil trailed off. He put a hand on Anil's shoulder. "Thank you, *bhai*."

Anil smiled as he remembered it, a satisfying exhaustion permeating him. It was only a few minutes before sleep overtook him.

THE NEXT morning, Piya knocked on Anil's bedroom door before poking her head inside. "Get up, get up, brother. Look outside."

Anil, feeling groggy, hoisted himself out of bed and walked over to the window. Five or six people were waiting in the clearing in front of the Big House. "Who are they?"

"One of the field servants—a man you helped yesterday—he came back with his wife and children. They all have fever. The baby's lips are chapped and flaky, she must be dehydrated."

Anil looked over at his little sister. How, when had she learned such things? He craned to look out the window. Three bicycles and a few more people were coming down the lane.

"You'd better get dressed, *bhai*," Piya said.

He reached for his clothes. "What about Leena?"

Piya, already out the door, called back over her shoulder, "I'm going to get her."

WORD HAD spread across the village; throughout the day, people in need of medical attention continued to flock to the Big House. They came alone and in groups; by foot, scooter, and bicycle. They brought straw mats on which to sit, and tiffins of food to see them through the long hours of waiting. With the assistance of Leena and Piya, Anil set the broken wrist of a young woman, removed a ball of ear wax the size of a grape from an elderly man, and treated a blacksmith with a severely burned hand. They kept going until their medical supplies were depleted, and even then, some people refused to leave, believing Anil could perform some miracle of healing without so much as a cotton ball.

After the crowd finally began to dissipate, Piya walked toward him, holding the hand of a five- or six-year-old girl. Anil watched the girl's face as Piya explained that she had severe pain in one of her molars. Anil glared at his sister. She knew he couldn't do anything about tooth pain. But the girl's eyes were welling with tears. Anil knelt down and asked her to open her mouth. There was no swelling of the gum, no visible infection or decay.

"We could try a clove," Piya offered. "I remember Ma doing that when I was little."

Anil shrugged, having nothing else to offer. Piya went inside the house and returned with a small handful of dried cloves. She picked one out, placed it inside the girl's mouth atop her molar, and told her to bite down. The little girl did as instructed, a tear spilling out of her eye. "Keep chewing on it, okay? Don't eat it, spit it out. Then take another one." Piya held the girl's palm in hers and poured the rest of the cloves into it.

"Where are her parents?" Anil asked.

Piya pointed to a couple standing next to a coconut tree, some twenty meters away. "Untouchables," she said. They were standing at a distance out of respect for the Patel family's higher caste. Another difference from Parkview, where anyone could walk into the ER to receive treatment, and quite often berate him as he provided it.

Anil touched the girl's head as he walked past her and she looked up at him, chewing vigorously with a smile on her face. Her parents greeted him with folded hands but did not touch him. He explained that their daughter likely had a cavity in her molar and needed to see a dentist in town. In the meantime, the cloves would provide some temporary relief from the pain she was suffering. He took several hundred-rupee bills out of his pocket and pressed them into the father's hand.

"Bring some fresh coconut water for these people," Anil shouted to the nearest field hand. "Quickly!" he added when the boy hesitated, prompting him to scramble up the nearest tree. The girl's father smiled and pressed his palms together in appreciation. Piya brought the child back over to her parents, then went inside to appease Ma, whose calls from within the house were growing louder.

Anil turned back toward the porch. He'd been able to treat many, but not all, of those who'd come—not those who needed surgery or more acute care, and these were the ones who stayed in his mind. There was a diabetic woman who'd developed a foot ulcer from poor blood supply. He'd treated and dressed her wound, but what she really needed was antibiotics, ongoing care, and insulin to control her diabetes. There was the little boy born without an ear, whose parents had been taking him to every temple within fifty kilometers to try to rid him of what they believed were evil spirits; Anil explained that their son suffered from microtia, a congenital deformity unrelated to spirits or demons. They looked hopeful for a moment, until Anil explained there was nothing he could do to help the little boy, whose condition required surgery.

It was the plight of being a doctor, Anil now understood. He would never stop thinking of those he couldn't save.

He and Leena cleaned up outside, using the pump. Anil hoisted the iron handle up and down, and Leena held her sari out of the way to wash her feet. Anil saw the skin above one of her ankles was severely contracted and mottled with red. The scar, from what must have been a second-degree burn, extended up her calf and disappeared beneath her sari. He blinked rapidly to clear his vision and looked up at Leena's face. Her eyes turned away quickly, and she dropped her sari to the wet ground and stepped backwards. "Your turn," she said, offering to take the pump handle.

"W-will you stay for dinner?" he asked. "You're welcome to bring your mother."

"Thank you, but she prefers to eat at home," Leena said. "I should go."

Anil took a step after her. "You . . . you were a big help. Thank you. I'll bring your things back tomorrow." Leena smiled and brushed a strand of hair away before turning to leave. Anil watched her walk down the path, recalling Piya's question about burn treatments months earlier.

MINA PATEL stood at the window inside the gathering room, watching Anil clean his hands at the outdoor pump. He could easily have come inside to wash up, but he stayed out there because of Leena, who was now walking down the lane, the breeze lifting her sari behind her. A discomfort brewed inside Mina, edging out the pride she'd felt earlier in the day. How quickly her emotions could shift these days, without her husband's rocklike presence at the center of her world.

Yesterday had been one of the best days she'd had since Jayant had passed away. All of her children were around, in relative harmony with one another. Anil had shown great wisdom in managing some very complicated disputes. He'd begun to understand, as his father had, that he couldn't solve a problem without understanding the people behind it, the dynamic of the family and the community. Jayant would have been proud to see Anil stepping into the role he'd always wanted for his son: healing ailments, both physical and unseen, in their community.

But that was yesterday. Today, Mina had to look on while her son watched that girl walk down the lane, without any understanding of where she'd come from.

Mina should have intervened earlier, as soon as she saw Leena here, helping Anil with his medical clinic. But she didn't want to be inhospitable to a friend of Piya's, and in some corner of her heart, Mina took pity on the girl.

She stepped outside and approached Anil at the well, where he was drying off. "Son, I need to speak with you," she said. "I don't know what's going on, but it's not right for you to be so friendly with Leena. It's one thing for Piya, she's a girl. But with you . . . it doesn't look good. There are things you don't know—"

Anil interrupted, holding his palm up. "I know about the marriage, Ma, if that's what you mean."

"You *don't* know, Anil, the kind of girl she is—the kind who would betray not only her husband and parents but yours as well. She let us down, Papa and I, after everything we did for her." Mina drew in a deep breath and told him the whole story.

SOON AFTER Anil had left for America, Leena's parents came to the Big House on the last Sunday of the month, the day Jayant usually conducted arbitrations for the villagers. Although Nirmala and her husband were neighbors to the Patels, their interactions had been limited. As the Memsahib of the Moti Patel clan, Mina couldn't be on familiar terms with everyone. Jayant had had more contact with Pradip, on occasions when they both sold their crops at the market in town. Jayant said he was honest and hardworking, and he seemed to have a fondness for the man.

Leena's parents had come to the gathering room on previous occasions but only to observe, so Mina was surprised to see them step forward for help that day. When Jayant greeted the man like an old friend, Mina knew her husband would be inclined to help him whatever the need. They wanted to marry off their daughter, but the only boy they could find was from a more prosperous family, one who rightfully wanted a greater dowry than Leena's parents had offered. Nirmala and her husband were at odds over whether to accept the proposal and take on the debt of a larger dowry.

"She is my only daughter, Sahib," Leena's father had said. "Naturally,

I want the best for her. So what if it costs me more?" His wife was fearful of going to the moneylender, who had a reputation for unsavory practices and usurious rates. Nirmala was small-minded about money matters, as Mina had observed some women were, accustomed to managing household budgets with a tight fist. She had learned from Jayant that improving their farm yields or earning more for superior crops was better than counting grains of rice. Even so, in Mina's mind, her husband was often overly generous with others.

Jayant listened patiently to both Nirmala's concern about the financial burden, and Pradip's worry over his daughter's future. Here, Mina recalled her husband digressing into his beliefs about the dowry system. As Jayant pointed out, although the practice had been banned by the government decades ago, he could not think of a marriage that had taken place without some kind of gift from the bride's parents. The very silver *thalis* on which he enjoyed special meals, with the Patel name and their wedding date hand-engraved in tiny Gujarati script around the edge, had been a gift from Mina's parents. The dowry used to be a well-intentioned practice, meant to bolster the economic security of girls at the start of their married life. It was a shame the way the original purpose of the dowry had become twisted through the years, Jayant explained—the way some greedy families appropriated resources intended for the bride.

Leena's parents waited patiently during this discourse. Even before Jayant delivered his opinion, Mina knew what he would say. Her husband had made clear his disdain for moneylenders. People often came to him with financial troubles, and he'd seen many of them fall prey to the threats and violence of those swindlers. As Mina expected, Jayant said he wanted Nirmala and Pradip to provide the best for their daughter without having to worry. He would loan them the additional money himself, without interest. It was not a small sum either—fifty thousand rupees would take several years to pay off. Leena's parents were appreciative, rightfully so. Her father even offered the Patels the most honored seats at the wedding.

MINA TASTED a sour acid in her mouth when she'd finished the story. In the impending night, a guard dog began to bark in the distance. "So you see, son, we've done a great deal for them, for Leena. More than most people would do. Without our generosity, her wedding would not have been possible. Because of your father, that girl got a better marriage than her parents could afford." The emotions were now stirred up within Mina, her heart aching anew at the loss of her husband.

"But Leena did not honor that generosity. She brought shame on her parents and spat on our kindness." Mina did not need to say more. Her son knew what it meant for a woman to be put out of her marital home, for a marriage to end in disgrace. It was a stain that girl would carry for the rest of her life, but one Mina would not allow to spread to her own family.

ANIL FELT his mother watching him carefully for a reaction. He replaced the bucket under the well and slowly toweled off his arms and feet, anger swelling inside.

"I just want you to be careful, Anil," Ma said. "For your own good. When you come back next year, we'll begin looking for a girl. I've already been getting inquiries."

"Well, Ma, you won't need to worry about that," Anil said.

"Good." She patted his arm. "I knew you'd understand."

"No, *you* don't understand." The words he'd been deliberating over came tumbling out. "I'm not coming back next year. I'm applying for a fellowship in interventional cardiology. If I get a spot, and I hope I do, I'll be there for five more years."

Anil disregarded the look of alarm on his mother's face; perhaps he even took some small pleasure in it. He explained the specialty and its advanced technology in enough detail to overwhelm her, to quell her forthcoming questions. He described the new research project he was undertaking—omitting that he still needed to find a sponsor, one of the many things that had slipped after the attack on Baldev, and resolving to redouble his efforts when he returned. "Don't you see, Ma? This kind of medicine would have saved Papa's life," Anil said. "He would have wanted me to do this."

Ma shook her head slowly. "Don't tell me what your father would have wanted. Your father was a great man. If he were still here, none of this would be happening." She waved her arm through the air. "I don't know what's happened to you, Anil. I don't know who you are anymore. I've done everything for you, and now you're doing this? You can't just rewrite the past to suit yourself." Ma turned abruptly and climbed the porch steps.

Anil exhaled deeply, feeling a strange relief at hearing his mother verbalize his own sense of guilt. When he closed his eyes, he pictured Papa at the head of the table in the gathering room, adjudicating the matter of Leena's marriage. Even after he opened them, the idea continued to haunt him.

❀

TWO DAYS later, Leena sat on the floor of the drawing room, replacing the misshapen pottery pieces on the shelf. She traced the rim of a cracked drinking cup that had held cotton balls; she balanced the wobbly bowl they'd used for discarded syringes. Pieces deemed futile had nonetheless found purpose. Over the last few days, she'd seen people from all over Panchanagar and beyond, many of them for the first time since she'd gotten married. If she'd stopped to think before climbing those steps to the Big House's porch, she might have worried about facing them. But none of the villagers she treated at the medical clinic had shown signs of disapproval. It was something Leena had noticed about people who were suffering: their vulnerability seemed to make them more caring—or perhaps just less concerned—about the circumstances of others.

Anil had helped her gain back some measure of respect. He hadn't shunned her after learning about her marriage, yet it was clear he didn't know everything. Piya had kept her word and told no one, not even her brother. Leena knew there was a risk in telling him now, but he deserved to know the truth. She settled onto her bed, her knees folded in front of her and her notepad resting on top of them, and she began to write.

❁

NIRMALA WALKED past Leena's room, watching her daughter from the corner of her eye. She could tell Leena was crying, though she never made any sound when she did; it was the way her daughter pressed her fingertips to the outer corners of her eyes, as if her *kajal* were smudged. It pained her to see her daughter without any of the joy and spirit a young person should possess. Leena deserved happiness, but she wouldn't find it with Anil Patel. That boy was no good for her, not even as a friend, as Leena insisted he was. There were things about that family Leena didn't know, and which Nirmala had resolved never to tell her.

The Patels had gladly participated in the arrangement of her marriage, accepted credit for their role, then turned their backs once the marriage went bad. When Nirmala had gone to Mina to beg for mercy from the crushing burden of their debt after the extortion began, the woman had refused to see her—sending her son out in her place. Nirmala had brought her most precious sari as an offering—to appeal, one mother to another, for the well-being of her only child. And Mina Patel had handed her heartbreak over to a mere boy. The humiliation of it stung to this day. But there was no need to burden Leena with this ugly truth; the girl had suffered more pain in the last few years than many adults did in a lifetime. Nirmala had wiped the tears from her daughter's face, had treated her injuries until they healed. Now she was afraid this Patel boy was opening those wounds all over again.

23

For the first time, when Anil landed at DFW airport in late July, no one was there to receive him. Baldev was still recovering in the hospital; Mahesh was unable to leave work. And his time with Amber now felt like a hundred years away, in another lifetime when they were both much younger. Still, Anil scanned the watchful waiting crowd at the airport. He felt a yearning he hadn't experienced since leaving Dallas. As he anticipated the empty evenings and lonely bed ahead of him, the loss was palpable; he was overcome with the thought of being alone again. But this is the way it would have been, he realized now, if he and Amber had tried to build a life together—the two of them alone in the world, without her family, without his. It was a life he could no longer imagine.

Anil stepped outside into the blinding sun. Even the heat was different in Texas, its own phenomenon, unrelenting from early May through late September. Not that anyone spent much time outside in the Dallas summer: they all scurried between their air-conditioned homes, cars, and offices. Playgrounds and fields stood largely empty as families flocked to well-chilled shopping malls and movie theaters.

Anil was accustomed to hot weather in India, but that was heat of a different nature. In Panchanagar, the early mornings were cool and the ground was coated with dew. Later in the day, occasional breezes rustled through the palm and coconut trees. And on the hottest days of late summer, the skies broke open with monsoon rains, drenching the parched land along with anyone caught outside. In India when the heat was unbearable, relief usually came through nature, or people retreated to their beds for long afternoon naps. In Texas, nobody waited for nature to deliver such relief; they produced it themselves with small armies of air-conditioning units outside every building. In July, the hospital was so cold, Anil often had to wear a sweater under his white coat.

ANIL WANDERED through the empty apartment, expecting to find something changed in his absence, which felt much longer than ten days. The kitchen counters were bare, and only two teacups stood in the draining rack. The fridge held a single carton of milk, past its expiration date. There were none of the usual plastic tubs filled with leftovers of Mahesh's vegetable curries. Anil hoped the man wasn't starving himself out of guilt.

Baldev's room looked chaste without the Bollywood starlet posters. His parents had returned to Houston a week ago, after his surgeries were complete and he'd been transferred to the rehabilitation ward. They had to get back to the gas station they owned, which had been operating in their absence under the watch of employees they didn't fully trust. They couldn't afford to stay away any longer, particularly with the medical bills they now faced for Baldev's hospital stay. Anil thought of his friend in the ward reserved for those with the most broken bodies, those who needed additional time and help to heal. He felt the impulse to leave the apartment—his suitcase still standing at the front door, his body stiff from the journey—and drive straight to the hospital to see his friend. But then he pictured Baldev's limbs in casts, his face bruised, his eyes unavoidable, and Anil decided to wait until morning, when he was due at the hospital for his shift.

Anil unpacked his suitcase and retrieved from one of the outer pockets the prescription bottle containing chai masala powder that Ma had pressed into his hand before he left. His mother never wasted anything: the bottle had once held beta-blockers Anil had brought back from Ahmadabad to treat Papa's angina.

The first sip of Ma's chai always reminded Anil he was home, and he longed for some now. On this visit, he'd followed her into the kitchen, watching how she crushed a nub of gingerroot and tore fresh mint leaves into the simmering milky liquid, sometimes adding lemongrass or cloves. He opened the bottle to take a sniff. How could this dusty beige powder possibly deliver the flavor he craved?

As he waited for the milk to simmer, Anil looked around his living space. It was drab and lifeless, its beige walls, blinds, and carpets all merging into a single undistinguished backdrop for their scant furnishings. A temporary home. Anil spooned tea leaves and a sprinkling of masala into the pot, and while he waited for the color to take hold, he looked at the prescription bottle. How strange to be holding this same bottle bearing his father's name, now across the ocean and filled with spices ground by his mother in the brass mortar that had belonged to his grandmother.

He pulled a teacup out of the kitchen cabinet and examined it. The cup was clearly made by machine, smooth and identical to the three others in the cupboard. It was perfect, not beautiful. It did not have the thin ridges imprinted by Leena's fingertip, the small swirl at the bottom, the evidence of her hands, her touch. He closed his eyes, felt himself sitting so close to her, he could smell the jasmine woven into her hair. The person Ma had portrayed—the one who had walked out on her marriage and dishonored his father's generosity—was not the same woman who had shown him her flawed work and helped him bandage wounds at the Big House, nor the brave girl he remembered from childhood. Anil was troubled by the thought of Papa's involvement in Leena's marriage; he could not stop speculating about what his father had known. And he could not stop thinking of Leena.

He imagined her now, sitting on her terrace, molding lumps of clay into beauty. How would it feel to create magic with your hands, to experience the power of your craft? Was it even possible for him? Anil didn't measure his mistakes in misshapen pots but in death certificates and weeping relatives, in the pained, desperate eyes of a patient he was unable to help.

Medicine had once seemed like a noble profession, but most of the time it was messy and imperfect. Anil had not anticipated the interplay of power between doctors, or the reality that some patients inspired him to give his best and others, he could now admit, did not. He had not imagined the guilt he would carry from making a bad judgment call that could never be undone.

Those days he had spent treating patients in Panchanagar were tiring but ultimately satisfying. But was it better than the work he did at Parkview? Did he belong where he could strive to do his best, or where he could do the most good?

When the tea was ready, Anil took his first sip standing there in the kitchen. It wasn't as richly flavored as Ma's chai, but it wasn't too bad either. He couldn't detect any mint, but he clearly tasted cardamom and cinnamon. Some elements survived the journey better than others.

The tea stirred his appetite, and Anil realized he was ravenous. He checked the fridge again, then the freezer. Even the kitchen cabinet was depleted of its usual supply of canned chickpeas.

Anil returned from the Indian grocery store with a half-dozen boxed dinners, a tub of yogurt, and fresh onions, tomatoes, cilantro, and limes for a salad. On impulse, he'd also bought a bag of frozen samosas and a quarter pound of freshly made sweets. He called to let Mahesh know he was preparing dinner, then went to check the mail. Resuming this habit felt like a small but necessary step. Their box was crammed full, including three large brown envelopes addressed to Mahesh and adorned with Indian postage. Anil smiled, realizing that Mahesh's future wife might be awaiting discovery in one of these packages. He took the envelopes to Mahesh's room, where the desk held a neat stack of similar envelopes, at least seven or eight of them, all unopened. Anil added the new envelopes to the pile and pulled the door closed behind him.

❁

"THAT IS a lot of food." Mahesh surveyed the dishes Anil had spread out over their dinette table. "You got used to eating like a king back home?"

"Too much?" Anil said. Undoubtedly it was, for just the two of them. He reached for the radio. It was quiet without Baldev. "Maybe I should go next door and see if Amber wants to join us?" He'd thought about knocking on her door since coming home, just to see how she was.

"*Bhai* . . ." Mahesh hesitated. "She came by to tell you herself, but you'd already left for India." He wrapped his fingers around the top of a chair. "Amber moved out."

Anil pulled out another chair and sat down. "Oh."

"She wanted you to know it had nothing to do with you," Mahesh continued. "It was them . . . those guys."

"Did they bother her again?" Anil asked.

Mahesh shook his head. "She said she just couldn't live here anymore. She felt like it was her fault, what happened to Baldev. Which it wasn't, of course. I tried to tell her . . ."

Anil nodded. The infection of guilt had spread farther than he knew.

"She has a roommate now, and a security guard at the gate where she lives. *Bhai*, you okay?" Mahesh asked him in Gujarati.

Anil served himself *matar paneer* and handed the plastic tray to Mahesh, who was still standing, watching him. "Yes, fine," he said, trying to end the discussion. He reached for the tub of yogurt. "Speaking of love interests," he shifted gears, "you got a few packages in the mail today. I left them on your desk."

Mahesh sat down and served himself some rice. "Okay."

"Any interesting prospects? Have you found the future Mrs. Shah yet?"

Mahesh shook his head, scooping up rice and curry with his fingertips. "I haven't had time to look, I've been so busy at work. We have a big release coming up next month—they've just put another development team on it. Now we have eight people working on it, but it'll still be a stretch to hit the release date."

"Another team? You have to manage all those people?" Anil asked. Mahesh preferred to work alone; his anxiety level correlated with the number of colleague interactions he had.

Mahesh added another dollop of yogurt to his plate and mixed it with the rice. Unlike anyone else Anil knew, Mahesh always finished off his Indian meals with a few tablespoons of rice and tart yogurt, like some unsweetened pudding. Mahesh shook his head again. "The other team has its own leader, so we coordinate with each other."

"I guess I did make too much food," Anil said, taking in all the dishes left on the table. "You want to take it for lunch tomorrow?"

"No, that's okay," Mahesh said. "We've been going to this place near the office, Dosa Palace. Really good; I'll take you there some time."

"Since when do you go out for lunch?" Anil asked. "I thought you didn't like to leave your desk. And who's we?"

"Just . . . Yaalini," Mahesh said. "She's the other team leader."

"Yaalini?" Anil smiled. "Really?"

Mahesh shook his head. "Nah, it's not like that. We have nothing in common. She's from Tamil Nadu, she speaks Telugu. It's just work." He stood up and carried his plate to the kitchen. "Hey, why don't we take this stuff to Baldev in the morning? He's always complaining about the hospital food."

❁

PARKVIEW'S REHABILITATION ward was in the east building, on the opposite side of the hospital complex from where Anil usually worked. Patients stayed there for anywhere from a week to a few months, until they regained enough mobility to be at home. The rehab ward had a different layout from the others. Across from the elevators was an enormous open room, covered with floor mats and equipment. Sunlight streamed into the space through long vertical windows lining the outer wall. And notably, the cinder-block walls here were painted a cheery yellow rather than the drab pastels elsewhere in the hospital. It was the most hopeful space at Parkview. Although these patients were badly injured, they all had the capacity to get better. That knowledge alone must have been reassuring: rather than teetering on the edge of death or severe illness, they could move slowly toward progress.

In his room, Baldev was sitting up in bed, holding the remote control at an awkward angle toward the television. "Anyone want a samosa?" Anil asked, holding up a plastic bag as he entered.

"Hey, Anil—welcome home, man." Baldev dropped the remote in his lap and reached out his good arm. The bruises on his face had turned to a lighter olive green, and only the deepest lacerations were still visible. Both his casts had been removed, though his right arm remained in a sling. He'd made tremendous improvement in the past couple of weeks.

"You look good, man." Anil took Baldev's hand and gave it a gentle slap. Mahesh pulled two chairs over and they sat next to the bed.

"I feel good," Baldev said. "Starting to get my strength back, you know?" He held up his arm in a weightlifter's pose. "I'll be back causing trouble in no time."

"Oh, he's already causing trouble." A female voice came from the doorway, and Anil turned to see a young woman dressed in deep-purple scrubs. She had a fringe of sandy-brown hair across her forehead, and the rest was held back in a ponytail. "Mahesh, good to see you." She touched Mahesh on the shoulder. "And you must be Anil." She smiled at him. "Or should I call you Dr. Patel?" She indicated the badge clipped to his white coat.

"Oh no, Anil's fine." There was a tiny diamond stud on the left side of the woman's nose. She was pretty in that natural way of girls in soap commercials, all glowing skin and bright eyes.

"Well, it's a pleasure to finally meet you. I'm Trinity," she said, extending her hand. "Baldev's physical therapist."

"Good to meet you too." Anil shook her hand, noting she'd pronounced all three of their names correctly.

"And how's my second-favorite patient feeling today?" She walked over to the far side of Baldev's bed and stood back to assess him.

"What?" Baldev threw his good arm up in the air. "I got bumped down again?"

"Sorry," Trinity said. "But until Mr. Naderi goes home, I have no choice." She winked at Anil and Mahesh. "His wife brings me baklava. I have a weakness."

"Understandable," Anil grinned. "Frankly, I'm surprised Baldev is even in second place."

"Oh, come on, don't gang up on me." Baldev slapped Anil's knee. "Now, hand over that samosa, will you? I'm starving for decent food in this place."

"Samosa?" Trinity said.

"Yes, and if you're very good to me, I might let you have one." Baldev reached inside the greasy bag.

"Well, you better build up your energy, Mr. Kapoor, because I have a serious regimen in store for you today. I'll be back for you in an hour, okay?" Trinity headed toward the door. "And don't forget to save me some chutney," she called over her shoulder.

After Trinity left the room, Baldev grinned as he chewed. "I think she likes her men spicy too, if you know what I mean." He moved his eyebrows up and down, and with that single gesture, Anil recognized his friend again.

24

After the mornings turned chilly and the trees had dropped their leaves into great piles of ocher and crimson, Anil was assigned to an elective rotation in Oncology. The Oncology ward was populated by chronically ill patients: the nineteen-year-old student whose brain tumor resisted radiation, the young mother whose bilateral mastectomies rendered her unable to hold her toddler, the businessman diagnosed with advanced colon cancer the year he finally retired. The few good stories were quickly usurped by the hopeless ones. It was also Anil's first chance to work alongside Sonia Mehta again since the death of Jason Calhoun during his ICU rotation, and he was eager to redeem himself.

"Mrs. Templeton," Anil said, entering a patient's room. "How are you feeling today?"

"Good, doctor, but please call me Marilyn." The patient, an older woman in her seventies, smiled brightly at him. Her short gray hair was growing back after her second round of chemotherapy for breast cancer. "'Mrs. Templeton' makes me feel old," she whispered.

Anil smiled. "Okay then, Marilyn. How's your appetite today?"

"Oh, fine," she said. "Isn't the snow beautiful?" She gestured at the fluffy white flakes falling outside. "So nice to have a window room."

Anil followed her gaze outside. It had started to snow during the night while he slept. On his drive to work, the radio broadcasts had been full of school closures and traffic warnings. No one was prepared for snowfall in Texas except the emergency room, which already had seen a sharp increase in injuries from motor vehicle accidents. It was the first time Anil had ever seen snow. "Yes," he agreed with Mrs. Templeton. "It is beautiful." He glanced around her room and noticed her lunch tray untouched. "Did you eat breakfast this morning?"

"Oh, well, I didn't really feel like eating today. I'm not one to complain, doctor, but the food here isn't very tempting, you know?"

Anil checked her chart. "Looks like you haven't been eating much the last few days."

"I'm sorry, doctor." Marilyn looked remorseful. "I tried. It's just that nothing tastes quite right." She was a small woman with a sturdy frame and a soft drawl that reminded him of sitar music. Even her negative words landed softly.

Anil gestured to the lunch tray. "Well, I'd like you to try to eat something so you can keep up your strength. I'd rather not have to put you on an IV." He noted her thin arms and barely visible veins. "I'll be back to check on you later this afternoon, Mrs. Templeton."

"Marilyn!" she called out as he left the room.

ANIL FOUND Sonia at the nurses' station. "I'd like to get a CT scan for Mrs. Templeton," he said. "She's three months out of chemo for stage-two breast cancer, and I think she may be having some new neurological symptoms."

"You think?" Sonia asked as she wrote in a chart.

"Loss of taste sensation. She hasn't eaten a meal in days, just sips juice through a straw."

Sonia looked up at him. "Have you done the neuro exam yet?"

"No," Anil said. "I thought I'd do the scan first."

Sonia collected her papers and began walking down the corridor. "Why?"

Anil scrambled to catch up. *Why? Because we always scan first.* "It's faster, more accurate." In more than two years at Parkview, no one had ever questioned the diagnostic superiority of a CT scan.

"See if you can figure it out on your own first, Patel," Sonia said. "Do a complete neuro exam—all five components, no shortcuts—to determine if and where there's a lesion. Then you can do a CT to confirm."

"But that'll take an hour, and I still have eight patients—"

"At least an hour, if you do it right," Sonia interrupted. "And not enough physicians are skilled at doing it right." She lodged a pencil behind her ear. "Don't look so glum, Patel, you'll still get your scan. I just want you to have an opinion first. And if you're right," she called over her shoulder as she walked away, "I'll buy lunch."

ANIL HADN'T done a full neurological examination since practicing on a classmate in medical school. He started with the cranial nerve section, testing Marilyn's sense of smell, vision, and eye movements, all of which appeared normal. He went on to assess the sensory functions of her face, stopping when she didn't seem to feel the sharp end of a cotton swab he touched to her left jaw. He repeated the test, with the same result. She also had trouble moving her jaw from side to side. Although she didn't appear to have any facial asymmetry, Anil went through the steps of testing every facial nerve for dysfunction. He tested her hearing and her gag reflex, and the mobility of her tongue.

Marilyn was an agreeable patient, cooperating as Anil progressed through the lengthy sensory and motor examination, testing the reflexes in her feet, ankles, knees, and arms, and finally evaluating her coordination and walking gait. "Honestly, doctor, if I knew I'd be putting you through all this, I would've eaten the tuna sandwich." Marilyn smiled, her eyes twinkling. Anil had a hollow feeling in his stomach when he left her room.

He found Sonia in the break room. "I think she has a lesion between the mandibular branch of CN5 and CN7," he said. "It must be small because she hasn't lost any facial nerve function, just the taste sensation on the anterior of the tongue, and some motor function in the masseter. Everything else on the neuro exam had a normal finding, so I think it's localized to that one site. Likely metastasis from the breast cancer."

"Okay, Patel," Sonia said. "Go do the scan and see if you're right."

When Anil returned with the CT scan, it showed a pea-sized lesion between the fifth and seventh cranial nerves. Sonia handed the scan back to him. "Good work, Patel. Call her oncologist, then let's go." She clipped her pager onto her belt. "I'm hungry."

"For someone who enjoys being right, you certainly are morose, Patel." Sonia sat across the cafeteria table from him. They'd both chosen the grilled-cheese platter, but Sonia's was largely finished while Anil's remained on his plate.

"I wish I were wrong in this case." Anil said. "What a depressing specialty. Everybody's dying."

"Everybody's dying anyway." Sonia reached over and took a few of his french fries.

"Oncology just seems so hopeless. At least in cardiology you can do something to help most people get better—stents, angioplasty." Anil stabbed at a thick slice of cucumber, breaking his plastic fork.

"Cardiology?" Sonia asked.

Anil nodded. "I decided to apply for a fellowship in interventional cardio. You think I have a shot?"

"Honestly, I don't know, Patel," Sonia said. "But you should think about whether that's the right specialty for you. Is it the best use of your skills? Is that how you want to help people? I know it's easy to get seduced by all the technology we have here, but look at what you did today." She leaned across the table. "You diagnosed a brain tumor using only your eyes and hands."

"CT scan would have been faster," Anil said. "Why'd you have me do it that way, anyhow?"

Sonia shrugged and sat back against the bench seat. "When I was a junior resident, a huge tornado struck Dallas. Power went out all over the city. The hospital was running on backup generators, but we were told not to overload Radiology with nonurgent cases. So I had to rely on all the skills I had systematically unlearned my first year here." She shook her head. "I found a peripheral nerve dysfunction in a chronic diabetic patient that day. I don't know who was more surprised, me or my attending." She drained her glass of iced tea. "The thorough physical exam is a lost art, Patel, but done properly, you can diagnose more than you'd think."

"So why this case, today? You think this snow's going to take down the power grid?" Anil nodded toward the window.

"I don't take bullets from the firing squad for just anybody," Sonia said. Anil stared at her, not comprehending. "You've got your flaws, Patel, that's for damn sure. But you've also got the potential to be more than just a technician, which is what most of your peers will be. I know you've got a chip on your shoulder, coming here from India, but at least you learned how to perform a full physical exam, since you didn't have a scanner on every ward." She chewed on a crust of her sandwich. "Patients always want a solution and we like to feel invincible, but medicine is not a perfect science. If you want to be a truly great physician, you've got to learn the art as well."

Anil's pager buzzed in his pocket. He glanced down at it and let out a deep breath. "Her oncologist is here. God, I really wish there was something else we could do for her. She's such a sweet old lady. The last round of chemo really wore her down, and now we have to ask her to go through it all again."

"Well, maybe you shouldn't ask her." Sonia stood up, carrying her tray. "Maybe that's not the right question."

"What do you mean?" Anil followed her, taking half his grilled-cheese sandwich with him. An elevator ride had become an adequate length of time to consume a meal. "Isn't that the best course of treatment for this kind of metastasis?"

"This is a woman who's been living with a terminal illness for years. You can ask her if she's thought about how she'd like to spend her remaining time," Sonia said. "You might get a different answer."

LATER THAT afternoon, Anil sat with Marilyn Templeton while her oncologist explained that the cancer had metastasized to her brain. He showed her the CT scan and presented her with treatment options, recommending she start a third round of chemotherapy immediately. Before leaving the hospital for the night, Anil returned to Marilyn's room and found her sitting by the window, staring outside. The snow had stopped falling, and what remained on the streets was a slushy mess.

Marilyn's dinner tray remained covered. Anil handed her the bottle of juice he'd brought and sat down in a chair next to her. "Marilyn," he said deliberately, and she smiled. "What do you think about the options Dr. Heasley laid out?"

Marilyn stirred her juice with the straw. "I don't want to disappoint anyone—my family, friends. Even Dr. Heasley—he's been so supportive over the past two years. Such a *smart* man. You know he has three boys?"

Anil smiled, waiting for her to continue.

Marilyn sighed. "I've been fortunate. Two kids, five grandkids, a wonderful husband—God rest his soul." She made the sign of the cross on her chest. "This"—she gestured around the hospital room—"isn't really living to me. I can't enjoy my garden or help out at church. I've had a good life. It's inevitable now, isn't it?" Her voice caught on the words. "It's all up to God now."

Anil hesitated before nodding. Even the most spiritual of his patients rarely wanted to discuss it, but in her case, the end was inevitable. "Yes, now it's a matter of the time you have left. But you can choose how to spend it." He reached over and held up the juice bottle, encouraging her to take a sip.

Marilyn looked out the window. "Everybody wants me to fight. They say I'm a fighter." She turned back to Anil. "But you've got to decide what's worth fighting for, right?"

❁

MARILYN SPENT three more days on the oncology ward, and Anil went to see her each evening before he went home, sometimes staying for an hour while she tried to get down some of her dinner. They discussed God and heaven. She was a devoted Catholic, but she asked Anil about the Hindu belief in reincarnation. "If it were me, I'd like to come back as a bird of some sort, maybe an eagle," she told Anil as she fingered rosary beads. "Wouldn't it be lovely to fly, to see the whole world from up there?"

Another evening Marilyn asked, "Are you married, Dr. Patel?"

He shook his head.

"Girlfriend?"

Anil shook his head again, thinking of his mother's reminders to begin looking for a wife. Marilyn's question felt different somehow. As she rested her head back against the thin hospital pillow and gazed out to some point over Anil's shoulder, Marilyn said, "My husband wrote me a poem every year on our anniversary. The first one was simple: *Roses are red, violets are blue. You love me, and I love you.*" She smiled and shook her head. "He said he didn't know what else to get me the first year, since it was our paper anniversary, but then it became a tradition. Every year, no matter what other gift he bought, there was always a poem with it." She laughed. "He got better at it too. The year our daughter was born, he wrote a limerick:

There once was a lady from Dallas,
Who no one would ever call callous
Until she went into labor,
And then every neighbor
Heard her curse her husband with malice!"

Her deep throaty laugh seemed incongruent with her thin frame, and Anil couldn't help but join in her merriment.

"How did you meet him?" Anil asked.

Marilyn sighed and wiped a tear from the corner of her eye. "At a dance hall. He was in the service, and he'd just come back from a tour in Korea." She shook her head once. "He looked so tall and strong in his uniform, that's what drew me in initially. But that's not why I fell in love with him."

"No, why then?" Anil crossed his legs and leaned back into his chair. His shift had ended a half hour ago.

"He walked me home after the dance and we sat on the porch, talking all night." Marilyn turned to look out the window again. "He told me what he saw over there, terrible things." Her forehead creased. "He opened his heart to me. He wasn't afraid to show me his weakness. It was a remarkable thing, in that time, for a man to do that. That's the key thing about a strong marriage. It gives you a safe place to be yourself, entirely, even the weak parts." After a pause, she added, "Especially the weak parts." Marilyn grew quiet and continued to gaze out the window.

Anil thought of Amber, of how hard he had tried to show her the best version of himself—the one who could run fast, tell funny jokes, even line dance. He had thought it a good sign, an indication of the strength of their relationship, that he wanted to reflect his best self with her. But had it even been a version of him at all, that idealized person who bore little resemblance to him? His flaws, his weaknesses—those he'd hidden from Amber.

Clay has a memory, Leena had said. Where it had fractured was always the weakest part, obvious if you looked for it. And yet, she'd kept those damaged pieces, just as she'd held his weaknesses comfortably.

Marilyn elected not to pursue further treatment. There were no eagles in the hospital gift store, but Anil brought her a colorful stuffed parrot, which made her laugh out loud. She gave him a worn copy of her favorite book, an illustrated version of the poem "Desiderata." "I know it by heart." She winked at him.

On the day Marilyn was due to check out of the hospital, Anil brought in milkshakes from the fast-food joint across the street for them to enjoy on the roof of the hospital. Then he wheeled her down to the front lobby, stuffed parrot on her lap, where her daughter helped her into the waiting minivan. As he returned with the empty wheelchair, it occurred to Anil that the patient he felt best about treating during his two months on the oncology ward was not one whose life he'd saved but one who was going home to die in peace.

FOR THE next week, Anil met up with Charlie every night at the diner to rehearse his pitch to Dr. Tanaka for the research project. He practiced until the words came smoothly and Charlie agreed he was ready.

Anil located Dr. Tanaka's office in the Cardiology Department and approached it with a quivering stomach. He knocked on the door, then waited for Dr. Tanaka's muted response to enter. Anil reintroduced himself when Tanaka showed no sign of recognition and launched into his pitch. He was able to get through the first sentence, proud of himself for not stammering, before Tanaka held up his silver pen to interrupt.

"Dr. Patel, I'm glad you enjoyed the cath lab. I don't believe in veiling it off like some people. I like to take all my residents in there at some point, so they can see the true power of cardiology. I believe there's no finer specialty. But, unfortunately, I'm already committed to overseeing one resident research project, and I don't have time to take on another. Do you know Dr. Crandall?"

Anil nodded, his ears humming in harmony with the fluorescent lights.

"Perhaps you can team up with him," Tanaka continued. "Trey has a very interesting research study on early incidence of MI. I'm excited about the prospects."

Anil thanked Dr. Tanaka for the suggestion. After leaving the office, Anil bypassed the elevators for the privacy of the stairwell, raced down three flights of stairs, and pushed through the exit door into the frigid air.

When Anil returned home, a thin blue slip addressed to him was lying on the kitchen counter. He held the frail aerogramme between his fingers and studied it. Alternating navy-blue and red-cadet stripes chased each other around the perimeter of the pale blue envelope. He didn't recognize the handwriting. Instinctively, he brought it close to his nose and detected the faint aroma of something—cardamom? He took a knife from the kitchen drawer and slipped its sharp tip into the seam.

Back home, aerogrammes were always treated with great care and respect. The onion-skin paper folded onto itself to make its own envelope, and there was a prescribed space in which to write: one small page and one-third of the other side, favoring writers with small penmanship and readers with strong eyes. When Anil had first moved to Dallas, his mother sent him monthly aerogrammes to update him on all the family news; at the bottom were a few sloppy lines written in his ailing father's hand, a visual sign of his decline. Anil had not received an aerogramme since Papa died.

He read Leena's letter standing in the kitchen. When he looked up afterward, the room shifted a bit, tilting on its axis. He gripped the counter to stabilize himself, then slid over a few paces to the sink and pulled up the faucet handle. He stayed in that position for some time—he couldn't be sure how long—watching the stream of water, the compressed bubbles changing its hue from clear to white, changing its shape. When the urge to vomit had finally passed, Anil splashed water onto his face and neck, then immersed his whole head under the current. He longed to rid his mind of the images, but one was etched there permanently—Leena's leg covered in angry, red, puckered skin.

Anil tore off his hospital scrubs and put on his running clothes. He left the apartment with only the house key clutched in his palm, digging into his skin. He ran without knowing where he was going, across busy intersections and down unfamiliar streets, afraid that if he stopped running he would explode. He was seething with anger, but he knew his rage was aimless: the offenses against Leena had occurred long ago and far away. Who was there to punish now?

By the time Anil returned home, his lungs burning, dusk had set in and he had found a viable object for his rage. His mother had judged Leena without knowing a thing about her.

25

It was two o'clock in the morning and the ward was empty. Anil was on call overnight and looking for a nurse to help move a large patient. Walking toward the nurses' station, Anil could see down the entire length of the vacant corridor. He was about to turn around and head for the break room when he spotted a figure crouched down under the nurses' station. He drew closer; the person was not wearing the scrubs typically worn by nurses, but a white coat. The upturned heels of dark loafers were visible under the hem of the coat, and a patch of rugged blond hair could be seen above the collar.

Anil stopped a few meters short of the station. He watched Trey rummage through the bottom shelf of the drug trolley, used by the nurses to move between patients' rooms. Anil's vision became blurry, then crystallized again. His ears filled with the abnormally loud ticking of a clock and the regurgitation of a fax machine. He saw Trey slip something into his pocket, then stand up and turn around to face him. Panic flashed through Trey's eyes, but it was so quickly masked by his confident grin, Anil thought he had imagined it. "What's up, Patel?"

Anil stood, unmoving. His eyes drifted to the drug trolley, then back to Trey's face.

"Yeah, no nurses around. Had to get some meds for a patient."

Trey chuckled. "Gotta do everything myself around here." He put his hands in his pockets and stepped away.

"Wait." Anil reached for Trey's arm. "What did you just put in your pocket?"

"I told you, Patel. I had to pick up some meds for a patient." Trey shook Anil's hand off his arm. "Now, if you don't mind, I need to get back—"

"Why are you on this floor? Why didn't you get the meds on your own ward?"

Trey's stubble-covered face showed the weariness typical of a resident on night shift. But there was something else, a sort of nervous energy uncharacteristic of him. "Christ, Patel. What's with the inquisition? What's it to you?"

"You know you're not supposed to pull meds off the trolley like that," Anil said. "You need to have someone present and sign everything into the log. What's in your pocket?"

"Christ!" Trey said. "It's just a couple of tabs of Adderall for a patient with TBI." He reached into his pocket and pulled out a small plastic cup with two tablets. "Ward 6 was out, so I came down here. Happy now? I'll follow the procedure next time, officer." Trey stormed off down the corridor.

SEVERAL HOURS later, after Anil was done with morning rounds and on his way home, he stopped off on Ward 6, glancing at the patient board as he passed the central station. He found Trey in the break room, recapping the weekend's football games with the other residents, smiling and energetic.

"Trey, can I have a word?" Anil asked. Trey glanced up at him, the earlier trace of panic in his eyes now gone. He slapped another resident on the shoulder, excused himself from the group, and followed Anil out to the corridor and into an empty patient room. Anil closed the door.

"What is it, Patel?" Trey asked. "You want to rap me on the knuckles again for forgetting to follow procedure? I told you I'd write it up next time."

"You don't have any patients with TBI," Anil said.

"What? So?"

"You said the Adderall was for a patient with traumatic brain injury, but the board shows no patients on this ward with TBI."

"He was discharged this morning, okay? Look, Patel, I don't need you looking over my shoulder. I can take care of my own goddamn patients. Why don't you just worry about yours?"

"Really? Shall I check the discharge papers, then?" Anil was fed up with Trey getting everything he wanted. He didn't get to play by his own rules, not this time.

"Holy crap, Patel." Trey rolled his head back and shook his head at the ceiling. "What are you, the self-appointed ward policeman? I know how to do my fucking job, okay? You want me looking over your shoulder all day long, finding every little mistake? I bet I could find a whole lot of them. Now will you please back the fuck off?" Trey tried to push past him but Anil put his hand up, stalling until he could think of what to say next. He swallowed hard, the vague fear of a physical altercation creeping into his mind.

"What are you gonna do, Patel, huh?" Trey jammed his hands into his pockets and leaned forward. "There's no written record, you said so yourself. So it's your word against mine. You think anyone around here's gonna believe you? Over me?" The corner of his mouth curled up.

Anil thought of Dr. Tanaka and Trey's father on the hospital board.

"I didn't think so." Trey leaned in closer. "Don't fuck with me,

Patel. Mind your own goddamn business." He swung open the door and left.

❁

"HE'S RIGHT, who's going to believe me?" Anil said, pushing the salt shaker around the Formica tabletop after relaying the incident to Charlie as they sat in their regular booth at the diner.

"Tough call," Charlie agreed. "If you're not sure what happened, it's tricky. Maybe you should try talking to him again, see if he'll come clean?"

Anil shook his head. "He didn't seem very agreeable to talking. He looked more like he wanted to punch me."

"I don't know what to tell you, mate," Charlie said. "You'll come up with something. Don't they call you the Great Decider back home?"

Anil laughed. "Yeah, that's right." He picked up the laminated menu card standing on the table. "And I just decided we need some pie. Banana cream or apple?"

While they waited for their dessert to arrive, they discussed their infectious disease research study. The data analysis had yielded some interesting conclusions, and they were beginning to map out the report they would write. Eventually, they reverted to their default topic: what their peers would be doing after residency. Rumors were swirling about who was applying for which specialties, and who was likely to be chosen. Anil had started his fellowship applications and was moving ahead with his cardiology research project, even without a sponsor. The conversation brought them back to Trey, who was favored for one of the few cardiology fellowships, and anger began to stir again in Anil.

"Hey, I heard the new CMRs are going to be announced at the end of the week," Charlie said, cutting into a thick slice of apple pie with his fork. "Kirby, Choi, and your friend Mehta."

"Really?" Anil spoke through a mouthful of whipped cream. "Sonia Mehta? Chief medical resident?"

Charlie wiped the crumbs from his mouth with a paper napkin. "You could not pay me enough to do that job—all that responsibility, all those *interns*." He shivered.

Anil placed a forkful of pie in his mouth and let the cream melt away, thinking how it would feel pretty incredible to be selected as a CMR, to be recognized as the very best. "Sonia will make a great CMR. She deserves it."

"Yeah," Charlie said. "God knows she's bloody well sacrificed enough for this job—her marriage and all."

A prickling sensation traveled around Anil's temples. "Marriage?"

"Yeah, you didn't know about her divorce?" Charlie reached over and dug his fork into Anil's pie. "I thought you guys were tight."

Anil pushed the dish toward Charlie. "I'm done." He took a long drink of water, then held the cool glass between his palms. "Where did you hear that?"

"One of the other senior residents went to med school with her. I guess she and her husband got married halfway through school, and split up their first year here. I suppose it would be pretty intense going through this with your wife, the competition and all."

Was he Indian? Anil was curious but didn't ask. Instead, he craned his neck to look for their waitress, whose voice had been raspier than usual today. "Where is she, out for a smoke?"

"What's the rush, mate?" Charlie said.

Anil checked his watch. "I need to get back and finish some charts." He was suddenly eager to complete his rote paperwork. What a relief it would be to check medication dosages, to think about blood pressure readings and blood sugar levels instead of the new layers of unsettling information in his mind. *Trey. Sonia. Leena and Ma.* The accumulated stress of the past week had frayed Anil's nerves. He felt ready to burst from the secrets he was holding on to; he wanted to let it all go, but not here in the diner, not with calm and cheerful Charlie.

"It's all right, you go on," Charlie said. "I'll get the check."

What Anil needed was to blow off steam with his favorite unbridled Punjabi, but ever since Baldev had come home from the rehabilitation ward a few weeks ago, he'd been inseparable from Trinity. She'd practically moved into their apartment, her yoga mat rolled up in a corner of the living room, her copies of *The New York Times* accumulating on the coffee table. Generally, Anil didn't mind her presence. She cooked vegetarian meals for them, and brightened up the place with live plants she said would improve the energy flow. But right now, Anil wanted to vent his frustrations, and he couldn't do it in front of Trinity.

After pulling into a parking space at the hospital and turning off the ignition, Anil rested his forehead on the steering wheel. If he wanted to, he could scream here—scream as loud as he wanted and no one would hear him. He waited for some sound to erupt from his throat, for the release of tension that would accompany it. Nothing.

Anil sat there, his fingers wrapped tightly around the steering wheel. He was incensed at Trey for stealing the meds and lying about it. And he was furious about the things he'd read in Leena's letter, unable to reconcile what he knew of her with Ma's scathing judgment. And, perhaps unjustifiably, he felt disappointed Sonia had not trusted him enough to share more about herself.

No one was who they pretended to be. Nothing was as it seemed. Sometimes, it was impossible to know which of the things he'd learned would endure and which would be proven wrong at the next turn. Anil stayed in his car for several more minutes, breathing in and out, waiting for the emotions to subside before he returned to the hospital.

Anil was sitting at the break-room table with a stack of charts when Sonia entered the room. "Hey Patel, I thought you were gone for the day." She walked past him to the kitchen counter.

"Just came back to finish some charts," Anil said. He tried to focus on his work, debating whether to say anything.

Bubbling sounds and the aroma of fresh coffee filled the room. "Coffee?" Sonia asked.

"I heard about CMR," Anil said. "Congratulations. You're going to make a great chief."

Sonia warmed her hands around her mug. "Well, thanks, but it's not public yet, so I'd appreciate you keeping it quiet until next week. They have to notify the other candidates first. I haven't even told my parents yet. How did you hear?"

"I didn't know you were married." The words slipped unchecked from Anil's mouth.

Sonia looked at him for several moments. Anil could feel light perspiration on his nose, his spectacles slipping down its bridge. "I'm not married," she said.

"I know it's none of my business—"

"No, it's not, Patel." Sonia stared at him for several moments, then pulled out the chair on the other side of the table and sat down. "We met in medical school, on the first day of Gross Anatomy, as clichéd as that sounds. Everything was easy. We fell in love and got married after third year. We both matched at Parkview. We were going to suffer through residency together. Romantic, huh?" Sonia looked up at him and smiled. "Yeah, we were clueless." She paused to let out a deep breath. "On graduation day, I started having sharp pains in my abdomen. I thought it was just indigestion or reflux. I must have taken a whole roll of antacids, but the pain got worse, until I couldn't stand up anymore. It was my right side, so we thought it might be appendicitis. He drove me to the hospital." Sonia gave a weaker smile now. "We joked in the car about what a good story it would make one day . . . that he'd have to roll me across the stage on a gurney to get my diploma after getting my appendix out." She stopped and looked out the window, past Anil. "Turns out it was an ovarian cyst that ruptured. When they opened me up, they found cysts all over both ovaries. They had to take them out."

"The cysts?" Anil twisted the cap on and off his pen, unable to stop.

"My ovaries," Sonia said. "Both of them." She leaned back in her chair and closed her eyes for a moment. Her voice was tighter when she continued. "When all our classmates were getting their diplomas, I was waking up in a recovery room to find out I no longer had any ovaries." She shook her head. "And my husband was learning his new bride would never have children." Sonia placed her coffee mug on the table very gently, as if it was more fragile than it was. "He was really supportive, but we never got past that. It was too much. There are some things a young love can't survive. We'd only been married a year. He was twenty-five. He wanted his own children. And I thought he deserved that." She reached for her mug again and raised it to her lips.

Although he'd never stopped to think of Sonia as a mother, Anil found the idea that she never would be now profoundly sad. "Sonia, I'm so sorry."

"It's okay," she said. "It's for the best."

"How?" Anil said. "How is it for the best?"

"Well, I love this." She held up her hands. "All of it. I've wanted to be a chief medical resident from the first day I stepped into a hospital. And next I want to be an attending, and then chief of staff. How many female chiefs do you see? It's impossible to do what I want to do and have a family. I would have had to choose at some point. And now I don't have to. That's the way I think of it anyway. Everything happens for a reason, and now I'm free to pursue my calling without guilt. Or without disappointing anybody—my husband, my parents. I got all that out of the way early." She tried to smile. "Always an overachiever."

"What happened . . . to him?" Anil asked.

"We split up at the end of our internship year, and Casey transferred out to a program in San Antonio." She traced her finger around the rim of the coffee mug. "Married his high school sweetheart, a preschool teacher. Baby on the way. See, all for the best." She looked up at him. "I didn't tell you because . . . well, I didn't get a lot of support from the Indian community. Turns out it's quite a black mark to be divorced by twenty-five." She raised an eyebrow.

Anil nodded. "Yes, not a lot of tolerance for imperfection in our culture."

They shared a warm smile, then Sonia stood up, walked over to the sink, and poured the rest of her coffee into it. "So how's your fellowship application coming? Did you get Tanaka on board with your research project?"

"No," Anil said. "He's already overseeing another project for Trey Crandall."

"Trey? Oh, he's sharp." Sonia returned with a fresh cup of coffee. "Very sharp. I remember him from the ICU. You should see if you can team up with him."

Anil snorted and shook his head. "No way. He's the last person I'd work with."

"You know, you're just like him." Sonia smiled. "Cherished son. Important father. Trey's been a prince his whole life, but he's still trying to prove it to himself. The only difference is you left home, Anil. You're a fish out of water here, and Trey's still a big fish in his home pond. Other than that, you're not so different."

Anil looked at her with disbelief that quickly swelled into anger. "You're wrong." He pushed his chair away from the table. "I'm nothing like him." He stood up and walked out of the break room.

26

ANIL ENTERED THE HOSPITAL CAFETERIA SHORTLY BEFORE NOON and surveyed the specials posted on the board; as usual, there were no vegetarian choices. He contemplated yet another cheese sandwich and checked his watch, annoyed at Trey for making him wait. It was maddening, this feeling of powerlessness that lately had crept into every part of his life. Yesterday, he'd led a code that lasted forty minutes, certain he'd be able to revive the patient, but in the end he'd lost the sixteen-year-old girl. Despite his independent research project showing promise, he still hadn't been able to secure a sponsor within the Cardiology Department. And he'd been avoiding his mother's phone calls, her messages about disputes that needed his attention. He could not bear talking to her about anything since receiving Leena's letter. In all the areas that mattered most, Anil was utterly powerless, and it was a feeling he loathed.

Since the incident with Trey at the drug trolley, Anil had turned the quandary over and over in his mind, recalling what he'd seen and how Trey had responded, weighing the options before him. He'd pulled out the hospital handbook from orientation and reviewed the pharmaceutical checkout protocols. He'd even made an appointment with Human Resources, then canceled it. Parkview had a zero-tolerance policy for substance abuse, and the penalties were severe. Trey could be suspended from the residency program and lose his medical license, and Anil was simply too uncertain about what had happened. Could Trey have taken the drugs for a patient? Was it simply carelessness or poor record-keeping, or was it theft? Was it addiction?

Anil reconsidered everything he knew about Trey: the habitual gum chewing might be due to the dry mouth caused by amphetamines. He often paced the corridors, and always walked quickly. And there was Trey's formidable performance, both in regular duties and his extracurricular research. He seemed to operate at a superhuman level. The looming fellowship applications complicated things further: Trey's qualifications alone made him a strong candidate; his father's position on the hospital board made him unassailable. If Anil reported Trey, he couldn't be sure anyone would believe him. With those decisions on the horizon, he certainly didn't need to create waves at the hospital. Or to have Trey looking over his shoulder to catch a mistake, as he'd threatened.

Even as he tried to push all this aside, Anil knew, in some quiet corner of his mind, that he might stand to benefit without Trey in the race. He had spun himself into a knot to find the right answer before realizing he needed to know more. Resisting his tendency to work things out for himself, Anil had taken Charlie's advice and asked Trey to have lunch today. Glancing at his watch again, Anil was now ready to condemn Trey for tardiness on top of his other shortcomings when he felt a hand on his shoulder. Trey was dressed impeccably, as always, in a blue shirt that fit his shoulders squarely and a designer silk tie uncharacteristic of a resident's salary. He smiled and leaned toward Anil. "You don't want to eat here, do you? Let's go get some real food."

Anil hesitated.

"You like Mexican food? I know a great spot," Trey said. "Come on, I'm parked right outside."

Anil's salivary glands betrayed him, and he followed Trey to the exit doors.

❁

TREY DROVE an early-model BMW with unblemished navy-blue paint and a convertible top. As they roared out of the parking lot, Trey shouted over the chugging diesel engine, "Have you been to Oak Cliff?" Without waiting for an answer, he drove several miles on the highway with the top down, negating any possibility of conversation, before taking an exit unfamiliar to Anil.

They followed a winding road into a valley and up a hill, until the scenery changed to something Anil had never seen before in Dallas. All he'd observed in his three years here was flat terrain with large building complexes like Parkview or strip malls with the same branded stores. Baldev once told him Dallas repeated itself every five miles, and after seeing a CVS, Tom Thumb, and Wells Fargo at each major intersection, Anil agreed. And yet, they were now driving along a hilly crest with a view of the entire downtown skyline in the distance, a vantage point he'd never seen in this city that had become his home.

Less than fifteen minutes after leaving the hospital cafeteria, Trey pulled into a large dirt lot across from a gas station and parked the car. The centerpiece of the lot was a white truck with a hand-painted sign hanging on its one open side. A handful of beat-up cars and pickup trucks were clustered around the truck at odd angles, and a dozen men, all Hispanic, sat on scattered wooden stumps and overturned milk crates, eating and talking. Soda bottles and cans littered the ground around their feet.

"Ditch the coat, Patel," Trey said as he climbed out of the car. Anil slipped off his white coat and tossed it onto the backseat along with

Trey's. As they approached the white truck, apprehension rose within him. Trey was the only fair-skinned person in the vicinity, even more conspicuous with his blond hair, but he showed no hesitancy as he strode toward the truck, rolling up his dress-shirt sleeves. "Jorge," he bellowed into the window of the truck, reaching inside to slap hands with a man whose round terracotta face glistened with sweat. They bantered in fluent Spanish for a few moments before Trey motioned toward Anil. "Okay, Patel, what's your pleasure? *Carnitas? Al pastor?*"

Anil looked over the menu, which listed two kinds of beef, plus pork and chicken, and realized this had been a bad idea. He shook his head. "I don't eat meat."

Trey stared at him for a second, then turned back to Jorge and spoke in rapid-fire Spanish. Anil stepped closer to the truck to peer inside the window at the kitchen operations, then thought better of it and stepped back again.

"Hot or mild?" Trey asked.

"Hot," Anil said. "Extra hot."

When Trey turned back around after ordering, he was holding two glass soda bottles. "Coca-Cola Light." He handed one of the heavily scuffed bottles to Anil. "Ever tried it? It's only sold in Mexico. I think these guys smuggle it over the border. Tastes different from the American version, sweeter. Reminds me of the family beach trips we used to take to the Gulf when I was a kid." He gestured to a couple of sun-bleached rickety lawn chairs sitting in the shade of the truck.

Anil sat down, discreetly wiping the top of the bottle with his shirt cuff before taking a sip. The soda bubbled into his mouth and slid easily down his throat, making him smile.

"Good, huh?" Trey held up his bottle for affirmation.

Anil held up the bottle and inspected the contents in the sunlight. "Yeah. Tastes like Thums Up—that's the only cola we had in India years ago before Coke and Pepsi came in."

From the window of the truck, Jorge leaned out and shouted to Trey, who went to retrieve their order. He returned with two flimsy paper plates bowing under the weight of the food, and handed one to Anil. "Three beans and cheese with hot salsa. Extra chilies on the side. I didn't know you were a vegetarian."

"I didn't know you were Mexican," Anil retorted.

Trey grinned before he sank his teeth into a taco dripping with meat juices. Anil picked up one of his tacos, its inner contents shrouded by the mound of chopped lettuce on top.

The first bite reminded Anil of the *chaat* stalls on the streets of Ahmadabad he used to frequent until one of his friends contracted an infection that put him down for a week. A single mouthful brought together creamy pinto beans, tangy crumbles of cheese, crunchy lettuce, and salsa so spicy it left his tongue burning. Anil didn't dare ask if the beans were prepared with lard, as Mahesh always did when at Mexican restaurants.

"So what do you think?" Trey asked.

"Mmm." Anil followed Trey in topping his second taco with extra jalapeños. "You don't find this spicy?"

"Nah. I love it," Trey said, wiping at his nose.

"It's really good." Anil was grateful to have avoided another tasteless meal at the Parkview cafeteria but hadn't forgotten the reason for their meeting. "Listen, Trey." He balanced his plate on his lap. "We need to talk about what happened that night, at the med trolley—"

Trey held up a hand and wiped his mouth with a napkin. He nodded a few times while he finished chewing. "I've been meaning to tell you, Patel. That was totally decent of you to keep it between us. You could've really screwed me."

"I haven't said anything yet, but it doesn't mean I won't," Anil said. "I-I-I have an obligation, you know. This isn't just about you." Anil looked around the lot, but no one was paying them any attention.

He lowered his voice. "Trey, I need to know whether you took the drugs."

"Yeah, Patel, you know I did. But it was an honest mistake. I've learned my lesson."

"No, I mean, did you *take* them?" Anil said. "Did you take the Adderall, yourself?"

Trey dropped his gaze and tapped on the gravel with his shoe.

"Trey, did you?" Anil pressed.

Trey kept his eyes on the ground as he spoke. "I just needed something to get me through the night."

Anil closed his eyes. Without realizing it, he'd been hoping for a different answer.

"I needed a little boost, like an espresso shot without the jitters. You know what it's like, Patel. You've got a dozen patients who all need something, your pager keeps going off, the nurses are too busy to help. Sometimes you need a little . . . edge, that's all." Trey was rubbing his palms back and forth along his pant legs, getting more animated as he spoke. The sun had shifted overhead; it was beginning to creep into the periphery of their space.

"How long?" Anil asked.

"It's not a habit, if that's what you're asking," Trey said, meeting his eyes. "Just once in a while, when I need a little boost. And it's not just me. A lot of residents do it."

"Trey"—Anil lowered his voice—"you could lose your license."

"Look, I haven't done it since that night, and I'm not going to do it again. You scared the shit out of me, man."

"Yeah, well, you were a little scary yourself." Anil recalled the curl of Trey's lip, his overbearing physical presence.

"Sorry," Trey said. "I was worried you were going to report me." He stared at the remaining tacos on his plate but made no move toward them. "Are you?"

"I don't know." Anil shrugged. "We're all under a lot of pressure, Trey. And it's not going to get any better. How do I know you're really going to stop?"

Trey nodded. "I have already, man. It's just been rough for me lately. I can't sleep on my days off because of my research project with Tanaka. My dad expects me to have an article ready to publish by the end of residency. 'You have to make a name for yourself, Trey. You can't rely on my reputation to build your career.' Which is ironic, because I don't even have my own damn name." A wry smile came across his face. "You know that, right? *Trey* means the third. It's not even a real name." He took a swig from his Coke bottle and leaned back in the lawn chair. "William Adam Crandall the third. My grandfather's William, my dad goes by Bill, and all I get is a little footnote, number three. Trey." He closed his eyes for a moment, then continued speaking. "I used to like that when I was a kid: being part of this great tradition, the family lineage. That was before I understood the price it came with."

The sunlight now engulfed the lower halves of their bodies; it wouldn't be long before it reached their arms and faces and became unbearable. Trey continued talking, almost oblivious to Anil's presence. "First, it was SMU for undergrad, where I had to double major in biology and chemistry, then off to Baylor for medical school." He turned his head sideways toward Anil. "Because the Crandalls are Baylor men. And then residency at Parkview, of course. But we're not done yet." Trey held up his forefinger. "Oh no, I still have to publish this article, score a cardiology fellowship at Parkview. Then a few more years to chief medical resident and full-steam ahead to head of Cardiology. And after all that, I'll be perfectly positioned to rake in the big bucks at my old man's private practice, *if* he thinks I'm worthy. But more likely, it'll be because he needs more time for all his board work—Parkview, MedTherapy, Children's Cancer House, the university. Everybody wants a piece of the Crandall magic." Trey tossed his empty bottle on the ground. "Everyone thinks it's so great to have my father on the hospital board, but the pressure." Trey shook his head. "Man, the pressure is *intense*—from him, from everyone who knows him—and it never lets up. They know who I am before I open my mouth, before I do a single damn thing." He nudged the Coke bottle with the toe of his leather loafer, now coated with dust. "What I would give to be totally anonymous at Parkview."

"What?" Anil said. "Do you have any idea what it's like to get no attention from senior staff? To have no one remember your name? Hell, not even know how to *pronounce* your name? To scrounge for references for your fellowship application, to have no one sponsor your research project?" Anil shook his head. "You don't know what the hell you're talking about."

"Hey, man," Trey said, "I didn't mean—"

Anil interjected, unable to stop. "You have no idea how lucky you are, Trey, how much harder it is for everyone else."

"Sorry, man." Trey stretched out his foot to reach the Coke bottle and rolled it back and forth under the sole of his loafer. "What's your research project about?"

Anil described his cardiology research topic in general terms, still a little leery of Trey's intentions. "I've been making good progress analyzing the ER data on my own, but it would help if I had a senior doctor to help navigate the other departments."

"I might be able to help with that," Trey said.

Anil shifted in his chair to avoid the sun beaming into his eyes. "How?"

"I can ask Singer or Martin if they're interested. They're both friends with my old man, but he made me work with Tanaka, since he's top dog. Give me your research brief and I'll ask them."

Anil cocked his head, squinting at Trey through the sunlight. "Why would you do that?"

"Why not?" Trey shrugged. "I owe you, man."

FOR THE rest of the afternoon, as Anil finished out his shift, he felt a slight lift from the stress overshadowing him. For the first time in months, there was hope for his research study and, therefore, his fellowship prospects.

Lunch had not been at all what he'd expected; he found himself empathizing with Trey and the pressure he felt from his father. Anil could easily recall the weight of obligation he felt when returning to Panchanagar. It was no excuse for the amphetamines, but Trey seemed sincere about quitting, and that was the point, after all. Everyone could be forgiven a transgression here or there. Like Leena's shelf full of wobbly clay pots, mistakes were a part of life: the inevitable and essential element that helped make sense of everything else. The nakedness of the unglazed bowl revealed the imprint of her fingertips. Invisible cracks rendered a cup impractical for water, but not gauze. Many people had tolerated Anil's imperfections: Sonia had kept teaching him after he failed her, and Baldev hadn't blamed him for the attack he suffered, nor had Amber for failing to defend her. And now, Trey was offering him a real shot at his dream.

If Anil reported him, Trey's career would almost certainly be ruined, not to mention his relationship with his father. Anil still carried a deep void for Papa—a longing that could never be filled, a guilt that would never be eased. How could he inflict that kind of damage on someone else? Regardless of the mistakes Trey had made, Anil had seen him at work for years now, and although it stung to admit, there was little doubt Trey Crandall would make an excellent physician, probably better than Anil himself.

27

Anil arrived home to an unfamiliar aroma from the kitchen. Brown paper bags littered the floor, and the counter was covered with ingredients in various stages of preparation. Trinity was stirring a pot on the stove. "Anil!" she called out. "Perfect timing. Dinner's almost ready."

"Hi, Trinity." After a day of complicated and disheartening conversations, Trinity's unfailing serenity was the perfect antidote. Anil understood why Baldev enjoyed her company so much. He peered into the pot and caught a pungent combination of spices and onions.

"Moroccan vegetable curry," she declared. "Totally vegan."

Anil was confounded by this concept. He was accustomed to vegetarianism as the norm in India, and some strict religious sects even wore masks to avoid inhaling bugs, but he didn't understand the elimination of dairy products as Trinity explained it. No animals were killed by the use of dairy. In fact, cows and goats were an integral part of their farming community in Panchanagar. To not use the milk they produced was to defy the natural order of things he'd learned on the farm, not to mention wasteful. He couldn't imagine chai without milk, or any Indian meal without yogurt, or any dessert made without ghee.

Fortunately, for all her veganthusiasm, Trinity was not imposing about her beliefs, and Anil was grateful for anyone cooking dinner.

"Smells delicious," he said.

"It'll be ready in half an hour. Baldev's in the shower. We just got back from the gym."

On his way to his room, Anil ran into Baldev, emerging from the steamy bathroom with a towel wrapped around his waist. The definition of new muscle in his shoulders and chest was evident. "Hey, man, come talk to me while I get dressed," Baldev said.

Baldev had no trouble strutting around unclothed. Normally, Anil would avoid such a situation, but he wanted to discuss what had happened with Trey, so he followed Baldev into his room and sat on a corner of the unmade bed. "The curry looks good," he offered. "So this vegan thing, are you—?"

"Nah." Baldev waved away Anil's question. "I get a burger for lunch every day so I can make it through dinner." He smiled. "Trinity knows. She's cool with it."

"So is it serious?"

"What, with her?" Baldev pointed his thumb toward the kitchen. He closed the bedroom door. "I don't know, man. I thought it was just fun, but she's really cool, you know? So yeah, maybe I can see it getting serious. If she doesn't get fed up with a knucklehead like me. She's probably too smart for me."

"Doesn't take much," Anil said. Baldev grinned and dropped his towel and Anil kept his eyes trained on the floor. "Hey, let me ask you something. Something happened last week at the hospital—" he began.

From the hallway came the sound of the front door opening and closing, then Mahesh's voice followed by Trinity's. "Dinner's ready!"

"Yeah?" Baldev sprayed an excessive amount of scented deodorant under each arm.

"Never mind." Anil stood up. "Let's go eat." This was not the kind of matter he wanted to discuss around Mahesh, whose tolerance for shades of gray was the same as for Mexican beans of uncertain origin.

THE MOROCCAN vegetable curry was quite good, despite Trinity's experimental addition of Anil's tea masala she'd found in the kitchen cupboard. Over dinner, they discussed the success of Mahesh's recent big software release at work.

"It has the fewest bugs reported of any release in the company's history, despite its size and complexity," Mahesh said.

They clinked their glasses in congratulations. "And"—Trinity wrapped her arm around Baldev's shoulders—"I'm proud to report Baldev hit a major milestone today. He's regained full mobility in his knee and his arm, and he's stronger than he was before the injuries."

Baldev held up his hands while they cheered. "Six long, hard months that would have been even longer and harder without this wonderful lady." He pulled Trinity toward him and kissed her cheek.

"And, there's more . . ." Trinity glanced over at Baldev.

"Yes." Baldev wiped his mouth. "I've been asked by the company to take on a new position, overseeing a large team." He looked at rinity, then around the table. "In Bangalore."

"Bangalore?" Anil laid down his spoon.

"Wow," Mahesh said.

"Yeah, the company wants to groom me for a management position, so I need to spend a couple of years learning customer support. I'd be managing the call center in Bangalore."

"Bangalore," Anil repeated. Of the three of them, Baldev had always been the most removed from India, the only one who never spoke about going back. "Really? Are you . . . you're not . . . thinking of going?" He was reluctant to say more in front of Trinity. Did Baldev really want to give up his whole life here, his girlfriend?

Baldev shrugged. "You know, at first I didn't consider it, but it's only for a couple of years. And if I do well, I'll get a big promotion when I come back. It's a good career move."

"It's a great opportunity," Mahesh concurred. "Bangalore is on fire right now."

"Well, I think he should do it," Trinity said. "I would love to go to India." She gave Baldev a prolonged kiss on the cheek. Their outward giddiness was at odds with the melancholy Anil felt descending upon him.

"So much good news! We should celebrate." Trinity clapped her hands together. "Let's throw a party. Isn't Diwali next weekend?"

"How did you know that?" Baldev asked, leaning toward her.

She winked at him. "The lab tech told me."

"Yeah, I think a Diwali party's a great idea," Mahesh said. Anil and Baldev exchanged a glance. Crowds of people and loud music in their home ran counter to Mahesh's preference for meticulous order. "We can get the food from Taj Chaat House—"

"And make a dance floor." Baldev motioned to their sparsely furnished living room. "I've got a great bhangra mix, and there are some new speakers at the store I've had my eye on."

❁

OVER THE next week, their dreary beige apartment underwent a full transformation; each night when Anil came home he noticed a new change. Cases of beer and soft drinks were stacked next to the dining area. The furniture in the living area was pushed out to the perimeter. Strings of Christmas lights were wrapped around the potted plants, and floral garlands were hung in doorways. Anil invited Charlie and a few other residents to the party, but despite Baldev's prodding and the fact that she was the only other Indian person he knew in Dallas, he did not invite Sonia, wary of not being able to relax around someone who still wrote his evaluations.

The night of the party, Trinity's friends were the first to show up: earthy, athletic girls like her who had all gone to UT Austin together.

Not one of them wore makeup or heels. They brought bottles of light beer and hard cider, and devoured samosas as they discussed their latest book club selection, the memoir of an Afghani schoolgirl. Baldev's buddies from work clustered around the sound system he had rigged in the living room, testing the upper limits of its volume. Soon, the bhangra dance mix was pumping through the speakers and people were milling around, drinking and eating.

In between shuttling trays of food from the oven and refilling bowls of chutney, Mahesh hovered around the front door to welcome guests as they arrived. Anil found the sudden onset of Mahesh's hosting persona amusing, and was about to urge him to join the party when the doorbell rang again.

Yaalini was not at all what Anil had expected of a hard-driving software engineer. Dressed in a deep-blue and silver *salwar khameez*, she was no taller than five feet, with a sweet face framed by curly hair. Mahesh's expression was transformed into a broad smile. He took her purse and shawl, then walked her over to the buffet table. Anil watched from the couch as Mahesh leaned closer to her when he spoke and Yaalini threw her head back and laughed freely. His roommate was not known for his sense of humor.

❁

"WHY DIDN'T you tell us?" Anil asked the next morning over breakfast.

Mahesh shrugged, stirring his tea. "I didn't even know what was happening. It took me by surprise. We started as friends—well, we really started as colleagues—and as we spent more time together, it just grew . . ." He smiled. "She's so easy to get along with. We can talk about Bollywood films and music, we enjoy the same food—she makes the best *masala dosa*, by the way. And she understands my work. I can talk to her about anything."

"It's like dating the female version of yourself." Baldev grinned. "Only you're much uglier." Mahesh pushed Baldev's shoulder and he groaned, already nursing a hangover.

"How long has it been?" Anil asked.

"I don't know, a few months?" Mahesh said. "Four and a half, actually."

Baldev clucked his tongue and exaggerated his Indian accent. "All this time, you've been lying to us, your family?"

The smile on Mahesh's face faded.

"Come on, you know I'm kidding." Baldev slapped his arm playfully. "We're happy for you, man. You've finally found love, and not in a bio-data envelope. Think of all the money you could've saved your parents on matrimonial ads."

Mahesh stared into his mug, stirring absentmindedly.

"You haven't told your family, have you?" Anil asked.

Mahesh shook his head. "I didn't think of her that way, in the beginning, because she's Tamil. I thought she wasn't what I was looking for; we were too different. But all those differences—Gujarati and Tamil, Vaishyas and Brahmins—they don't matter over here. No one knows the difference between a South Indian and a Sikh, or a Patel and a Punjabi. People at work tease us about being brother and sister just because we're both Indian. Maybe if we met in India—*if* we even met in India—we wouldn't have anything in common. But over here, everything that's important we do share." Mahesh's voice was gathering strength as he spoke. "We can stay here. We can get married and build our lives here."

"Good man," Baldev said. "It's your life. You can do what you like. You don't need your family's approval."

"But I do need them. I want their blessing." Mahesh sipped his tea, which must have been cold by now. "And so does Yaalini. We both do. I was waiting until I was sure, and now I am. I'm going to tell my parents and ask for their approval to get married."

"And if they don't give it?" Anil asked.

Mahesh dropped his teaspoon into his empty mug with a clang. "I don't know. I don't want to spend my life with anybody else. Every time I see one of those envelopes from my mother, I feel sick to my stomach. But I don't want to disappoint my parents, or be an outcast from my family. I can't imagine living that way either." He carried his mug over to the sink.

A heaviness descended from Anil's chest to his stomach. They all played by the implicit rule that they could do as they pleased over here in the United States, as long as their parents didn't know. Anil had avoided telling his family about Amber. Even Baldev, whose parents had been in America for years, had not yet told his family about Trinity. As long as they didn't know, no harm was done. But what if, like Mahesh, you fell in love with the wrong girl, a girl to whom your parents objected, a girl you still could not forget?

ANIL SAT with Charlie next to the coffee cart, a permanent fixture in the hospital lobby. "I'm proud of you, mate," Charlie said. "Must have taken a lot, knowing how you feel about the guy, but sounds like you've thought it through and you're doing the right thing."

Anil forced a smile, unsettled by the implication of nobility in his actions. He hadn't told Charlie about Trey's offer to help him find a research sponsor in the Cardiology Department, only edged up to it a few times in his mind.

"Like I said." Charlie patted him on the back. "The Great Decider." He leaned closer and lowered his voice. "He really said a lot of residents use speed?"

"Yeah. Who knows?" Anil shrugged. "The research says it can be taken safely in low doses on occasion. I even read a study on college athletes whose performance improved on amphetamines. Maybe Trey's right, and we're the odd ones out."

Charlie shook his head and held up his coffee cup. "I'll stick with this stuff, thank you. Americans are so tightly wound, the way they kill themselves to get ahead. It's no way to live, I tell you. In Sydney, my mate Jeremy, he's on staff at the public hospital—plum job, nice income. He and his wife have a great house in Balmain. Nothing like these ridiculous mansions you see in Dallas, but plenty of space, three bedrooms, backyard. Jeremy drives a new Saab, he's got a nice life, y'know?"

Anil nodded, removing the lid of his cup to pluck out the soggy tea bag. He was due for rounds in fifteen minutes.

"But here's the difference," Charlie continued. "Jeremy goes surfing every morning before work, he has dinner with his wife most nights, and they travel all the time because he's on call only every other weekend. He works to live, y'know? Here, everyone lives to work. It's backwards, if you ask me."

"You have a point," Anil concurred, though he tended toward the American side of Charlie's lifestyle spectrum. The intensity of cardiology was part of why he found it such an attractive specialty.

"I'm thinking of going back in July when we're done," Charlie said.

"What?" Anil said. "Where?"

"Sydney," Charlie said. "Jeremy said his hospital's hiring a few more docs, he can put in a good word for me. Apparently, they're looking for doctors with research experience. I might be able to get into their Infectious Disease Department." He slapped Anil's shoulder. "Come on, mate. I'm thirty-six. I need to find a nice Aussie girl and settle down." Charlie beamed his magnetic smile, but Anil was immune to it. "My folks are getting older, I want to be near them while I can."

There was a gripping in Anil's chest from the guilt he felt over his father's death, which presented itself at unexpected moments.

Charlie laid his hand on Anil's arm. "Sorry, mate. I only meant . . ."

"No, it's all right," Anil said. "When will you decide?"

"I won't hear about the job until March or April. But don't look so glum, mate. We've got at least six more months to hang out. Plenty of time for you to learn to drink a proper pint." Charlie grinned and excused himself to the restroom before rounds began.

Anil returned to the coffee cart for a fresh cup of tea, to which he added generous portions of milk and cinnamon powder, a poor substitute for his mother's chai masala.

"Hey, man." Trey approached the cart. "Triple espresso," he said to the barista. Anil noticed the shadows under his eyes. He'd been watching Trey's behavior carefully but hadn't seen any signs that he might be using again. "Listen," Trey said. "I spoke with Singer and Martin about your project, but they're both too busy to take on anything else." He took his espresso cup from the barista. "But listen, I've got another idea." He led Anil away from the cart. "I can add your name to my paper. Tanaka doesn't know what's going on day to day. I'll tell him we've been working on it together, okay?" He pulled the lid off the paper cup and took a sip. "Let's meet up after work tomorrow, and I'll fill you in on the study. Horseshoe, eight o'clock?" Trey drained his espresso and tossed the cup into the trash.

Anil had a sunken feeling in his stomach. "Okay."

"Trust me, Patel, it'll be fine," Trey said, resting a hand on his shoulder. "Just make sure you have some solid recommendations."

❁

HEEDING TREY'S advice, the next week, Anil sat across from Sonia, separated by their lunch trays. The cafeteria had recently introduced a vegetable lasagna he was eager to taste, but first he launched into his speech about why he'd decided to apply for a cardiology fellowship and believed he was qualified. Sonia waited until he finished, then smiled. "Look, Anil, I'll write you a recommendation letter for whatever you want. If it's cardiology, so be it. Personally, I think it's a waste for you to spend your days with electronics and draped patients, but that's your choice. It's your career, not mine."

"Thanks, Sonia." Anil sat back in his chair, the tension leaving his shoulders. Sonia's reference was the last piece he needed for his fellowship application. "I know I haven't always been the easiest guy to work with."

Sonia shrugged. "I don't place a lot of value on easy, Patel. And I wouldn't mind having you around here a few more years. How's the rest of your application coming along?"

"Pretty good." Anil took his first bite of the lasagna, which was surprisingly good. "Eric Stern said he'll write me a letter as well, and I'm waiting to hear back on one more."

"And that research project you were trying to get going in Cardiology?"

"Yeah." Anil pushed the wavy noodles around his plate with a fork. "It's going well."

"Oh good," Sonia said. "You found a sponsor, then? Who is it?"

"You want some hot sauce?" Anil put down his fork. "This is kind of bland, huh?" He got up from the table and meandered around the cafeteria. How could he explain his partnership with Trey, his sudden reversal of opinion? A bottle of Tabasco taunted him from a nearby table. He picked it up and returned to Sonia, then doused his food with it.

"You were saying, about your cardio research? You got a sponsor?"

"Yeah, actually I . . . I took your advice and teamed up with Trey Crandall on his study. So it's all good. Thanks for that suggestion." Trey had blown him off twice. Anil didn't know anything about the project other than the subject, and that, he'd only learned from Tanaka months ago. He hoped Sonia wouldn't ask him any more questions about it.

Sonia sat back in her chair. "Really?" She smirked at him and shook her head. "Patel, you really surprise me sometimes. Well, good for you. I have no idea how you can manage two research projects, but it'll definitely help your applications."

Her approval seared him with guilt. Anil took the opening to change the topic, asking about her new role as chief medical resident. They chatted about one of his patients waiting for a liver transplant, and the scandal of a junior resident who'd driven over the border to Mexico on his weekend off and hadn't come back for four days. Sonia even spoke about her family for the first time since he'd known her—about the younger sister who was soon graduating from medical school and oblivious to what lay ahead in her internship.

Although their conversation never veered too far from the professional, there was an undeniable warmth between them. Anil thought of the first time he'd worked with Sonia, in the ICU on call overnight, when he'd missed the ruptured aneurysm. The mortality and morbidity conference, where she'd saved his ass. How she'd stitched him up the night after Baldev had been attacked. The ridiculous gauntlet she'd put him through in Oncology, forcing him to diagnose a brain tumor with nothing more than his eyes and hands. Anil had learned a tremendous amount under Sonia, and he'd become a better physician for it. As uncomfortable as that conversation about her divorce had been, their relationship seemed to have grown after having broached it. They were not yet equals, and perhaps they would never be. But he had earned her respect and support, and her opinion mattered to him—perhaps, he was surprised to realize—more than anyone else's at Parkview.

The Suspicious Engine

Anil climbed into the car with Mahesh and Baldev, on their way out for a celebratory dinner. "Listen to this," he said to his roommates. "My family called me a few days ago, and I have to call them back this weekend."

"Again?" Baldev shook his head. "Anil, why don't you tell them to use one of those services? For two, three hundred rupees, they can go to someone to broker their disputes. There are businesses now—you can be done with the whole thing."

"What are you saying?" Mahesh cocked his head to one side. "This is his family coming to him, not some stranger. It's his duty to help, his honor."

"Well, I'm stuck with the role for now," Anil said. "So listen to this one and tell me what you think." He leaned forward from the backseat. "One of my cousins decided he didn't want to be a farmer like the rest of the family. Everyone says he's too lazy to do the work. He says agriculture is an old practice that doesn't generate enough income, so he decided to start a business converting car engines to run on natural gas rather than diesel."

"Why?" Baldev asked.

"Because diesel petrol is so expensive in India," Mahesh said. "The government charges a huge tax."

"Right," Anil said. "Natural gas is much cheaper, but they don't sell cars that run on it. So my cousin started this business converting the engines."

"Very clever." Baldev nodded approvingly.

"Yes, but the converted engines are a little more unstable," Anil said. "That is, there's more of a risk something will go wrong, and there can be . . . an explosion."

In the rearview mirror, Anil could see Mahesh's eyes widen.

"Of course, nobody knew this in the beginning, and my cousin needed help getting the business started. He had no capital, so he went to another uncle who owns one of the bigger plots of land. My cousin asked him to make an investment in the business—twenty thousand rupees to buy some tools and supplies. That was about six months ago, and everything was going well. My cousin's business was getting off the ground, he was getting more customers. He was starting to pay my uncle back, a little bit at a time."

"Then?" Baldev said.

"Then one of his customers suffered an accident. He filled his tank with natural gas and, when he turned on the ignition, there was a small explosion. He didn't die, but he lost one of his legs." Anil looked back and forth between them before continuing. "So this fellow, the customer, has come to our family for compensation. He can no longer earn a living with only one leg, and he says it's my cousin's fault, he did something wrong to the engine. My cousin says he warned his customer about the dangers, and the customer was careless when he filled the tank. No one else was there, so no one really knows. But here's the problem: my cousin has no money, so there's no way he can satisfy the man. No one else in the family has the kind of money this man needs to take care of his family. Except my uncle."

"The one—" Mahesh started.

"Right, the one who made the initial investment," Anil said. "But that uncle already gave a lot of his savings to my cousin to start the business, and now he feels betrayed. My uncle was trying to be supportive, and now he's mixed up in all this business. And to make matters worse, apparently this fellow, the customer, has a reputation for trying to scam money out of people. According to my brother Chandu, who has some shady friends himself, he tried to squeeze money out of his factory boss not long ago. So no one can really be sure of his story. But," Anil held up a forefinger, "he is missing a leg. That much has been verified."

His roommates silently deliberated on the situation for a few moments as they waited at a red light. "Well, I say buyer beware," Baldev offered. "That fellow knew there was some risk involved, like there is with everything. If he purchased a machete to break open coconuts and chopped off his own hand by mistake, would he go to the man who sold him the machete and complain? There are always risks involved. At least it's a leg, not an arm. The streets of Delhi are full of one-legged men who travel on their wheelie-boards faster than me. There are plenty of ways he can make a living."

Mahesh shook his head forcefully. "I don't agree, Baldev. Think of their karma. Anil's cousin and uncle are involved, even indirectly, in the maiming of another person. If they don't do something to atone, they'll come back as . . . *ants* in the next life. Is that really worth a few rupees?"

"My mother always says, never step on an ant." Baldev grinned.

Mahesh continued, "Anyway, if it were me, I would offer some compensation to the customer's family, and a nice box of sweets. Maybe the whole family can pitch in together?"

"That would be nice," Anil said. "The problem is, everyone in the family's fighting over this. Some people are angry with my uncle for encouraging my cousin's scheme in the first place. My uncle's really mad at my cousin—well, everyone's mad at my cousin. But my cousin's upset too. He feels like the family's abandoning him because he went out on his own and tried to do something different." Anil paused. "And I understand him, in a way. It's not easy to strike out on your own when everyone expects something of you."

Mahesh shook his head as he pulled into a parking spot. "Well, I think you should encourage your family to take responsibility for this fellow, the one-legged one. A tragedy has occurred, and someone has to pay. Your family is in a position to do so."

"No way," Baldev said. "It was an accident, pure and simple. It's not your cousin's fault. Are you responsible for every patient in the hospital who dies on your watch?"

Anil climbed out of the car, no closer to an answer than before. *Primum non nocere*, he recalled from the Hippocratic oath he'd recited when graduating from medical college. First, do no harm.

❁

AFTER WAITING for forty minutes in the crowded bar of the hottest new Asian restaurant in Dallas, Anil and his roommates were seated in a black leather semicircle booth.

"To new beginnings." Mahesh held up his drink, a silly grin plastered on his face. Months had passed since he had told his parents about Yaalini, and he was smiling again.

"New beginnings," Baldev toasted. "And to the prospect of Mahesh finally getting laid."

Mahesh shook his head, but the grin remained. He took a deep sip from the small ceramic cup, then squeezed his eyes shut and pursed his lips. "God, what is this stuff?" He stared into the clear liquid remaining in the cup.

"Sake." Baldev reached over and slapped Mahesh's shoulder. "Japanese rice drink. Very good for your health." He winked at Anil.

"Improves masculine virility, which you'll need for your wedding night. One hundred percent guaranteed." He refilled Mahesh's cup. "Drink up."

"Have you set a date?" Anil sniffed at the sake, which reminded him of antiseptic solution.

Mahesh popped an edamame pod into his mouth. "Not yet. We're waiting on her parents, still hoping they'll change their minds." He took another big gulp of sake. Anil wondered how long it would take for an alcohol novice to start feeling the effects. Mahesh was already so giddy, it would be hard to tell. "Yaalini doesn't say so, but it's important to her, I know it is. How can you get married without your parents?"

"What else can you do?" Anil stabbed at a tempura-crusted onion with his chopsticks.

"They're really hung up on caste," Mahesh said. "My parents tried to explain it works differently in our community, but they're stuck on the idea we're all descended from farmers." Mahesh tipped his sake cup to his lips. "Never mind I have a master's degree from IIT."

"Well," Anil said, "at least you have your parents behind you."

After several difficult conversations over the past few months, Mahesh's parents had come around to the idea of his marrying Yaalini. Their prejudices had a hierarchy and, as it turned out, Yaalini met their most important criteria of being Hindu and vegetarian. With their friends fretting over their children marrying Muslims and meat-eaters, Mahesh's parents came to the conclusion that their son's choice could have been much worse. In Yaalini, they'd even found some things they could boast about, such as her high caste and master's degree. Mahesh's mother insisted on planning the wedding herself in Ahmadabad, as good preparation for the marriage of Mahesh's younger sister in a few years.

"True, true." Mahesh wobbled his head, his eyes beginning to lose their focus. "So, Baldev, what did you decide? Are you going to tell your parents about Trinity?"

"Man, I don't know," Baldev said. "They're just so crazy happy about my moving to India. I haven't had the heart."

Baldev had decided, with Trinity's urging, to accept the assignment in Bangalore. They would move there together for a contractual minimum of two years and live in Palm Meadows, an expatriate enclave far from the bustling city core. Baldev would be responsible for hiring and managing IT support staff at the electronic giant's new call center, a role for which he would be paid handsomely. After the successful completion of his assignment, he would return to the company's headquarters in Dallas with a promotion.

Trinity had resigned from her job at the hospital and signed up for a six-month course in therapeutic yoga at Bangalore's leading yoga college. She planned to incorporate new techniques she learned there into her physical-therapy practice. The boom of companies in Bangalore, their employees working on computers and phones around the clock, had led to a rise in carpal tunnel syndrome and other repetitive stress injuries. Trinity's American experience would help her find work, but Baldev's expatriate package was generous enough that she didn't have to. Anil was impressed, and a little envious. He couldn't imagine Amber, for whom Dallas had been such a drastic change, offering to move to India with him.

"Don't be a coward, man." Mahesh slurred his words slightly. "If you love her, you should tell them."

Baldev laughed. "Oh, look who's talking like a big man now, heh?" He picked up a sushi roll with his fingers. "Yeah, I might just have to do that. She might be worth breaking my parents' hearts."

"What would be worse, do you think, for your parents?" Anil asked, the sake having loosened his tongue. "An American? Or a Muslim? Or a lower-caste girl?" He leaned forward. "Or a divorcée?"

"Ohhh!" Baldev howled, slapping his leg. "That girl from the hospital, Sonia? You finally going to give it a go, Anil?"

"No." Anil shook his head. "No way."

"Then who? You got your eye on someone else?"

"No, no," Anil said, "just a hypothetical question. There's a . . . situation in my village back home. A dispute I'm sorting out. A woman who . . . So the question is, could you get your parents to accept someone who'd been married before?" He tapped his feet alternately under the table, waiting for their responses.

"Not my parents," Mahesh said. "No way. They barely came around to Yaalini, and she's only from a different region of India. No Muslims, no Americans, and *definitely* no used goods. My parents would not stand for any of that." He swigged the rest of his sake.

"I don't know," Baldev said. "Depends on the circumstances. I think my parents might be open to Trinity if they thought she could take care of me as well as an Indian wife. And she's been doing a damn good job of that, I'd say."

"And her parents?" Anil asked.

Baldev shrugged. "They're hippies from Seattle; they're fine with me. Trinity's dated every color of the rainbow. Her folks are planning to come visit us in India." He thumped Anil on the shoulder. "Listen, you can't think your way out of these questions, doctor." He pounded his closed fist against his chest. "You've got to go with your gut. Your heart." He poured more sake into each of their cups and held his up in the air. "Courage, gentlemen!" They toasted again, Mahesh sloshing some onto the table.

Part IV

28

THE DATE OF MAHESH AND YAALINI'S WEDDING IN AHMADABAD was set. Mahesh's mother had taken on the wedding preparations with fervor. Over one thousand guests had received invitations with embossed illustrations of Ganesha, the elephant-headed god invoked for marriage ceremonies. Five days of activities had been planned, including a henna night for the women, and a party with live folk music and dancing the night before the ceremony. It was not an extravagant wedding by urban Indian standards, but it was a meaningful demonstration of Mahesh's parents' enthusiasm for the nuptials. The way they had warmed to the idea over the past few months made Anil unexpectedly hopeful.

Anil had requested two weeks of vacation, fully expecting Casper O'Brien to approve only one, as he had every other time. When he was granted both weeks, Anil felt a modicum of guilt over listing the purpose of his trip as a family wedding, but it passed quickly. He was, after all, closer to Mahesh than to his own brothers. As a third-year resident, Anil had seen his value at Parkview rise, and it undoubtedly would grow even more as a cardiology fellow. He would submit his application soon after returning from India. Anil could already see his life changing ahead of him, a brighter path than the one he'd traveled the past few years.

Mahesh's wedding festivities in Ahmadabad would occupy his first week in India, but he didn't make any plans for the second. If he received the cardiology fellowship, this would be Anil's last opportunity to visit home before it began, but he still couldn't bear the idea of facing his mother. Anil booked himself a seat on the same outbound flight as Baldev and Trinity, and a return flight to Dallas by himself two weeks later. He told no one in his family he was coming.

The weeks leading up to the wedding were hectic for everyone. Mahesh and Yaalini had to prepare their company to survive their simultaneous absence, and vacate Yaalini's apartment so she could move in with Mahesh after the wedding. Every night after work, they shuttled over a car full of her belongings. By the end of the week, the hallway outside Mahesh's room was stacked high with sealed cartons. On the other end of the apartment, Baldev sifted through his possessions to decide what to take on the plane to Bangalore and what to send via shipping container. Some items, such as his barbells and the Bollywood posters, he bequeathed to Anil.

As Anil prepared for the trip, his mind kept drifting to Leena. He pictured her slender fingers tracing the inner rim of the imperfect bowl in her drawing room. Leena's hands were beautiful, but not in the glossy, manicured way of the hospital clinic receptionist. Nor did she have the delicate, thin wrists he remembered on Sujata, his lab partner in medical college, with her tinkling glass bangles. Leena kept her fingernails trim, with only a thin strip of white. The backs of her hands were darkened by the sun. Her fingers were long and slim, with remnants of clay dust in the creases of her knuckles. When Leena had shown him those enormous urns she'd made, the ones for the fancy hotel, Anil had been astonished they had come from her slight hands. He longed to go back to that day, to grasp one of her hands and decipher the lines on her palms, the way his grandfather used to do for all the children in the family. How long was her life line? Was the wealth line unbroken? How many children would she have? Now, after reading her letter, he knew more about her destiny than he ever would have found in her palm.

Anil continued to think of her as he boarded the late-night flight out of DFW airport, and while Baldev and Trinity slept curled up together in the two seats next to him. During their layover at Heathrow, as they strolled through the duty-free shops, Anil wondered how the Tahitian black pearl earrings would look in her earlobes, or a tiny diamond pendant in the hollow of her neck. He said nothing to Baldev or Trinity as they traversed the terminal and stopped for tea. If he spoke about Leena, she would become real, along with the complications of her past and his mother's judgment. For now, it was better that she remain safe in his thoughts.

ONCE THEY landed in Ahmadabad, the wedding festivities provided Anil with ample distraction. Mahesh's mother was in constant motion: directing vendors, welcoming guests, and fussing over Mahesh and his friends. She doted on Anil, because he too was Gujarati, and because doctors were the only professionals who trumped engineers in their cultural hierarchy. There was no hint of the Shahs' initial reluctance about their future daughter-in-law as they proudly introduced Yaalini to their circle of friends and relatives. That Baldev had shown up with his American girlfriend, with whom he planned to live unmarried, seemed to render Mahesh's choice less scandalous. For her part, Trinity managed to win over everyone with her willingness to dress in a sari for every occasion and eat so adeptly with her hands.

On the morning of the wedding ceremony, the atmosphere in Mahesh's family's home reached a heightened frenzy. Yaalini's parents had finally agreed, just days earlier, to attend the wedding. They'd arrived the night before the ceremony and were staying in the same hotel as Baldev and Anil, declining the Shahs' offer to stay in their home. Their discomfort was clear as they entered the ceremony hall wearing tight smiles and avoiding eye contact with the other guests. They answered inaudibly when asked by the pandit for their blessing of the couple. But Yaalini seemed impervious to any tension. She was beautiful in her wedding sari, her head crowned with flowers and dramatic makeup flaring her eyes. Mahesh looked like a smiling robot, a permanent grin etched on his face as he drifted around the room, greeting guests and accepting the envelopes of cash they pressed into his hands.

Despite being exhausted by the end of the evening, Anil, Baldev, and Trinity lingered in the reception hall until it was appropriate to leave. Even Trinity's appetite for Indian culture had been depleted after so many wedding functions.

"Only one more event," Baldev groaned. "Lunch tomorrow." He sank into a chair. "All I want to do is stay in bed and order room service."

"We have to go." Trinity held up the skirt of her heavy sari as she sat down next to him, layers of fabric billowing around her. "Mahesh's mother will definitely notice if we're not there. She even loaned me an outfit of his sister's." She glanced over at Anil and smiled. "What do you think of Mahesh's sister, by the way? Pretty, don't you think?"

"Auntie could probably get that wedding arranged lickety-split, doctor." Baldev elbowed Anil in the ribs. "Just give us some time to recover from this one."

Trinity rested her head on Baldev's shoulder. "I'm so glad we're going on vacation after this."

"You sure you don't want to come with us, Anil *bhai*?" Baldev asked. He and Trinity were going to a beach resort in Goa for a few days on their way down to Bangalore. "You could use a rest too, before you go back to Dallas. It's your last chance to spend time with us. Beautiful beaches, nothing to do but eat and drink and swim all day."

"Sounds tempting," Anil said. "But I can't. They're expecting me in Panchanagar." It was not true, of course. No one was expecting him. His mother did not even know he was in the country, much less a hundred kilometers away. But it wasn't his family he was going to see. On that long, lonely flight from London to Ahmadabad, when the cabin was darkened and the other passengers slept, Anil had stared out the window into the black sky. He'd wrestled with his thoughts, trying to make order out of the chaos: Leena, her marriage, the kerosene, the dowry money, his father's advice, his mother's sharp disapproval. He could make no sense of it. The only place his mind found solace was in those early memories of his childhood with Leena: rolling in the gully between their homes, play hunting for tigers in the brush, scrambling up the coconut trees. A time before everything became so complicated.

Over the past week in Ahmadabad, Anil still hadn't sorted out anything in his head, but he'd felt a deep, driving need to return to Panchanagar, and that instinct was stronger than any reason to the contrary he could conjure. He wanted to see Leena again, and he was prepared to face his mother to do so. He had allowed Ma to constrain his behavior when they were younger, but he would not do it again. What might Leena have been spared had he stood up to his mother that first time, if he had followed his heart back then? He could barely allow himself to consider it.

EARLY THE next morning, Anil awoke feeling refreshed, despite the exhaustion of the preceding week's activities. He showered, shaved carefully, and dressed in the crisp white shirt he'd kept unworn until now. After checking out of the hotel, he confirmed the arrangements he'd made for a car and driver, then paced the lobby, waiting for Baldev and Trinity.

The Shahs' home was bustling with people by the time they arrived. Trinity was hurried off to provide a therapeutic massage to Mahesh's mother, who was suffering from lower back pain after being on her feet all week. Anil and Baldev found Mahesh and pulled him out onto the private balcony.

"So?" Baldev asked Mahesh, sliding the balcony door shut behind him. He dropped his voice. "How was the wedding night?"

A grin spread across Mahesh's face as he cast his eyes downward and put his hands into his pockets.

"Look at that." Baldev slapped the balcony railing. "Proud as a peacock."

Mahesh smiled and wobbled his head. "I can't lie. Happiest day of my life." He put a hand on each of their shoulders. "Thanks for coming, brothers. It wouldn't have been the same without you."

"Are you kidding? We wouldn't have missed it." Baldev leaned against the balcony rail and let the sun warm his face. "It's the end of our collective bachelorhood. Mahesh was the first to fall, no surprise."

"And Baldev's become totally domesticated," Anil said. "Which *is* a surprise."

Baldev gave an exaggerated shrug of his shoulders. "Who would have predicted three years ago when we met that we'd end up here? Mahesh in a love marriage, staying in America. And me, moving to India?" Baldev shook his head. "Life is funny, man. You never know where the road leads."

"And then there's Dr. Patel," Mahesh said. "Who is exactly where he planned to be."

"And soon to be a cardiologist." Baldev extended his hand toward Anil, who grabbed it and embraced his friend. They shared one last collective farewell—big bear hugs and slaps on the back—before going their separate ways, not knowing when they'd all be together again. Mahesh and Yaalini would return to Dallas after their honeymoon in

Rajasthan, but it would not be the same as before. Mahesh had told Anil he was welcome to stay in the apartment indefinitely. They would not need to replace Baldev as a roommate, and Anil could have the other bathroom to himself. It was a generous offer, but Anil had other plans. Before leaving Dallas, he had already inquired about the vacated apartment next door.

After explaining to his hired driver how to get to Panchanagar, Anil settled into the backseat of the air-conditioned Ambassador and closed his eyes, bold with the anticipation of doing the first rash thing in his life.

❁

LEENA WAS sitting on the edge of her bed, braiding her hair, when there was a knock at the front door. Her mother was rolling chapatis in the kitchen, so Leena held the loose tail of her braid and went to answer the door, expecting to see Piya. Instead, it was Anil. An immediate fluttering rose in her chest. Was it her mind playing tricks on her, conjuring up the person who'd just been occupying her thoughts? Leena had mailed the letter months ago; she had received no reply, and had stopped expecting one. She held the end of her hair, waiting for the apparition to move.

Anil smiled and took a step toward her. "Come for a walk?" He gestured with his head to the fields behind him.

Leena watched him for a moment, trying to read his face. She looked toward the kitchen, where her mother would be occupied for some time, then turned back to Anil, held up her forefinger, and closed the front door, leaving him out on the terrace. Leena stood still for a moment, trying to calm her spinning mind. She could not blame him for not responding to her letter. Not many people, even those who'd been friendly when she first returned, cared to associate with a ruined woman. She had long ago stopped hoping for anything else. *And yet.*

Leena breathed deeply a few times, then told her mother she was going for a walk. She opened the door just enough to slip through and closed it behind her. She skipped barefoot down the front steps without waiting to see if Anil followed. Leena could move quickly through the fields, picking her way expertly in and out of rows. She didn't slow down for his benefit. He hurried behind her, through a patch of trees and down a valley on the other side. Finally, she reached a point where they were completely isolated in the brush. Her house, far in the distance, was obscured by the tall reeds surrounding them on all sides. Leena slowed her pace along the edge of the sugarcane field, planting one foot squarely in front of the other, as if walking a tightrope. Anil fell into step beside her. She could hear him trying to catch his breath. They walked quietly for several moments.

Anil stopped at a guava tree and laid his hand against its python-skin trunk. "You remember that time you climbed a guava tree to get fruit for all of us? And my mother came looking for us, angry because Kiran and I were late for dinner?"

Leena smiled. "You were so scared of getting in trouble, you ran off and left me there at the top of the tree by myself!"

Anil laughed. "We knew you could get down on your own. You were the only one who could do it without help."

Is that how he thought of her, as she used to be? Strong and carefree, not needing anyone else? It was no longer who she was, of course. Had he even received her letter, Leena wondered, or would she have to tell him everything again?

Anil turned to face her. "Leena, remember the last time I was here, I told you about the hospital I work at in Dallas, about the cardiology program?"

She nodded, recalling their conversation after the Big House medical clinic, during which he came alive describing how he could do more than just bandage people up, how he could actually mend their hearts, save their lives.

"I'm applying for a fellowship in cardiology, to become a specialist. It's not certain yet, but I have a very good chance." Anil's face was flushed. "It's going to change everything. It means another four or five years in America."

Leena smiled. "That's wonderful, Anil." *So that's why he'd come, to share his good news.* She turned her eyes to the ground. With the curl of her big toe, she pushed at the earth; wrapped around her second toe was a thick silver band, the last remaining piece of jewelry on her body. In the still air, she could hear Anil breathing.

"Come with me, Leena," Anil said. "It doesn't matter to me. Everything you told me, your letter. The past. It doesn't matter anymore." Leena looked up, met his eyes, and examined his face for a moment. *What was he saying?* She turned and continued walking along the edge of the sugarcane field, the heel of one foot in front of the other's toe. She heard him scramble after her. "Leena?"

She shook her head. "You don't know what you're saying, Anil."

He reached over and grasped one of her hands, pulling her to face him. "What don't I know? I know I loved when I was twelve years old and you beat me up that coconut tree, because everyone else always let me win. I love the way you make those beautiful pieces with your hands. And I love that you keep the crooked ones."

Leena's smile widened and she automatically moved her hand to her mouth.

"And I love that." Anil caught her hand. "I love your smile, *that* smile. Don't cover it up. It's the best part of you."

The smile remained on her face as Leena's eyes filled. They were words she'd never heard, words she'd given up believing she would ever hear. "I love the way you slow down your speech when I start stammering, and it helps me stop. I love the way you know me better than I know myself." He cupped his hands around her face and wiped the tears from each of her cheeks with his thumbs. The roughness of his skin surprised her. She'd imagined someone so educated would not have the same hands as her.

She shook her head. "Anil—"

"It will be different with me, Leena. You know me." Anil's eyes glistened. "You've always known me. I can come back this summer for the wedding. I even found an apartment for us to live in. It has a big patio you can use for your pottery studio. We'll live right next door to my friend Mahesh and his wife, Yaalini. You'll love them. We'll start a new life together. It's a different world there, Leena. The lights never go out, the water runs all the time. I'll be making a good living. You can work on your pottery, and you don't even have to worry about selling it. You can keep it all, even the good ones. We'll have shelves from floor to ceiling. Have you ever seen a motorized pottery wheel? We'll get you one." He was talking without pause, running out of breath again, his shirt damp with sweat. He looked into her eyes, holding her face in his hands. "A new life, just the two of us. What do you think?"

Leena smiled, shaking her head. He'd been like this even as a boy, a big dreamer, always talking of faraway places. "What about my mother? I can't leave her alone." Even as she said it, Leena knew her mother prayed every day for her happiness. It was the only thing she asked of God after her husband had died.

"She can come with us," Anil said. "Whatever you want, Leena."

Leena had to laugh at his brazenness. Could it be true? Could those dreams she'd tucked away in a corner of her heart still be possible?

"Your mother can take care of our babies," Anil said. "Make them fat on her delicious *chundo*."

Leena felt an unmistakable pang from somewhere deep inside her as Anil stepped closer to her, slowly. Only after her skin was already burning with the anticipation of his hands did he embrace her. Despite everything else they knew about each other and all the things they'd done, this was the closest they'd ever been physically. How different his touch was, how safe she felt in his arms. He lifted her off the ground and spun her around and she laughed.

Anil stumbled on the uneven ground and they fell together onto the earth, splayed out like awkward children. Leena moved her sari to cover her bad leg, but Anil caught her hand. He sat up, drew the sari away from the area, and touched the scar lightly. With his fingertips, he traced its outline from the top of her foot past her ankle, up her calf to her knee and back down again, sending a tingling sensation up her leg. When he finished, he draped the sari over her leg again carefully and smiled. Leena felt a warmth spread through her body, a feeling of security she hadn't had in a long time. She stood up and brushed herself off. Anil followed and took her hand, and they started walking again, back through the reeds. "I'll take you to a very good plastic surgeon in Dallas," Anil said. "He can do skin grafts on your leg, the scar would hardly be visible." He squeezed her hand.

❁

NIRMALA WAS finishing up the chapatis when Leena returned to the house and retreated to her room. Nirmala turned off the kerosene stove before stepping out the back door, where she saw Anil Patel walking toward a black car parked at the edge of their property. She felt her blood seethe as she marched outside, clutching the wooden rolling pin.

"*Namaste*, Nirmala Auntie." Anil pressed his hands together and bowed. He was grinning like a child.

"Why have you come here?" Nirmala asked. "What do you want from us?"

Anil took a deep breath, then another. "Auntie, I came to see Leena." He paused for several moments, as if he'd forgotten how to speak.

"You leave my daughter alone." Nirmala rapped the rolling pin against her legs. "We don't need any more involvement from your family."

"Please, Auntie. I know there was some dowry business between you and my parents, but it doesn't concern me—"

"Doesn't concern you? That's what you think?" Nirmala laughed and shook her head. "You listen to me—listen and then say it doesn't concern you."

She started at the beginning, with the day everything changed, when she woke up to find the folded paper her husband had left on his pillow. He'd never had any formal schooling, but he'd learned to read and write enough to sell his crops in town. Since she'd been accompanying him to the market, Nirmala had learned a few numbers as well. On the paper was a hand-drawn map: it showed their home, the main road they took into town, and the market where they sold their crops. This was all familiar to Nirmala, but Pradip had also drawn a small square with an *X* on it, a few blocks from the town market. Below the map was written his name, and next to it a single number: *78,000*. What did it all mean? She went to find him, searching first through the fields where he'd spent his life, and finally reaching the river where he'd ended it.

"He couldn't swim?" Anil's face was pinched, the expression of a young boy who'd skinned his knee and was trying not to cry.

"He was an excellent swimmer," Nirmala said. "He taught Leena to swim." Anil drew in a ragged breath. She looked out to the rolling hills on the horizon. "After what happened to Leena, I worried about the revenge he might take against those people. But my husband only exacted a punishment against himself."

Anil was shaking his head, his pinched expression threatening to burst open.

"We brought him home. We held our own cremation. No one else came. We could not afford any ceremony. We were too ashamed to call the pandit. After the cremation, Leena and I went into town and found the place he'd marked on the map." Nirmala paused, then continued in a softer voice. "It was the police station," she said, looking up to see if he understood. "He was the giver of the dowry. As her father, full responsibility could be placed on him. And since he was dead, he could not be prosecuted. Everyone else—me, Leena, your parents who gave money—we could all be spared. He saved your father's reputation, but did your mother ever acknowledge that sacrifice? No, of course not." She exhaled slowly. "Seventy-eight thousand rupees, the price of my husband's life."

Anil was rubbing his chin furiously, as if to wipe something away.

"We filed the complaint," Nirmala continued. "Leena gave her statement. That was when I learned the full extent of the evil she encountered in that house. She had to show them her wounds." She swallowed against the tightness of her throat. "They took photos of each and every one."

"What happened?" Anil demanded. "They must have been prosecuted?"

Nirmala smiled. For all his knowledge and travels, this boy didn't understand how things worked. He still thought bad people were punished and good ones rewarded. He still believed in justice. "We filed the complaint," she said. "They told us they would investigate. I don't know if they ever did. Those scoundrels probably used our money to bribe the police to look the other way." She shook her head. "But they never came back. My husband gave his life so we could be free." Nirmala's throat was tight, and her whole body ached for her husband. "I came to learn that he also paid back your parents the day before his death—all our outstanding debt. He decided he would rather take his own life than be diminished in front of the great Patel family. God knows how he got that money. I came to you, remember? I came for help, for mercy. Your mother refused to see me."

Anil had stopped fidgeting and was now quietly watching her.

"We did everything on our own," Nirmala said. "I pulled my husband's body from the water myself." She clenched the rolling pin with both fists now. "Leena and I carried him back from the river. We cremated him ourselves. No one came. No one helped us." She gestured to the land around them. "And we rebuilt our lives, stick by stick: this home, our land, Leena's business." She watched Anil, waiting for the meaning to sink in. "My husband paid the last rupee of our debt to your mother before he took his life. We are free from your family and that's how we will remain. We don't need anyone, understand? The great Patels have given us more than enough help for one lifetime. We are still recovering from your family's generosity." She stepped close enough to smell his pungent sweat. "So leave here. And leave us alone."

29

Anil stood in place, a droplet of sweat trickling down the back of his neck as he watched Nirmala Auntie return to her house. His driver was leaning casually against the hood of the Ambassador, probably having heard every word of the conversation. "Let's go," Anil barked. "Rest time over."

"Where now, Sahib?" The driver spat betel-nut juice on the ground.

Anil slammed the car door. *Where now?* His family wasn't expecting him. He could easily have the driver take him back to Ahmadabad to catch the next flight to Dallas. Or hop on a plane down to Goa to drink cocktails on the beach with Baldev. Both of those alternatives would be easier than the one he knew he had to face. "All the way up the road."

❁

"Anil!" Ma cried when he entered the Big House. Eyes wide, she rushed over and grabbed his face between her palms before pulling him into an embrace. "But when? Why did you not tell us you were coming? Where did you come from?" She looked past him out the front door, but the car and driver were gone. It was the quietest arrival to Panchanagar he'd ever made.

"I came from Leena's house," Anil said. "I asked her to marry me and come to Dallas."

The smile drained away from his mother's face. She let go of him and stepped back, clutching herself with her own arms. Her face contorted a few times, then went blank as a mask.

"Ma, listen, you don't know what happened."

"I know everything that matters. That girl brought shame upon her family, and she disrespected your father." She spat out the last words, turned and moved toward the kitchen.

Anil followed her. "She didn't walk out on her marriage," he said, trying to keep his voice even. "And her husband didn't throw her out. She had a good reason."

A sharp noise of protest emanated from Ma's throat. "What reason?" She went into the dark cellar and yanked on a chain, illuminating the single bulb overhead. From the bin, she began picking up onions one by one, sloughing their papery skins onto the cellar floor.

Anil followed her into the cellar, which was scarcely big enough to hold both of them. "Ma, he tried to *kill* her." Anil spoke in a low voice, feeling as if he were betraying a confidence. "He doused her with kerosene and lit her on fire."

Ma stopped fussing with the onion in her hands. Her expression was inscrutable except for a twitch at the corner of her eye. "She told you that? And you take it as truth, simply because someone said it?" She turned away.

"No. I saw it," Anil said. "With my own eyes. Severe burns, all the way up her leg." Ma swiveled to look at him, her face shocked by the implication. Anil closed his eyes and shook his head once. "When she was washing her feet at the well, the day we held the medical clinic outside. I saw it then. It's true, Ma."

Ma studied his face for a moment, then marched out of the cellar and unloaded the onions onto the kitchen counter. She smoothed the front of her sari with both palms. "I can't believe such a thing could happen. That boy was from a good family."

"They treated her like a servant, Ma," Anil said. "Worse than a servant, like a slave. Like a *dog*. They worked her to the bone and they beat her, and they burned her—"

"It is not possible!" Ma interrupted, her voice climbing to an unnaturally high pitch. "Your father looked into the family himself. He had excellent judgment in these matters."

Anil drew in a breath. "What do you mean, Papa looked into the family?" The idea of his father meeting Leena's husband was at once intriguing and horrifying. "He went to their home?"

"No, they came here," Ma said. "The groom and his father. They sat right out there." She nodded toward the gathering room. "They wouldn't even take tea, only water. They brought gifts, a box of very good sweets. Your papa said they were well-mannered and kind. He had excellent judgment in these matters," she repeated.

"Not this time, Ma." Anil gently shook his head. "They manipulated him. They were only after the money. If he'd gone to their house, he would have seen it was in shambles and no one was working their fields." Anil watched his mother's profile, the continuous twitching near her eye. "Ma, it wasn't a marriage, it was a scam. The dowry was all they were after. If Papa hadn't given the money, they never would have agreed to the match and Leena never would have been in danger." Anil paused. "It was a mistake, Ma. Papa was wrong."

His mother spun toward him with fury glittering in her black pupils. In one quick movement, her hand flew out and she slapped him hard across the face. "How dare you?" she spat in a loud whisper. "How dare you blame him?" Her eyes bore two holes into him. "You think you know better than your father? You think your judgment is equal to his?" She held his eyes as firmly as if she had his chin in her grip, then pushed past him and left the kitchen.

Anil touched his own hand to his cheek where it burned with the imprint of hers, then turned and followed her into the gathering room. "Isn't that what you expect, Ma? When all these people come here and ask for my opinion, when I make decisions about their lives?" He slapped his hand on the table. "It's fine for me to make judgments about other people, but not us?"

Ma stood with her hands on the back of Papa's reading chair. Anil closed his eyes and felt them burn before opening them again. "Look, Ma, everyone makes mistakes. I've made plenty." His voice rose in an impatient crescendo. "My mistakes have *killed* people. Patients have died because I screwed up. My best friend was nearly beaten to death because of a girl I dated. That was *my* fault." When his mother's eyes filled with tears and shock, Anil nodded. "Yes, that's right, Ma. I had an American girlfriend, and I had a *full* relationship with her." He slumped into another chair and rested his head in his hands. "Leena's not the only one with a past, Ma. I'm not sure you'd like my history any more than hers."

Ma moved away from Papa's chair and toward the front window, her back turned to Anil. From the rise and fall of her shoulders, he could tell she was breathing deeply.

"All I'm saying is, Papa wasn't perfect. He made mistakes like the rest of us." Anil stood and took a few steps toward the window but did not reach out to touch her. "His intentions may have been good, but this decision was wrong. Leena almost died. Her family was ruined financially." Anil's voice dropped to a near whisper. "Her father killed himself to save them, to pay you back."

Ma stared out the window, a deserted look in her eyes. "You don't have to marry her out of guilt, Anil."

"No. It would be out of love," Anil said, waiting a few moments for her to take this in. "But Papa still made a bad decision, Ma. And we have to make it right." *First, do no harm.*

"I don't know what's happened to you, Anil," Ma said. "You've lost your way. After your father died, you should have come home and stepped up to your responsibilities like a man. Instead, you're disgracing his memory. You should be ashamed." She climbed the staircase and disappeared behind her bedroom door.

ANIL FOUND Piya in her room, sitting on her bed with an oversized sketchbook propped up against her knees. On her nightstand sat a tray of watercolors and a cup of muddied water. She was leaning forward, the tip of her nose a few inches from the paper, making precise flicking motions with a thin brush.

Anil stood in the doorway for a few moments, then knocked lightly on the door frame. Piya looked up, her face marked by surprise. "Anil?" She stood up, overturning the water cup at her elbow. "Shoot," she said, righting the cup and stepping over the puddle on the floor. They moved toward each other and embraced. Not for the first time, Anil felt a pang of gratitude for his younger sister. "*Bhai*, what are you doing here?" She kissed his cheek, where Anil could still feel the sting of his mother's hand.

"My roommate Mahesh got married in Ahmadabad last weekend. It was a last-minute decision to come for the wedding," Anil lied. "I didn't know if I could get the time off."

"Did you see Ma? Oh God, you must have given her a heart attack." Piya grinned and sat back down on the bed, tucking her legs under her. She moved the large sketchbook aside to make space for him.

Anil sat on the end of the bed, leaned against the footboard, and closed his eyes. His mother had never laid a hand on him. He'd witnessed her anger many times, but always directed toward others.

"Oh God," Piya continued. "The kitchen will be total madness by the crack of dawn. You know she usually starts cooking an entire week before you come? She must be beside herself." Piya, seemingly delighted about this prospect, rocked back and forth to get comfortable.

"She slapped me." Anil pulled at a loose thread in the bedspread, watching it pucker. "Ma. She slapped me across the face just now."

Piya's eyes grew large. "Oh, shit. The golden son has fallen. What happened?"

The thread broke in Anil's fingers. He ran his palm over the surface of the bedspread, searching for another loose end. "Leena."

Piya leaned back against the pillow. It was a while before she spoke. "I could see it last summer. At the clinic, the way she looked at you."

"She did?" Anil looked up. "You did?"

Piya nodded. "Anil—"

Anil held up a hand. "I know everything," he said. "It doesn't matter to me. I want to marry her. I asked her to come with me to Dallas."

Piya rocked backwards on the bed and looked up at the ceiling. "Oh, Anil. Why do you always have to choose the difficult path?"

"What, you don't approve either?" Anil asked, an edge of anger creeping into his voice.

Piya shook her head. "No, it's not that. Just be careful, *bhai*. She's been through enough."

The volume of the crickets chirping outside escalated. Piya went over to the window and cranked it halfway closed. Anil picked up her sketchbook from where it sat next to him. Underneath was another book, a thick volume resembling one of his textbooks. "*Complete Guide to Ayurvedic and Homeopathic Medicine?*"

"Yes." Piya smiled. "Actually, it's quite interesting, the number of natural remedies that have been proven to work. I bet you could even learn something, Doctor Sahib."

Anil handed the book back to her. "I'll leave that expertise to you."

"People kept coming here, you know," Piya said. "Last summer after you left. Word spread about the clinic, and people traveled here from sixty, seventy kilometers away. That one man, whose son was born without a proper ear? He came every day for months. So I started to look things up." She tapped the cover of the reference book. "I helped a few people, not too many."

Anil stayed in his sister's room, talking with her until after midnight, when he was finally tired enough to sleep. Walking down the hallway to his own room, he saw the lamp on through the cracked door of his mother's bedroom. Several hours later, when Anil got up for a glass of water, the same light was still burning.

MINA PATEL sat cross-legged on the floor of the small alcove adjoining her bedroom. In addition to the altar containing statues of several gods and goddesses and the framed picture of her guru, was a portrait of her deceased husband. It was not one of the photos taken shortly before his death, when his face was sunken and his eyes held a look of defeat. Nor had she chosen, as some widows did, a picture from his youth, in which he looked more like a movie star than the man she woke up next to every morning. Mina had selected a picture of Jayant in his early forties, in the prime of his health and life. That was how she preferred to remember him: after he'd become comfortable in his leadership of the farm and other family duties.

Jayant was not always the confident man others saw. In the beginning, when his father had first asked him to serve as the family arbiter, he had been uncertain a lot of the time. They used to discuss cases together—at night when they lay in bed, or on long afternoon walks through the fields when everyone else was resting. Mina helped him think through the marital disputes or find solutions between siblings who fought. In time, Jayant developed his own way of talking to people and solving their problems. People listened to him, they trusted him. He had a gift.

And yet, if what Anil had said was true . . . If that other family had convinced Jayant of their decency only to secure the big dowry? Mina recalled the way they'd praised Jayant's farmland and his expertise, the elaborate box of sweets they'd brought, the gold coins she hadn't mentioned to Anil. Her husband had always enjoyed such admiration. Had he allowed it to affect his judgment in this case?

Mina closed her eyes and bowed her head toward the ground, as far as her joints would allow. Her husband was the most decent man she'd known in her life, including her own dear father and her respected guru. It was one thing for a man to behave in a holy way in an ashram; it was quite another to maintain that spirit in the real world. If what Anil said was true . . . An involuntary image came to her, flames rising around a sari, licking their way up a leg.

Mina hadn't seen her husband make such an error in judgment since his early days as an arbiter. Jayant's father had pushed him into the role too early, forcing him to bear the responsibility before he was ready. It was the one thing Jayant had resolved not to impose on his own son. He'd encouraged Anil to study, move away, pursue his own education and career in the way he wanted. Jayant's deepest hope was for Anil to return to Panchanagar one day, but he would not force him to do so. A tear escaped Mina's eye, and she allowed it to run all the way down her cheek without wiping it away. *God rest his soul*, she prayed to the picture of her husband. What would he do now?

Mina rose from the floor and reached for the large ring of keys she kept tucked into her waistband. She unlocked the metal cupboard next to Jayant's portrait and retrieved the slim journal in which he'd recorded the names, dates, and amounts of various loans he'd made through the years. Then she opened the lockbox in which she kept the cash and counted out fifty thousand rupees.

30

ANIL AWOKE THE NEXT MORNING UNDER THE SHADOW OF Nirmala Auntie's fury. The revelation that Papa had met that boy's family—entertained them, been charmed, perhaps even coerced by them—it was almost too much to bear. Such a terrible course of events had been set into motion by a single bad judgment of his father's.

On his dresser, next to the chessboard, Anil spotted a notebook that hadn't been there the night before. Its lined pages were filled with Papa's handwriting. Anil turned to an envelope tucked into a back page, where the names of Leena's parents were listed at the top, with a tally of numbers below. Their account took up several pages, and at the end was written a single figure: 50,000. The number of rupees, paid in full.

Inside the envelope were fifty bills, each in the denomination of one thousand. A thin sheaf of folded paper slipped out of the notebook and onto the floor. Anil sat down at his desk and unfolded it.

❁

Dear son,

I will not hide the truth from you. This is not an easy job. You will be asked to make judgments without having all the information, without knowing how people will take your counsel or what will happen in the future. You will never be able to please everyone, and you will make mistakes. Often, you will feel you are not equipped to bear such a heavy burden. Do not let this prevent you from acting. It is important for people in our village to know someone will hear them and consider their problems. But this does not mean you must always substitute your judgment for theirs. Often, if you ask the right questions and listen very carefully, people will lead you to the answer. You are already smart, like the mathematician who created the game of chess so many centuries ago—you can outwit others if you want. Now you must also learn from the king, and do not squander what you have.

I know your mother can be challenging, but she possesses wisdom too. She helped me with many of the disputes I faced in the beginning. As a woman, she knows and understands things differently, and I found her counsel to be invaluable. You and your siblings are young and have new ways of thinking, and that too is valuable. There is wisdom in both approaches, and I have often thought, if we could merge the old and the young into one person, that wisdom would multiply.

All this is to say, don't be afraid to look everywhere for the wisdom you will need. This role is difficult, but it is important. It has been a privilege for me, and I have done my best. I know you will do yours.

Papa

ANIL BRUSHED a tear from his cheek. He read the letter three times before tucking it into his backpack. The house was unusually quiet as he emerged from his bedroom. Down the hallway, Piya's room was empty. His mother's bedroom looked as it always did, its uncreased batik bedspread betraying no signs of a sleepless night. Through the window, he could see Kiran working in the fields.

Anil climbed down the stairs and followed his mother's voice into the kitchen, where she was chiding a servant for allowing moisture to accumulate in the potato bin. Anil watched her issue instructions for lunch preparations, ever detailed in her requirements of how the vegetables were to be diced. When Ma looked up, she caught him smiling. They held each other's gaze for a moment; he could detect a softness in her eyes, a wordless apology. Then she turned to the cook. "Don't you see Anil Sahib has come? Quickly, make him a fresh cup of chai."

Anil was sitting outside on the porch chair with his tea when Piya ran up the front steps, panting. "Anil, come quickly!" Damp strands of hair were matted to her forehead.

"What, where?" Anil asked, rising slowly from his chair, but she'd already run off. He followed her, running all the way down the lane, past Nikhil and the field hands, past Chandu and the outer reaches of the rice paddies. When Piya turned toward Leena's house, Anil's heart began pounding in his chest and ears. He followed Piya up the terrace steps, through the front door, and into one of the bedrooms, where he saw Leena kneeling on the floor next to the bed. On the bed lay a young girl, about eleven or twelve years old. She was motionless, except for the labored breath with which her chest rose and fell. Her eyes were closed, and one of them was badly swollen. A deep aubergine bruise radiated out from that eye and disappeared under her hairline. Blood was crusted at her nostrils.

Leena stood up and touched his elbow. Anil was conscious of her fingers against his bare skin. "She showed up here this morning," Leena whispered. "She must have slept outside last night, or longer."

Anil now noticed the rest of the young girl's body. Her skirt was caked with dirt and dried grass; the hem was torn apart. On the front of her blouse was a large stain from what appeared to be dried blood. The same rusty color was streaked down her bare forearm and the back of her hand. "She just showed up on your doorstep?" Anil asked. "You don't know her?"

Leena did not take her eyes off the girl. "I do know her," she said. "It's Ritu. My niece."

Anil turned to Leena. "Your . . . ?" He lowered his voice. "What is she doing here?"

Leena explained how, earlier that morning, Ritu had knocked on the door and collapsed into her arms. "I didn't recognize her at first. Her hair used to be much longer, and her cheeks were rounder. I thought she might be a beggar, but then I saw her clothes were too fine." Leena touched the edge of the girl's skirt, the tiny mirrored jewels stitched into the forest-green cloth. When she spoke again, her voice came out in a whisper. "She was crying. I couldn't understand what she was saying, but then I heard her call me *didi*. And I knew. It was her." Leena knelt down again and stroked the girl's forehead. "Poor, sweet Ritu. What happened to you?"

She looked up at Anil. "I don't know how she got here, but she could hardly stand up, so I brought her in here to lie down. She was so dirty, covered with blood. I wanted to clean her, but she wouldn't let me touch her. I went to get a glass of water and when I came back, she was asleep, just like this. She hasn't moved in over an hour. I'm worried, Anil. Can you check if she's okay?"

"Yes, but I'll have to touch her to examine her," Anil said. Piya offered to run back to the Big House to retrieve the medical bag he'd left from his last visit.

Leena nodded. "Should we wake her?"

"Yes, I think so. From that contusion, it looks like she's had a serious head injury. She could have a concussion or internal bleeding. She might need to go to the hospital."

"Can't you just help her here?" Leena's voice quickened.

"I'll try," he said. "I'll do my best."

LEENA WOKE Ritu, but even after she introduced Anil as a friend and a doctor, the girl would not allow him to touch her. She drew back when Anil tried to look at her injured face, so Leena served as his hands during the examination. She held open Ritu's eyelids while Anil shone a light to inspect her pupils. It was Leena who slipped the stethoscope under the girl's blouse and held it, first to her back and then to her chest, moving it according to Anil's direction while he listened to her heartbeat and breath. Together, like two halves of the same person, Anil and Leena moved quietly and deliberately through each step of the physical examination. They spoke little, communicating mainly through their eyes and gestures. He'd never worked with someone with whom he fit together so easily.

Leena held the girl's hand as Anil asked questions to test for memory loss or mental impairment, but Ritu would not respond to him. So Leena repeated Anil's questions to Ritu and relayed her answers back to him. Anil recognized that the girl's skittish behavior could be a sign of physical abuse.

Leena's tenderness helped to calm not only Ritu but Anil as well. He worried that Ritu's family, the very people who had beaten and burned Leena, could show up at any moment, demanding money or revenge. His anxiety rose at the prospect of confrontation or violence. A sense of helplessness engulfed him, the same sense he'd felt when watching those men attack Baldev.

After his examination, Anil removed the stethoscope from his neck and gestured for Leena to follow him outside. They joined Piya on the terrace. "She has some infected wounds on her hands and feet, which look like they've been festering for a while. I'll need to drain the abscesses with a scalpel, but it will be painful. I'll come back tomorrow morning. Can you prepare her?"

Leena nodded. "I'll try, but she seems so frightened." She bit down on a fingernail.

"I have something else that might work," Piya offered. "I'll be back in a little while." She trotted down the steps, leaving Anil and Leena alone on the terrace.

"Most of her injuries are superficial," Anil continued, "but she's had some blunt force trauma to the frontal lobe."

Leena peered at him. "What does that mean?"

"Something hit her hard, right here." Anil touched his right eye and forehead to illustrate. "Or she hit something, like a wall or the ground."

Leena was nodding almost imperceptibly, as if her head were vibrating with the comprehension of what had happened.

"She may have suffered a mild concussion at the time of the injury, but there's no lasting brain trauma, which is good. Her remaining symptoms—the dizziness and nausea—those should disappear on their own over the next couple of weeks. We should keep an eye on her for a day to make sure, but after that, she'll be fine." Anil waited for the tension to ease from Leena's face, but she still looked deep in concentration. "Leena, we need to call the police to come and get her. Soon. Before her family comes looking for her."

Leena's head jolted up. "I can't send her back there," she said. "They hit her, you said so yourself."

"You're not sending her back there. The police will make sure she's safe. They'll take her to the hospital and get her the medical care she needs." Anil reached for Leena's wrist and held it gently. "Leena, her family will be looking for her. If they find her here, you have no idea what they'll do. Do you really want to get mixed up with them again, after you've finally got free?" Leena was pressing down on the terrace with her pointed toes. Her wrist was limp in Anil's hand. "Have you forgotten, Leena, what they're capable of? These are dangerous people."

Leena slipped her wrist out of his grip and looked Anil directly in the eyes. "Yes, I know, and the police are not so trustworthy either." Her hand went to her mouth and she nibbled on a fingernail. "How can we be sure what they will and won't do with a young, helpless girl?"

Anil shook his head. "You have to alert the authorities. That's the right thing to do. You're not equipped to deal with this." When Leena shot him an angry look, he reached out for her hand again. "You have to think of your own safety, Leena. And your mother's. Where is she?" He'd been relieved earlier not to see Nirmala Auntie, but now he was worried.

"She went to the market in town. I stayed back to finish some glazing."

"Look, keep an eye on her overnight. Make sure she drinks plenty of water and eats something. I'll come by in the morning, and we can decide then. I also have another matter to speak to you and your mother about tomorrow, okay? It's good news." He embraced her tightly, relishing the feel of her in his arms.

❁

EARLY THE next morning, Anil left the Big House after a fitful night of dreams about Rudy and Lee, and their swinging six-pack of beer. As he walked down the lane to Leena's house, he marshaled a list of reasons they had to call the police today. He saw situations like this all the time at Parkview—neglected and abused children. His job was to treat them medically, then alert the proper authorities: that was the right thing to do.

Nirmala Auntie opened the door, her eyes narrowing when she saw him.

"Auntie." Anil bowed his head. "I'm just here for the girl." He held up his medical bag, and she stepped aside to let him enter.

He stopped in the doorway of the bedroom. Piya was wiping a dark green paste from the girl's foot. "Anil, look," Piya said, nearly breathless. "See how much better it looks."

Anil peered over her shoulder and was astonished to see that the abscess was half the size it had been the day before. "What did you do?" he asked. "What is that?"

"Leaves from the neem tree. I boiled and mashed them into a paste and left it on overnight." Piya beamed. "Another day or two and these wounds should be all drained." She stood up and gathered the dirty cloths into a bag. "I'll come back with another batch."

Leena embraced Piya. "Thank you," she whispered.

Anil walked his sister to the front door. "I suppose I could learn a few things from you." He hugged her before she left. When he returned to the bedroom, Leena was sitting on the edge of the bed next to the girl.

"You left us without saying good-bye, *didi*," Ritu said. "You said you wouldn't leave. You promised."

Leena looked up at the ceiling, then down to Ritu's hand, which she was holding in hers. "I had to. Forgive me." Her voice cracked with emotion.

"I know," Ritu said. "He would have killed you too."

Anil heard Leena's sharp intake of breath. "Ritu, what are you saying?"

"He would have killed you," Ritu said. "Like the other woman, before you came to live with us."

Leena straightened her back. "Ritu, please, slow down. You're not making any sense."

"One day she was just gone. Dev was too young to remember her, but not me. She took care of me all the time, she gave me handfuls of puffed rice from the cellar." A small smile pushed at the corners of Ritu's mouth. "And she wore jasmine flowers in her hair. She always smelled good. Dev was just a baby. She bathed him, she sang to me at night."

"I don't understand," Leena said. "Girish? My husband?" Anil flinched at the reference. Leena rubbed at her forehead. "There was another woman? He had another . . . wife? Before me? You called her *didi* too?"

Ritu shook her head, a look of confusion spreading across her face. "No . . . I don't remember. It was so long ago . . . even before I started school. I remember the puffed rice. She . . . I think she called me *beti* . . ." She shook her head again. "One day she was gone. Grandmother told me she went on a long trip. Later she said there was no such person." Ritu dropped her head. "She told me I had just imagined her. After that, I couldn't speak about her or I got a spanking. But I never forgot."

"God," Leena whispered. "Oh God. Ritu baby."

"When you came, Leena *didi*, I felt like my prayers had been answered. But then you went away too." Ritu took in a big gulp of air before continuing. "Grandmother said you ran away, but I didn't believe her. You promised me you wouldn't. And Dev was old enough to remember you too. We asked if we could visit you. After Grandmother died—"

"Your grandmother died?" Leena said sharply. "Only Rekha is left now?"

Ritu nodded. "Whenever we asked her about you, she got so angry. One day, she turned around and screamed at us that you were dead." Ritu dropped her head, choking on her tears.

"Rekha told you that?" Leena asked.

Ritu nodded and began sobbing.

Leena leaned in close to Ritu and stroked her hair. "Shh, baby. Shh."

"They told me you were dead, *didi*." Ritu sat up in the bed, her arms entwined with Leena's, her hands clenching Leena's shoulders. "But that night, after I was supposed to be sleeping, I heard the men talking—they were saying they should have killed you, like the first time. It would have made less trouble afterward." Ritu wiped her face with both hands. "I knew they were lying about you, *didi*. I knew you wouldn't run away. I had to come find you."

ANIL WALKED back and forth across the patch of packed dirt in front of Leena's house. "We have to call the police today, Leena. *Now.*"

Leena shook her head slowly, twisting the end of her sari around her palm. "It makes sense now, it does. Rekha was so unfeeling to those children. She had no love for them at all. It made no sense to me, but now it does." Leena looked up at Anil, her eyes a little wild. "Those children are not Rekha's. She took them from Girish's first wife when they were too young to remember. You heard Ritu—that woman called her *beti*, daughter. It makes sense now."

"That doesn't prove anything," Anil said. "I call my little cousin *beti* sometimes; my grandmother always called Piya *beti*."

Leena continued speaking, faster, her words gathering speed as they came out. "One night, I heard Rekha's husband, Girish's elder brother. He was drunk and yelling at her. He called her names, so many terrible names. 'Whore,' 'animal'—" She stopped and turned her piercing eyes on Anil. "'Barren.' He called her barren. It made no sense to me because she had two children. But now it does. And no wonder Rekha acted so badly! She was just trying to survive. She was terrified of them, terrified she would be next." Leena kept moving her head in slow motion. "They are his children too. Girish. That's why the children were so fond of him. It makes sense."

The way she kept repeating that phrase filled Anil with a sense of helplessness. "It *doesn't* make sense. You're not making sense. Leena, do you hear yourself? They killed another woman. They wanted to kill you, *tried* to kill you. What do you think they'll do to you when they find Ritu here? We have to call the police."

"No!" Leena cried.

He threw his hands in the air. "What are you going to do, Leena? You can't keep her here forever."

"Why not?" Leena glared at him.

Anil stopped pacing and looked at her.

Her expression was stern, her eyes unflinching. "I can keep her. She can live with me. It's only me and my mother here. We don't have much, but we have space for one more." Her eyes opened wider. "Oh God. Dev!" she said. "He's still there. God knows what they'll do to him without his sister to protect him."

"Leena!" Anil grabbed her arm. "This is not your problem anymore. They are not your family." He stopped and took a deep breath. "How can you take such a risk with these people who almost killed you?" He pictured the envelope of cash, fifty thousand rupees, back in his room, ready to return but insufficient to repair the damage it had caused. When Leena didn't respond, he rubbed his forehead furiously with his hand and sank down to the ground. "You don't have to do this, Leena." His felt his life, his dream, slipping away.

"Perhaps that is true." Leena's voice was steel, her eyes unyielding. "But those children were the only ones who treated me kindly in that home, the only ray of hope I had for more than a year." A tear slipped down her cheek. "Ritu kept me alive when I thought I would rather be dead." She pointed toward the house. "And I will not turn my back on her now."

"They're his children, his flesh and blood," Anil said. "You'll never escape that."

"At least some good might come of the bad," Leena said. "It won't have been for nothing."

31

Anil's bedroom door swung open and banged against the wall. He jolted awake and reached for his specs on the nightstand. When he put them on, the figure of his younger sister came into focus—hands on her hips, jaw set. "What is it?" Anil sat up. "What's wrong?"

"She's gone."

"Who?"

"Who do you think?" Piya said. "Ritu! She's gone."

Anil swung his legs out of bed and went to the window, as if he might be able to see her out there. The fields were still and empty, the morning light filtering into the broad sky. From downstairs, he could hear the sounds of mealtime and chatter. "What do you mean she's gone? Did the police come for her?"

Piya's eyes bore into him. "She overheard you and Leena fighting last night. She told Leena she didn't want to put her in any danger. Leena assured her everything would be fine, but this morning, Ritu was gone." She walked over to the window. "She's *gone*, Anil." Piya crossed her arms across her chest. "You've been away too long, *bhai*. You don't even see how you've changed. Maybe that's the way you deal with things in America, just call the police and wash your hands. But not here, *bhai*. It's not right."

In that moment—from the sick feeling that rose in his stomach at the thought of Ritu walking alone in her battered condition—Anil knew he'd been wrong. Under different circumstances, this was a child he would've admitted to the hospital. Instead, he'd seen her as a sort of threat to their safety, their independence, their life. He'd already been thinking of himself and Leena as *they*, an entity together, one that had become imperiled. He'd allowed his judgment to be compromised by the loss of his dream. Anil cursed himself as he hastily pulled on his clothes.

"Where are you going?" Piya called after him as he left the room. "Don't go over there, Anil." Her voice rose after him. "She doesn't want to see you."

Anil ran down the stairs and into the gathering room. Everyone was sitting around the table, eating breakfast. "Oh, look who managed to get up before noon." Chandu smiled. "Good morning, Anil *bhai*. Everything okay?"

Anil shook his head. "Nikhil, can you part with Kiran and Chandu for the day? I need their help, for just one day, I promise."

"Of course, *bhai*," Nikhil said. "You need my help too? We're just puddling the rice paddies today. The field hands can do it without me."

Anil considered the offer and what it meant coming from his brother, but he shook his head. "No, you need to take care of things here, keep everyone settled." Nikhil nodded and Anil gestured for his other two brothers to follow him outside. He led them to the far end of the porch, where they huddled over a small table and formulated a plan.

❁

WITHIN THE hour, they were ready to go. They met up in one of the distant crop fields, out of sight from the Big House. Chandu had borrowed a truck and some provisions from his delinquent *bhang*-growing friend. Kiran had persuaded two of his larger cricket teammates to come along. Anil wasn't sure what his brothers had traded for these favors, but he was grateful to them. When Piya became aware of their plan, she wanted to come as well, but Anil convinced her she was more valuable at home, keeping Ma occupied and unaware.

Kiran drove the truck, with one of his teammates next to him, providing rough directions to Dharmala. Anil and the others rode in the rear of the truck. Once they had cleared the outer limits of Panchanagar, Chandu unzipped a bag he'd brought and pulled out a pistol. Anil felt a gripping in his chest. "You think we need that?"

Chandu took a ragged square of cloth from his pocket, rolled it up, and tied it around his forehead. "With people like this, you have to show strength." He tucked the pistol into the back of his waistband.

Anil's palms began to sweat. He had never held a gun, much less fired one. Perhaps it would have been wise to go duck hunting with Amber's brothers after all.

Over the next hour, as Anil anticipated the confrontation ahead and the violence that might ensue, bile rose in his throat. Strangely, it calmed his nerves to watch Chandu, who made such a convincing bandit that Anil wondered if he should worry. But today, his youngest brother made him feel secure, as did Kiran's friends, each of whom held a cricket bat across his lap.

When they drew close to their destination, Anil recognized the small white house Piya had described, with marigolds out front, and after another kilometer or so, the dilapidated croplands. Chandu shook his head as they drove by the fields of wilted wheat stalks and rotted cotton bushes. Stray goats with visible ribcages wandered through the pastures nosing at the plants, looking for sustenance. Kiran parked in front of a house with a decrepit grand facade and revved the engine to announce their arrival. His two buddies hopped out of the truck, cricket bats swinging at their side, and Anil climbed out after Chandu.

The house was large, nearly as large as the Big House, with a similar porch wrapped around the front. Anil spotted Ritu, camouflaged in the earth surrounding the water well as she crouched down on the ground, her torn clothes caked with dirt, her hair wild, and her eyes frightened. She scrambled backwards, away from them, then stopped abruptly. Anil saw a chain joining her wrists to the well. She was tied up like an animal, an image reinforced by the frantic scanning of her eyes and her whimpering sounds.

Anil told the others to stand back and took a few slow steps toward her. Ritu crawled away again, shielding her head with her chained hands. With a rush of shame, Anil realized she considered him an enemy. He squatted down and held out one hand as slowly as he could. "Ritu, we're not here to hurt you. We're going to take you away from here."

Ritu's eyes darted from Anil to Chandu, to Kiran's buddies with their bats. She began to cry and shake her head.

"We're not going to hurt you," Anil repeated in his most calming voice. "We're here to protect you. You remember, I'm a friend of Leena? Your Leena *didi*? We're going to take you back to her."

The front door burst open. "What's the meaning of this?" a potbellied man in an undershirt and dhoti shouted. "You hoodlums get off my property before I kill you myself."

Anil froze, still crouched on the ground. Was this the man, Leena's husband? The one who'd hurt her, desecrated her? His stomach tightened. Kiran's buddies swiveled toward the front door.

A second man came through the front door, younger and more handsome than the first. "What do you want? Who are you?"

Anil realized that must be him. He stood up and walked toward the house. "Anil Patel, son of Jayant Patel."

The younger man's face shifted with recognition. "I know your father." His face grew a sly smile. "He gave me a bad deal. Why has he sent you here? I won't take that wretched woman back, no matter how much you pay me. I'm done with that garbage."

Anil clenched his fist at his side and took a deep breath. "I'm here for the girl." He nodded toward Ritu. "We're taking her away from here, from you . . . animals."

"Oh-ho?" The potbellied man laughed. "Who's the animal? She's the one who came crawling back here in the night, hiding in the back of a truck until they found her and dumped her on the road."

Anil fought the urge to lunge at the man. "Let the girl go. Leave her and Leena alone," he said. "They are dead to you, understand?"

Potbelly leaned forward and spat a stream of betel-nut juice onto the porch, adding to the smattering of old stains. Papa would have whipped anyone who soiled the Big House porch like that. "Dead is what they should be." He snorted. "Less trouble that way."

Chandu was standing at Anil's right shoulder, Kiran at his left. Anil stepped forward onto the bottom porch step, and his brothers followed, flanking him. Anil could see the face of a small boy inside the house peering through a window. He lowered his voice. "Listen to me. If you ever come anywhere near them again, I will go to the police and have you both thrown in jail."

Girish smirked. "The police already investigated that bitch's lies and found no wrongdoing." He raised an eyebrow. "Unreliable witness."

"Yes, but that was a long time ago," Anil said. "People forget. Memories fade. Wallets empty."

"That's right," Chandu added. "Once wallets empty, memories fade very quickly, it's true."

"Maybe the police will want to investigate again," Kiran said. "Murder is a very serious crime."

"What murder?" Leena's husband said. "That bitch Leena isn't dead, is she?" He laughed and looked over at his potbellied brother. "Too bad."

"But your first wife is." Anil watched recognition dawn on the men's faces. He climbed two more steps toward the porch. "Did you know, even when you burn a body, even when there's nothing left but ash, you can still find traces of that person left behind in the soil? It's called DNA. Deoxyribonucleic acid. You can find it years later, decades even. One hundred percent guaranteed."

"What nonsense are you talking?" Potbelly said, but Anil noticed the stricken look on Girish's face.

"It's true," Kiran said, throwing an arm around Anil's shoulders. "My brother here is a very educated man, a doctor from America. He knows all kinds of advanced scientific techniques. You should see the special tools he has back home."

"What, you think a person can just vanish into thin air?" Chandu clucked his tongue. "Poor, stupid village idiots."

"Nonsense," Potbelly said, elbowing his younger brother. "Don't listen to him. He's trying to pull our chain."

"No, it's true," Anil said. "And the interesting thing about DNA is it's like a fingerprint, absolutely unique to each person. Except it's also passed down to your children." He nodded toward Girish. "So we can tell exactly who this girl's true mother is. Her father too. With one simple test."

"Fine, take the girl," Potbelly spat. "We don't want her anyway. She's useless, another mouth to feed."

Kiran walked over to the well and unknotted the chains that tethered Ritu's wrists. When she was free, she stood and slowly walked toward Kiran's extended hand. Anil watched incredulously as the girl allowed Kiran to lift her in his arms. His brother carried her back to the truck, her face bobbing above his shoulder. When they passed in front of the porch where the two men stood, Ritu raised her head and spat at the ground.

"The boy too." Anil nodded toward the window. As he spoke, the front door creaked open and the little boy who'd been watching from inside darted out past Potbelly and Girish, calling out Ritu's name as he ran toward her. One of Kiran's friends caught him in mid-run and picked him up.

Potbelly spat on the porch again. "Good riddance," he muttered. But Anil caught a look of regret in Girish's eyes as he watched Dev being carried toward the truck.

Chandu leaned toward Anil and touched his arm. "Come on, *bhai*, let's go," he whispered. "You got what you came for."

Anil shook his head. "Not yet. They still have to return what they've stolen."

"Heh? Now you're calling us thieves?" Girish said. "I haven't stolen a thing from anybody. If anyone's a thief, it's your father. He took those gold coins from me and promised me a good wife in return. Instead, I got nothing but trouble with that woman."

Anil's palms were sweating again, but he refrained from wiping them on his pants. "I want the things you took from Leena's family—the jewelry and saris, everything."

"Those were gifts," Girish said. "Part of the girl's dowry."

"They were not given willingly."

"Well, people change their minds. That's not my problem." Girish snorted.

A man who paid off others to absolve his own moral failings could surely be bought himself. The envelope filled with fifty thousand rupees sat in Anil's back pocket. His stomach curdled as he thought of its origins: money paid once already by Papa to this man who'd abused Leena, repaid to his father by Leena's parents, who had sacrificed everything to do so.

Anil turned toward the truck. Ritu's face was framed by the open window on the passenger's side, where Kiran had settled her and Dev with a blanket and bottles of Limca. Anil could detect the faintest tug of a smile at the corner of her mouth as she watched them from her safe perch. Kiran looked like a palace guard, standing outside the truck, his arm resting on the window frame.

"If I let you keep the jewelry, you leave them alone," Anil said. "Forever, understand? Otherwise my brothers and I will be back, and we won't be so understanding next time." Chandu took the pistol out of his waistband and let it dangle from his hand until both men wobbled their heads in agreement. Potbelly spat another red stream of betel-nut juice onto the ground and retreated into the house, Girish following behind.

32

As soon as they were a safe distance away, Kiran stopped the truck and Anil opened the passenger door to take a better look at Ritu. This time, she allowed him to gently examine her wounds: there were lacerations all over her body, bruising on her ankles and wrists where she'd been bound, and capillaries had erupted in one of her eyes, making it seem as if she were crying tears of her own blood.

"We have to get her to the hospital," Anil told his brothers. "She has so many injuries, there might be internal bleeding or broken bones." They drove directly to Ahmadabad, to the hospital where Anil had completed his clinical rotations in medical college. Kiran carried Ritu into the hospital and stayed with her and Dev while Anil went to find the senior doctor in charge. It was decided Chandu would drive the others back to Panchanagar and return the next morning.

"Chandu." Anil grabbed his brother's arm. "Do you know anyone with the police?"

"I'll check into it," Chandu said before leaving.

❁

Three hours later, Anil and Kiran sat by Ritu's bedside as she slept deeply, Dev curled up at the foot of her bed. Her X-rays had revealed broken bones in both wrists, which had been set in casts. Her lacerations had been cleaned and stitched, and she'd been given several units of saline for dehydration, and antibiotics for infection. The ER physician who examined Ritu told Anil that, despite the extensive physical trauma, there were no signs of sexual abuse.

The physical healing would be the least of the challenges Ritu faced in the days ahead, and Anil knew Leena was the right person to guide her down that long road. But his own wounds were fresh, his heart ruined over losing Leena from the life he'd envisioned. He tried to console himself with thoughts of the fellowship and everything he had to return to in Dallas, but it all felt hollow.

Unable to sleep, Anil decided to wander around the hospital. Some of it looked familiar: the simple front lobby without a single plant, the elevator with its overhead fan. But much had changed in the past several years, including the addition of a full-scale radiology lab on the basement level and a neonatal intensive care unit. Two more wings were blocked off for construction. How different this was from the rudimentary medicine he'd practiced in Panchanagar years ago, on a warm summer night when the midwife called. He could conceive of coming back here now and having a real medical career, one without compromise.

Anil found his way to the cafeteria, where the smell of food pricked his appetite. He realized he hadn't eaten anything all day. Glancing at the menu board, he smiled when he saw the third item listed under Vegetarian, after *chana masala* and *saag paneer*, was cheese pizza.

After eating his fill of the vegetarian *thali* and finishing his second cup of strong chai, Anil began to wind his way back to the Emergency Department. He took the long way, strolling up and down corridors, passing through wards, nodding to the nurses in their starched white uniforms. When he returned to the room, Ritu and Dev were awake, watching Kiran enact a puppet show with bandages wrapped around his fingertips. Ritu paused her giggling when she saw Anil. "Where's Leena *didi*?"

"I will bring her back with me," Anil promised. "As soon as I can."

❁

THE CAR was waiting in front of the hospital when Anil came out. Anil almost didn't recognize Chandu when he stepped out of the sedan, dressed as he was in a crisp suit. His younger brother pulled another suit on a hanger from the backseat of the car and held it out to Anil. "Get dressed," he said. "We have an appointment."

Twenty minutes later, they were parked outside the Central Ahmadabad Police Station. "You think this will work?" Anil asked. "They already tried going to the police in Dharmala. They wouldn't do anything about it."

Chandu shook his head. "These big-city cops are different. They love to have a reason to lord their power over those small-village policemen. You just have to know how to talk to them." He nodded toward a bag sitting on the floor by Anil's feet. Anil reached down and unzipped the bag, and saw bundles of rupees. He looked up at his brother with an unspoken question.

"Where it came from, nothing good," Chandu said. "Where it goes now, different story."

❁

BY THE time Anil and Chandu arrived back in Panchanagar, dusk was beginning to settle. Anil had been gone for over twenty-four hours and hadn't slept, bathed, or shaved in that time. He'd phoned Piya from the hospital to tell her he'd found Ritu, but he knew his mother would still be frantic with worry.

He rubbed at the stubble on his chin as the car pulled up to Leena's house. She was sitting on the terrace at the pottery wheel; when she saw the car, she gathered her sari and stood up. As Anil drew closer, he noticed the deep crease in her forehead.

"Ritu's at the hospital in Ahmadabad. She has some injuries, but she's going to be fine. Dev too."

Leena's shoulders rose and fell in disproportion to her small frame—once, twice—and Anil realized she was beginning to cry. He moved closer but stopped short of putting his arms around her. The front door opened and Nirmala appeared in the doorway. She took in Anil's disheveled appearance, Leena's tear-stained face.

"Piya told me you'd gone there," Leena said. "I was so worried about all of you."

"They won't bother you again," Anil said. "She's safe now. You all are."

Leena nodded, her eyes holding on to his. "Can I go see her?"

"Yes, but there's someplace I'd like to take you and your mother first." He nodded toward Nirmala Auntie, who, he was surprised, bowed her head slightly in return.

❁

THEY LEFT early the next morning. When Anil pulled up to the large dilapidated house in Dharmala, Leena's body tensed beside him. From the backseat, Nirmala leaned forward. Anil cut the engine. "It's okay. They're not here." Leena's knuckles were colorless, gripping the seat at her side. "The police came and took all of them yesterday. The men have been arrested on multiple charges and will be in jail for months until the trial. Rekha was taken to a family shelter. She's making no claims to the children, so they can be released into your custody, since you are the only other living family member. The old woman, your . . .

mother-in-law—as Ritu said, she died several weeks ago. The police speculated that may be why Ritu decided to run away. No one left to look out for her."

Leena exhaled slowly. She unlatched the car door and stepped out. Anil opened the door for Nirmala Auntie, who took his arm for support as she climbed out. He was surprised Leena did not hesitate as she climbed the steps, avoiding the rotted ones without even having to glance down. It made him uncomfortable to think of her familiarity with this house, and of everything that had gone on here. He considered waiting outside rather than having to see the room and the bed she'd shared with her husband. But Nirmala Auntie was still holding on to his arm, so they entered the house together.

LEENA WENT first to the kitchen, then outside the back door to the well. She stood there for some time, daring herself to summon the memory. Closing her eyes, she conjured the odor of kerosene, the sound of angry words, the welts and bruises on her arms, the tears dripping from her face into the food she had prepared to nourish the family into which she had married. The family she had left. The family that had abandoned her.

She returned to the kitchen, where dirty dishes sat on the counter and a pot of cold tea was on the stovetop. Leena went into the small cellar and ran her hands over the sacks of lentils and rice. On the top shelf, she found the box of chocolate biscuits Dev liked to steal, reached inside, and took one out. It smelled sweet and vaguely like coffee or tobacco. She bit into it and felt the crisp wafers break between her teeth, the soft chocolate cream on her tongue. She tucked the box underneath her arm and continued walking through the house.

In Rekha's room, inside the metal cupboard, Leena found three of her good saris, which she took out and placed on the bed. On another shelf, next to Rekha's hairbrush and coconut oil, sat the white metal canister of rose talcum powder. Leena removed the lid and leaned forward to inhale the sweet fragrance. She held the can in her hand—feeling the smooth metal under her fingertips, tracing its raised edge, brushing away the soft powder—for several more moments before she returned it to the cupboard and closed the door.

Leena found her mother with Anil in the living room, sitting in the chair where Girish used to play his card games and tell rude jokes. On her lap was a bundle wrapped in white cloth and tied with a string. Her mother looked up at her, her eyes glistening. "I found this in your mother-in-law's cupboard." She pulled at the string and the white cotton sheath fell away to reveal a sari the brilliant burnt orange of sunset. Leena's mother stroked the silk with her palm, back and forth, then lifted it to reveal the next sari, in bright peacock blue. There were a dozen more saris, made from silks and chiffons, each one a different hue and design. The last sari was the most ornate, red and white, embroidered with tiny mirrors and gold thread. Tears welled in Leena's eyes as her mother leaned down and buried her nose in the traditional garment she'd worn for her wedding ceremony.

Anil reached forward, holding out three small red boxes. Leena's mother looked up at him. "The police didn't let them take anything," he said. Leena went over and sat next to her mother. One by one, her mother opened the boxes and lifted out each piece of jewelry: she delicately fingered the ruby and pearl waterfall earrings, and slipped all four of the gold bangles easily over her wrist. She shook her head. "I never thought I would see this again," she said as she held her gold wedding band between her fingertips.

Leena put one of her hands over her mother's and clasped it tightly. Her mother, to Leena's surprise, reached out her other hand to grasp Anil's. "Thank you," she whispered.

Anil nodded. "We should get to the hospital."

"I'll collect some of the children's things," Leena said, blinking away tears as she stood.

❁

AT THE hospital in Ahmadabad, Anil led Leena and her mother through the now-familiar maze of corridors to Ritu's room. Inside, Kiran sat next to her bed, trying to convince her to eat some of the meal on her tray. Ritu was shaking her head when she glanced up and saw them.

"Didi!" Ritu's face exploded into a smile and she knocked over the tray as she sat up. The contrast from her sullen expression a moment earlier was startling. Ritu wrapped her arms around Leena's waist and buried her face in Leena's sari. "Oh *didi*, I'm so sorry if I caused more trouble. I was so scared—"

"Shh," Leena whispered, stroking Ritu's hair until she settled down. "It's fine now. I'm here. No one will hurt you again."

The door creaked open, a nurse entered, and Dev darted out from behind her. He ran toward Leena, who lifted him up and held him on her hip. "What is this?" Leena ruffled Dev's shaggy hair. "Who's been cutting your hair? Such a mess. I will have to fix it, no?"

Dev grinned and nodded with slow, exaggerated movements, his chin pointing up in the air, then down to his neck. "Can we come live with you, Leena *didi*?"

"Of course you can!" Leena pinched his nose. "Who else will get my chocolate biscuits for me?"

"Do you still get sad, *didi*?" Dev asked.

Leena tilted her head and smiled at him, a slight and melancholy smile. "Not as much anymore," she said, her voice hoarse. Anil watched her reach for Dev's hand, covered with a large pigmented birthmark, kiss it, and hold it to her cheek. "But I have missed you, little monkey." Dev threw his arms around Leena's neck.

Anil swallowed hard. He could see them already as a family, with their own roles and their unique dynamic: Dev the mischievous clown, Ritu the moody adolescent, Nirmala the benign disciplinarian, and Leena the nucleus who pulled them all together. *Was there any place for him?*

Anil drove back to Panchanagar while Kiran slept in the passenger seat next to him, and Ritu and Dev curled up in the back between Leena and her mother. At one point, when Anil glanced in the rear-view mirror and saw everyone asleep, he tried to imagine himself among them, this unlikely and automatic family—not the kind he'd expected to have, yet one he found himself drawn to.

Kiran stirred as they turned down the bumpy lane to Leena's house and the others followed, all awakening except for Dev, who remained dead asleep with his head in Ritu's lap. Kiran carried him into the house, trailing the others; after he came back out, Anil handed him the car keys and told him he would see him later at the Big House.

Anil sat down on the top step of the terrace and looked out over the fields as he waited. The sky had darkened to gray. After the few small noises emanating from the house faded, Leena came outside closing the door behind her. She gathered the folds of her sari in her lap and sat down next to him. Leena held out a closed fist and slowly unfurled her fingers. In her palm lay a king chess piece made of sandalwood.

Anil's mind could not process what he was seeing, the impossibility of it. He looked at her, then took it from her hand and turned it around between his fingers. It was a near-perfect match to the one he'd lost from his father's set. He looked up at Leena again. Her smile began small, then grew wider, unguarded—illuminating her eyes and bringing a lump to his throat.

"I know a woodsmith at the market," she explained. "I drew a picture for him and he carved it by hand."

Anil nodded, staring at the delicate crosshatch pattern on the crown of the piece. The thickening of his throat threatened to tear him open.

It was a few moments before Leena spoke again. "When are you leaving?"

"Tomorrow," Anil said.

Leena nodded but didn't say anything, and Anil allowed a long silence to stretch out. "You know, when it's all done," he said at last, speaking carefully, "once the adoption has been finalized, I can come back for you. You can all come to Dallas—your mother, Ritu, Dev. I'll find a house, I can apply for visas. I'll be earning enough to support all of us." He glanced at Leena. "There are good schools. We can be a family." His eyes burned, tears accumulating at the edges. "I love you, Leena. I always have. I'll fix things with my mother, and even if I can't, it doesn't matter. We'll have our own family." He gestured toward the darkened house behind them. "We'll have everything we need. The rest won't matter."

Leena reached over and grabbed his hand with surprising strength. She continued to grip it tightly as she spoke, as if wanting to distract him from the pain her words would cause. "I do love you, Anil. But that is not the life I want. This is." She let her eyes travel across the fields surrounding them. "If you'd asked me a few months ago, I might have said yes. I wasn't sure I could make a life for myself here. But then Ritu came, and I knew what I wanted. I can live on this land I've loved my whole life, in this house. I can make a living with my pottery. I want to be with my mother, I want to raise these children, to give them the love they deserve. And now I know, after everything that's happened, I can do this. I choose this life." She loosened her grip on his hand and Anil felt the loss immediately. "Just as strongly as you know you don't belong here anymore, I know I do." Her voice was a whisper.

"It won't be easy for you, to stay here," Anil said.

Leena thrust out her chin, the determined gesture Anil recognized from their childhood when she'd stood up to the landowner who raped the servant in the fields. "People may never respect me. I don't expect it. I've survived this long. Damaged, not broken." She turned her head toward the house behind them. "They are the only ones who matter to me now."

Anil tightened his hand around hers once more. Then he let go. He did not try to speak. His throat was tight and there was nothing left to say. Leena's past was an indelible part of her, like the scars burned into her skin he could not simply graft away with surgery. After having so many choices made for her, she deserved to make this one for herself.

❀

MA WAS sitting on the front porch, a teacup in her hands and another on the table beside her. "Sit." She nodded at the chair next to her. "You've missed your tea today," she said, as if that were the most notable thing to have happened.

Anil sat down, feeling relief from the deep ache in his knees, and reached for the teacup.

"Your brothers told me what happened in Dharmala. The house, those . . . men." She paused, then added in a whisper, "The girl." Ma closed her eyes and shook her head once. "Your father . . . we . . . would never have encouraged the marriage had we known."

Anil nodded. "I know, Ma." *Do no harm.* It was not, as he'd learned, an easy principle.

"How is she?"

"They released her from the hospital. She should recover in a few weeks."

"And . . . Leena?" Ma did not look at him as she asked. "Are you . . . Is she . . . ?"

Anil slid his hand into his pocket and tightened his fingers around the king piece.

"Son, I really think you should let this go—"

"And if I do . . ." Anil turned to her, setting down his cup. "If I do agree to let this go, let *her* go, then you have to do something for me. You will make sure Leena can hold her head up in the village, that she can sell her goods at the market. You make sure she and Nirmala Auntie are treated like anyone else in the community, with respect."

"Son, how can I do all that?" Ma chuckled. "I'm only one person. I can't control how people think, what they say. What nonsense." She shook her head.

"Well, I've been giving that some thought," Anil said. "I'm leaving tomorrow, and I'll probably be gone for a few more years. Maybe . . . longer." He closed his eyes for a moment. "I can't be the family arbiter, Ma. Not anymore."

His mother held up an open palm to him, eyes closed, as if she couldn't bear to hear any more. Anil took a deep breath and continued. "In the hospital, we have a team of people who work together across specialties and seniority levels. When something goes wrong—when a patient dies unexpectedly, for example—this team holds an open forum to look at the case, to discuss what happened, so everyone can learn from it." He took another deep breath. "I think we should have a council of arbiters, not just one. You, Kiran, and Chandu." He waited for her reaction, for her questions, but she only turned to him with that concerned look she used to get when he stuttered as a child.

"You hold more respect in this community than anyone else since Papa died," Anil continued. "You know the families, the culture, and you've seen Papa broker a lot of disputes. You've seen the successes and the mistakes. And Kiran . . . " Anil smiled, remembering Ritu and her Limca. "Ma, Kiran has a special way with people. They trust him, they'll talk to him. He knows how to make others feel safe." His mother nodded, acknowledging this. "And Chandu, I know he can be trouble, but he's so sharp. Papa always used to say that about him and I didn't believe it, but Chandu knows how things really work in the world, how to get things done. He understands people in a different way than the rest of us." Anil leaned back against his chair. "Nikhil will continue to run the farm operations, that's his domain. Piya has her own interests to pursue."

His mother's eyes darted back and forth as she considered Anil's proposal. "You've thought it all through."

"It's the best way, Ma," Anil said. "Old and young. Man and woman. The wisdom will multiply." He placed Papa's account journal on the table between them, along with the envelope containing fifty thousand rupees. "Your first order of business is to return this money to Nirmala Auntie. We can never restore what she's lost, but perhaps they can start again." He watched his mother as she stared, expressionless, out over the fields. "It has to come from you, Ma."

His mother nodded slightly, and without another word, collected the journal and cash, stood up, and went into the house.

Anil rested the back of his head on his chair and allowed his eyes to close. He hadn't had a proper night's sleep in days, and the emotional turmoil of the past week had left him drained. He felt himself drifting away and let himself go.

He awakened with a start to the sound of his sister's voice. "Where's she going?" Piya stood in the doorway of the Big House. The sun was low on the horizon, its last arc visible just before slipping away. The coolness of dusk settled onto Anil's skin and brought him a shiver.

"I guess I'll tell the cook to hold dinner," Piya said, nodding toward a figure on the path: their mother, holding a silver *thali* with coconut, bananas, and fresh blossoms, walking through the fields toward the gully and the house just on the other side.

❁

BEFORE LEAVING Panchanagar, Anil spoke to each of his siblings to explain his decision. Nikhil was pleased to accept full control of the farm operations. Piya hugged her big brother and praised him for the resolution he'd found. Finally, Anil sat with Kiran and Chandu, reiterating what he had discussed with Ma before handing over Papa's letter. "This is for you, both of you."

Chandu unfolded it and glanced across the page. "From Papa," he said, showing it to Kiran. "You sure it's not for you, Anil?"

Anil nodded, explaining what he'd realized upon his third reading of his father's letter. It was addressed not to him, but simply to the next family arbiter.

33

PARKVIEW HOSPITAL WAS REASSURING IN ITS PREDICTABILITY: everything sparkling clean, white, and sterile. There were no odors, nothing in the air but the scent of brisk efficiency and lingering antiseptic. It was an environment that made Anil feel at home, one he could slip right back into, yet it also made him acutely aware of everything he'd left behind, the lushness of India that had penetrated his being once again.

"Patel! Welcome back." Trey grabbed one of his shoulders. "Two weeks and counting 'til applications are due. You ready?" He leaned in closer and lowered his voice. "Hey, the research project's going well. I got the preliminary results back, and I think we'll get a strong brief out of it by the end of the year. It's going to look good for the fellowship." He smiled his million-dollar smile, and Anil caught the faint scent of mint chewing gum.

"Yeah," Anil said. "I need to talk to you about that, Trey."

Trey glanced at his watch. "I've got thirty minutes now, want to go outside?"

They sat on the low perimeter wall of the courtyard, which had been landscaped to resemble a peaceful Japanese garden. "Listen, Trey," Anil said. "I don't want you to include my name on your research project. It's your work, not mine."

Trey squinted. "What are you getting at, Patel?" The corner of his mouth curled up. "You're not reneging on our deal, are you?"

Anil shook his head. "We didn't have a deal. Listen—" He took a slip of paper out of his shirt pocket.

"You're breaking your word? Are you an Indian giver, Patel?" Trey snorted with laughter, evidently at some joke Anil didn't get. "You think you're going to push me out of the way to make a spot for yourself? Good luck with that shitty little MRSA project and your chances at a cardio fellowship without my help."

Anil should have been prepared for Trey's threats, though they were unnecessary. He'd already determined it would be futile to report Trey's behavior. While Anil had been away in India, Parkview's new Heart and Stroke Center had been named for the senior Dr. Crandall, in honor of his sizable donation. Between the prominence of his father and the support of the Cardiology head, Trey was untouchable. No one would believe Anil, particularly so long after events had transpired—or worse, he would appear to be a rival with an ax to grind.

"Trey, listen. I'm not going to report you," Anil said. "But I do think you should seek help. There's a confidential program in Richardson, designed for health professionals. Completely private; one-on-one counseling." He handed the slip of paper to Trey and saw the muscles in Trey's jaw pulse visibly as he chewed harder on his gum.

"You don't want it to become a problem, Trey. You're too good a doctor for that." After everything, Anil knew at his core this was inarguably true. Even the technically correct action, in this case, would not result in the greater good.

Trey stood up and walked back toward the hospital, spitting his gum into the slip of paper and tossing it into the trash before he passed through the sliding doors.

Anil watched him go, then removed his specs and rubbed at his eyes. America, despite its billing as the ultimate meritocracy, was just like everywhere else. Trey would always come out on top because of his confidence, his connections, his charm. Others would continue to be fooled by him as Anil had been. Anil would not be able to solve every problem that came before him, just as he would not be able to save every patient. His new life in the modern world would still retain many of the problems from the past.

THE DECISION arrived in a thin envelope a few months later. Anil took the mail back to the apartment before opening it, but he had a sense even as he turned the key in the lock. He scanned down the page until he reached the word *regret.*

We regret to inform you we are not able to offer you a fellowship in the Department of Cardiology at Parkview Hospital . . .

At the bottom of the letter was a handwritten note from Dr. Tanaka explaining that it was a particularly competitive year, and encouraging Anil to apply again.

News of the fellowship decisions had spread by the time Anil arrived at the hospital the following day. Charlie offered to take him out for a drink at the Horseshoe after work. They sat with their beer glasses in front of them, trying to hear each other above the din of other residents quickly on their way to inebriated celebration. "I heard Trey and Lisbeth were the only two who matched at Parkview for Cardiology," Charlie reported. "Everyone else came from other programs. Competition was tough this year." He made a halfway attempt to smile. "I know it's not much consolation. Sorry, mate."

Anil tried not to think, as he had since receiving the news, of the near-holy quiet of the catheterization lab, the precision with which Tanaka had operated, the images on the monitor delivering the promise of a whole new interior world, all now out of his reach. He cleared his throat. "When do you leave for Sydney?"

"First of July, just in time to catch a bit of ski season before the job begins." Charlie held his glass up. "Couldn't have done it without you, mate. The hospital loved our MRSA study. It totally sold them on hiring me, even though I told them you were the brains of the operation. You sure you don't want to come make your home at Infectious Disease at Sydney General?"

Anil raised his glass and clinked it against Charlie's. "I'll miss you, mate."

IN THE break room on Ward 4, Sonia listened while Anil lamented the outcome of the fellowship decisions. "I should have taken your advice and applied to more programs," Anil said. "Now it's too late for cardiology or any other specialty."

"Haven't I taught you anything, Patel?" Sonia shook her head. "You don't need a specialty. You're already a doctor, and a damn good one—maybe even exceptional, one day. You're supposed to learn the basics of clinical medicine in your residency, which you've done. But you've also learned to trust your eyes and your hands, how to use technology when you need it, how to relate to patients. Those are all important skills. Not all residents figure it out while they're here—or ever, frankly. Not everyone can do what you did in your village in India, despite what O'Brien says at orientation." She pointed her finger at him. "And don't let that go to your head."

"Don't worry." Anil smiled. When he'd told his Oncology team about the impromptu medical clinic he'd set up at the Big House last summer, Sonia was the only one who understood how treating lacerations and minor infections all day could be interesting.

"You know, Patel, we could use a few more doctors with your skills in Internal Medicine—someone to help me keep all those fresh-faced interns in line." Sonia smiled. "You remember what that's like, don't you? Give us a year and see how it goes. You can always apply to Cardiology again next year, if you still want to."

"Thanks, Sonia." Anil smiled. "I appreciate the offer."

"Always happy to help, Patel."

"Actually, I could use your advice on something." Anil reached into his backpack, pulled out a small glass jar filled with thick green paste, and slid it across the table.

"You made me pesto?" Sonia grinned as she unscrewed the lid and peered inside, then pulled back at the strong odor.

"It's a paste made from the leaves of the neem tree, also known as Indian lilac," Anil said. "They're plentiful on my family's land. It's a natural and highly effective topical antibiotic. Reduces the size of an abscess by half in the first day. No need to see a doctor to lance or drain." Anil pointed to the bottle. "That's easily a million-dollar-a-year over-the-counter product. Safe, effective, no regulation, and I've got a reliable supply."

"Hmm." Sonia dabbed her finger into the open jar and rubbed the paste between her fingers. "My little sister, Geeta, just moved to town to start her internship at Baylor. One of the senior docs she works with is into this kind of stuff." Sonia scribbled something on a slip of paper and handed it to him. "Geeta doesn't have much free time as an intern, but you should give her a call."

The Farmer's Sons

Anil had practiced the national anthem for months—in the shower, in the car on the way to the hospital, any time he was alone. Geeta teased him about this, but he was determined to sing each and every word at the citizenship ceremony. After eight years in America, at the age of thirty-one, he would pledge himself to his adopted country.

On the day of the ceremony, in an auditorium with thirteen hundred people and with his wife's family in the gallery, Anil watched the film of Ellis Island with tears in his eyes, then stood up when the country of India was announced and took his oath. When it came time for the anthem, he could only manage to get out the first couple of lines before the swell of emotion choked off his voice.

He was living in two worlds comfortably, or at least as comfortably as he could. There were times he still felt like a foreigner in America, like when he got up in the middle of the night to watch live cricket games on television. And there were times he felt like an outsider in India. The moments he felt most at home were those he spent practicing medicine, whether he was treating patients at Parkview Hospital or at the simple clinic in Panchanagar. What brought him a sense of home was what he carried within: his knowledge and experience, his compassion for his patients—all of which helped him make the right judgments most of the time. Mistakes and failures still happened, and when they did, he ensured his residents understood their value.

"ONE MONTH sabbatical, Dr. P?" a junior resident asked at the send-off party. "That's pretty sweet. I didn't think you could get that kind of time off as an attending."

"Yes, well, I know the department head pretty well." Anil chuckled. "Dr. Mehta seems to think I'm very dispensable around here."

"Not true, not true," Sonia interjected, pointing a finger at him in playful accusation. "But I might change my opinion if you don't take good care of my sister over there. You've got the IV bags and antimalarials?"

"Yes, yes," Geeta said as she joined them. "Don't worry, we have an entire suitcase full of medical supplies. Two suitcases, in fact."

"Good," Sonia said. "Bottled water only, no street food. Don't take any risks with my future niece." She patted her sister's belly, which was beginning to show a slight rise under her white coat.

Anil smiled as he watched their interplay. Geeta had some things in common with her older sister: besides being doctors, they shared a killer competitive spirit for board games and a taste for very spicy food. But Geeta didn't have the same ambitions as Sonia: she'd chosen to specialize in dermatology so she wouldn't be subject to the vagaries of call schedules. She freely admitted that Sonia was the better student and had a more natural aptitude for medicine. Geeta enjoyed her work but had other interests: she was a voracious reader and maintained a large vegetable garden in the backyard of their Lakewood house. She wanted to start having children soon after they got married, so they could have three or four if they wanted.

Their daughter was now due in four months. Anil had already

painted the nursery a pale shade of butter yellow and assembled a crib with the aid of Mahesh, who had built one last year for his son, and Baldev, who was now back in Dallas.

It hadn't been easy to get Ma to come around to Geeta. She resented the idea that Anil had found a woman himself, without the involvement of his elders or the village pandit. That Geeta was an American, born and raised in the West, who spoke only a few words of Gujarati and had little knowledge of cooking, made things more difficult still. Anil was up-front about the fact they had met and dated before choosing to live together. Before Geeta moved in, he went to his mother and told her in calm, unequivocal terms that he had met the woman he planned to marry; he hoped for her blessing but didn't need it to carry on with his life. Ma found it easier to object to Geeta in the abstract, grumbling to Anil's siblings in his absence about the corruptions of the West and women who tried to be no different from men. Once she met Geeta, though—the first time Geeta had traveled to Panchanagar with Anil—Ma had fallen under the same mesmerizing spell he had.

Geeta had held his mother's hand loosely in hers as they sat on the couch together, leaning forward as Ma told stories of farming adventures, and raising five children, and her late husband. Geeta asked questions and listened intently to Ma's answers, nodding while she mentally filed away every detail to retell the stories later to their friends in America. "Can you believe she once nursed three children at the same time? Two of her own and a niece, after her sister died. And she never stopped cooking meals for all of them. Such an amazing woman!" She told the stories with a sense of pride and enthusiasm that reflected how she saw the world, as if wondrous things were around every corner, and she was fortunate to witness them. Each time she did, Anil felt a swell of love for her, and his own eyes opened to the wonder of the world they occupied together.

Some of the stories Anil overheard Ma telling Geeta were new to him, such as the first time his mother had made tea for Papa's parents after Anil had been born. They'd insisted she stay off her feet and look after her new baby, but she was eager to impress them and went into the kitchen early one morning after she'd been awoken by Anil—"Only in the night and the morning was he hungry, wouldn't you know? He slept all day long." Ma shook her head at him with a pursed-lip smile. She'd been so sleep deprived that she'd mistaken the salt for sugar. She was so appalled when she'd tasted the tea later, after it had already been served, that she hid away in her bedroom for the rest of the day.

As Geeta sat in the gathering room listening to Ma, her tea grew cold. Ma dispatched the servant back to the kitchen repeatedly to reheat the tea, then implored him to bring some snacks for the poor girl, who barely ate anything. Before long, Ma was fussing over Geeta's too-thin figure and making sweets laden with ghee to fatten her up. "Golden son has been replaced by soon-to-be golden daughter-in-law," Piya had teased Anil in a whisper.

That was Geeta's first visit to India, over three years ago, and they had returned every year since. This trip would be their last before the baby's arrival, and he expected his mother would be in full doting mode.

MORE THAN a dozen people were lined up outside, awaiting their turn to enter the small cottage. There was not much to look at inside, only two beds and a few chairs. A counter along one wall held a number of imperfect ceramic bowls filled with antiseptic, gauze, bandages, syringes, and pills of varied shapes and colors. In addition, there were cloves, ground turmeric, ointments, and tinctures not found on any pharmacy shelf—a mixture of coconut oil and aloe used to heal burns, the extract of a particular plant leaf that alleviated swelling and bruising. And there was the Neem product line, now bottled and sold in America, which generated enough profit to fund the clinic on an ongoing basis..

Despite its modest furnishings, the clinic was well equipped, with a portable ultrasound, electrocardiograph, and ventilator. They were older models, shipped over from Parkview after the hospital had upgraded to the latest technology, but they were more than adequate for the clinic. When Anil was here, he and Piya could see fifty patients in a day, but today they were preparing to close up early. Their last patient was a woman Anil suspected of having early symptoms of hepatitis C. He gave her some medicine and instructed her to return the following week when his friend, an infectious disease specialist from Australia, would be visiting.

❁

A REPORTER from the town paper had arrived in Panchanagar to do a story on the medical clinic. The spindly man with thick black spectacles was particularly interested in interviewing Nirmala and Leena, as the widow and daughter of the late farmer for whom the clinic had been named.

"People come from all around to receive treatment at this clinic bearing your husband's name. Your family name has become synonymous with good medical care for everyone, regardless of caste, religion, or gender. You must be very proud."

"Yes," Nirmala said, leaning forward to speak into the reporter's recording device. "My husband was a good man. He devoted himself to his family, and he loved this community. We were very proud when this clinic was established in his memory." Nirmala smiled at Anil, standing at the edge of the small crowd.

"The clinic operates on the land your father once farmed? And you still live there?" The reporter pointed his recorder toward Leena.

Leena smiled and tucked a lock of hair behind her ear. "Actually, the clinic—where we are standing right now—the land and cottage were donated by Mina Patel, and we are very grateful. Our home is over there." She pointed beyond the gully.

"And the doctor is tireless." Leena smiled over at Piya. "She is training my sixteen-year-old niece, Ritu, to assist in the clinic after school. I wish I could spend more time here, but my pottery business keeps me busy."

❁

ANIL AND Piya watched the reporter follow Leena to her house to get some photographs of her pottery. "How is she doing?" Anil nodded toward Ritu, standing at the outskirts of the assembled crowd.

Piya moved her head in a noncommittal gesture, not quite a nod or a shake. "She's a little hard to reach. Stays very close to Leena. And she loves Kiran. He's like a true older brother to her. Not the kind who tortures you with early-morning math lessons." She elbowed Anil. "But she picks things up quickly. She's quiet, but I can see she's taking it all in. Last week we were so busy, she did her first sutures. Can you believe it?"

"She's got a good teacher," Anil said.

"Almost as good as mine," Piya said, raising one eyebrow. "Which reminds me, I'd like your help with a child who has a nasty rash. Doesn't seem to go away no matter what I do."

"You probably want Geeta," Anil said. "She's the nasty-rash expert."

"Oh yes," Piya said. "Where is she?"

"In the kitchen with Ma, getting an unsolicited cooking lesson."

Piya groaned. "Poor thing. I think Ma's given up on my marital prospects and she's turning her energy elsewhere."

Anil smiled. Their mother was like the last stubborn embers of a fire that refused to go out. When thwarted by one person, she turned somewhere else. She still asked Anil if he and Geeta would move back to India; she was probably lobbying Geeta right now in the kitchen. Ma wasn't willing to give up her dream of how she envisioned her family. It was the same relentless drive that had propelled Anil on the improbable journey from these sugarcane fields to senior physician at Parkview. Although he'd made the right decision for himself, he would have to live with the reality that his choices would always be a disappointment to her.

Nirmala Auntie approached them, bowing her head in greeting. She wore a proud smile as she held out two large jars wrapped in newspaper. "Mango pickle for you to take home." She gestured to a distant horizon to imply he should take the pickles all the way back to America, not just to the Big House.

"Thank you, Auntie." Anil embraced her and they caught up for a few minutes while Piya closed up the clinic for the night.

The reporter returned and began asking questions of the patients who'd been treated that day and had stayed around for the spectacle of the camera. Anil looked up to see Leena smiling at him, and they simultaneously began moving toward each other. They embraced with the familiarity and duration of old friends who had not met in a long time.

"Good job," Anil said. "You'll be on the front page of the paper tomorrow and you won't be able to keep up with all your new orders."

Leena threw her head back and laughed. "I don't think so. More likely, Piya won't be able to keep up with all her new patients." Her voice was strong and her smile now uncompromising, but Anil also detected the steel in her eyes; they held the unmistakable history of the challenges she'd endured. Despite the contentment he knew she felt, Anil doubted he would ever stop feeling guilt and regret about what she had lost along the way.

Dev ran up to them and hurled himself at Anil, who leaned down and scooped him up, swinging his legs into the air. "Oh God, you're getting so big," he said. "And I'm getting so old. Soon you'll be the one picking me up."

"Anil Uncle, will you bowl for me? I have to practice my batting." Dev swung an imaginary cricket bat.

"Yes, tomorrow, I promise. Geeta Auntie likes to sleep late, and I need my exercise." Anil patted his tummy, though it was no bigger than it had ever been.

"Oh yes," Leena said, pulling a small bottle out of her pocket. It appeared to be filled with a golden-tinted liquid, no doubt some herbal extraction she and Piya had cooked up. "For Geeta. It's a tree oil, good for the skin, for stretch marks."

"Thank you," Anil said. "I'll give it to her."

Anil walked the long way back to the Big House through the golden fields and under the majestic canopy of the coconut trees, enjoying the scent of the earth filling his nose and the soil pushing into his sandals. In some ways, it always felt the same when he came home: this familiar touch of his senses, the way his gait slowed and his speech patterns shifted to fold in with his family. Yet, as the years passed, he felt the distance growing between his two worlds: he began to look forward to returning to his adopted home as much as he missed the one he'd left behind. It would always be like this in some form, he had come to realize, the undeniable push and pull between the land that had borne him and the one he had chosen.

INSIDE THE gathering room, people were starting to assemble. Kiran and Chandu walked to the head of the table and took the two empty seats on either side of their mother. Ritu stood at the back, leaning against the wall.

The first dispute, among three brothers, had erupted after the unexpected death of their father. The man had died of a sudden stroke without leaving any instructions about what to do with his large plot of farmland. He had three sons: the eldest, to whom property rights naturally fell by law; the middle son, who had the most experience tending the land alongside his father; and the youngest, who owned no property and had the most need. The brothers each claimed they had the greatest right to their father's land. The simplest solution, the one most discussed by those in the room before the meeting started, would be to divide the property equally among the brothers.

"It's a terrible loss. Your father was a good man," Ma said. "But we have the matter of the farmland before us today, and while we cannot ascertain what your father would have chosen to do, I do know what he would have wanted. Your father would wish to see all three of his sons undivided by his death. He would want to see you working together in cooperation, each of you bringing your strengths to the land that was so dear to him." The eldest son looked angry; the youngest, sheepish; and the middle one wore no expression at all. "Your father worked hard to cultivate his land. Dividing it would diminish its value." Ma turned to Kiran.

Kiran pointed to the eldest son. "You will be responsible for the selection of crops and the designation of where to plant them. Your leadership is important, and so is the knowledge you will glean from your brothers." He turned to the middle son. "You know the land better than anyone, so you will oversee all the tilling, planting, and harvesting." Finally, Kiran spoke to the youngest brother: "And you will manage the daily care of the crops: irrigation, pest removal, weeding. It's hard work, but that is how we all learn the nature of farming."

The eldest son pushed his chair away from the table and stood up.

"We're not finished yet," Chandu said, motioning for the young man to sit down. "Listen, now: these are the areas you will each lead, but when it comes to doing the work, we expect each of you to be there every day, working alongside one another." Chandu looked at each of them in turn. "At the end of two harvests, you will come back to us with your proposal of what to do with the land. You may propose anything you like: dividing the land among yourselves; selling it and splitting the proceeds. But whatever you decide, all three of you must agree."

The eldest brother exhaled a deep, audible breath and crossed his arms over his chest.

"If you cannot come to agreement," Ma said, "we will take the land back into the family's name and give it to someone else." She stood, looked up toward the ceiling for a few moments, then turned back to the young men. "You are being entrusted with your father's greatest earthly possession. If you fail, you will not only disappoint yourselves, you will disgrace his memory."

She ordered the servants to make more tea after the other visitors left, and the three brothers stayed behind and sketched out plans for rows of sugarcane and corn, using cardamom pods and rice grains to symbolize their crops on the long table. The council of arbiters understood the farm was too large for any of the brothers to do his part alone; they would have to work together to fulfill the tasks assigned to them. They knew that, after the first year of intensely tending the land, in the second year it would yield such great harvests, they would be convinced of their success. That day in the gathering room, three rivals would become partners.

Anil watched as Ritu left her position against the back wall and wandered over to a table in the corner upon which his old chess set was displayed. She sat down at the table, picked up one of the pieces, and examined it from all angles. Anil made his way over to her and took the seat on the other side of the table. He began arranging the pieces in their correct positions, aligning them on the squares. He smiled at Ritu. "Have you ever heard the story of how the game of chess was invented?"

Author's Note

In India, there is a long tradition of settling disputes between individuals and families within a community. In its original form, the *panchayat*—the assembly (*ayat*) of five (*panch*) respected elders—was the inspiration for the name of the fictional village in this novel, Panchanagar.

In less formal ways, I have witnessed the same practice of navigating disputes in my own family and that of others, usually by an elder male in the family. When I was younger, I was not often privy to these conversations, so my imagination took over.

Even as a child, I was fascinated by this practice of sorting out troubles at the kitchen table rather than in a courtroom or by a formal authority figure. I became further intrigued as an adult, once I realized that grown-ups don't have all the answers and that, in fact, often there is no clear answer to be had. I began to consider the burden of such a responsibility on an individual, and how different people might react to the role of being the arbiter.

For the purpose of this narrative, I chose an individual, the eldest son of the clan, to be the arbiter; in reality, the practice of informal dispute resolution can be carried out in as many different ways as there are families. While historical experience provided the inspiration for my story, all of the details of specific cases in this book are purely fictional, as are the village of Dharmala, India, and the town of Ashford, Texas.

❁

THIS NOVEL follows a young man through the three years of his internal medicine residency program at an urban American hospital in the early 2000s. During my research process, I had the generous help of many people, including patients, hospital staff, physicians, nurses, and current and former interns and residents at several medical centers across the country.

The fictional Parkview Hospital in this book is not modeled after any one hospital, nor is Anil's experience a perfect representation of any single residency program at a moment in time. Rather, it is a composite based on my research. While I have tried to remain true to the spirit of the medical residency experience, which has evolved significantly over the past two decades, I have also taken creative license to change some details and compress timelines to suit the narrative. There are undoubtedly errors in this kind of interpretation, and those belong solely to me.

The more exposure I gain to this world, the more I am humbled by the nobility of the medical profession. I only hope I did it justice.

Acknowledgments

This novel was a labor over five years, and I have many people to thank.

My literary agent, Ayesha Pande, has been a steadfast adviser over many years and was instrumental in guiding this book, first editorially, then into the world. I feel fortunate to have her in my corner.

I am so very thankful to the formidable team at William Morrow for taking a risk on my first novel, and continuing to invest in my career as a writer with this one. Publisher Liate Stehlik has been a wonderful champion over the years and my editor Kate Nintzel brought her detailed attention, unique insights, and enthusiasm to this novel. It has been a pleasure to work with them, along with Margaux Weisman and the wonderful marketing and publicity team of William Morrow.

Iris Tupholme at HarperCollins Canada showed early faith in this story and tremendous patience over the many years and drafts it took to bring it to fruition. Even as I tore the story apart and started over from the blank page (twice), her belief that I would eventually write something decent never wavered, even when mine did. I am grateful for her confidence, without which this story might never have seen the light of day. I would also like to thank Helen Reeves for providing invaluable feedback on the latter drafts of the manuscript; her keen insights helped shape this story into what it is. Noelle Zitzer ushered it smoothly through the entire process. Judy Phillips brought her exacting attention to the final draft as the copy editor, and Mumtaz Mustafa, her brilliant artistic skills to the cover design.

The entire HarperCollins Canada team (current and former) are a shining example of publishing at its best, and I'm lucky to be on their roster: David Kent, Leo MacDonald, Sandra Leef, Cory Beatty, Emma Ingram, Colleen Simpson, Julia Barrett, Michael Guy-Haddock, Alan Jones, and many others who've worked with enthusiasm to support my books.

I also owe a huge debt of gratitude to all the independent bookstores, passionate booksellers, reviewers, and readers of my first novel, who helped make it possible for me to write a second.

As someone who didn't study science past high school and is squeamish about blood, it was not a likely (or wise) choice for me to write about a young doctor in his residency. But that was the story that captivated me, and I'm fortunate that many people in the medical profession graciously helped me learn what I needed to know.

My brother-in-law, Dr. Vikas Desai, an emergency room physician, helped me with the details of the GHB drug overdose case, along with illuminating the unique culture of the ER.

My father-in-law, Dr. Ramayya Gowda, a cardiothoracic surgeon who has spent many days and nights saving patients in the ICU, helped me construct the case of an abdominal aortic aneurysm that could end so badly.

Dr. Ritvik Mehta helped me understand the nature and treatment of severe burns and, based on his own extensive experience, how medicine is practiced in rural areas of developing countries.

Like the main character in this novel, I was fortunate to see inside the hallowed chamber of a cardiac catheterization lab. Thanks to Dr. Pam Rajendran Taub, a cardiologist at UCSD, for her tenacity in gaining me such access. My appreciation also goes to Dr. Shami Mahmud, chief of Cardiovascular Medicine at UCSD, for clearing all the necessary hurdles and spending time with me. Finally, I am indebted to interventional cardiologist Dr. Mitul Patel, who, along with his staff and patients, allowed me to observe their remarkable work and answered my many questions.

Several other friends were generous in sharing experiences of their time as residents and in reading over my medical scenes, including Dr. Melissa Costner, Dr. Katherine Dunleavy, Dr. Bella Mehta, Dr. Sheila Au, and Dr. Cindy Corpier.

I could not have written this book without the generosity of these incredible physicians. Any inaccuracies in the story are my responsibility alone.

Thanks to my generous family of Ulambra, India, for showing me their agricultural practices, and the numerous varieties of trees and vegetation in the area, and for explaining the ayurvedic remedies derived from them. A local potter there who practiced the art of ceramics passed down through three generations was instrumental in showing me how to throw and shape clay without the use of modern tools.

For reading parts of the manuscript, my thanks to Saswati Paul, Anne Miano, Erin Burdette, Lori Reisenbichler; to Satish Krishnan, for educating me on the finer points of cricket; and to Vanessa, for her keen eye and ready ear.

My deepest gratitude goes to my family, and to friends who might as well be. Whose depth and laughter sustain me. Finally, thank you—

To my mother and father, Rama and Raj Somaya, for showing me the way.

To my sister, Preety, for always having my back.

To my second parents, Ram and Connie Gowda, for expanding the circle of my family.

And to Anand, Mira, and Bela, for making all my days golden.